English
Animals

LAURA KAYE

ABACUS

First published in Great Britain in 2017 by Little, Brown
This paperback edition published in 2017 by Abacus

3 4 5 7 9 10 8 6 4

A CIP catalogue record for this book
is available from the British Library.

ISBN 978-0-349-14219-7

Typeset in Garamond by M Rules
Printed and bound in Great Britain by
Clays Ltd, Elcograf S.p.A.

Papers used by Abacus are from well-managed forests
and other responsible sources.

MIX
Paper from
responsible sources
FSC® C104740

Abacus
An imprint of
Little, Brown Book Group
Carmelite House
50 Victoria Embankment
London EC4Y 0DZ

An Hachette UK Company
www.hachette.co.uk

www.littlebrown.co.uk

for my parents

CHAPTER ONE

'The house is just down there,' the taxi driver said, pointing in front.

I took off my belt and moved between the seats to look. We were at the top of a big hill. Below were squares and diamonds of green and brown fields all the way to the sunset. Then I saw the house. It was more perfect than the one I had been dreaming about. A red cube in the middle of the land, like someone had thrown a dice. I could not believe that I was going to live there.

At the bottom of the hill we turned off the road and drove across the stones in front of the house. Out of the window I watched the line of pigeons sitting on the electricity wires. Suddenly there was a loud bang and I covered my head with my hands from the shock. A bird fell from the wire like a stone. The other pigeons flew off the wire in all directions, not understanding what happened to their friend. Then there was another bang and I saw the gun at the last window on the first floor of the house.

I got out of the car and pulled my rucksack from the seat next to me. When I bent down to pay the driver through the car window, there was another bang above us.

'Good luck,' he said, raising his eyebrows.

As the taxi turned and drove away, a woman came running towards me holding her green hat with one hand to stop it from falling. She was breathing hard and her cheeks were pink, her eyes wild. Two brown-and-white dogs ran next to her.

'What the fuck is he doing?' she said, looking at me as if I knew the answer.

I opened my mouth to say something but she ran up the steps and into the house. I had imagined arriving at the house so many times, but it was never like this. I realised I knew nothing about these people. Richard and Sophie sounded like good names for good people. But they could be anything, they could be completely crazy.

I waited outside on the step. After a few minutes I was too cold and decided to go inside. I brushed my feet on the mat, went into the dark hall and put my rucksack next to the empty fireplace. Upstairs I could hear a man and a woman shouting, their voices cloudy in the distance. On the wall there was a metal switch and I pushed it up. Above my head a big iron chandelier of yellow lights came alive.

The first thing I saw were the dead animals. They were everywhere on the walls, some in glass boxes, some not. Their eyes seemed to stare directly at me.

Next to the door was a white owl with bright yellow eyes landing on a branch with her wings open. Then there were two squirrels eating nuts inside a glass box, then another box with a black bird inside, picking up a worm from the earth in his beak. There were all kinds of birds, some foreign and colourful, some more English-looking brown ones, lots of mice and rabbits, a few small, long animals like the ones used for making fur coats, and a big grey animal with a black-and-white stripy face. I felt something powerful from them. They were not decorations like lamps. They had been breathing animals full of flowing blood. And now they lived together in a zoo of death, watching the people who came in and out of the house.

I walked towards the fox inside a big glass box on the wall opposite the door. When I arrived at the glass I felt that the fox had heard my steps and froze. Her head was turned towards me like she was listening. I stared at her. She was amazing. I had never been so close to a fox in my life. She had rich orange fur and a white chest. There was a bird between her teeth and she looked at me with suspicious eyes, as if she thought I was going to steal the bird.

The artist had made a beautiful natural home for the fox to live in. The back of the box was painted blue for the sky and her black feet were walking on grass with rocks and moss and ferns. She seemed so alive. But I knew she was dead, and if I looked at her for ever, she would look at me for ever too. But she would stay the same and I would grow old. My hair would grow long and grey, lines would cut into my face, my skin would become loose, until one day I would fall to the ground and turn to dust in front of the eyes of the fox.

I heard heavy steps on the ceiling coming towards the stairs. I went quickly and stood next to my rucksack with my hands held together, smiling politely.

'I've told you a million times not to do it from the house,' the woman was saying.

'Yes and I've got the message, thank you,' the man said. 'Now can you shut up about it?'

On the stairs, through the white railings, I saw a man's black boots. Then his legs in patterned trousers of different greens, the kind that soldiers wear. He was holding the strap of his gun on his shoulder. He had dark brown hair with curls over his forehead and the shadow of a beard around his mouth. I thought he must be about forty years old. He was handsome, very masculine. As he turned the corner in the stairs he saw me and looked at me like he wished I would disappear into the ground. I looked quickly down at my feet.

He went out of the door without saying anything to me and I heard his feet on the stones. The woman followed him, but stopped at the door and shouted, 'Did you hear what I said?'

'Mind your own fucking business,' he shouted back.

'It is my business, you prick,' she said quietly and closed the door.

She breathed deeply, turned to me and smiled.

'Right then, let's get you settled in.'

I let myself look at the woman as she took off her hat and threw it next to the telephone on the little table. She was younger than the man, maybe thirty-four or thirty-five with blonde, nearly white hair that finished just below her ears. She was beautiful, but also very unusual. Before I arrived I imagined she would be beautiful because rich men don't usually marry ugly women. But she was not beautiful in the way I imagined. I had a picture in my brain of a thin, hard woman with long nails, red lips and dried hair. Like a poodle in a competition. But this woman was more like a snow wolf with long pale blue eyes and a pointy chin.

'I'm Sophie,' she said.

She held out her hand and I saw the black moons of dirt under her nails and the holes in the ends of the sleeves of her red jumper.

'You must be Mirka,' she said, saying *Murka* like many English people did.

I took her hand and shook it. 'Meer-ka,' I said. 'Nice to meet you.'

'I'm sorry about my reprobate husband. He's a bit stressed.'

'That's OK.'

She spent some time taking off her long green boots using her toes against the back of the heels and bending her leg to pull them with her hands, jumping around on one leg. Then she sighed and pushed the hair out of her eyes, as if it had been a lot of hard work.

'Right, follow me.'

I picked up my rucksack and walked behind her up the stairs.

'How was your journey?' Sophie said, twisting her head. 'I know it's a nightmare to get here with all those crappy trains.'

'It was nice to look out of the window.'

'Yes, it is a beautiful part of the world,' she said, almost sadly.

When we got to the corridor on the first floor we turned and went up more stairs to another smaller corridor with four doors. We were at the top of the house. Sophie opened the door on the left and switched on the light. I followed her inside. The room was so pink it hurt my eyes. Pink walls, pink curtains and a pink carpet. Even the lamp next to the bed was pink.

'This was my room when I was a little girl,' she said, looking with dreamy eyes at the wooden desk and wardrobe and drawers.

I was surprised because I thought the house must be Richard's and only became Sophie's when she married him. But it seemed to be the opposite. I told myself I should not make judgements before I knew things.

'You must have really liked pink,' I said.

'Oh, I don't think I had any choice. My sister got the blue one and I remember being extremely jealous. Will you be able to get used to it, do you think?'

'It's perfect,' I said to be polite.

She pointed to different things in the room: 'Towels over there on the chair. You've got your own little kettle if you want to make tea in the morning. The radiator can be turned up and down like this.' She bent down and showed me how to twist the white circle. 'I think that's it.'

'Thank you.'

'I'll show you the bathroom.'

As we were walking past the other doors, I said, 'Are these rooms where the children sleep?'

Sophie turned her head and her eyebrows came together. 'We don't have any children. Didn't they tell you that at the agency?'

I felt hot blood in my cheeks. 'They did not tell me a lot. Just Mr Richard and Mrs Sophie Parker, Fairmont Hall. I'm sorry, I did not mean to say anything—' I stopped talking, embarrassed.

'That's OK, don't be silly. I suppose most of the jobs must be for au pairs. But we only need an assistant. To help out with bits and bobs, here and there. Help Richard with his latest grand money-making scheme.'

She raised her eyebrows and I had the feeling she did not think her husband was good at making money. I wanted to ask her more about the bits and bobs, now that I was not looking after children, but I did not want to be rude. Whatever the jobs were, I would have to do them.

I followed her into the bathroom to the toilet with a cracked lid. The air smelt of the black fungus growing in the corners of the ceiling.

'Now,' Sophie said, putting her fingers into the hole at the top and pulling out a piece of string. 'Pull this to flush. Sorry it's broken. And if you could not do it in the middle of the night, that would be great. Especially when we have guests, as it makes an absolute racket.'

She went to the bath with a metal shower resting like an old telephone on two stands and turned the tap on.

'You need to run the water for a few minutes before it warms up. If you want a shower then you push this lever here to the other side.' She pushed the lever to the left and water came from the shower in thin, weak lines.

'Is that the shower?' I said, looking at how short the metal tube was, and thinking that I could never get my head under

7

the water. I could not believe people like Sophie and Richard lived in such bad conditions.

Sophie looked embarrassed, as if she knew what I was thinking.

'Yes, you have to crouch, I'm afraid. Sorry, the fixtures in this house are all about a century old. If you are desperate for a proper shower you can have one in our bathroom. We've just put one in. I'm more of a bath person really, but Richard kept complaining.'

We went outside into the corridor again and Sophie looked at her watch.

'I'll leave you to it. Come down to dinner at about eight, or whenever you're ready.'

I closed the door to my room and stood there for a moment thinking about my life in the strange pink room. But then I smiled. The room was nice. It was warm. And it was mine, only for me.

From the side of my eye I saw some pen marks on the edge of the door in the white paint. Next to a blue line, it said, *Sophie, August 1988*. I looked down and a few centimetres below there was another line in red pen, *Sophie, November 1987*. I followed all the marks down to the first mark, less than a metre from the carpet, *Sophie, June 1984*. I thought of Sophie growing against this wall, from the first mark to the last, and it seemed beautiful to me, but also sad for some reason, maybe because I thought how far from my home I was. How strange, I thought, to live in the same house all your life. I always imagined it would be nice to live in a few places and then one day to find your own home that would be different to the one chosen by your parents. But if I had a beautiful home like Fairmont Hall maybe I would never leave either.

I folded my clothes carefully in the drawers. In the top drawer there was a little cushion with lavender inside and I took it out and breathed the smell and then put it back with my bras and pants. I put my trainers under the bed with the rucksack and made a line of my bottles and creams and hair gel on the top of the chest of drawers. On the desk there was a pile of magazines called *Country Life* with pictures of beautiful houses, horses, dogs or owls on the covers. I thought that I should read them so that I would learn about the English countryside. Next to them I put the frame with the photograph of my family standing on a beach next to a lake. For a moment I stood stroking the glass over the faces with the end of my finger, remembering the holiday when it was taken. I was fourteen. Unusually for my family, everyone is laughing. It was because the woman who was taking the photograph was strange-looking with a lot of green make-up on her eyes and yellow hair. Her dog, like a white rat, was taking a crap next to her shoe and his expression was very shameful. The woman did not know that we were laughing at her dog and thought she was being funny taking the picture. My sister – on the left side, in a blue dress – was touching her long hair like the tail of an animal sitting on her shoulder. I was on the opposite side wearing denim shorts and a black T-shirt with one eye closed because of the sun and my mouth open, laughing. I had the same haircut as always, just below my ears. In the middle were my parents. My mother was dressed in an elegant white dress, and my father was wearing his grey hat, like always. Seeing them made the back of my eyes get hot and I blinked a few times so I would not cry. I remembered my father sitting in his favourite chair reading books about chess and my mother in the kitchen talking on the telephone. She was always on the telephone. I had not seen my family for two years. They had no idea that I was in England. I had left them and now I could not go back, not after everything that had happened. But I thought my parents would be proud if they could see me living in such a big house. One day, I thought, maybe I would see them again and show them a photograph.

When it was eight o'clock I followed the smell of onions and meat down the stairs and along a dark corridor to the kitchen. I pushed open the door. Sophie was bending over the table looking closely into a steaming dish. She saw me waiting and stood up.

'Come in, come in. Richard's gone to the pub.' She bit the side of her lip. 'I've had a slight disaster with the lasagne.'

I walked to the table and stood next to her. The lasagne looked OK, with circles of brown bubbles in the cheese and a big hole in the corner where someone ate some already. I was so hungry.

'What is wrong with it?' I said.

'Scrabble got up on the chair and took a couple of bites out of it.' Sophie looked towards the dogs in the giant basket and waved her finger. 'Didn't you, you bad dog?'

The dogs had their chins resting on the edge of the basket and looked guilty. I realised who Scrabble was and what had happened. I wanted to kill the dog.

Sophie put some lasagne on the plate and looked at it closely before giving it to me.

'There you go. I think I've got all of it. Anyway a bit of dog saliva won't kill us,' she said laughing. 'Sit down, sit down.'

I tried to laugh politely, but I felt the hairs rising on my arms. I could not believe Sophie was going to eat the dog lasagne, and that she thought I was going to eat it. I thought I must have not understood something.

She went to the drawer and took out knives and forks and white napkins in silver rings. I looked around the kitchen properly for the first time and everywhere I looked, I saw dirt. Sauce stains on the blue tiles behind the cooker. Old teabags turning red on the edge of the sink. The necklace of egg foam on the outside of the saucepan. Two brown circles of coffee on the envelope next to my elbow. Dog hairs covering every surface like the first snow. I could smell something like old meat in the rubbish bin. There was a bloody bone in the middle of the floor and I stared at it, trying to see if there were patches of fur on it, or whether it was just dirt. My hands started to shake and saliva filled my mouth. I told myself, *Mirka, get yourself in control.*

'Can I wash my hands please, Mrs Parker,' I asked.

'Only if you never call me that again,' she said. 'I hate my name.'

I got up and went to the sink. There was a thin blue soap with black cracks in a metal dish next to the sink. My fingers nearly dropped it when they touched the other side. It was soft and melted like jelly from sitting in water for a long time. I stroked the top of the soap with my fingers and washed my hands carefully. The water was not flowing away quickly because of the pieces of onion and celery in the sink hole. I washed my hands again and I felt Sophie's eyes looking sideways curiously at me but I ignored her because my hands still felt dirty and I needed to clean them.

I sat down again. 'Why do you hate your name?'

'Sophie Parker. It sounds like *nosy parker*,' she said.

I did not know who Nosy Parker was, so I said nothing. Over the sink she poured the peas into a sieve. While she was busy I cleaned my knife and fork with the inside of my sweater.

'My name means mosquito,' I said. 'Komárova.'

'Hmm, Mirka Mosquito,' she said. 'It has quite a ring to it.'

In the middle of the table there was a mat with a picture of a man in a red coat and tall black hat riding a horse. Sophie put the dish of peas on top of it.

'Would you like some wine?' she said, holding the end of the bottle over the wine glass in front of me.

'No thank you,' I said. 'I don't drink alcohol.'

A drop of red wine fell in the glass. Sophie looked at me as if she did not hear me correctly. She kept staring, like she was trying to imagine how somebody could live without alcohol.

'Why not?'

'Because I don't like being drunk,' I said.

'Why not?' she said, looking more surprised.

I paused. 'Because I like being in control,' I said. I had never said this to anyone before.

'Fair enough,' she said. Then panic came into her eyes. 'Oh my God. You aren't a vegetarian, are you?'

'No, don't worry. I eat meat.'

'Phew,' she said, putting her palm against her chest. 'I

completely forgot to specify that with the agency. I know we said that you must be comfortable handling dead animals, but we eat so much game, it would be a nightmare if you were a veggie. You wait until the shooting season starts. You'll never want to see another pheasant again in your life.'

I remembered the woman at the agency asking me about touching dead animals and I had been surprised, but I nodded because I needed a job and did not want to look like someone who was difficult. I thought I must be doing a lot of cooking and I was happy because I wanted to learn how to cook.

When she put the plate in front of me I tried to look closely for dog hairs without being obvious. Sophie was busy squeezing ketchup all over her lasagne and peas. Then she mixed everything together and used her fork like a spade to eat it. I brought my fork slowly towards my mouth. In the cheese I saw a white dog hair. I put the fork down again and pushed the dirty piece of lasagne to the side of the plate. But then I felt a sharp pain in my stomach. I had only eaten a Toffee Crisp and a packet of cheese-and-onion crisps on the train. I watched Sophie eating quickly and taking big sips of wine and I thought it must be OK. Like she had said, it would not kill me. I took some of the pasta and meat from the bottom and put it in my mouth. It was delicious. Once I started eating I could not stop and I ate all of the lasagne, taking the hairs out of the cheese with my fingers and wiping them on the napkin.

As I ate, I looked at all the postcards on the fridge: pictures of beaches and European cities, tourist images of the Eiffel Tower, a Spanish bullfighter, or girls in Austrian national costume holding beers in front of their big breasts. Some were bright and new, some were faded yellow. They were held by magnets in the shape of miniature national objects, like a paella dish or the Leaning Tower of Pisa. I thought they must like Europe a lot.

Sophie put down her fork and pushed her plate to the middle of the table. Then she reached behind her to take a small yellow plastic package from a drawer. She took tobacco from the packet and put it into a cigarette paper on her palm. As I watched her rolling a cigarette, she became more and more unusual to me. Her fizzy white hair in the shape of a triangle. Her zigzag bottom teeth and strong jaw. She was not wearing a bra and her small breasts under her red jumper were like little volcanoes. She lit the cigarette and held it with two fingers next to her face like she was pointing a gun behind her shoulder. Only some people can make smoking into an art and Sophie was a pro, she smoked like a movie star.

'Did you grow up in the countryside in Slovenia?' she said, with smoke curling out of her mouth.

'Slovakia,' I said.

'Oh God, I'm so sorry,' she said, looking guilty. Then she frowned and I knew she was trying to think where Slovakia was. It was an expression I had seen many times before.

'I grew up in a town near the castle where *Nosferatu* was filmed.' ·

'What's that?'

'It's a vampire film.'

'You look a bit like a vampire,' she said.

I was shocked, but then I saw the laughter in her eyes. I lifted up my lip with my finger and showed her my teeth at the side, which are unusually pointy.

'Maybe I am a vampire,' I said, making my accent heavily Slovak. 'Are you sure you want me in your house now?'

For one second, Sophie's face was confused and I thought I had made a mistake and ruined everything. But she smiled.

'So you would prefer a coffin to sleep in instead of a bed? I'm sure I can arrange it.'

'And I only work at night. Did the agency tell you?'

She laughed. I was happy that I had made her laugh and I had not done something wrong. Then we were silent like we were embarrassed. Behind me something made the noise of a bird.

'Blue tit,' Sophie said.

I turned. It was a clock with pictures of birds in a circle. A different bird for every number. Nine o'clock was a blue and yellow bird. Under the picture it said, *Blue tit*.

While Sophie smoked, I picked up the plates and went to the sink.

'Dishwasher's over there,' Sophie said, pointing to the cupboard next to the fridge.

When I pulled down the door to the dishwasher, the dogs stood up and ran towards me, fighting each other to arrive first. They put their feet on the door and licked the plates. I tried to push in the tray and shut the door.

'It's OK, you can let them,' Sophie said. 'It's their little treat. We call it the pre-wash, don't we, boys?'

My God, I thought, she *is* completely crazy. What kind of barbarians share their plates with their dogs? Why not put the lasagne in the big metal bowl on the floor and kneel down and eat it with her mouth? Every time I ate something from a plate in the house I would know that the dogs had eaten from it too.

When the dogs had finished licking the plates I closed the door to the dishwasher with my foot and sat down again. I felt dirty.

'How old are you again?' Sophie asked, staring at me.

'Nineteen.'

Sophie nodded her head like she was impressed. 'And is this your first job since you arrived in the UK?'

'I had one job working in Pret A Manger outside Euston station.'

'How was that?'

'It was not so bad. The people were nice – I mean, the people working there, not always the people coming in to buy things. There were a lot of Spanish and Italian and Polish people working there who were good people. But every day was exactly the same.' I gave her a polite smile, the same smile I always had when I was standing behind the till. 'Who's next, please? Can I help anyone? You, sir – can I get you any hot drinks today? Would you like milk in that? Can I get a white tea, please.'

'Wow,' Sophie said. 'You are so good at that. But yes, I can imagine that it would get a bit tedious, doing that all day every day.'

'It was not a good life in London. It was very hard and I was lonely. I shared a room with two people. I could not see my future, do you know what I mean?'

'Yes, I think so.'

'One day I woke up and I could not make myself go to work. I stayed in bed and I thought about what I could do. I remembered one of the girls at work told me about an agency that had jobs in nice houses all around England. I wanted to feel safe and have a home, only for a while, so that I could save money and think about what to do with my life.'

'I can't imagine how hard it must have been.'

In the entrance hall the door banged.

'That will be the B&B guests coming back,' Sophie said.

We listened to their feet going up the stairs. Sophie smoked her cigarette with an empty expression in her eyes.

'Richard hates having people in the house. But we need the money.' She sighed and put her cigarette out in the glass ashtray like she wasn't thinking about what she was doing. 'Personally, I don't mind having people around. It's funny that you said you were lonely in London, because I get a bit lonely here too sometimes.' She seemed sad, but then she smiled as if she was being brave. 'Well, I am really happy that you came here, Mirka.'

'Me too,' I said.

'It will make a refreshing change from Richard and David.'

'Who is David?'

'He's the gamekeeper. He also helps me in the garden with a few of the bigger jobs, but we're not allowed to call him a gardener. Not exactly a barrel of laughs.'

Then there were three loud knocks on the door.

Sophie looked confused and sat forward. 'I've no idea who that is.'

She walked out of the kitchen. After a moment, I followed because I felt strange being alone. But when I came around the corner, I saw that it was a policewoman in a bright yellow jacket and black hat talking to Sophie, so I stayed hidden behind the wall, watching.

A policeman came up the steps with his hand around

Richard's arm. Richard's head was hanging down as if he could not hold it up.

'He hit the landlord and another customer,' the policewoman said to Sophie. 'They managed to restrain him before he did any serious harm. And luckily nobody wanted to press charges.'

Richard looked up for a second, then his head fell again. One eye was swollen and purple, and there was some dark dried blood under his nose. Sophie put her arm around his waist.

'Thank you for bringing him home,' she said.

'That's all right,' the policewoman said.

The policewoman looked at Sophie for a long time as if she was trying to see in her face if there was a problem with Richard. Then they left and the door banged shut behind them.

Sophie turned Richard towards the stairs. 'Come on then.'

'What are you doing?' he said. His head lifted and fell again.

'I'm trying to help you.'

Richard pulled his arm away. 'Get off me. I'm fine.'

Sophie stepped backwards and crossed her arms. Richard nearly fell over. Then he stood straight, trying to stay still, and concentrated his eyes on the stairs. He stepped forward, but his foot went to the left. Then he tried to step forward again, but his foot went to the right.

'Let me help you,' Sophie said, putting her arm around him again.

'Get off me, you stupid bitch!' he said, and pushed her hard on the shoulder.

Sophie fell on the floor. I was so shocked I put my hand to my mouth. It all happened very quickly. Sophie was lying on the rug. She stayed there for a few seconds, then slowly pushed herself up. Richard was looking down at her, his eyes full of hatred. I thought I should go and help her. But I did not move. Then Richard turned and started to pull himself up the stairs by the railings. Sophie watched him. I could not see her face but I heard an angry noise in her throat as she started crying.

I did not know if I should go to help her or if I should leave her alone. I nearly went to her, but then instead I walked quietly back towards the kitchen because I decided that it was better that Sophie did not know that I saw anything. I waited, but in the end she did not come back and I sat for a while at the table, feeling guilty that I was such a coward. Then I went to bed. I lay there for a long time thinking about everything that had happened. Had he pushed her before? Did he hit her? Why didn't she leave him? I realised that I had imagined people from a piece of paper. But the people were real and messy and I was going to be in the middle of them.

In the night I woke up in the darkness and I did not know where I was. I did not know who I was. It was like I was dead. I tried to remember the day before and there was nothing in my brain. I tried to remember something from my life and there was nothing. I could not breathe and I felt like my heart had stopped. Who was I? I was nobody. Then, suddenly, images from my life flew to me like bats in the night. I lay breathing in air deeply, like someone who had nearly drowned.

After a few minutes I got up to go to the toilet. I sat there for a long time in the bathroom, feeling empty and strange. When I stood up again I saw the toilet was full of blood. For a moment I thought I was dying, until I realised what it was. It was stupid, because I had seen it so many times before, but on this night it was such a shock. I felt like it was a sign. And worse, I could not flush it away because of the guests. After this, I could not go to sleep again. Any optimistic thoughts had gone away. I had a bad feeling about being in the house and that the blood was the symbol of this feeling.

CHAPTER TWO

In the morning, after breakfast, I went out from the kitchen door and walked along a stone path next to a wall. Cold drops of water were falling from the black branches of the cherry trees into my hair. I looked over to the fields where white birds were flying in a cloud and I saw, almost hidden against the earth, eight or nine deer. They were standing very still as though they were listening. Suddenly, all together, like dancers, they turned and ran to the side of the field, their white behinds floating up and down, until they made a big jump over the fence into the trees. Seeing them made me feel better after such a terrible night.

Through an arch of hedge there were two barns made from grey stones with red roofs and metal symbols like an S backwards on the walls. I went into the second barn where a ladder, a metal saw and a spade were leaning on the wall next to a pile of wood. A black cat came out of the darkness and made circles around my ankles. I bent to stroke the soft fur on her head.

'Hello,' I said.

I knocked on the small door cut into the wall at the end of the barn.

'Come in,' Richard said. 'Whatever you do, don't let the cat in.'

It was too late. I was already pushing the door as he said this and the cat ran into the room.

'Oh bugger,' I heard Richard say, and the noise of a chair scraping the floor.

I followed the cat into the bright room, a kind of studio. Directly in front of me was the skull of a deer hanging by its horns from a hook on the ceiling. The skin had been peeled off and the skull was white and red from the fat and muscle still on the bone. It was twisting gently and in the space between the jaws I saw a light bulb behind shining through. One eyeball of black jelly was sticking out from the skull, but when the head twisted around, I saw the other eye was gone and there was only a red hole. It was disgusting. What was Richard doing to the deer? What was this place? I saw all the stuffed animals around the room and I realised Richard was the person who made them. Then I remembered about handling dead animals and felt sick in my stomach. This could not be what they wanted me to do, I thought.

The cat was on the table, staring at Richard. I stared at him too. The skin around his right eye was purple. He was smaller than I thought, approximately the same height as me, because I am very tall for a girl, but I was narrow and he was wide, with big muscles in his sloped shoulders and in his arms. His shape reminded me of a bull.

He suddenly reached out and picked the cat up by the fur around her neck. Everything about him was rough and strong, and reminded me of what he had done the night before. But then he held the cat next to his face and spoke to her in a gentle voice, full of love, as if he was talking to a baby.

'Sammy Twinkle you know perfectly well you aren't supposed to be in here. Don't you, sweetie?'

He walked across the room, put the cat outside the door and turned to me.

'Take a seat,' he said, pointing to the stool opposite his.

On the table there was a brown bird, scissors, a thin knife and a ball of yellow wool. Richard went to the side of the room to the wooden chest and opened a drawer full of metal tools.

I looked around the room. Dusty plants with long leaves were blocking the light from the milky window. Old grey spiderwebs hung from the ceiling like dirty tissues. The surfaces were covered in paintbrushes, scissors, knives and pieces of wood and grass. In the corner a big owl looked down at all the mess with her yellow eyes. On the floor, in a plastic tray, there was a fox's skin lying flat like a rug. She had no eyes, I noticed, only holes like ones for buttons.

Richard saw me staring at the fox. 'Vicious fucker,' he said, shaking his head. 'They go crazy with bloodlust, foxes.'

From the drawer he pulled out a metal tool, the same kind as the one for pulling hairs from eyebrows, and put it on the table. I was still thinking of a fox with bloodlust. Then he went to the giant freezer in the corner of the room and opened the lid. I saw an orange leg of a bird sticking up. I stepped closer to see. It was full of bodies covered in fur and feathers. Richard was moving them around, looking for something, and their stiff, icy bodies made a scratching sound like plastic rubbing. He pulled out a squirrel and put it on the shelf above the heater.

'Right,' he said sitting down and drinking everything in his cup. 'I take it you have never done any taxidermy before?'

'No. Taxidermy,' I said, trying the word. 'You are a taxidermer?'

'I am a taxidermist,' Richard said. 'But you're up for it?'

'Up for it?'

'I need an assistant. We asked the agency for someone who wasn't squeamish. You're not squeamish, are you? Not afraid of a bit of blood and guts?'

So it was true. He wanted me to help him stuff animals. I did not know what to say. Richard was looking at me, waiting.

'I'm not afraid of blood and guts,' I said nervously. 'But I would prefer not to touch any. I thought I would be cooking animals.'

'O-K,' Richard said slowly. 'Well, how about I just show you and then you'll see that it's not too bad. Not that different to cooking really.'

He moved his head to one side, cracking the bones in his neck, then did the same on the other side.

'Ahh,' he said. 'Nothing like skinning an animal on a hangover.'

In very quick movements, he picked up the bird from the table and with the other hand he took the thin knife and cut through the skin in the middle of the bird's chest. Then he peeled the skin gently with his thumb so I could see the purple shiny meat behind.

'Oh God,' I said by mistake.

He looked up at me and smiled. 'You get used to it.'

He continued making small cuts towards the wings, pulling the skin back gently with his fingers. The bird's legs were wide open and his yellow feet jerked with the movements of the knife.

'Is that the bird you shot yesterday?' I asked.

'No, this one's a kestrel someone found on the road. I don't bother with pigeons. It's like trying to skin up with wet papers.'

I felt like I was in a dream as I watched Richard slowly pull the skin away until the purple body was naked and the skin was over the head, completely inside-outside. It seemed sad and humiliating for the bird, even though I knew he was dead and did not know what was happening. I thought, this is death, exactly this. When you were gone, and only a body, people could do anything they liked with you because you were nothing. As I thought this, my throat became narrow and tears came into my eyes and ran down my face. I was swallowing, trying to control myself, but I made a loud sniff. Richard looked up, frozen with the knife in his hand. I was embarrassed and wiped my face with the sleeve of my sweater.

'I'm sorry,' I said. 'I don't know why I'm crying.'

But the tears did not stop. Richard looked sideways as if he thought someone might be in the room who could help him, then looked back at me like he did not know what to do with a crying girl. After a few seconds he got up, put down the knife and walked around the table. He put his arms around me with his hand on my hair.

'Come here,' he said. 'The first one is always a bit of a shock.'

My cheek was pressed against his shirt and I smelled his male alcohol sweat and pine laundry soap. I thought, who is this gentle, kind man? It was not the same man as the one from the night before. I let him hold me until the tears stopped, thinking how nice it was to be held by someone. It was the first time someone had done this to me for a long time. Then I got control of myself, took a big breath and pushed him away. I did not want him to think I was weak.

'I'm OK,' I said.

'Are you sure?' he said.

'Yes, I'm sure. Please continue.'

He finished pulling the skin over the head, cutting gently around the eyes and pulling out the little pointy tongue. The meat and the skin were now separate. I thought there would be organs and blood everywhere, but it was just a tidy purple body in the white dish. He made cuts at the neck with the scissors until the head fell off.

'Next I'll measure the body with these things—' He picked up a big tool like scorpion claws. 'Callipers. But I want to show you the whole process, so . . .' He got off his stool and picked up a smaller bird-skin from the table under the window and showed it to me on his palms quite theatrically.

'And here's one I made earlier,' he said, smiling like he thought he was being very funny.

When he saw my face looking confused and not laughing, he stopped smiling and said, 'Anyway.'

He picked up a small cushion made of straw with wires sticking out.

'This is his new body. Neat, no? But first we need to do the eyes. See that book over there?' He pointed to a fat book on the shelf called *Birds of Britain*.

'Yes.'

'Go and look up the song thrush and then fetch some appropriate eyes from that drawer over there.'

I found the song thrush in the list at the back and went to the page with the drawing of the bird. The eyes were small and black. I closed the book and went to the drawers and looked in the top one. It was full of little plastic packets of pairs of eyes. There were red eyes, yellow, orange, white, brown, black and blue, in all different sizes. I took Richard a pair of small black eyes and he glued them into the plastic skull.

'Why did you want to be a taxidermist?' I asked Richard as he pulled the skin of the bird over the new body.

'For the cash mostly. But I suppose I became interested in it in the first place because I hunt and I thought, instead of sending animals to someone else, why not do it myself? So I started, and it just took off. The demand for taxidermy is unbelievable. It's really trendy right now, for some reason. Pubs and hotels want it. All those pretentious wankers in East London can't get enough of it. I've got this guy called Caleb who looks like something from Central Casting. He wears a bolo tie and snakeskin boots. Runs a shop near Bethnal Green where they sell taxidermy and have absinthe-tasting nights. You get the picture. He got in contact with me and comes down now and again to pick up some pieces to sell in his shop.'

Richard was pulling the end of the bird's beak out of a circle of fluffy feathers. Then the bird was looking like a bird again. Richard turned him around on his palm for me to see.

'Need to pad out the stomach a bit more, but it's looking good.'

'Do people kill animals to decorate their houses?' I asked.

'Most of the animals would be dead anyway. Except for maybe deer, I suppose...' He paused, thinking. 'But even then, they aren't killed *for* decorating houses, exactly. I guess people just want to preserve them, for whatever reason.'

'Do people want to preserve their dogs and cats?'

'They do. You'll see we get a few calls. But I won't do them. People are too emotionally attached to them. Sometimes they keep them for days after they die, stroking them, so when you get hold of them the skin is in an awful condition and they are starting to rot. And then when the owner sees the finished result they're never happy because it's not their precious Rover or Tigger.'

I thought of someone crazy stroking their rotting pet for days and days. Richard saw my expression and he nodded at me as if to say, *Yes, exactly*.

When the bird was standing on his feet on the wooden branch inside the glass box I felt better for him because he had a nice home with some moss. He seemed to have his dignity again. I knew it was not true, but I felt it very strongly. I felt that the bird was lucky because he would never rot and would live for ever.

'So we will just make him look over here,' Richard said,

twisting the bird's head to the side. 'Like he's listening. What do you reckon?'

'It's good. Maybe the tail feathers can go up.'

'Yes, I like it. More alert,' Richard said. He opened the beak. 'Beak open or closed?'

'It is too violent with the beak open. Like he is hungry or frightened. It is more peaceful with the beak closed.'

'OK, beak closed. You're getting the hang of this.' He smiled. 'Sometimes you know when you get the right pose to capture the essence of the animal.'

He went to the shelf and stood on his toes to take down a huge black bird standing on a block of tree. The bird had pulled his wing across his body like a shining black cape and was looking over his shoulder.

'This one is probably the one I am most happy with.'

'He is very dramatic.'

'Isn't he?' Richard said, looking proudly at the bird.

'Like Batman.'

'Well, yes, except he's a raven.'

Richard finished making the song thrush into a peaceful but alert pose and turned it around so I could see. I had the same feeling as when I saw the fox: like the bird would come alive and start jumping along the branch or open his wings and fly away.

'Voilà,' Richard said. 'It wasn't so bad, was it? Do you think you could give it a go?'

He looked at me hopefully and I did not say anything, but I must have looked worried because then he said quickly, 'It's OK, maybe we can work up to it slowly.'

He went to the shelf over the heater and touched the squirrel with his finger and frowned. He came back and started to measure the purple body of the kestrel with callipers.

'Richard, can I put the eyes in the drawer in order of colour and size?' I asked him, because I could not stop thinking about the mess in the drawer.

'Knock yourself out.'

I tidied up all the mess in the room and washed the splashes of dried blood and dust from the surfaces. In the little metal square on the front of each drawer I put a piece of paper with the name of the objects inside: *Pins & Needles, Thread & Wool, Bodies, Bird Legs, Scissors & Pliers, Tweezers, Modelling Tools, Knives* and *Wood Wool*.

At one o'clock Sophie came to the barn with ham sandwiches cut into triangles. She put two plates on the table and looked round the room like she was impressed.

'Is this for Richard's benefit or yours?' Sophie said, laughing.

'I don't care who it's for, it's brilliant,' Richard said, putting his arm around my shoulders and squeezing me until I was smiling, feeling shy from the praise but also happy that I had done a good job.

Later, in the evening, we were in the kitchen eating chicken stew and mashed potato.

Richard raised his wine glass. 'Here's to your first day as a taxidermist.'

Sophie and Richard touched their wine glasses against mine, which had apple juice in it.

'I am not sure I can be called a taxidermist,' I said.

'Give it time,' Richard said. 'Give it time.'

They were telling me stories about getting married and when they were first in a relationship. Everyone in the stories was always drunk and Richard and Sophie were laughing a lot. I could tell that they had told the stories many times, but were enjoying having a new person to tell them to. I liked being that person. They seemed happy. It was like the day before had never happened and they were just a normal couple who loved each other very much.

'How did you meet?' I asked them.

'We were at a house party and Sophie was dressed as a jelly-fish,' Richard said.

'Which basically consisted of me wearing a blue dress and holding an umbrella with long bits of plastic hanging from it.'

'I was impressed anyway,' Richard said, leaning forward to light Sophie's cigarette.

'Yes, but you're easily impressed.' Sophie stroked Richard's arm. 'It wasn't too sociable, being under an umbrella. I couldn't see anything.'

'It was pretty sociable once you got inside the umbrella with her,' Richard said, winking at me. When he laughed, he had deep birds' feet next to his eyes and looked very handsome.

We had finished eating so I got up and put the plates in the dishwasher and waited for Ringo and Scrabble to give them a pre-wash. I wiped the surfaces, feeling a little sick about the dogs' licking noises, but I told myself it was not a big thing, the plates would be washed in the machine and I would have to get used to it if I was going to live in the house.

'Don't worry about that, Mirka,' Sophie said, but I did not

stop wiping until the sauce stains were gone. I put the oven dish in the sink and filled it with soap and water.

'Enough, dogs,' I said, closing the dishwasher door with my foot.

Richard took a metal box from the tobacco drawer. From inside he took a brown rectangle and started burning it with the lighter and breaking crumbs from it into a paper. I realised it was marijuana. When he had finished making the cigarette, he lit it, took two breaths and passed it to me.

'No thank you,' I said.

'Suit yourself,' he said, and passed it to Sophie.

After two deep breaths of the cigarette, Sophie gave it back to Richard and went to the fridge. When she opened the door I could smell sweetcorn and cold vegetable soup. Everything in the kitchen, the colours and the smells, seemed very clear to me and I did not know if it was the marijuana smoke or if it was because I was bleeding, which sometimes made my senses extra sharp.

'Shall we have another bottle of Chablis?' Sophie said, turning from the fridge.

'I'm going to polish off the red from last night, but you go ahead,' Richard said, picking up another bottle on the table and filling his glass.

Sophie was still looking into the fridge. 'It seems a bit extravagant. We don't want Mirka to think we're complete alcoholics.' She turned and smiled at me to show that she was joking.

'Oh, just open it. We're celebrating.' Richard blew out smoke and said to me, 'Got another booking for a wedding today.'

'A big one in August,' Sophie said. 'Which means we have one almost every week from June until the beginning of September. Not bad.'

'It's bloody good,' Richard said.

'Well, I don't expect we will get any more now. People seem to like to plan about two years in advance these days.'

Sophie sat down again with a full glass of white wine and took the end of the marijuana cigarette from Richard.

'So, given that you don't drink,' Richard said to me, 'how would you feel about driving us to a dinner party on Saturday night and picking us up again?'

I had already been worrying about what I would do on Saturday night. I did not know if I should leave the house to make space for them. But where could I go?

Sophie said, 'Come on, Richard, she has to have a night off.'

'I'm not expecting her to do it for free.' He turned towards me. 'So if you want to earn some extra cash maybe we can come to some kind of arrangement.'

'OK,' Sophie said. 'But, Mirka, you must make yourself at home. I'll show you where you can watch TV. Or you can go out. I'm happy to give you a lift anywhere you like.'

'Thank you,' I said.

'Do you have a boyfriend?' Sophie said. 'I'm only asking because we wouldn't allow anyone to stay the night here. But if you want to go out and meet him, or have him over for dinner, that would be fine.'

'I don't have a boyfriend,' I said.

'I'll take you down the Dog and Duck on a Friday,' Richard said. 'There are some pretty choice specimens down there.'

'Don't listen to Richard,' Sophie said, hitting him gently on the shoulder. 'And you can always use the house phone, as long as you don't spend hours talking to Slovakia. Nobody gets any reception down here.'

'I don't have a mobile phone anyway,' I said. 'But I won't call home, don't worry. Do you have a computer so I can check my emails?'

'I'll show you my laptop,' Sophie said. 'You can check them any time or use it to go online.'

'You know, I really admire you,' Richard said to me suddenly. 'Coming over here, not knowing what you will find. Getting on with it. We need more people like you in the world.'

'I just wanted to have a different experience,' I said, feeling shy.

'And you're so young,' Sophie said, looking at me like a proud mother. 'It's so brave. I don't think I could have done anything like that at nineteen.'

'Anything you need, you let us know,' Richard said. He reached his hand over the table and put it over my hand and looked me in the eyes. 'If you have any problems. Anything at all, you must tell us.'

He was looking at me very seriously and I felt that he really meant it. It seemed like he left his hand there for a long time, looking at me with so much kindness, that I felt like I was going to cry again. I had never imagined I would feel so welcome and safe after feeling so lost and alone in London, with no control over my life and what direction I would go. And now I was here and I would be OK, at least for a while.

'Is it OK for me to go to bed?' I asked, because I did not want

Richard to see me cry twice in the same day. I did not usually cry so often.

'Yes, of course, don't be silly,' Sophie said. 'Good night.'

Sophie asked me to come to the kitchen at eight o'clock to help her make the Full English. When I came into the kitchen she was leaning over the newspaper on the table holding a cigarette between two fingers covered in ink. She was wearing jeans and a pale blue jumper with no bra again, even though she probably should wear one because I could see the points of her nipples through the material. But she did not seem to care.

'Did you see anyone about?' she asked.

'No.'

'Eight was probably a bit keen,' she said, yawning.

I pulled up the silver lid on the cooker and put the kettle on the hot stone circle. In front of the dirty window on the shelf there were three plants with blue flowers growing in glass bowls with thin white roots under the water like worms. Outside the sun was shining on the grass. Small nuts of pink flowers were starting to grow on the cherry trees.

'Conservative deeply stained,' Sophie said.

I turned around and looked at Sophie, confused.

'The clue to the crossword,' she said explaining. '*Conservative deeply stained*. A four-letter word, then a two, then a three, then four. Hmm.'

'I don't understand anything you are saying.'

'Well, usually in crossword clues you get the definition of a word, or sometimes two alternative definitions. For example in this one, it is probably an expression that we use to talk about someone who is conservative.'

'Like someone who does not like change?'

'Exactly. And then you have other words that signal how you should look at the clue. Like "jumbled" or "scrambled" usually means an anagram where the letters are all there, but in the wrong order. You just have to know what to look out for. And then—'

Sophie stopped and smiled.

'I've worked out what it is. Stained, dyed. It's *dyed in the wool*, which means someone who is stuck in their ways. As in, my father is a dyed-in-the-wool traditionalist who hates change.'

'Was he?'

She looked up from writing the letters into the boxes.

'My father?' she laughed. 'Oh my God, yes. We are talking about a man who, when Robertson's Marmalade removed the golliwog from their packaging—' she stopped. 'Do you know what a golliwog is?

'No.'

'It's a kind of black doll. They used to be everywhere, but now they are regarded as racist. So Robertson's stopped printing their labels with a picture of a golliwog on them, and my father was so upset that he cut out a picture of Ian Wright – who was a famous black footballer at the time – from the newspaper and sellotaped it to the jar in protest over what he called the PC brigade's insidious corroding of our national culture. So yes, you could say he is pretty old school.'

'My father too,' I said, though I thought Sophie's father sounded much worse than mine.

'What's your father like then?' Sophie said.

'He's sweet and shy. But old fashioned. My mother is the one who is in charge and she is not a nice person.'

'What do you mean?'

'She is a very big person in a small community—'

Sophie interrupted me: 'A big fish in a small pond.'

'What?'

'It's a phrase we use to talk about someone like that. Sorry, ignore me, carry on.'

Sophie poured some more coffee and lit the half-cigarette resting on the ashtray.

I continued, 'She knows everybody and talks about everybody badly. Who has a bad marriage. Which husband is cheating. Someone's daughter is having sex with someone's son. Everyone in the town is afraid of her, but they continue being friends with her.'

'I know the type well,' Sophie said. 'Best thing to do is ignore them.'

'I wish I had,' I said. 'But it is hard when it is your mother.'

There was the sound of feet on the stairs. Sophie quickly folded the newspaper and put out the cigarette again.

'Right, let's go. You're in charge of slicing the mushrooms.'

She went to the fridge and took out packages wrapped in paper and passed them to me. I sliced the mushrooms and cut the tomatoes in half while Sophie went to take the breakfast orders. When she came back she made coffee and tea in a teapot with a pink wool jacket and poured milk into two jugs shaped like cows and took them to the dining room on a tray.

When everything for the Full English was ready, she put

it on the plates. The arrangement of the fried eggs, tomatoes, sausages, black pudding, baked beans and bacon was a master-piece. There was also some toast cut into triangles on a metal rack with a handle for the finger, and a rectangle of butter on a small plate. Everything was so perfect.

'You can take this,' she said.

'Really?' I said.

I went down the corridor, through the entrance hall and into the dining room, carrying the tray carefully. An old man and a woman with the same thick white hair and healthy faces were sitting at a small table near the window and two Japanese women, mother and daughter, were sitting in the other corner underneath a pheasant with a long tail.

'Will you look at that!' the white-haired woman said in an American accent, clapping her hands when I put down the plate. 'Now that is something.'

I felt proud. 'I hope you enjoy your breakfast.'

When I came back to bring two more plates to the Japanese women, the daughter took photographs of her breakfast with her mobile phone. It made me remember the tourist magnets on the fridge. I tried to think of another dish that was more English, but I could not.

There was a plate of breakfast on the table in the kitchen when I came back.

'That's for you, if you want it.'

I thought that the Full English was only for the guests so I was happy. I had eaten one before in a café in Bratislava, but this was the first time I had eaten one in England.

'It is delicious,' I told Sophie.

'Well, it's hardly rocket science,' she said, making a small wave with her hand.

After I finished my breakfast I went to collect the dirty plates from the dining room. The American woman was talking to the Japanese women.

'The village was just precious,' she was saying. 'You can walk along the stream and there is a little post office with a red postbox. And there are ducks swimming, and willow trees. And the cottages were so cute. It was like something from a movie set.'

The Japanese mother and daughter were nodding to each other as I picked up the plates.

'Now that was delicious,' the American woman said to me. 'Would you tell Sophie it was delicious.'

'Of course I will,' I said. 'I'm happy you liked it.'

'You don't sound like you're from here,' the man said suspiciously.

'I'm from Slovakia.'

'Where's that?' he said.

'It is in the middle of Europe. Next to the Czech Republic, below Poland.'

They were nodding politely, but I saw in their eyes some disappointment that the person who gave them the Full English was not English.

When I came back to the kitchen Sophie had gone and there was mess everywhere. I washed the pans and oven dishes and put the white paper packets into the fridge, the broken eggs into the brown bin and the tins in the green recycling bin. I wiped all the stains from the surfaces until the yellow cloth was black. A frozen piece of meat tied with string was melting on a wooden board next to the sink and blood was dripping on to the surfaces and running down the door of the cupboard. I didn't understand how anybody could live in such a dirty place. Under the sink I found some bleach and I washed the floor.

I was just thinking how much I loved making the kitchen clean when Sophie came in and put the kettle on the cooker. She put a teabag in a cup. Then she looked around the kitchen like she knew something was different but she was not sure what it was.

'I cleaned everything,' I said.

'You really don't need to do that,' she said, frowning.

'It's OK, I wanted to help.'

'It was fine how it was,' she said in a sharp voice.

'I'm sorry,' I said, shocked.

'Well you can stop now, I need you to come and help me strip the beds.'

Her cheeks were pink. She turned and finished making the cup of tea. First I thought it was because she was embarrassed about the dirt, but then I thought maybe she liked the kitchen dirty for some reason. Like the dirt was something old that reminded her of the history of the house and all the people who had lived there and made it.

I followed her up the stairs and she stopped on the corridor.

'Hang on a sec, while I give this to Richard,' she said, looking down at the cup in her hand. She did not seem angry with me any more, as if nothing had happened.

She went into their bedroom and through the open door I heard Richard saying in a sleepy voice, 'Mmm, come here and get back into bed.'

'Get off,' Sophie said. 'Someone has to do some work around here.'

'Get Mirka to do it. Surely that's the point of her.'

'Shh,' Sophie said. 'She'll hear you.'

I could hear the sounds of them kissing, and Richard speaking between the kisses: 'I don't give a fuck if she hears us. Take off your clothes.'

'OK, wait here. I'll be back in a minute.'

Sophie came out of the door pulling her jumper down over her breasts. We went along the corridor to a bedroom with walls printed with a pattern of small green leaves. The curtains were green with gold lines in diamond shapes and the carpet was green. Whoever decorated the house did not like to mix their colours, I thought.

'Right, strip the beds in here and then do the yellow room and take them to the kitchen,' she said speaking quickly, her body half behind the door. 'You can manage on your own, can't you?'

'OK,' I said.

'Great,' she said, and was gone.

She left the door open and I closed it so that I would not hear anything. I felt like they were my parents and I did not want to know what they were doing.

On Saturday night Richard and I were waiting in the entrance hall for Sophie. Richard took two logs from the basket and put them into the fire.

'Keep an eye on it when we're gone,' he told me. 'There's more coal and wood in the cellar.'

Sophie came down the stairs in a blue dress and black boots.

'Ah, my dearest wife, how lovely of you to grace us with your presence,' Richard said. 'You're only' – he looked at his watch – 'twenty-one minutes late.'

'I don't want to go,' she said, standing at the bend in the stairs with her arms crossed. 'Can you ring them and tell them I've come down with something.'

'You ring them. You got us into this.'

'Don't be like that. You know I can't say no.'

'I'd absolutely love to stay here and get quietly stoned in front of the telly. Call them and tell them you've got a vicious bout of haemorrhoids or something.' Richard's eyes moved up and down Sophie's body. 'You aren't going like that, are you? You can't wear boots to a dinner party. Come on, Sophie.'

'Are you telling me how to get dressed?'

'Yes. To be honest, I think you can do better. Haven't you got a nice pair of heels?'

Sophie sighed and gave Richard an angry look, but it seemed like she already thought the same thing about the boots. She walked up the stairs again with heavy feet.

'A little bit of haste, perhaps,' Richard shouted to her. He turned to me and shook his head. 'This is going to be a long night.' He put his hand on my shoulder and looked sincerely into my eyes. 'But at least, thanks to you, I can get completely smashed.'

Richard and Sophie did not talk in the car. Richard sat in the front pointing to me where to turn. Sophie looked out of the window into the dark forest. The trees were like an army of ghosts. I saw a sign at the edge of the road, a glowing white triangle with a black deer. The deer was running and I thought he looked like he wanted to escape from something. Then we arrived at another house with thick plants growing up the walls.

'See you at midnight,' Richard said to me.

'Eleven,' Sophie said.

'We can't leave at eleven,' Richard said to her. To me he said, 'Midnight, OK?'

'Half past.'

'No, Sophie.'

I went home and ate dinner and watched television with Ringo and Scrabble sitting next to me on the sofa. I did not like being alone in the house. I kept hearing noises. If anyone came to rob the house, I thought, there would be nothing I could do. But I told myself it was only the wind moving in the trees or the old house cracking. I was glad the dogs were there, at least they would bark to warn me so I could hide.

At twenty to midnight I drove again to the house. As soon as I switched off the engine, the door to the house opened and Sophie walked quickly to the car with her arms holding her coat tightly around her. In the door behind I could see the black figures of Richard and a woman kissing on the cheeks.

Sophie opened the back door of the car. 'Thank God you're here.'

'Are you OK?'

'Not really,' Sophie's voice became high and wavy. 'Sometimes I feel like I can't do anything right.'

I looked in the mirror and saw her face folding and tears running down her cheeks.

Richard got into the front of the car and pulled the door. 'Perfect timing,' he said. He seemed drunk and happy.

As I started to turn the car, Sophie sniffed loudly and Richard turned around and looked at her.

'What now?' he said, like Sophie was being very boring.

'Why do you have to constantly undermine me?'

'I don't undermine you.'

'You interrupted everything I said.'

'I had to. You were wittering on about fracking for a good two hours.'

'I was not!'

'Oh, stop crying.'

Sophie was making wet sniffing noises, trying to make her breathing normal.

'I said stop fucking crying!' He hit the plastic in front of him with his fist. 'Jesus, why do you have to make such a big deal out of everything? Why can't we have a night out without you getting all hysterical about something and ruining it?'

Sophie wiped her cheeks with her hand and looked sadly out of the window. Richard was breathing hard next to me. I tried to think of something to say to make the atmosphere less heavy but I could not think of anything.

After a few minutes of driving through the dark, narrow roads, Sophie said, 'Anyway, it's important to talk about fracking. I care about these things.'

'Oh, don't start.'

'You don't care about anything that goes on in the world. You're not interested in anything except getting stoned and your stupid fucking animals. The government could be taken over by blue aliens and you wouldn't even notice.'

'The country is already run by aliens.'

Sophie said in a flat voice, 'I knew you were going to say that.'

Richard took off his belt and turned around. 'Do you know why I don't care about fracking, or feminism, or tax havens, or any of the things you go on and on about? Because none of it makes the slightest bit of difference to my life. And quite frankly, I've got enough on my plate trying to keep this ship afloat.'

'As if I don't.'

'We are on a knife-edge, Sophie. Sometimes I don't think you realise.'

Sophie made a loud noise through her teeth. 'Oh, just sell the fucking house. Let's be done with it. I can't take it any more. I don't want to live here, withering away, counting every penny.'

There was a lot of anger and pain in her voice. Richard sighed and his body went soft.

'We are not selling the house,' he said quietly. 'Come on, we can get through this together. We've got Mirka now, so you can concentrate on the weddings and really getting our name out there. And the taxidermy business is picking up.'

Sophie said nothing. We drove along a road through the woods. Then, in front of the car, I saw a dark lump in the road. It was a dead animal. I turned the wheel so we would not drive over it.

'Wait, stop the car!' Richard said.

I put my foot on the brake until the car stopped. Richard opened the door and ran back to the animal.

'You are fucking kidding me,' Sophie said, turning to look through the back window. 'He is! He is actually picking up a dead animal from the road!'

Richard put the animal, whatever it was, in the boot of the car and got in again.

'Nice fresh tawny owl,' he said, rubbing his palms together.

There was something about the way he said it that made me want to laugh, but I was careful not to because of Sophie.

Then I heard Sophie saying, 'Who is this person I am married to?' And I knew she found it funny too, and she forgave him because he was completely crazy.

Richard turned around and put his hand on Sophie's knee.

'Don't knock it, sweet cheeks. I can get three hundred quid for that.'

The next afternoon I was in my room when I heard Sophie calling my name.

'Mirka, do you want to go for a walk with me?'

I was trying to give Richard and Sophie space to be alone on a Sunday, but it seemed like they did not want to be alone. I looked out of the window. The sky was perfect blue.

'OK,' I shouted back.

I did not know what I should wear so I came down the stairs in my black jeans and trainers. Sophie was standing on the mat with her hand on the kitchen door, putting her foot into a wellington boot. Ringo and Scrabble were making noises like they were singing, their tails waving from side to side.

'Aren't you lucky?' Sophie said, pulling Ringo or Scrabble's ears – I did not know which dog was which yet. 'You are a lucky boy. Yes, you are. Because you are going for a walk. That's right. A walk.'

The dogs obviously understood what Sophie was saying to them because they started barking and turning in circles like it was too much excitement. Sophie looked down at my feet with a worried expression.

'You're not going out in those are you?'

'I don't have anything else.'

'Let's find you some wellies. What size are you?'

'Forty-three.'

'Forty-three – what's that?' she said, looking up to the ceiling to think. 'Jesus, that is huge. You'll have to take Richard's boots.'

She went through a white wooden door in the corner of the kitchen and came back with a pair of green wellington boots and a dark green jacket made from a waxy fabric.

'How are those?'

I pulled one boot on to my right foot. 'Perfect.'

We walked down a road between the two lines of tall trees. The air seemed to clean my skin and my lungs. Sophie was wearing her green hat with feathers at the side, always whistling and calling to the dogs. With her wooden stick I thought she looked like a character from another century.

On the other side of the road was a green sign pointing through the hedge. Someone had built a wooden gate with two steps on both sides to help people climb over. Sophie held out her hand when I was at the top and I took it as I climbed down.

'It's called a stile,' she said.

'Did you build it?' I asked.

'Not personally,' she said. 'But it's our responsibility if it is on our land.'

We walked along a path in the grass towards some woods. Scrabble and Ringo were running all over the field with their noses close to the ground. There were so many exciting smells they did not know which one to follow. They would go in a line and then stop and decide this new smell was more interesting and turn and run in a different line.

We walked up a long hill with trees at the top like a crown. There were sheep eating the grass and they lifted their heads to watch us go past. I became so hot I had to take off the coat and put it over my arm.

Both of us were breathing deeply when we arrived at the gate at the top and turned to look back. The greens and browns of the fields and trees were milky in the weak sun. I looked sideways at Sophie, who was staring at the view. This was her world, I thought. She belonged here like a plant growing in the soil. It would never be my life. It was Richard and Sophie's life and I could only borrow it for a while, like a book from the library. One day I would have to give it back and leave the house to find my real life. But how would I know when a life was really mine? How did you know when you had found a home? I could never go home to my town and live there again. My old life was not mine any more. Perhaps I would never belong anywhere like a plant, I would move through different lives for ever. I wondered if Sophie had ever wanted a different life from this one.

'When did your family buy the house?' I asked when we started walking again.

'My grandfather bought it in 1947 in complete disrepair.

It had been requisitioned during the war and used as a billet for soldiers, and I think the old owners were killed or went bankrupt.'

We followed a path around the top of the hill below the trees.

'My mother grew up here,' Sophie continued. 'She lived in London for a while, working at Christie's as secretary. That's how she met my father, who was an art dealer.'

'He liked art?' I asked.

'He was passionate about art. Twentieth-century masters mostly. Kandinsky, Matisse – you name it.'

'Wow,' I said, impressed. Maybe Sophie's father was not so bad as she said.

'After my mother died, he couldn't bear to be here any more. He married my godmother, fucked off to France and has been there ever since.'

'I'm sorry,' I said.

I had thought that both her parents were dead, which was why Sophie was living in the house. Now I knew her father was alive. I remembered the marmalade jar and felt a shiver at the idea that I might have to meet him.

'You'll meet him sometime, no doubt,' Sophie said, as if she could hear my thoughts. 'And Caroline, who is a complete wet blanket. She drives me bananas. But she lost her husband too. He died of some rare form of leukaemia, leaving her with two boys. So they had that in common. And Dad wasn't going to survive for long without a woman to wash his clothes and cook for him. I doubt he could boil an egg if his life depended on it. So he grabbed the nearest woman and said, *She'll do.*'

We walked in silence and I could tell Sophie was thinking

about deep things. The path went down the other side of the hill between two hedges.

'I wish I hadn't married so young,' she said after a while. 'I was only twenty-four. I thought a wedding would cheer Dad up.' She sighed and said bitterly, 'Sometimes I wish I hadn't married Richard at all. He can be such a dick.'

I did not know what to say. I could not agree with her and say that Richard was a dick.

Sophie continued, 'I was so bowled over by him, I was blind. He was older and so good-looking. I know it's hard to believe now, but back then everyone fancied him. I was incredibly flattered he chose me. I didn't think things through. And once you're married, you're sort of stuck with it. You have no choice but to make it work.'

The path between the hedges was long and became narrower. We walked in a line, Sophie first, then me. I wanted to be in the open fields again. I had heard people say the things that Sophie said about marriage before. It was the kind of thing people said in books or movies.

'Do you want to get married?' Sophie said after a minute.

'I think so,' I said. 'One day I would like to fall in love with someone and know that I want to be with them for ever. But I do not want to be blind or be with the wrong person just to be with someone.'

Sophie looked hurt. 'You are so naïve. It doesn't work like that in real life. You have to compromise and weigh up what you have with the alternatives.'

'Then I will be alone.'

'OK, well good luck with that.'

'Thank you,' I said.

Sophie smiled. 'You know, I do love him. Even though he is completely ridiculous sometimes.'

'Ridiculous?'

'Oh, Mirka!' Sophie started laughing. 'Some of the things he comes up with. We've had the barn turned into storage units for people to hire. Except that he didn't damp-proof them and everything went mouldy. Then one year he thought it would be a good idea to have a festival in the grounds but only eighty kids turned up, and they were off their heads on whatever drug it is that they're doing now, and hardly bought any of the booze or food. We had about a million sausages left over. The list is endless. Bless him, he tries so hard. Fingers crossed, this taxidermy thing works out.'

There were muddy pools in the field at the bottom of the hill and Scrabble and Ringo immediately jumped into them. When they came out, they were covered in mud. Drops of brown water fell from the hair under their bellies.

We walked along the road towards the house.

'Did you have a boyfriend before you came to England?' Sophie said.

'I had a girlfriend,' I said.

'Oh,' Sophie said. 'Sorry, I didn't mean to assume ... Oh, that's terrible of me. I just thought—'

'It's OK,' I said. 'Everyone is the same.'

I turned and smiled to show her I did not care. I saw that her cheeks were pink and she was looking down at her hands. Her thoughts were so loud I could almost hear them.

'I mean, so you're gay then? Or was it only one girl?'

I already knew all the questions she would ask. 'I'm completely gay.'

'I wouldn't have guessed.'

I watched her looking at me. Behind her eyes I could see her brain was making new calculations about my character and appearance.

'But now you say it, it makes sense.'

'I thought you said you wouldn't have guessed.'

'Well, you aren't exactly very feminine,' she said.

'It's true I don't wear dresses and high heel shoes, but I think I am elegant.'

'I suppose you do have your own unique brand of elegance.'

Sophie was laughing, then she was silent. I waited.

'Who was the girl?'

'She was my English teacher.'

'Ha! That's why your English is so good. What happened?'

'She was married. We were together for about six months. I liked her, but it was never a real relationship. And then her husband found some text messages from me. He asked her about them and she said that it was nothing, that she made one mistake but I was obsessed with her and would not stop texting her. He came around to my house and told my parents and said that he would call the police if I did not leave his wife alone.'

'That's awful. How could she do that?'

'She had so much to lose. People are afraid to live like they should live.'

'Then what happened?'

'My mother told me to get out of the house and never come back. She was ashamed because everyone knew.'

'I'm so sorry,' Sophie said. 'That must have been awful. Where was your father?'

'He was there. He could have argued with my mother, but he said nothing.'

'Well, perhaps he didn't feel the same way as her, it was just that he wasn't brave enough to stand up to her.'

'That was exactly it. And I was not brave enough either. And secretly I wanted to go. I never wanted to be hated by my parents and community, but I never felt at home there with those people.'

'I'm sure they don't hate you. You'll go back one day and make it up with them.'

'Maybe,' I said. 'But I would like them to make it up with me first. I am not the one who is wrong.'

'What did you do?'

'I went to Bratislava and worked in a café. I was very unhappy for a while. I knew I had to leave my country. It is not good, being gay in Eastern Europe. So I decided to come to England.'

'Poor you.'

'I was OK. It is life. It's better than staying in my town and marrying a boring man like my sister.'

'I don't know what my dad would do if I told him I was gay,' Sophie said. 'All my life he used lesbian as an adjective for things that he didn't like. Herbal tea was *lesbian* tea. Flat shoes were *lesbian* shoes. There was a woman in the village – she's dead now, but she used to ride around on her bicycle. She was a spinster and Dad used to refer to her as *the lesbian*. Or *that dreadful lesbian*, if he was feeling charitable. Poor woman.' Sophie shook her head sadly.

We arrived at the kitchen door. Sophie put leads on to the

dog's collars and pulled them through the door. The dogs, still muddy, did not want to go inside and pushed against the floor with their feet.

'Come on, you stupid dogs. You know this has to happen.' She walked backwards, dragging them towards the white door in the corner of the kitchen.

'Shall I help you?' I said.

'Can you get the light?'

Sophie pulled the dogs into the little room with both hands and I switched on the light. Along one wall there were more wax coats and shelves full of boots and shoes. Opposite was a big rectangular sink. Sophie turned on both taps. Scrabble and Ringo started to run in circles around the room like they were trying to find a hole to escape.

'Oh, stop making such a fuss,' Sophie said.

When the sink was half-full of water Sophie picked up one of the dogs with both hands and dropped him in the sink with a splash. The dog stood still like he was trying to be dignified in the horrible situation. Sophie washed his legs and under his body with the water.

'There, it's not so bad, is it?'

The water turned brown and little twigs and leaves floated around on the surface. Sophie left him standing in the sink and put a towel on the floor. She lifted him up against her chest and put him on the towel. The wet dog shook his body so that water flew everywhere.

'Do you want to do Ringo?' she asked me.

I looked at Ringo the mud monster, who was looking up at Sophie and me.

'No thanks,' I said.

'No thanks? No thanks?' Sophie looked up at me while she was rubbing. 'What do you think this is, a holiday camp?'

For a moment I thought I had been rude, but then I saw that she was smiling and only teasing me. She released Scrabble from the towel and he ran towards the closed door, his nails scratching on the floor.

'Your turn, Ringo,' she said, trying to pick up the dog, but he ran past her. She dived after the dog, laughing. 'Come here, you little shit. You think you can escape from me, do you?'

I loved the way she spoke to the dogs, not like they were humans exactly, but as if they could understand her perfectly. I watched Sophie chasing the dog in circles until she caught him and lifted him into the sink. I wondered how many times she had practised these exact actions with the dogs in this little room. It seemed like a private ritual that I had been invited to watch, and it made me feel special, but at the same time I felt our difference very strongly.

CHAPTER THREE

Two weeks after I arrived at the house I was in the barn making grass, brushing green raffia paper with a steel brush, when the telephone rang. The fox on the table was watching me with her orange eyes. She still had pins in the skin of her face to hold them in the right place. Richard was out in the woods burning old trees. I could see the smoke in the distance from the window. I went to the desk and picked up the telephone.

'Good morning, Nose to Tail Taxidermy,' I said.

'Hello,' a man with a nervous voice said. 'I wanted to check it was all right to bring in my guinea pig this afternoon.'

'Is it a pet?' I asked. 'I'm sorry, we don't do pets.'

'Oh no,' the man said, sounding worried. 'Your colleague said it would be all right.'

'I guess it is OK then,' I said, confused. 'When did he die?'

'She died a week ago but I put her straight in the freezer like he said.'

'Bring her in and we will look at the skin,' I told him.

I went back to making the grass. It was one of my favourite jobs in the studio because I liked to watch the raffia break into pieces. After a while, I heard a scratching at the door and I went and opened it. On the stone floor there was a dead mouse. I could not see the cat anywhere.

'Thank you, Sammy Twinkle,' I said into the darkness of the barn.

I put on some blue plastic gloves from the box next to the sink and using some paper tissues I pushed the mouse on to a newspaper, put it into a plastic bag, zipped it and put it in the freezer. The skin was in good condition with no blood or bite marks. Richard would be pleased.

The grass I had made was for the home of a grouse. I had already painted the back of the glass box blue for the sky. Now I glued some bunches of grass in different places between the rocks on the floor. While I was waiting for the glue to dry I got a tube of brown paint from the paint drawer and a thin brush from the tin and put them ready on the table next to a sparrow. I took the white tape off his beak and started to paint it. I did not mind touching the animals after they had been stuffed when all the insides were gone.

Outside I heard the wheels of the car on the stones. The door opened and Richard came in smelling of fire smoke. Behind him I saw a tall man wearing a green wool hat rolled above his ears. I knew it must be David. He had a big head and small dark eyes like someone drew them on a potato with a black pen. In his left hand he held a dead squirrel by the tail. He stayed in the door with his head bent down as if he did not want to come inside.

'Hello,' I said.

Richard turned around from the sink where he was washing his hands. 'Have you two never met? Mirka, this is David.'

'Hello,' I said again.

David looked at me suspiciously and nodded without smiling.

'All right, David, I think we are done for today,' Richard said. He leant against the sink and put his hand down his trousers to scratch himself. 'We can do the rest on Thursday.'

'Still need to think about crop cover on Beech Hill for the new drive,' David said quietly. His lips almost did not move when he spoke and his accent was hard for me to understand.

'Yes, thank you, David. We will turn our attention to that straight away next time you are in, I promise.'

David looked at Richard like he wanted to say something he could not say.

'Well, don't forget to put that squirrel in the freezer before you go.'

After what seemed like a long time, David walked across the room to the freezer, lifted the lid and put the squirrel inside. His hands, I saw, were covered in mud and blood. Then he turned and put them in the pockets of his wax coat and walked out of the room.

Richard waited a minute, until we could hear David's steps outside, and then said, 'Fucking hell, that guy could really do with some cheering up. What the fuck is his problem? Why do I have to spend my precious days on this earth with someone so devoid of personality? I've known David for ten years and I have never seen him laugh. Not once. It would be nice to be mending a fence while indulging in a bit of hearty banter, instead of exchanging monosyllables with a man who has never stepped outside the confines of the parish.'

'Why don't you get a new gamekeeper?' I asked.

'Oh, I wish. But David's been working here since he was seventeen. I can't fire him, I'm not that much of an arsehole. And he's William's – Sophie's father's – favourite. God knows why. The son he never had, I suppose. David's all right, anyway. I just wish he would get a girlfriend or something. Bit of pussy down the Dog and Duck would sort him out. Sorry, I shouldn't say things like that in front of you.'

Richard was smiling as if he did not really care. I smiled back to show him I did not care either.

'Thank God he's only part-time. We share him with the adjacent estate. So at least I get every other day off.' He came and sat on the corner of the table, picked up the glass box and looked closely at it. 'Nice job, that. Anything come in today?'

'A man is bringing his guinea pig,' I said.

'Oh yeah, him. I remember. Weird bloke.'

'I thought we didn't do pets.'

'We don't do cats and dogs. Other things, like pet rabbits and hamsters, are fine. You can't get that attached to a hamster.'

'Also a woodcock that flew into a window arrived.'

'We've got to clear this backlog,' Richard said, frowning. 'I've got more dead animals than I know what to do with.'

He was silent, looking down at his crossed arms. I knew what he wanted to say. He had already told me a few times that

I should feel free to help him taxidermy the animals any time I wanted. I concentrated on making the straw body for the grouse, waiting for him to say it again. But he said nothing and went to peel the skin from a weasel.

Later, there was a knock on the door and a thin, pale man came in holding a purple cushion carefully with both arms. On the top there was something wrapped in a white napkin.

'Let's have a look then,' Richard said.

The man put the cushion on the table and unfolded the fabric. In the middle was the guinea pig, lying on her side with four stiff legs sticking out. She had orange fur and a little white bunch of hair between the eyes. When the man saw her, he sniffed and looked away.

'Can you do her?' he said, looking at Richard with a worried expression and blinking his dark eyes a lot.

Richard picked up the guinea pig with one hand and turned her around in front of his eyes without saying anything. I had a feeling he was playing with the man, making him suffer deliberately.

'I put her straight in the freezer, like you said,' the man said.

'Was she, er, one of the children's?' Richard said curiously.

'No, no. I know it must seem a bit odd,' the man said, looking down at his hands, his fingers moving quickly like he could not control them. 'But I've had her for five years and she's been a good friend to me.'

Before the man left again, he put his hand on the guinea pig's head and whispered, 'Bye, Misty.'

When we heard the engine of the man's car switch on, Richard said, 'God almighty, he gives me the creeps!'

'He was just sad.'

'What kind of man gets attached to a guinea pig?'

'Someone lonely.'

'You've got to be a bit of a bender.' Richard nodded at me with his eyebrows raised.

I did not understand exactly what Richard meant, but I knew he meant that the man was strange.

I frowned. 'You are cruel.'

'I guess he's perfectly harmless.' Richard shrugged and picked up the guinea pig and put her into a plastic bag. 'When is he coming back for her?'

'You said two weeks.'

'Put Misty on the shelf and I'll do her later.'

After two hours, when I had nearly finished the body of the grouse, Richard came and sat on the table next to me. I stopped and waited to see what he was doing. Then he bent his head towards mine.

'One little guinea pig,' he whispered in my ear.

'No.'

'Come on.'

'No.'

'Honestly, guinea pigs are a piece of piss.' He saw me looking confused and said, 'I mean, easy to do.'

'No.'

'You saw how upset the guy was. You can bring Misty back to life for him.'

I thought about this as I looked at Misty on the shelf. It would be good to help the man, even though I was not sure having a pet stuffed was definitely the right thing to do. But the man obviously thought it was the right thing and I felt sorry for him. I decided that the man knew that Misty was not going to come to life again, but I understood that maybe it would make him less sad to look at her body and remember her. She would be like a ghost, but the opposite of a ghost. Misty's skin would be a real object for the man to stroke after the ghost inside had died.

When Richard saw I was thinking about the possibility, he jumped off his stool, picked up the box of blue gloves and shook it under my chin.

'Look, gloves. What else?' he said, looking around the room with an excited expression. 'Anything you need.'

I kept looking at the floor. Richard came to me and held my shoulders with his hands. 'I'll give you ten per cent commission on top of your wages for whatever you do.'

'OK, I'll try,' I said. I sighed because I knew he would never stop asking me. 'But only try.'

Richard punched his fist in the air. 'Yes.'

I put the bag down on the table and went to take a pair of gloves. Richard took Misty out of the bag and put her on the table next to the knife and scissors. He stood there, still smiling.

'Stop being so happy,' I said.

Misty was lying on her back with her four legs open in the air. I took a deep breath and picked her up. She was soft and heavy like meat, and cold, so cold. But even so, I felt the strange energy of her life. I thought I would feel sick, but I did not. With the gloves on I felt safe because I knew nothing would get inside.

Richard was watching me. 'Are you OK?'

'I am surprised to be touching a dead animal,' I said. 'I never thought I would do something like this.'

'You know you are a bit OCD, don't you?'

I looked at him, confused.

'Obsessive Compulsive Disorder. Do you have that in Slovakia?'

'Yes,' I said. 'But I don't think I am very bad.'

'Don't think I haven't seen you washing your hands every two minutes and wiping your cutlery before you eat.'

'Ha ha,' I said, blushing because I did not think anyone had seen me do these things. I never really thought about it. 'OK, I am quite bad. But I am getting better.' I held Misty towards him. 'Look at me now.'

I took the knife in my right hand and made a small cut in Misty's throat. Slowly and gently I cut the skin down the middle of Misty's body over her belly to her vagina hole. As the skin opened I could see the shiny fabric of the bag holding the organs inside, and I was careful not to break it with the knife. I peeled the skin until I could touch my fingers around her back and her body hung like a purple bag with the little ribs against the surface like sardine bones.

Suddenly blood started coming out of Misty's mouth and nose, staining the fur on her face. Saliva came into my mouth and I thought I was going to vomit. I put Misty on the table.

'I can't do it, I can't do it,' I said, bending over and closing my eyes.

Richard stroked my back. 'It's normal, don't worry. You're doing really well. Keep going.'

I opened my eyes and picked up Misty again.

'Now pull the skin down her legs and tug the hip joint out,' Richard said.

When I had got all the legs out, Misty's skin was lying on the table inside-outside, a pool of shiny pale yellow fat with fur at the edges. Her purple body was in the white tray. Richard put his arm around me.

'That's the worst part over with,' he said. 'I'm extremely proud of you.'

It was not as bad as I thought it would be. But as I put the skin to cure in the chemicals I could not help feeling that what I had done was wrong and not natural.

It rained every day. Richard needed his wellington boots and wax jacket and I could not borrow them any more. So one afternoon Sophie took me to the town to go shopping. We drove in the rain and turned into the car park behind the supermarket.

'Keep your eyes peeled,' Sophie said as we drove slowly past the parked cars.

'There's a space,' I said, pointing to a car coming backwards towards us.

When we were parked, I got out from the car and Sophie opened a big umbrella. I had to bend to fit underneath.

'Maybe I should hold it,' I said, taking the curved wooden handle.

Sophie put her arm through my arm and we walked to the main street and I remembered Richard's story about how it was sociable to be inside the umbrella with her. I stopped to look in the window of a shop full of old objects like Chinese vases, wooden boxes and gold mirrors. There was a sign saying, *Quality is a thing of the past*, and in the next window there were more objects like a silver hairbrush and a trumpet, and another sign saying, *Hundreds of previous owners*, which I thought was funny of the owner of the shop. Above the street there were strings of red, white and blue triangles as if there was going to be a party.

Sophie stopped and got out her purse and put her card into the bank machine in the wall. When the fat pile of money came out she counted five twenty-pound notes and gave them to me. Every Wednesday she gave me cash in my hand. I had nothing to spend the money on so I ended up with much more money than I had in London, where I had spent everything on rent and tube tickets.

We arrived at a shop with a small wooden horse in the window and I put down the umbrella and Sophie opened the door, which made a bell ring above our heads. A little man, even smaller than Sophie, came out of a different room. I had never seen a man who was so small in my life. I tried not to stare at him too much.

'Right then, ladies, what can I be helping you with?' he said in a whistling voice.

'Some wellies and a Barbour for this one,' she said, pointing her thumb towards me.

The man looked at my feet. 'What size will you be wanting?'

'Nine,' Sophie said.

'Right ya are,' the man said, raising his eyebrows as if he had never seen a girl with such big feet.

He went into the other room. The shop smelt of leather. On a shelf above the glass desk was a line of pretty silk hats with squares and stripes in different combinations of colours. I went to the rail of wax jackets at the side of the room and picked up a white label on one of those coats and read the price. It was more than my wages for two weeks! I did not know if I was going to be paying or Sophie, and I could not pay for the jacket and the boots.

'Sophie,' I whispered.

Sophie was looking at some black leather gloves. She turned and the black fingers flapped over the back of her hand.

'I don't have money for the jacket and boots.'

Sophie smiled. 'Don't be silly. I'm getting these.'

I was relieved, though also embarrassed to be bought such expensive things. The man came back with a pair of green wellington boots.

'There we go. Give these a try.'

I sat on a stool and took off my trainers. The boots were the perfect size.

'They come in green, blue, red, black and yellow.'

'Black please,' I said.

The man brought a pair of black boots and some green wax jackets for me to put on.

'Give us a twirl then,' Sophie said when I put on the first jacket.

I looked in the mirror. I loved my outfit, elegant but also a little rough, not too feminine. I looked like a real English country person. Sophie was staring at me and I turned around in a circle and made some poses like I was a supermodel. I pointed my boot behind me and pushed out my lips. Then I walked to the window, twisted my feet, took off the jacket and held it over my shoulder as I walked back, moving my hips as if I was in a fashion show.

'How do you feel?' Sophie said.

'I feel like *Pretty Woman*,' I said.

Sophie laughed and clapped her hands together. 'You're so funny,' she said.

I could feel my cheeks blush. And as I stood behind Sophie while she paid for the boots and jacket, I realised I was still smiling. I thought how much I enjoyed making Sophie laugh.

After we had left the shop, we went into a coffee shop on the opposite side of the street. I put the wet umbrella against the wall and the shopping bags under the table. Sophie picked up the plastic menu with one hand and brushed the wet hairs from her face with her fingers. I made a hole in the mist on the windows with my sleeve and looked at the street. It was so dark the cars had their lights switched on.

'It's funny, but I don't mind the rain,' Sophie said. 'I wouldn't last two minutes in Dubai or somewhere like that. I'd have to walk around with an umbrella all day to keep the sun off me.'

The waitress had her arms inside the curved glass display case to put a black rectangular box of prawns inside. When she pulled the glass door sideways she smiled at us and picked up her notepad from next to the till.

'What can I get you?' she said, with the end of her pen resting on the paper.

'I'll have one of your cream teas with Earl Grey please,' Sophie said.

'Black coffee and a banana muffin please,' I said.

The waitress went away again.

'Sometimes I do wonder what on earth I am doing here,' Sophie said.

'Everyone thinks about what they are doing on earth.'

'No, I mean here. Why I'm not doing something more interesting with my life.'

'Your life is very interesting.'

Sophie looked at me under her eyebrows with narrow eyes. 'I mean something exotic. I should be living in Paris or working in New York like my sister. I get so restless sometimes. I wake up in the middle of the night and think to myself that I will just get up in the morning, pack a bag and go somewhere on my own. But I never do. I can't.'

I had wondered whether Sophie was always happy with her life at the house. Now I knew.

'You can.'

'Not really. And anyway, I feel an enormous sense of duty. To my mother, I suppose. Not that it seems to trouble the other members of my family.'

'What duty?'

'To keep the house going. My mother loved the house so much. And of course, I do too. I know it's a privilege. It just doesn't seem that way sometimes. I see what is going on in the world, so much excitement and change and drama, and I feel like I'm stuck in some strange sluggish pocket of time, ironing sheets all day and listening to Radio 4, my brain turning to mush.'

'What would you have done instead?'

'I wanted to be a journalist or maybe a historian,' Sophie said. 'Something to do with writing, anyway. A biographer, perhaps.'

'You should write something now.'

Sophie was playing with the pot of sugar, putting her finger over the top of the silver tube and turning it upside down.

'I'm going to. Now that you're here and I'm not constantly having to do household chores. It's funny, but when I was growing up, my mother used to always say to me, "Don't get stuck with a husband. Make sure you have your own career and you can support yourself." I was raised to believe I could do anything I wanted. I went to Oxford and got a first.' Sophie stopped and looked up at me. I nodded to show her I was impressed. She continued, 'And now I've basically turned into a housewife.'

'You run a business. Many different businesses. You should be proud.'

'Hmm, I suppose so. What about you?'

'I think my mother would only be happy if I was a housewife. Marriage is the most important thing and everything else is extra. Anyway, tell me about your sister,' I said, curious to know more about Sophie's family. She had never talked about having a sister.

'Camilla. She works for a fashion label. She's a total bitch.' Sophie smiled and licked the sugar from the end of her finger.

'Like my sister!' I said.

The waitress came with a tray and we leant back at the same time so she could put our cups and plates on the table. I took a bite from my banana muffin. It was a bit dry. Sophie was spreading a lot of cream on to her scone with the back of the spoon and I wished I had the same thing as her.

'Camilla is unbelievably self-entitled and single-minded. She has a clear vision of what she wants her life to be and it involves a very rich man paying for it. She's into yachts and private planes and that kind of thing. And not so much into working. She was never interested in the whole rural thing.' Sophie took a bite of her scone and wiped the cream and jam from her moustache. 'She couldn't wait to get as far away from the house as possible. What about your sister, what does she do?'

'She's a nurse.'

'Well that's admirable.'

'She's still a bitch,' I said, and Sophie laughed. 'It just makes her worse because she thinks she is perfect.'

At that moment, a man who looked like a poet, with round silver glasses and curly hair, came through the door and gently shook his umbrella towards the floor. He went to a table near the bar and took out a book from the pocket of his jacket. I turned my head sideways to read the name of the book, but his fingers were covering the words. When I looked back to Sophie, she was staring at him. She saw me looking at her and blushed.

'What? I'm only looking!' She looked sideways at the man again. 'He's handsome, right?'

'Not my kind,' I said.

'Obviously,' Sophie said, smiling. 'But try and be objective about it.'

'He's OK.'

'There is something sensual about him. The lips.'

I did not see anything sensual about him. To change the conversation, I said, 'Please tell me more about when you were growing up in the house with your sister.'

'Camilla and I were allowed to do pretty much what we wanted. I don't remember where Mum and Dad were half the time. I used to climb a lot of trees.'

'I liked to climb trees too,' I said. 'My sister never came with me. I always wished I had a brother to climb trees with. I wanted a brother more than anything.'

'I wanted a brother too. But in some ways I'm glad I didn't have one, because maybe I would have been treated more like a girl and not been allowed to be so free. Do you know what I mean?'

I nodded and Sophie continued, 'When my sister was born and my dad realised there were not going to be any sons, he decided that I would have to do. I went on all the shoots with him and did the picking up and beating. He taught me how to use a gun. It was our thing, I suppose.'

'Have you killed anything?'

'I've shot a few pheasants in my time,' Sophie said, smiling like she was secretly proud. 'But I can't say I get what all the fuss is about. Standing in the freezing cold, shooting some dumb birds out of the sky – it's not even a good sport. Anyway, that's Richard's arena now.'

When we came outside, the rain had stopped and the sun was burning white on the wet road. Sophie went into the newsagent's to buy tobacco while I waited outside, spinning the display of postcards of grey churches, swans swimming on a river, houses with straw roofs and other perfect English scenes. I picked a postcard up with a picture of the street where I was standing and I thought about buying it to send to my parents. But in the end I put it back. They did not care where I was, and even if they did care, I was not sure yet if they deserved to know that I was OK.

*

On Friday afternoon I was twisting yellow wool around the new body for Misty. Richard was peeling the skin from a deer's head. He made a noise through his teeth and threw the knife on the table.

'Argh, fuck it,' he said.

'What is wrong?'

'Made another fucking rip in the skin. I can never do the ears. I don't have the patience for this shit.'

'Let me have a look,' I said, going over to look at the deer's head. There was a big rip by one of the ears. I was beginning to realise that Richard was not the best taxidermist. He was not careful and did not like detail. For him it was only about the money.

'It will be OK,' I said. 'Finish taking off the skin and I will fix it.'

'How about we knock off early and go for a pint instead?' Richard said with a naughty smile.

We went outside and climbed into Richard's car.

'Shall we ask Sophie if she wants to come?' I said.

'Sophie's with a couple who have come to see the house for a wedding next year.'

As we drove past the house I saw Sophie with the couple on the front lawn. Sophie was standing a few metres away from the couple. They were shouting and their arms were waving and pointing angrily. Then the woman put her hands over her face and ran away from the man. We could not see any more because we were driving up the road between two hedges.

'Ouch,' Richard said. 'That didn't look like it was going too well.'

After about three kilometres we arrived in a street full of

small houses made from brick and grey glassy stones. There was a red telephone box and postbox, like the ones I had seen on the postcards. An old woman with a scarf on her head and her chin lifted high walked along the street with two small brown dogs. She reminded me of the women in my parents' town who had lived there all their lives.

On the left side of the street I saw a red-brick building with a sign saying *The Dog and Duck* hanging above the door. On the sign there was a picture of a brown-and-white dog, the same kind as Scrabble and Ringo, watching a duck with a green head flying away. Richard turned into the car park.

Inside the pub there was a fat man sitting at the bar.

'Hi, Richard,' he said, turning to shake Richard's hand. 'Good to see you.'

'Jimmy, this is Mirka who is helping us down at the house.'

Jimmy had small drops of sweat around the edge of his hair. When he shook my hand, it was very weak and sweaty and I wiped my palm on my trousers afterwards. He looked back at the horses racing on the television screen above the bar.

'I've got a fifty quid each way on April Showers in the ten to four.'

Richard whistled. 'Get a tip-off from Derek, did you?'

'Just fancied it. He put in some terrific performances the last season.'

A woman with short spiky dyed red hair and a lot of lines around her lips came through an arch behind the bar.

'Richard my love, how are you?'

Richard leant towards the woman on his elbow with his hand under his chin.

'Not bad, Sally. All the better for seeing you.'

'Oh stop it, you old flirt,' she said, shaking her head as if she was angry, but I knew she was enjoying herself. 'I'm old enough to be your mother.'

'Still got it, though,' Richard said.

The woman laughed. 'All right, that's enough of that. What can I get you?'

Richard turned to me and said, 'What are you having? I'll get these.'

'A coke.'

'You're not coming to the pub and having a coke.'

'Why not?'

'Because it's gay, that's why. I'll let you away with a shandy, but that is as low as I'm prepared to go.'

He turned back to the woman. 'A lager shandy and a Fat Badger, if you please.'

'And a packet of cheese-and-onion crisps,' I said.

Richard smiled. 'That's more like it. Make that two.'

I went to sit at the table next to the fire. The pub was plain and simple with green walls and stripes of black wood and white paint on the ceiling. Two men were playing cards at a table in the blue light from the window. Richard ripped open a crisp packet and put it open on the table so the crisps were in a pile on the silver square.

'So how are you feeling about everything?' he said, crunching a crisp.

'I'm very happy,' I said.

'Good, because I think we are on to a winner,' he said. 'And although it pains me to admit it, I think you are going to make a better taxidermist than me. You're a natural. Together we can make a killing.'

I took a sip from my glass. I had never liked the taste of beer before but I liked the shandy. Richard pushed his glass towards me.

'Try this, this is the real thing.'

I drank some. It was bitter and warm.

'You can have the real beer,' I said. 'It's disgusting.'

Richard laughed and leant back against the wood bench behind him.

'So, in an ideal world, what would you want to do with your life?'

'I don't know,' I said.

'Come on, there must be something.'

'Sometimes I have ideas. I don't know how to explain . . .'

'Ideas?'

'I look at something and it gives me an idea about something I could do.'

Richard frowned. 'Could you be a little more specific?'

'For example, when I worked at Pret A Manger I used to look at the people choosing their sandwiches and some of them would take a long time, as if they had forgotten what they were doing and were thinking of something completely different. Just staring at the sandwiches. I wished I could put a camera inside the fridge and make a beautiful film of their expressions when they thought nobody was watching.'

Richard looked at me curiously. 'Fair enough. We all have to have a dream.'

'Did you know what you would do when you were my age?'

'I was at agricultural college at your age. I always wanted to work on the land. That, or join the army.'

'The army?'

'Anything but sit behind a desk.' He shook his head seriously. 'It's not what we were made for.'

'Lucky you did not join the army.'

'Depends on how you look at it,' he said, pouring all the rest of his drink into his mouth and wiping his lips with the back of his hand. 'Drink up.'

I still had three centimetres of drink and I poured it all into my mouth. I swallowed and did a small burp. Richard bent his chin towards his chest, opened his mouth and did a huge burp. We both laughed.

I stood up. 'I'll buy you a drink.'

'Don't be silly. This is my treat.'

Richard went to the bar and came back with two more pints.

'Now admit that this is a hell of a lot better than London,' he said, and before I could say anything he continued, 'I used to visit Sophie in London when we first started going out. Full of absolute cunts.'

'There are nice people there too.'

'Full of cunts who don't give a toss how people in this country actually live.'

'Everyone is just trying—'

'No respect for ancient ways of life. They've got no idea what it's like to live out here. All they care about is the latest fashion, what's the newest restaurant, where they should be seen. It's all a load of bollocks. All that matters is money. And the politicians are the worst of the lot. They've all got their noses in the trough.'

After some more pints I noticed there was something wrong with my movements. When I put down my drink on the table I did it too heavily. I realised I was drunk. As I walked to the bathroom, my legs felt lazy. I looked in the mirror and thought that I looked beautiful and I started to laugh. Being drunk was not as bad as I remembered. I felt quite free and careless.

When I came back there was a new drink on the table for me. 'Richard!' I said, suddenly thinking. 'How will we get home?'

'Good point,' he said, frowning. 'Soph can pick us up.'

'Do you think we should call Sophie and invite her?'

'She'll be all right,' he said, leaning towards me. 'I love her to bits and everything, but it's nice to get away once in a while. Do you know what I mean?'

'I guess,' I said.

'I like having you around, Mirka. You're a good egg. And Sophie does too, I can tell. She seems happier already.'

'Happier?'

'Between you and me, I think she was a bit depressed. Or lonely. I was the one who wanted you to come. I thought she could do with some company. She was worried we couldn't afford it, but I was the one who insisted. And I think it was a brilliant idea.'

Richard looked very pleased with himself. I was thinking about Sophie being depressed and feeling sorry for her. But I liked the idea that I had made her happier.

The door opened and David came in. When he saw me and Richard he stopped at the door. His expression was as if this was the worst thing he could find in the pub. Then he realised he could not escape and walked to our table.

'All right, David,' Richard said. 'Didn't expect to see you here. Does Geoffrey know you're slacking off down the pub?'

'It was him who told me to go and have a pint.'

'It was only a joke. Come and join us. Please.'

As David walked to the bar, Richard gave me a strong look. I was sad to have my conversation with Richard ruined.

David came back with a dark brown pint and sat down. All of us picked up our glasses and took a drink.

'We should set those traps tomorrow,' David said.

'Let's not talk shop in front of Mirka, shall we?' Richard said in a friendly way.

There was a silence. I could see Richard trying to think of something to say.

'How is Geoffrey, anyway?'

'He's selling up.'

'Oh, that's a shame. You'll be fine though. Whoever comes will still need a gamekeeper, I'm sure.'

David nodded and drank some more beer. There was another silence.

'Are you from this village?' I asked, to make conversation.

'Next village,' he said.

'David has the local accent, can you hear it?'

'Not really,' I said. I was going to say that it was difficult to know because I had heard him say less than ten words, but I stopped myself.

'Where are you from?' David asked me.

'Slovakia,' I said.

'At least you're not from Poland. That's something.'

'Do you know what I heard?' Richard said quickly, before I

could say anything. 'Apparently there is going to be a Starbucks opening in town. Can you believe it? A Starbucks! Here I was, thinking that we were completely sheltered from the relentless march of globalisation. How wrong I was. You a big coffee fan, David?'

David made an expression of disgust and said nothing. It was hard to know if it was the idea of the coffee or Richard's behaviour. It was an uncomfortable atmosphere.

'Richard,' I said, 'I think we should call Sophie.'

'Fine. I'm going for a quick fag. I'll give her a call outside.'

When Richard was gone, David and I sat in silence for a minute. Then he turned to me and said, 'Like it over here, do you?'

'Yes, I like it very much,' I said.

'Couldn't get a job over there?'

'I had a job, but I wanted to live in a different country.'

'That's the problem, isn't it? Anyone who wants to can come over and get a job, just like that.' He clicked his fingers and stared at me. 'The country gets flooded with people who will work for less than the people here who are trying to feed their families.'

I was so shocked at how many words David was speaking that I did not realise at the beginning what he was saying. He did not blink and this gave him a dark energy.

'English people go to work in different countries in the world,' I said. 'Everyone has the right to find a better life.'

David leant towards me and said, like it was a real threat, 'You should have stayed in your own country.'

The door to the pub opened and David leant back again and

drank some beer. Richard came to the table and stood with the telephone on his ear. 'I'm sorry. I know. I know. I'm sorry. OK, see you in bit. Thanks, angel cakes.'

He pressed a button and put the telephone back in his pocket.

'Sophie's on her way,' he said.

Richard talked about what jobs they needed to do on the land in the next weeks until we heard two beeps from a car outside. Both Richard and I got up from the table immediately.

'Bye, David,' Richard said. 'Have a nice evening.'

'Bye,' David said, and as Richard turned to open the door, he gave me the same dark look.

Outside Sophie was sitting staring ahead with her hands on the wheel. When we got into the car she did not turn to look at us.

'Had fun then?' she said in a bitter voice.

'Don't be like that,' Richard said, leaning across to kiss her. 'We only went for one drink and it turned into a few, that's all.'

'Get your beer breath out of my face,' she said, pushing Richard's face with her hand. 'You know something? It would be nice to be asked. Just once.'

I could see her hard blue eyes in the mirror. Suddenly she looked up and her eyes locked with my eyes. They were full of hurt and anger, and I had to look away.

CHAPTER FOUR

'*Accommodation given to setter in disgrace.* Three, five,' Sophie said.

'I don't know,' I said, putting tomato and sausage on my fork. 'Prison?'

'Prison's not a bad guess. I don't think it's right though. Now, setter probably means something to do with the person who wrote the crossword.'

I put my knife and fork together and looked up. Sophie's white towel robe was open and through the gap I could see her nipple. I looked quickly again at my plate but I could still see it from the side of my eye and I could feel my cheeks getting hot. Sophie did not realise anything, and continued sucking the pen and brushing her messy hair with her fingers.

Somebody knocked three times at the front door. Sophie stood up, looked down and saw her robe was open. As she walked across the kitchen, she pulled it wide open and folded it again more tightly, showing me by accident her whole naked body. After she had gone from the room I shut my eyes and I could still see the image of her body, the small breasts with blue veins like lightning and the pale hair between her legs.

After a minute she came back with a big brown box in her arms. The dogs ran to her, sniffing the bottom of the box and waving their tails.

'I think this must be one of yours,' she said. 'The dogs can smell it.'

'It's a woodpecker.'

'Of course,' Sophie said, like she had just realised something. 'Setter not as in crossword setter. Setter is a kind of dog, you see. The answer is *dog house*.'

'What?' I said, confused by the way Sophie always changed conversation.

'As in, Richard is in the dog house because he didn't invite me to the pub. It's where you put someone, metaphorically speaking, when you are angry with them.'

Sophie took the letters from the top of the box and opened each one, making one pile on the table of torn envelopes and another pile of cards and letters. She took the pile she did not want to the recycling bin and opened the lid.

'Oh for God's sake!' she said. 'Honestly, what is wrong with him?'

'What?'

Sophie put her hand in the bin and pulled out a piece of newspaper with a chicken bone stuck to it, then an envelope stained with tomato sauce.

'You can't recycle chicken. What does he think they are going to turn it into? I swear he does it on purpose.'

Richard walked into the kitchen from the corridor wearing a green cap and his leather boots. Pieces of dried mud fell from the bottom of his feet on to the floor.

'Richard, please don't walk through the house in your boots,' Sophie said.

'I'll clean it up later,' he said, like he was not really listening.

'You won't though, will you? I'll end up doing it. And look at this,' she said, holding the chicken bone. 'How many times have I told you not to scrape your plate in the recycling bin.'

'Please don't give me a hard time this morning. I've got a million things to do.'

'And I don't?'

'You don't look like you do, no,' he said, looking at Sophie's newspaper and coffee cup.

Richard started taking things out of the bowl next to the telephone: a ball of string, rubber bands, pins, metal keys and some batteries, putting them on the dresser surface. The ball of string fell off and ran across the kitchen floor. I put my foot out and stopped it. I was used to these arguments now. They had them all the time and behaved as if I was not there. Tonight they would be drinking and laughing again.

'Actually,' Sophie said. 'I'm just having a coffee and then I'm going to start on the rooms. Then I have a load of planting to get on with, and I could do without having to pick your food out of the bin and go round hoovering the mud that you've traipsed up and down the stairs.'

Richard turned and made a noise through his teeth. 'Argh, shut up! Where are my fucking keys?'

'Probably in the bowl in the hall where they live,' Sophie said, picking up the newspaper again and looking very closely at the page.

'Well, obviously they aren't there or I wouldn't be turning the house upside down to find them.'

'Then they probably fell out of your pocket while you were up all night getting stoned on your own. Try the sofa.'

Richard's head jerked up and he walked quickly out of the room without arguing with Sophie again. After a minute he called the dogs from the hall and they got up and ran out of the kitchen. The front door banged.

'Don't say goodbye or anything,' Sophie said quietly.

I put on yellow gloves and washed the dishes. Sophie continued with the crossword, her eyebrows together and her lips sometimes moving as she said words to herself. I knew she had forgotten about Richard already. Outside the sun was shining on the daffodils that were growing everywhere in the garden, along the wall and in circles under the cherry trees.

'Maiden aunt,' Sophie said, sounding excited.

'What?'

'It's an anagram of *united a man*.'

'What is a maiden aunt?'

'It's an older woman who never married, but sometimes we use it to talk about someone who is naïve and innocent in the ways of the world. You would say something like, "It's enough to make your maiden aunt blush."'

When the kitchen was finished we went upstairs to take the

sheets and towels from the yellow room and put new teabags and biscuits with clean cups next to the kettle. Sophie went to the cupboard in the corridor next to her bedroom and pulled a short red vacuum cleaner on wheels along the carpet. Each side of the black tube, the vacuum had two eyes that made it look like a little red man wearing a black hat.

'Mirka, meet Henry. Henry, this is Mirka.' She bent down and looked at the vacuum as if she was waiting for him to whisper something. 'Aren't you going to say hello? No? He's a bit shy sometimes.' She stood up again and saw me laughing and looked at me happily. 'Can you hoover the halls and bedrooms?'

'Of course,' I said.

Sophie went to clean the bathrooms. I watched the colour of the carpet change darker or lighter blue as the vacuum head was swinging forwards or backwards. The telephone rang on the table in the hall and Sophie ran past me, jumping over the tube of the vacuum. I switched off the machine so it would not be too loud for her and went to the bathroom in the blue room.

All the bathrooms had books with funny expressions or cartoons for the guests to read when they were sitting on the toilet. From the shelf opposite the toilet I took a book of English quotations, opened the book in the middle and read: *A man is in general better pleased when he has a good dinner upon his table, than when his wife talks Greek.* Samuel Johnson.

I read some more sexist quotes about marriage while I took a pee.

'Mirka! Mirka!' Sophie shouted.

'One minute,' I shouted back, wrapping paper around my hand.

I leaned over the railing. Sophie was looking up at me, holding the ear of the telephone on her shoulder.

'Can you go into my bedroom and get my diary? It should be on the chest of drawers.' She put the telephone to her mouth. 'Won't be a second. Which weekend was it again?'

I went to the door at the end of the corridor. I had never been in Sophie and Richard's bedroom. It smelt of Richard's sweat and Sophie's rose skin cream, sleepy breath, a little of smoke from cigarettes and burning wood, alcohol, pine trees and dirty sheets. Like I expected, it was very messy. The chest of drawers was on the other side of the room and I had to walk carefully not to step on all the clothes on the floor. Sophie's jeans and red jumper were on the carpet like the person inside had burst into fire and disappeared. There were pink pants on the sheepskin rug, a cream silk vest on the end of the bed, and Richard's green trousers in the middle of the floor. Socks flowed on to the floor from the armchair, which looked more like a clothes fountain than a chair.

The diary was next to a glass of white wine with a small fly floating in it. As I picked it up I saw a photograph in a frame of Sophie and Richard on the day of their wedding. Sophie's face was round and fresh. Richard had his arms around her waist, lifting her. They were both laughing and looked happy.

When I turned around again to walk back to the door I saw something on the bed. The covers were pushed to the side and in the middle of the sheet there was a blue vibrator. I froze, staring at it. I was shocked to see something so private and sexual.

I thought that when Sophie came back to the room she would know I had seen it and she would be embarrassed. But I could not touch it because then she would know I moved it. I could not decide which was worse.

'Have you found it?' Sophie called from downstairs.

'One second,' I shouted.

I quickly went to the bed and pulled the cover a little so that the vibrator was hidden. I decided that when she came back to the room she would be happy to find that her vibrator was hidden and she would not think, *But I am sure I left my vibrator in the middle of the sheet.*

I started vacuuming the carpet again but the images of Sophie's naked body from the morning kept coming into my brain, even though I did not want them to. And worse, now I thought of Sophie lying in the bed using the vibrator. I felt ashamed because I knew I should not have these thoughts and also a little angry because it was not my fault I had seen anything. I made myself think about taxidermy and all the jobs I needed to do that afternoon.

I was sewing Misty's belly together with white cotton, gently adding more wood wool around the body so she would be as fat as when she was alive. When I went to the bench at the back of the room I looked through the window and saw Sophie in the distance on the path. She was on her knees, pulling plants from the soil. She had a black stripe on her forehead where she had wiped her face with dirty hands. I still felt strange about what I had seen earlier.

At lunchtime there was a knock on the door.

'Knock, knock,' Sophie said.

She put the plate of tuna and cucumber sandwiches on the

desk and stood next to my shoulder, looking down at my hands working.

'You have a real knack for it,' she said. 'Richard said so.'

'I like this part, after the insides have gone.'

'It's such a strange thing to want to do, isn't it? When you think about it. I suppose it made sense in the days before television or even photography, when the way most people would ever get to see a lion was to see a stuffed one. But someone wanting their pet guinea pig stuffed, that seems kind of sad.'

'Maybe,' I said, because I did not know what I thought about it.

'Anyway, look,' Sophie said, taking a magazine from under her arm and unrolling it on the table. 'Aren't these amazing?'

It was an article about a famous taxidermist who lived in the Victorian era. On the first page of the magazine there was a big photograph of a scene of about fifteen kittens wearing rich lace dresses and red and blue necklaces and posing like they were at a wedding in a church. A kitten with brown fur dressed as a priest was standing in front of the groom and bride, who were looking at each other like they were very in love. It was a beautiful and unusual scene with a lot of details. Underneath the photograph I saw the name of the scene: *The Kittens' Wedding*.

'Look at the little earrings. And look, he's got a pocket watch!' Sophie pointed to different places in the photograph. 'And the vicar is holding a tiny bible. They're just so cute!'

Like Sophie, I had a lot of pleasure from the tiny details and I thought the kittens were cute, but I also felt strange for the animals who had to live forever dressed in human clothes, posing in a human scene. It was somehow different to animals living in their own homes with grass and sky, even if the homes were fake. There was something unnatural, almost frightening about the scene, but this was why it was so interesting.

I took off my blue gloves and looked more closely at the magazine. On the next page there was a photograph of taxidermy rabbits studying mathematics at school. They were sitting at tiny desks and had little black squares to write on with mini white sticks. All of them had different personalities that you could see in their faces. One naughty rabbit was looking secretly at the work of the rabbit sitting next to him. There were old maps on the wall of the school and pots full of ink and perfect little pens. On the other pages there were scenes of drunk squirrels playing cards and telling funny stories in a bar, and guinea pigs playing cricket. It was the work of a real artist. I looked again at the name of the taxidermist. He was called Walter Potter.

Sophie was watching me looking at the photographs. I was already having lots of ideas, images in my brain.

'What do you think?' Sophie said.

'They are amazing,' I said. 'The detail is so rich.'

'I thought maybe you could do something similar. We have rats, mice, squirrels and rabbits coming out of our ears.'

'All the cute, small animals.'

'I actually meant the unwanted animals.'

'I thought kittens were pets,' I said, looking at the first picture again.

'I guess in Victorian times cats were seen more as mice killers than pets. Like Sammy Twinkle. And if there were too many kittens they would probably drown them. I don't think they were as sentimental in those days.'

I was silent, looking at the pictures. What Sophie said about the small animals made me realise there was a possibility to do something. But I was still not sure it was right to dress animals in human clothes.

Sophie continued, 'I'm sure Richard could sell something like this and you would take a cut. You are so good at detail.'

I reminded myself the animals were already dead. It was about the pleasure for the humans looking at them, and the truth was, I loved the scenes for their power and strangeness and I had a lot of respect for the imagination of the artist.

'Maybe I could try it with some mice and dress them in modern clothes,' I said.

'But people love all that Victoriana stuff, don't they?'

'But I can't make the same as the past.'

'Hmm,' Sophie said, not sounding sure.

The light was bright in the windows and I suddenly wanted to go outside. I needed to think more about the taxidermy later, without Sophie.

'I think I will eat my sandwich in the garden,' I said.

'I'll come and keep you company.'

We walked along the path to the garden and sat down on a curly white bench between two cherry trees. The sun shone through the heavy branches of pink flowers on to our faces. It was much warmer now than when I arrived at the house.

In the middle of the grass was a stone stool with a shallow dish of water on the top. A bird with a yellow chest and blue hair was jumping around the edge of the circle and putting his beak in the water to drink.

'Blue tit,' I said, remembering the clock.

'Very good,' Sophie said.

'He's having a lot of fun.'

I ate my tuna sandwich and looked at the daffodils shaking gently in the wind. I liked the way Sophie cut the cucumber so thin. Another bird with black feathers and a yellow beak landed on the edge of the bath and the blue bird flew away.

'It is a magical place to grow up,' I said.

'I know. I was very lucky,' she said in a dreamy voice. 'One day I'd love to give my children the upbringing I had.'

'I'm sure you will,' I said. I had not thought about why they did not have children and now I understood that it was not a choice.

We sat silently watching the different birds arriving at the bath and flying away again. I felt that Sophie was far away, somewhere sad.

'Richard's gone to Devon for a stag party for the weekend,' Sophie said after a while. 'Do you know what a stag party is?'

'Of course I do,' I laughed. 'British men come to Bratislava every weekend for stag parties. They get drunk, vomit all over the city and use prostitutes. They are famous in my country, and all over Eastern Europe.'

Sophie laughed and put her hand over her mouth. 'Oh, that is so awful. I do apologise on behalf of my country.'

'That's OK.'

'It makes me feel sick whenever he goes on one because I wonder what he is going to get up to.'

'I don't think Richard is going to do anything bad. He loves you.'

'Hmm. He has a funny way of showing it sometimes.'

'I think a lot of men are the same.'

Scrabble and Ringo came round the corner of the house with their noses on the grass like they were following our smells and licked the crumbs of bread from the plates under the bench. Sophie was looking down at her hands on her jeans, picking skin at the sides of her nails.

'How did you know you were gay?' Sophie asked in a quiet, serious voice.

'I just knew,' I said. 'I think I always knew.'

Sophie frowned as if this was not the answer she wanted to hear.

'You never liked boys?'

'No. I remember all the girls talking about boys and I could not understand it. I was not very sexual when I was a teenager. I knew I was different. I never wanted to kiss a boy. I never cared if a boy wanted to kiss me. I felt nothing.'

Sophie looked surprised. 'I was completely the opposite. I wanted to fuck everything that moved.' She laughed. 'I was complete jailbait as a teenager. Like with David – I used to go out and sunbathe topless on the lawn on the days when I knew he was working.'

'You liked David?' I said, shocked.

Sophie made a face of disgust. 'No, of course I never liked David! Well, maybe a bit, but only in that way you do when you're fifteen and you fancy every single twenty-four-year-old.

But not seriously. I wanted him to want me, that's all. I wanted to torture him.'

'That's not kind.'

'Never underestimate the power of a ravenous ego. I can't imagine not wanting men to fancy me. It must be quite liberating.'

'I never thought of it before.'

'So when did you realise you liked girls?'

'I just remember imagining what it would be like to kiss a girl and thinking it would be nice. But I didn't know for sure until I met my English teacher.'

'What did you know?'

'That I wanted so much to kiss her. And it was incredible when we did.'

We both smiled and Sophie looked away as if she was embarrassed. She leant forward and stroked the head of one of the dogs.

'I had a couple of flings with girls at uni,' she said, still looking closely at the top of the dog's head and pulling his ears.

'You did?' I was so surprised.

'I guess technically I went out with one of them for six months. But it was only a sex thing.' She made a little wave with her hand and I saw her cheeks were pink.

'You never wanted to be her girlfriend?'

'I didn't really consider going out with her. I think she loved me a lot and I got scared. It was all too emotional and I wanted to have fun. Maybe I could have loved her if I had let myself. Maybe I was afraid of the consequences of making it real. I never even considered publically acknowledging that we were together, let alone bringing her home.'

'But you liked having sex with her?'

'Yeah, I loved having sex with her,' she said, her eyes glowing.

This information was too heavy for us and we sat in silence for a while. The idea I had of Sophie was changing quickly.

'I have to go back to work,' I said.

'I probably won't see you then. I've got to go over to the hen's house for dinner. I'll be back tomorrow.'

'OK,' I said.

'I'm not even friends with her, but I think she felt she had to invite me as Richard was going to the stag. There's some leftover pie in the fridge.'

I got up. 'Have fun.'

Sophie smiled. 'I won't, but thanks anyway.'

The next day I went to the barn. Richard and Sophie were still away. Misty was finished and ready on her purple cushion with her orange hair brushed. I opened the freezer and looked at the frozen animals. There were a lot of mice from Sammy Twinkle. I took one out and held it on my palm in front of my eyes. Then I had an idea. It would need some research but I thought it would be good. I put the mouse back in the freezer.

I worked all morning making a home for a squirrel in a big branch of a tree. At lunchtime I went to the house to get some food. I realised as I was walking along the path that I was nervous about seeing Sophie. It was because of the conversation the day before. I felt that the knowledge we had was dangerous. It could change our relationship somehow and make things that used to be clear, unclear, or things that were impossible, possible. It was confusing and I did not understand my thoughts.

The man came at four o'clock to collect Misty. When he saw her he went quickly to the table and put out his hand to touch her, but then took it back quickly again.

'It's OK,' I said. 'You can touch her.'

He put out his shaking hand and stroked Misty's head. He started to cry. He took a few deep breaths to control himself.

'It's such a relief to be able to touch her again,' he said. 'Thank you.'

'That's OK, it's my job.'

'A friend gave Misty to me after my wife passed away. He thought having something to care for might help lift me out of my depression. And it did, it really did. Now she's gone too,' he said with a sad voice, but he was not crying any more.

'I'm sorry to hear about your wife,' I said.

'It's funny,' the man said, bending to look closely at Misty. 'I know she isn't in there, but I can feel her so strongly, it's like she's looking at me from somewhere inside.'

He stood up straight. 'I suppose you think I'm completely mad.'

The man smiled with an embarrassed and helpless expression, but also with knowledge that the situation was funny. I wanted to go and put my arms around him.

'I don't think you are mad,' I said, smiling. 'When someone you love dies, you can do whatever you want to help yourself.'

'Exactly,' the man said, smiling happily. 'And one day, someone will peek through the curtains and I'll be eating my TV dinner off a tray and feeding bits of mashed potato to Misty and they'll come and lock me in the loony bin and throw away the key.'

He took Misty on the cushion and stopped at the door. 'You've done such a good job with her. I don't know how to thank you enough.'

'It was my pleasure,' I said.

I waited until eight o'clock in a kind of dream. I was not thinking about my conversation with Sophie any more, but about taxidermy and how powerful it could be. I kept thinking that I had brought something back to life. It felt good to know that I had stopped something from disappearing for ever and it existed only because of me. Now I could do this with other animals.

When I was finished, I walked along the path to the house. The moon was a thin curve above the fields. Through the windows I saw Sophie in the yellow light doing the crossword on the kitchen table. She had her chin resting on her hand, looking up, her expression thoughtful. It was a beautiful scene, like a painting, and I stayed there for a while watching her. I had always thought Sophie was interesting and pretty, from the moment I arrived at the house, but now she seemed to change in my eyes, becoming beautiful and extraordinary. I knew I could not hide my feelings from myself any more.

'Ah, there you are,' she said when I came through the door. 'Dinner is ready. I thought maybe we could go and eat it on our laps in front of the TV.'

I walked behind Sophie down the corridor, still feeling strange from what I had experienced outside. The lights in the living room were already on and a fire was burning. I sat next to Sophie on the sofa and put my tray on my thighs. She switched on the TV with the control, pressing buttons to try different stations.

'Why is it every time I want to watch television there is literally nothing on? It's Saturday night, for God's sake. OK, there is a new David Attenborough series starting, let's watch that.'

Sophie sat back and I could see her face in the television screen. I tried to concentrate on the programme. It was about animals in Indonesia. The old man on the television was talking about Komodo dragons. I watched the dragons dragging their heavy feet along a beach. They had strings of saliva hanging from their jaws and their long pale yellow tongues slid out of their mouths, whipping around their faces when they sucked it back up like a piece of spaghetti. The man said that there had been an important discovery at the London Zoo. One of the Komodo dragons had given birth to four dragons. But she had never had sex with a man.

When Sophie finished eating she put her tray on the low table in front of the sofa. She turned on her side and pulled a blanket over her body. After a minute, she sighed loudly as if she was not comfortable, and turned on her back.

'Do you mind if I put my legs over you?'

'No, of course,' I said, hearing my voice sounding strange.

She put her legs across my thighs. I had nowhere to put my hands so I crossed my arms. I felt as stiff as a dead animal from the freezer. Sophie's legs were heavy and hot on mine. I tried to concentrate on the television but I kept seeing Sophie's face in the screen. She seemed very peaceful, innocent, and I wondered how she could not be conscious of what she was doing, especially after our conversation. Once, when we were watching some Javan rhinoceroses walking through a muddy stream, Sophie's eyes changed distance and looked into my eyes. Instead of smiling like it was a coincidence, I looked away quickly, guiltily.

Then Sophie got up to go to the bathroom. I waited, not really watching the television, worrying that I had made her feel uncomfortable, that she would tell Richard. My mind imagined all the negative possibilities and I became sure that they would ask me to leave the house.

After a long time, Sophie had not come back and I wondered what had happened to her. I went out of the living room to the kitchen. The dogs were in their basket but Sophie was not there. I went to the stairs and shouted Sophie's name. There was silence. I started to walk slowly up the stairs. I was afraid she did not want me to come and find her, but at the same time I felt that something was wrong. It was dark upstairs and I felt along the wall with my palm for the switch. As I turned the corner, I saw the light underneath the door to Sophie's room. I knocked gently.

'Come in,' Sophie said, and I knew from her voice she had been crying.

She was sitting in bed with her knees bent. Her face was covered in red patches and her eyes were swollen. When she saw me, she started to cry again. I went quickly to the bed and sat next to her.

'What is wrong?' I said.

'I got my period, that's all.'

I knew immediately why she was sad. 'I'm sorry,' I said.

She put her head between her knees and cried some more. I stroked her hair. After a minute she lifted her head and wiped under her eyes with the ends of her fingers.

'Sorry,' she said. 'I'll be OK.'

'You don't need to say sorry.'

'I really thought I was pregnant this time. I was absolutely sure of it. I don't know why this keeps happening to me. I just want a child. Is that too much to ask?' She wiped her nose with her sleeve. 'Will you get me some loo roll?'

I went into the bathroom. On the white tile floor next to the toilet there was a drop of blood. I wiped it with some paper.

'I think nature is trying to tell me I shouldn't be a mother,' Sophie said after I had come back.

'That's not true.'

Sophie's face twisted and she closed her eyes. When she opened them they were full of tears again. She blew her nose on the paper.

'I'm not a good person, Mirka.'

'Of course you are a good person.'

'I've been unfaithful to Richard.'

'Oh,' I said, 'But becoming pregnant is not connected with being a good person. It is not a reward.'

'I only did it once, at one of the weddings here. It's so easy to have sex at a wedding. And I was feeling so insecure. I needed to feel desired. I was sure Richard was having an affair.'

'Was he having an affair?'

'I don't know. There was one summer, about three years ago when he seemed to have to go on some trip every other weekend. There was this woman called Georgia, the wife of an old acquaintance of ours. I don't know. But I felt different around him when he came back each time. I would recoil from him.'

'Maybe it was your imagination.'

'Maybe. But he would be so attentive and overly affectionate. Anyway, that's how I was feeling when we had this big wedding here. I had sex with the best man up against a tree. It wasn't my finest hour.'

I smiled because Sophie was smiling, then I said seriously, 'Sophie, this is completely separate to the baby.'

'I know, I know. It's just so hard.' She took my hand. 'Thank you.' She moved down the bed so she could lie down with her head on the pillow. 'Will you sleep with me here tonight? I don't want to be alone.'

She gave me a T-shirt to wear and I put it on in the bathroom. I felt nervous, so much had changed so quickly in one day. When I got into bed, she turned on her side with her back towards me. She reached behind and pulled my arm across her so that our bodies were locked together. I could feel my breasts pressing against her back through our T-shirts and her naked thighs were burning against my legs. I felt as though every nerve in my body was alive and I thought I would never sleep. Sophie's breathing became slower and slower until she was sleeping. I lay there, very still, trying to breathe normally for a long time, for hours, until my body and my mind relaxed from tiredness. As I fell asleep I imagined that Sophie was my wife, and this was my bed and that every night I went to sleep, holding her in my arms.

CHAPTER FIVE

It was the day of the first wedding. I was sitting at the table chopping vegetables. Everyone was always saying it would rain but so far June was sunny and hot and I could feel the summer waiting for me like a girl lying on a lawn. In front of me, the beetroots shone like jewels in the morning light. I cut the last one into fourteen faces and threw it into the bowl with the others. My fingers were stained pink at the ends. Sophie twisted the cigarette in the ashtray and waved the smoke away with her hand.

'Right, I need to go and have a shower.'
She pushed the folded newspaper along the table towards me.
'Look at fourteen down.'
'You know I can't do any clues.'
'It's an easy one. Remember, think laterally. Double meanings of words.'

'I don't know the first meanings.'

Sophie went to the cooker and took the saucepan from the hot circle to the sink. She turned on the cold tap until water was flowing down the sides. I pulled the newspaper towards me and turned it to look at the clues.

'*It won't be found in the pack*,' I read. 'Like a pack of cards?'

'Yes but what other kinds of pack are there?'

Sophie was smiling, waiting for me to know the answer.

'I don't know any other packs.'

The smile fell off Sophie's face. 'It's a wolf pack. The answer is *lone wolf*.'

'Don't be angry with me because I can't do the crossword.'

'I give up.' She put her hand on my head and messed my hair as she walked past.

I put the skin of the beetroots into the bin. The clock made the noise of the blackbird. It was eight o'clock. The doorbell rang and the dogs ran out of the kitchen. I switched off the tap and as the water in the pan became calm, I saw the small, patchy eggs gently bouncing at the bottom.

When I came into the entrance hall, the dogs were sniffing the bottom of the door. I pulled the lock and opened it. It was a woman with curly brown hair and red rectangular glasses carrying a giant pyramid of white roses. She pushed the flowers into my arms.

'Tell Sophie those are for the side of the hall. I've got three more to come.'

She ran down the steps to a long brown car and took another pyramid of flowers from the back. I was still holding the first pyramid when she tried to give me the second one. She looked at me angrily as if I was being stupid. I quickly put the flowers on the floor next to the door and took the second pyramid. She ran down to the car again.

After five minutes there were flowers all over the floor of the entrance hall. From the front seat of the car the woman brought a tray with six white roses with silver pins lying in tissue.

'That's the lot. Tell Sophie I'll give her a call. I've had a request for red roses and baby's breath for the one on the seventeenth. They seem adamant, but I thought maybe Sophie could talk them out of it. She's good at that kind of thing.'

The woman opened the door to the car and put one foot inside. Her head was nearly disappearing as she said, 'I do wonder about people sometimes.'

As I turned from the door I saw one of the dogs sniffing the flowers and lifting his leg to pee. I ran towards him and clapped my hands.

'Go, dogs,' I said, pointing to the corridor. 'To the kitchen.'

The dogs looked disappointed and walked slowly to the kitchen.

'Was that Sue?' Sophie's voice said above me.

She was coming down the stairs wearing a peach dress with her hands behind her head pulling her hair. I had never seen her looking so elegant. She had three pins between her lips and she reached and took one and put it in the side of her hair.

'Yes,' I said, guessing.

We stood silently looking at the flowers. I could not believe how many there were. The smell was so strong that I put my hand against my nose.

'Right,' Sophie said. 'I suppose we should get them into the great hall.'

She picked up the biggest pyramid and I followed her past the dining room to a white door with a pattern cut into the wood. She put her knee up against the wall to hold the roses while she turned a gold key and pushed the door.

The great hall was long and tall with dark red walls. Dusty light from the windows fell across the chairs, which were wearing simple cotton dresses tied with white ribbons at the back.

Sophie put her pyramid of flowers on the table and pointed to a black metal stand at the side of the room.

'Put yours on there.'

The white flowers looked beautiful against the red walls.

'Who is getting married?' I asked.

'I can't remember. I'll have to look up the names. I think the bride is called Josie or something.'

I helped Sophie put all the flowers into the big hall. I was picking up the last roses from the entrance hall floor when Richard ran down the stairs and took his keys from the bowl next to the telephone.

'I'm just popping out. Can you finish off the stoat? Caleb's coming at two. There's a list of the ones he's taking on the desk.'

'Sure,' I said.

Sophie came into the hall and Richard's eyes looked up and down her body.

'You look nice,' he said, kissing her on the cheek.

'Twenty points if anybody asks me where my dress is from. Fifty points if I get my arse pinched by the bride's uncle.'

Richard reached around and put his hand up her skirt on to her bottom. 'I'll be uncontrollably jealous if anyone gets anywhere near your arse.'

'Sixty points if the mother of the bride complains about the flowers.'

'You are so good,' he said.

He kissed her again on the lips and moved her hair away from her eyes gently. I looked away. I tried not to be jealous, but I could feel it in my stomach.

When he had gone, Sophie turned to me.

'OK, you can go now,' she said. 'Try and make yourself scarce today, will you? I don't want anyone seeing you lurking around in your black jeans.'

'I have better things to do,' I said, copying a phrase I had heard her say.

Sophie smiled. 'Oh really! Do you now?'

As I walked to the barn, I thought about how we talked sometimes, Sophie and I. It was playful and it was easy to think that it meant something, but it was just the way she spoke. I don't think she had noticed anything different in our relationship since we shared a bed. It was only me. It was already more than a month later and I still thought about that night every day.

I put on the radio and took a new pair of gloves from the box under the sink. Then I glued the eyes into the stoat's face and stuck pins in it to hold the skin in position. The stoat was standing up straight, his little brown head floating above his thick white neck and chest. I moved his lips to cover his teeth and lifted his nose so that he looked like he was smelling the air. He was nearly ready and I pushed him to the side of the table. All of the work was ready for Caleb, which meant I could work on my idea. That was my deal with Richard.

There were twelve mice skins hanging on a piece of yellow string above the table. I felt them to see if they were dry and took them down carefully and pressed the skin straight where it had turned curly at the sides. Ready on the table were twelve cotton bodies in a line like Tampax. I put the bodies inside the skins, one, then another and another, pushing more cotton in to make them fat. Then I sewed them closed, working quickly with the excitement. It was the first time I had made one of my ideas, and I wanted it to be good.

I was concentrating so much I did not see the door open. I looked up and there was a man with black hair to his shoulders standing in front of the table. He had grey, almost green skin and a nose like an eagle.

'You must be the famous Mirka,' he said. His voice was different to Richard and Sophie's, like the words were coming through his nose.

'You must be the famous Caleb,' I said.

'That's the one. Down from London to collect my wares. Now what have you got for me?'

'Everything is over there,' I said, pointing to the animals on the table next to the door.

Caleb went and looked carefully at the owl, then the puffin, the woodpecker and the two squirrels in the box. He seemed to bounce when he moved, like everything was exciting to him.

'You did these?' he asked.

'Yes.'

'Richard said you were good, but these are ace. They could be alive, don't you think?'

'Thank you,' I said.

'Richard's not a great taxidermist.'

'He's OK.'

'I've got a blog called *Bad Taxidermy* and I put pictures of Richard's on there sometimes. The shitter they are, the more people love them. Anyway, yours are very good.'

I said nothing, but I was happy. Caleb picked up the owl and took it out of the barn. I thought I should help him so I picked up the stoat and followed him.

'Thanks,' Caleb said. 'Put that one in the front footwell.'

'Where?'

'The bit where the front passenger puts their feet.'

After we had put all the animals in the car we walked back into the barn so that Caleb could sign the receipt.

'So what are you doing here? Shouldn't you be living it up in the big smoke?'

'Sometimes I don't know,' I said, which was the truth. 'But I like it.'

'I don't know how you stand it. Gives me the willies. All those narrow twisty roads and forests. I get paranoid that I'll break down and have to knock on someone's door. A man with eyes that look in different directions will open it, and it all goes a bit *Wicker Man*.'

'I have not met many people, but they look normal when I see them in the town or village.'

'But it's still a bit boring, let's be honest. Don't you miss the packed pubs and corner shops, the night buses, the pavements strewn with chicken bones?'

I smiled. 'Not yet.'

Caleb signed the paper and as he gave it to me, he moved his head to look behind me.

'What are you up to there?'

'I'm making a scene.'

Caleb made a laugh in his throat and showed his yellow teeth. 'You're making a scene, are you?' Then he coughed and stopped smiling. 'Please, tell me about your scene.'

'I don't want to say anything about it yet. Until I know if it is good.'

Caleb walked past me and looked down at the mice. He touched them and picked one up and turned it around.

'I'll tell you what, when it's finished, take some pictures and email me them. I know people who are in the market for things like this.'

'OK,' I said.

After Caleb had gone I started to dress the finished mice with the clothes I had made for them from old clothes of Sophie's. I put a denim jacket on one mouse and a red dress on another mouse and gave her a little white handbag to hold. I had a big black jacket for the biggest mouse and T-shirts and fashionable clothes for the others. It took a long time to pull the arms and legs through the holes gently and to glue the telephones or cigarettes to their hands. I was pleased with the details and wanted to finish it soon, it had already taken me so long to do the research and make all the tiny objects.

He passed the binoculars to me and I put them to my eyes. In the circles I saw two men in grey suits smoking at the side of the steps behind a bush. I moved the circles upwards. An old lady in a pale blue jacket and hat was holding the hands of a young man and moving them up and down like she was saying something important. At the bottom of the steps a woman in a one-shoulder purple dress was looking in a little mirror to put on lipstick. I moved the circles to the right. Sophie was standing on the grass talking to a man. Her hand was flat against her forehead to stop the sun. She was smiling. In her other hand she was holding a glass of champagne. I was jealous, I wished I was there with her, drinking champagne at an English wedding.

Suddenly everyone turned towards the door and started to cheer and clap. Hundreds of tiny colourful petals flew into the air. The bride and groom came out of the house and walked slowly down the steps underneath the floating petals. People kissed the bride and shook the groom's hand. Then a man standing on the grass holding a big camera in one hand started to shout at the crowd. The guests turned and followed his hand movements to come closer together for the photograph. I gave Richard the binoculars and rested my chin on the top of my hands.

Just as I was thinking how beautiful everything was, Richard said. 'It's always the same old shit.'

I hit him on the arm. 'Richard! Don't say that.'

'You only like it because it's the first one you've seen. Wait till we've had one every Saturday for the next two months. It's a wedding factory we're running here.'

Richard was moving the binoculars around in squares like he was looking for something and couldn't find it.

'I don't know how Sophie does it.'

'Maybe she likes making people happy.'

Richard smiled proudly. 'She's so good with people. I couldn't deal with all the emotional stuff. People are pretty highly strung when it comes to weddings. Sorry, I'll rephrase that. People are completely insane when it comes to weddings. You get the wrong shade of white for the bridesmaids' bouquets and it's game over. Once we had a mother of the bride completely lose it over the wastepaper baskets in the bogs.'

'What was wrong with them?'

'They didn't look vintage enough or something. Whatever happened to the days when you had a piss-up with your family and your best friends in the local pub? Everyone focuses on all the wrong stuff. Who gives a crap what colour the bridesmaids wear?'

'The bridesmaids do.'

Richard ignored me. 'Who remembers the salmon terrine? I certainly don't. Do I really want a pen with the bride and groom's name on it? No, I don't.'

He turned on his elbow towards me. 'Obviously it works in our favour. You can charge them anything you like. That photographer is probably charging a couple of grand.' He jerked his chin towards the house. 'A couple of grand for a day's work. People are nuts.'

'Some people think it is the most important day of their life. I can understand.'

'So what goes on at a Slovak wedding then?'

'Well, my sister's wedding was in a big country hotel. There was a traditional band and dancing. Lots of food and alcohol.'

'Sounds familiar.'

'On the way to the hotel there were some farmers who blocked the road and would not let us through unless we paid them. We gave them food and some alcohol. But they would not let us through until we gave them money.'

'That's awful.'

'No, it's what happens at a lot of weddings. Often people come and take the bride away and will not let her go until you pay them. It's OK, they always bring her back.'

'Right,' Richard said, looking confused. 'What happened when you arrived at the hotel?'

'My sister and her husband cut through a piece of wood. To show that they can work together. Then they smashed a plate.'

'To show that they can, er, destroy things together?'

'No.'

'Get completely smashed together?'

'No, they have to pick up the pieces together while everyone is moving around them with their feet. It is to show that they can work together again.'

Richard raised his eyebrows. 'Sounds like a hoot.'

'It is more fun than I explained,' I said. 'Anyway, do you think I can come to a wedding here? I would love to go to an English wedding.'

'You might be in luck. There's a big one here in a couple of weeks. I mean with a marquee and everything. A girl Sophie was friends with at Oxford. You can come to that. Not to eat, but you can hang around and help out.'

'Really?'

'We'll have to dress you up a bit though.'

He smiled in the way he always did when he was teasing me.

The groom and the bride walked on to the grass and the photographer bent down and waved them sideways so they would be in a position for the perfect picture in front of the green fields. The groom put his arm around the bride and they looked at each other with loving expressions. They kissed on the mouth and the crowd cheered again.

Richard was looking through the binoculars.

'Not a looker, is she?'

I took the binoculars. 'She's a little fat, it's true. But she looks happy.'

'A *little* fat? A *little* fat?' Richard laughed. 'You could park a bus under that dress!'

I punched Richard on the shoulder with my fist.

'You are very mean. It's her wedding day!'

Richard started to laugh and I caught his laughter until I could not stop. We were lying under the tree for a long time with our chests shaking up and down against the earth.

The weather stayed hot for a week. But I did not go outside much. I was always working in the barn on my scene. I carefully put the mice into the nightclub through the top of the big glass box. I checked the paper plan next to me on the table to make sure all the mice were exactly where

I wanted them. The walls and the floor of the box were painted black. Behind the bar, with tiny bottles of alcohol and glasses, I put the barman mouse. He was leaning over the bar to whisper to the mouse in the red dress that she was sexy and he wanted her telephone number. Then I put the bouncer mouse under the green emergency exit sign by the door and moved his head so he was watching the mice smoking next to the metal railings outside the club. I had thought a lot about the different characters and I wanted it to be easy for people to know immediately what they were doing and thinking. I had spent hours looking at pictures on Sophie's computer for research. The only thing I was nervous about was if I would be good enough at taxidermy. And looking at the mice as I put them into the scene, I decided that I was good enough.

I kept working, putting the DJ mouse into the special DJ box with the record player with some tiny records I painted exactly like the real ones of famous musicians like The Rolling Stones or Depeche Mode. I put the DJ mouse's arm in the air because he liked the song so much. In front of him, mice were dancing on the dance floor under the little coloured lights. Two mice were posing for a photograph that another mouse was taking on her phone. I put the last mouse lying down in the corner next to the speaker, sleeping even with the loud music, because he was so drunk.

When I was finished, I stepped backwards and looked at the scene. I hoped that people would get a lot of pleasure from the details like I did. There was something about the scene being tiny, like a complete world, that I found satisfying. I thought about the mice and whether they would be happy to be like that, in human clothes in a nightclub for ever, and I was not sure. But if I was a mouse, I thought, I would rather be in a nightclub than rotting under the ground.

Richard did not come back to the barn again that day. He was making a new pen for the baby pheasants who would arrive soon. At lunchtime I went to eat my sandwich on the bench in the garden. The sun was shining and birds were swimming and drinking the water in the birdbath. The air smelt of rose petals and cut grass. Suddenly, I saw a little white dog with black patches coming along the path towards the house. Behind him, on a lead, he was pulling a woman with long grey hair tied behind her neck. Her head was sticking forward and her big eyes were looking in every direction very obviously, as if she thought someone was watching her and she wanted to look like she was looking for someone. When she saw me her shoulders jumped and she put her hand on her chest. She had a guilty look in her eyes.

'You gave me such a fright,' she said.

The dog saw me and showed me his teeth. He started making angry noises and pulling the lead so his feet lifted from the floor.

'Whatever you do, don't look him in the eyes,' the woman said.

I looked away from the dog quickly. I tried not to look at the dog but I wanted to know where he was. I looked down carefully, without moving my head, but he saw my eyes looking down and barked like crazy. I was afraid the dog was going to bite me.

The woman bent down and said to the dog, 'It's all right Monty. Just relax. Take your time. She's not going to hurt you.'

I stood like a statue while the dog smelt my shoes and jeans. Monty decided I was OK and walked towards the bench and lifted his leg to take a pee.

'I was looking for Sophie, is she here?'

'She is somewhere here,' I said. 'Maybe she's in the kitchen.'

I started walking towards the kitchen door and the woman followed. When I got to the door, I said, 'Wait here.'

The woman's head made a small jerk of surprise. But I could not let her go in the house, I did not know who she was.

I went inside and closed the door behind me and shouted Sophie's name as I walked through the rooms. The radio was left on in the kitchen playing some classical music. The dogs were away with Richard. I checked to see if she was at her desk in the living room but there was only a half-smoked cigarette in the ashtray and balls of crushed paper on the carpet. I shouted up the stairs but there was no answer. I went back into the kitchen and out of the door.

'She might be in the vegetable garden,' I said.

I walked in front of the woman along the path, past the men building the tent. They had finished putting up the metal poles to make the shape and now they were hanging the pieces of white material in the spaces between the poles.

Through the arch of pale pink roses I saw Sophie on her knees, facing away from me. She was wearing a pink wavy hat, and her naked feet were sticking out under her white dress. I felt a pain in my heart because she looked so beautiful there in the garden. When I came closer I heard her singing softly, 'A holiday, a holiday and the first one of the year.'

I wanted the woman to go away so I could listen to Sophie singing.

'Sophie,' I said. 'There is someone here.'

'Oh,' she said, twisting her head in surprise.

Sophie pushed herself backwards on to her feet and stood up, taking off her dirty gloves and dropping them on the grass as she walked towards the woman.

'Hello, Celia,' she said, smiling politely, but she did not kiss the woman or shake her hand.

'I thought I'd find you here,' Celia said. 'You're just like your mother.'

Sophie's eyes froze for a moment. But the polite smile came back.

'Yes, well, I try.' Sophie bent down and put her hand towards Monty. 'Who's this? Hello little one.'

Monty showed his teeth and made an angry noise. Sophie pulled her hand back quickly.

'He's a rescue dog,' Celia said. 'They said he's likely to be carrying some residual trauma.' She bent her head and spoke in her dog voice again. 'You're OK, though, aren't you, Monty. This is Sophie. She's a friend. Yes, she is.'

While Celia was bending down to talk to the dog, Sophie looked at me, shaking her head to tell me she was not happy that the woman had come.

'And to what do I owe this pleasure?' Sophie said in a friendly way.

'Oh, I hope you don't mind me popping in like this. I was passing by and I thought I would come and say hello.'

'How nice of you.'

'Well, as you probably know, we're having a sale for the convalescent home on Saturday and I was wondering if I could put you down for a cake. You didn't reply to the invitation I sent.'

'I'm sorry, I've been so busy,' Sophie said. 'Yes, of course. We have a wedding here on Saturday, but I can drop a cake over.'

'That's wonderful dear. And do you think you'll make the fete? We're having a meeting about it next Monday at the village hall.'

'I'm so sorry, Celia. We're chock-a-block with weddings here. Otherwise I would have loved to come to the fete.'

'Well, you could at least come to the meetings. Show people you're committed. Communities don't make themselves, you know.'

There was an explosion of anger in Sophie's eyes and I thought she was going to say something rude to Celia, but instead she smiled and said, 'I feel terrible, but I'm sure you can appreciate how much work we have to do here over the summer.'

'Yes, of course, forgive me. It must be a terrible burden, trying to keep a place like this going.'

There was a silence and Sophie looked at me quickly while Celia was staring up at the house. I could not tell if Celia was saying what she meant, or if she was being rude.

'Anyway,' Sophie said smoothly. 'Apart from all that organising, are you well?'

'Very well. Grappling with the new bin system, but I'm getting there. We must all do our bit.'

'Yes, it is a bit complicated,' Sophie said.

'I don't understand if you can put those clear lids in the recycling. I'm so frightened I'll ruin the whole batch if I put the wrong thing in.'

'I know, it's a nightmare, isn't it? Do you mean the lids that you pierce before you put them in the microwave?'

I was watching Sophie, interested. Her eyebrows were together and she was nodding like she really cared about the woman's problems with the bins.

'No, I mean the firm plastic ones, like you get on packets of tomatoes, for example.'

'I'm not sure. I know the film lids you definitely can't. I can try and find out about those ones, if you like.'

As she was talking, Sophie started walking very naturally towards the gate at the other side of the garden and Celia followed.

'I can't seem to train Richard at all. I'm constantly having to fish out the things he has put in the wrong bin.'

Celia laughed and touched Sophie on the arm. 'Do send Richard my regards.'

'I will, I will.' Sophie opened the little wooden gate and said, 'Well, lovely to see you.'

'Is everything all right with him? Between the two of you?'

Sophie's face was cold now. 'What do you mean?'

'I heard about the incident in the pub. It sounded so unlike Richard and I thought to myself, there's something going on there. No smoke without fire. I've been meaning to drop round and see if you were all right.'

'Oh that! Celia, that was months ago. Richard was pissed, that's all. Everything is fine. Thank you for your concern.'

'Well, we must have a proper catch-up soon,' Celia said, nodding her head, as if she had not noticed that Sophie was making her leave the garden.

'Yes, we must,' Sophie said, waving.

When Celia and the angry dog had gone behind the house Sophie turned and breathed in deeply.

'God what an awful woman Celia is. She can go fuck herself and her cake sale. I've known her all my life, but honestly. We just live in the same village, it doesn't make her a friend. And it makes me angry when people turn up here unannounced like that. I might have been sunbathing naked, for all she knew. Why can't she use the phone like anybody else?'

'She reminded me a little of my mother,' I said.

'Poor you.'

Sophie got down on her knees in the same place on the edge of the vegetable garden. She picked up a miniature spade in her hand and was about to put it in the earth but she stopped, as if she had thought of something. Her eyes became narrow.

'I've always hated Jack Russells.'

'What are you growing?'

'I'm planting more courgettes. Look, we already have some new potatoes.' She picked up the silver bowl from the grass. Inside there were a few small round potatoes.

'Can I watch?' I said, sitting on the grass. 'I don't want to go inside yet.'

'Of course,' she said. 'Is everything OK? How's your scene?'

'Yes. It's very good,' I said. 'Caleb already sold *Mice Raving* for a lot of money. I can't believe it.'

'Richard told me,' she said. 'It's incredible. Maybe this is your calling. You'll be a world-famous taxidermist and we can say we knew you when you were starting out.'

'I don't think so.'

Sophie was digging in the end of one square of earth. At the other end there were some lettuces growing. In the next square I could see the fizzy green tops of some carrots. The smell from the pretty pale blue, pink and purple flowers growing next to the wooden pyramids was heavy and sweet.

I lay down and put my hands under my head. I fell asleep and woke up to Sophie saying, 'That'll do.'

She sat next to me on the grass with bent knees and stroked her dress up the back of her thighs. Her pale legs were covered in thin white hairs that shone in the sun. I watched her bend forward to scratch a cut on her knee with her dirty nail. The lumpy piece of hard skin was lifting from the fresh pink skin underneath.

'Don't do that, please,' I said.

'Sorry,' Sophie said, laughing. 'That's disgusting. I thought you were asleep.'

Now the hard skin was still joined to Sophie's knee but hanging like an open door.

'Just take it off,' I said.

I turned my head away.

'OK, gone.' She lifted her chin to look up to the sky from

under her hat. 'Let's hope the weather holds out for the weekend.'

'Are you good friends with the bride? Richard said you were friends at Oxford.'

'Not real friends. We used to see each other to say hello to in the pub. She didn't know it was my house until she came down to look at it, and then we realised the connection. But there'll be quite a few people I used to know at university. They'll all be bringing their children, I expect.'

I didn't know what to say. Sophie had her chin resting on her knees and her hand was pulling out pieces of grass from the earth.

'Are you OK?' I said.

'Not really,' she said. 'But it's one of those things. I'm going to see someone about it though. I'll go to London. I should have done it before.'

'I'm sure it will work out fine,' I said, but I felt like I was lying. Nobody could know what would happen.

'Thanks,' Sophie said. 'I know there are much bigger problems in the world than whether or not I can have a child.'

'It doesn't mean you can't be sad if you want a baby.'

'Anyway,' she said, lying back on the grass with her head next to mine. 'Not being pregnant means we can get completely wasted on Saturday and do lots of wedding dancing with pervy old uncles. It will be fun.'

'I can't wait,' I said.

Above us, small white clouds were beginning to float across the sky.

After a silence, I said, 'Sophie, what was the song you were singing earlier?'

'Oh, it was a favourite song of my mother's. She used to play me the record when I was a child.'

Suddenly she started to sing,

> *'A holiday, a holiday and the first one of the year.*
> *Lord Donald's wife came into the church, the Gospel*
> > *for to hear.*
> *And when the meeting it was done, she cast her eyes about,*
> *And there she saw little Matty Groves, walking in*
> > *the crowd.'*

She was leaning on one elbow, looking at me as she was singing, smiling a little embarrassedly, but pleased at the same time. She had a beautiful voice, sweet and low, but with something scratchy in it too that made it interesting.

Then she lifted her chin to the side and changed her voice as if she was speaking as a different character and sang,

> *'Come home with me little Matty Groves, come home*
> > *with me tonight,*
> *Come home with me little Matty Groves, and sleep*
> > *with me till light.'*

She was looking at me very strongly, as if she was really the Lady Donald and I was Matty Groves and she was inviting me to come home with her and sleep with her till light. It was difficult to keep looking at her eyes. I did not understand how she could do it. It was impossible to see in her face if she knew what she was doing, whether she was innocent and only acting, or not. But I was afraid that I was not good at acting, and she could see my feelings in my face.

Then she pushed her chin towards her chest and made her voice deeper to sing another character,

> *'Oh I can't come home, I won't come home and sleep*
> *with you tonight,*
> *By the rings on your fingers I can tell you are Lord*
> *Donald's wife.'*

Now it felt like Sophie was speaking for me, saying exactly what I would say. I looked in her eyes, but they seemed completely innocent, and her smile was too. She was just enjoying being the different characters in the song.

She lifted her chin to the side and sang in a high voice, looking at me strongly, playfully again,

> *'What if I am Lord Donald's wife, Lord Donald's*
> *not at home,*
> *he is out in the far cornfields, bringing the yearlings home.'*

A cloud went in front of the sun. Above the hedge behind Sophie I saw David's wool hat coming along the path. Sophie was still singing. David was nearly at the end of the path and was going to turn and see us lying there, with Sophie singing to me. For some reason I did not want him to see, even though we were doing nothing wrong.

I interrupted Sophie's singing. 'Sophie, I'm cold, shall we go inside?'

'Wait, there's more.' She sang again, *A servant who was standing by—*

David came around the corner and saw us. His expression was suspicious and satisfied, like he had been waiting to see something like this one day. I knew I looked guilty.

Sophie stopped singing. 'What?'

She turned her head to look where I was looking. I thought she would be natural, as if it was nothing. But she looked guilty and sat up quickly.

'Oh hello, David. How are you?'

'All right.'

'We were just having a bit of break. It's lovely today, isn't it?'

'Very nice.'

'Aren't you hot in that hat?'

David touched his hat and looked like he could not think of what to say. He could not look directly at Sophie, I noticed, but I saw his eyes move quickly to her legs as if he could not control them.

'The roses have come out well,' he said.

'Aren't they lovely? And have you seen the purple clematis in the front bed?'

'No, I'll have a look,' he said, almost shyly. There was a silence. 'Well, best be off. Tell Richard I'll see him next week.'

'Have a lovely weekend, David.'

After he had gone we got up to go inside. I followed Sophie along the path, dreamily watching her with the silver bowl resting on her hip. I thought about the way she looked when

David saw us. Why had she looked guilty unless she knew that she was doing something wrong? I remembered about the song, the way she sang it with her beautiful, rough voice. I wondered what would happen in the story between Lady Donald and Matty Groves. I knew that Matty Groves was going to go with her wherever she wanted him to go.

CHAPTER SIX

The kitchen was unusually dark when I came downstairs on the morning of the wedding. Outside the windows, the sky was the colour of pigeons. Sophie was hidden behind the open fridge door and I could see only her denim shorts and pale legs. I switched on the lights and walked towards her.

'Mirka, is that you? Could you scramble some eggs?' She put her head to the side of the door and passed me a box of eggs. 'When they're done, drape some smoked salmon over them. Yes?'

'Yes,' I said. I took the eggs and the greasy packet of salmon and put them on the surface next to the cooker.

Sophie looked down at a piece of paper on the table, her hair falling from behind her ears. She was talking quietly to herself. 'Flowers, done. Cake to Celia, done.' She drew a line with the pen through the words. 'Glasses, ironing, champagne.

Champagne!' She looked around the room as if she was going to see a bottle of champagne somewhere and then walked out of the kitchen.

I lifted the silver lid of the cooker and broke the eggs into the pan with some butter. The bottoms turned white and the six yellow circles were not broken so I took a wooden spoon from the pot and burst them all. I stirred the egg around until it became pale yellow and lumpy.

Sophie walked past and looked down into the pan.

'Perfect scrambled eggs. Well done. Are you OK to take those up to the bride in the red room?'

I carried three plates and a jug of fresh coffee on a tray up the stairs. I wondered how the bride would be feeling on the day of her wedding. Maybe she would be nervous or stressed, maybe she would be crying.

'Hello,' I said to the door. There was no reply. 'Hello. Room service,' I said, because it seemed like the right thing to say.

The door opened and a lady in a white towel robe smiled.

'Come in, come in. This looks wonderful.'

I followed her into the room. Her head was covered in pale blue tubes. Each thin piece of blonde hair was pulled over the tube making a slope, curling under the other side like a wave breaking on to the beach. The little waves were travelling in different directions, like the sea was very rough.

One girl was sitting on the bed with her knees inside her T-shirt. The other girl, wearing a grey T-shirt with a skull on it, was holding a cigarette and blowing smoke out of the open window. The two girls were obviously sisters, with the same long blonde hair and narrow backs. The girl on the bed, looking at me with a bored expression as I walked past, was about seventeen and I thought she was probably not the bride.

I put the tray on the chest of drawers next to the window and the mother took one of the plates and sat down with it on her thighs. The girl at the window put out the cigarette on the wall outside and threw it into the bin.

'Amazing, thank you,' she said. She lifted her glass, finished all of the champagne and wiped the drops from her chin with her arm. 'I couldn't be less hungry, but I know I should eat something. Don't want to faint at the altar. Or get completely hammered and pass out before, you know—' She whistled and made a clicking noise in her cheek at the same time as making a circle with her thumb and finger, putting the first finger of the other hand in and out of the circle.

It made me smile because I knew what the sign meant.

Her sister laughed loudly, then said, 'Are you scared?'

'Terrified.' The bride got on her knees next to her mother and put her hands around her waist like she was afraid. 'Mummy, does it hurt a lot? Tell me about your wedding night with Daddy. Is there anything I need to know?'

The sister on the bed fell sideways laughing. The mother shook her head, trying to be angry, but she was smiling.

'I think the fact that I had to take you for an abortion aged sixteen rather obviates the need for this conversation, don't you think, darling?'

'Ah yes, my first abortion. Happy times.' The bride sighed and let go of her mother. Then, as if she had another thought, she put her arms around her mother again and squeezed her body. 'Aren't you a nice Mummy?'

'Far too nice,' the mother said, making circles with her eyes at me.

I was a little shocked by their performance and did not know what to say. They were all looking at me, waiting.

'I hope you have a lovely day,' I said, walking backwards to the door.

'I'm sure we will,' the bride said. She got up and took a plate. 'Apparently the rain is going to hit just in time for drinks on the lawn. So that's great.'

'I can't believe it,' the mother said, pointing towards the window with her fork. 'It's bloody typical. Yesterday was sunny. Tomorrow is sunny. And today...' She paused. The muscles on her neck stood up like ropes on a ship. 'Today is a fucking hurricane.'

'Don't exaggerate, Mum,' the bride said. 'Anyway, we always knew it was a risk. This is England.'

'Let's face it, it couldn't be worse.' The mother's face folded as she started to cry. 'All the photos will have to be done inside. It's so sad.'

The bride put down her plate, put her arms around her mother's narrow shoulders, not joking now, but gently.

'Come on, Mum, it's not the end of the world,' she said in a serious voice. 'It will still be a wonderful day. No matter what happens.'

'It's just that you have the idea of what you want your daughter's wedding to be like and, and—' She took a tissue from the sleeve of the robe and blew her nose.

I reached the door and twisted the handle and went quietly out of the room. When I turned around, Sophie was coming up the stairs.

'How are they?' she whispered.

'OK, apart from the weather.'

'Well that's not our fault, thank God.'

She started walking down the corridor to her room.

'Sophie,' I said.

Sophie stopped and turned her head. 'Oh yes, of course. You need something to wear. Come with me.'

I followed her to her bedroom. Richard was lying in bed pointing the control at the television. The white covers were folded across the black hair of his chest. There was the sound of a crowd cheering from the television, then the noise of tennis balls being hit.

'Don't mind me,' he said. He turned the television off. 'Right, I'll leave you ladies to it. Chuck me a towel will you, Soph?'

Sophie took a towel from a hook on the back of the door and threw it to Richard. He tried to get out of bed and wrap the towel around him, but he dropped the corner and I saw his naked hairy bottom. I turned and looked at the wall.

'All right, safe to turn around,' he said as he closed the door to the bathroom.

The shower started. Sophie went to the wardrobe and opened the doors with two hands like she was opening a window to a beautiful view.

'I've got some dresses that are too big for me. We will definitely find something for you.'

She pushed the clothes up and down the rails, looking at different dresses. Then she reached and pulled out a dress with a pattern of coloured squares and held it under her chin.

'What about this?'

'Are you joking?' I said. 'I'm not a housewife in the 1950s.'

Her head jerked backwards and her eyes opened wide. 'OK, Jesus. Not that one then.' She put the dress back in the wardrobe, saying quietly, 'I happen to quite like that dress.'

She moved the clothes again and pulled out a bright blue dress that looked small enough for a child. I looked at her to see if she was serious.

'OK, I can tell by your face that you don't like it,' she said.

'It's a nice dress,' I said. 'But it's too small.'

'It's stretchy.'

'It is not really my kind of clothes.'

'Go on, put it on for me.'

'No.'

'Please. Come on, I want to see what you look like in a dress.'

She pushed the dress into my hands. We looked at each other for a few seconds and I sighed and turned around, lifted my T-shirt and put the dress over my head. I pulled down my jeans to my ankles.

'Off! And your socks.'

I took off the jeans and socks. Sophie got on to the bed and walked on her knees to the edge without taking her eyes off me. The dress stopped in the middle of my thighs and was clinging to my body like a swimsuit. I looked in the mirror inside the wardrobe door and turned to the side. I could see the shapes of my bottom and my breasts. I felt naked.

'Well?' Sophie said.

'I look like a prostitute.'

'No you don't! Don't be silly.'

'I've never felt so uncomfortable in my life.'

'I'd absolutely kill to look like that in that dress.'

Her eyes looked up and down my body like a man's eyes. I was not sure if she knew she was doing this, but I liked it. Then the shower switched off and Sophie, still looking at my body, turned her head slightly and shouted, 'Richard, Richard.'

'Yes,' Richard called from inside the bathroom.

'What are you doing?' I said, covering my body with my arms as much as I could.

Sophie ignored me and shouted, 'Come and look at this.'

The door opened and Richard came out in a cloud of steam wearing a towel around his waist. When he saw me, his eyes also looked up and down my body. He whistled.

'Wow, you scrub up pretty well.' He walked around me, nodding his head like he could not believe it. 'Who'd have thought?'

'She looks like a supermodel, doesn't she?' Sophie said.

'Mmm, will you look at the legs on that!'

'OK stop, both, please,' I said. 'Don't make me wear the dress, I feel very uncomfortable.'

'All right all right all right,' Sophie said. 'Christ, anybody normal would be thrilled to look like that. What shall we do then? I haven't got anything else.'

'Can I borrow something from Richard?' I said.

Both Richard and Sophie laughed at the same time. But then they stopped when they saw my face was serious and looked at each other. Richard bit his lip, thinking.

'I don't see why not. I've probably got a spare tux somewhere. As long as you don't mind everyone thinking you are a waiter.'

He opened the thinner door to the side of the wardrobe and

took out a black jacket with a pair of folded trousers hanging from the bar.

'Hold that,' he said. Then he pulled out a white shirt. 'OK go and try those.'

I picked up my clothes and walked quickly out of the room.

'Isn't she funny?' I heard Sophie saying as I was closing the door.

In my bedroom, I laid the tuxedo on my bed and hung the shirt on the door and went to have a bath. After I came back, when I was putting cream on my face, I could not stop looking at the tuxedo. It was like it was whispering to me. I wanted to wear it immediately. I quickly put on black pants and a bra. I only had black underwear so I hoped it would be OK to wear it under a white shirt. Then I put on the shirt and trousers. Everything was the perfect size for me. I could not find the button on the sleeves and they hung from my arms. But I put on the jacket anyway and looked in the mirror. I combed my hair back and put some hair gel on it so it stayed behind my ears. I stared at myself, turning my shoulders. I had never seen myself looking so sophisticated before.

I went downstairs and knocked on Richard and Sophie's door.

'Richard, what should I do about the sleeves?'

Richard came out in grey trousers, also with the sleeves of his shirt flying loose.

'You need cufflinks. Hang on.'

He came back with some small silver beetles in his palm. He pushed the bars through holes in my sleeves and twisted. Then he took a black tie in his hand and unfolded my collar.

'Hold still.'

He put the black tie over my head and around my neck, twisting the pieces. Then he let the pieces fall and looked confused.

'It's always impossible, doing it on someone else.'

He twisted them again in a different direction and pulled one piece up through a hole. His tongue was sticking out between his lips. I could smell his pine-tree smell. His face was so close to mine that I stopped breathing and looked at the ceiling.

In the mirror on the wall I saw he had made a bow. He made it straight with two hands and smiled proudly.

'There you go. You look like James Bond.'

Sophie came to the door and leant against the wall. She was holding a shiny silver dress like fish skin across her chest with one arm, showing a triangle of her pale pink pants.

'You look great,' she said. Then she looked very obviously up and down my body again before she went back into the room.

'You are going to absolutely kill it with the ladies in that,' Richard said, winking at me.

'Thanks,' I said, blushing. I did not know that Richard knew about me.

Behind him I could see Sophie putting the dress over her arms and pulling it down over her naked breasts and I thought it was lucky that Richard did not know what I really wanted.

I carried a bowl of potato salad across the grass to the dark entrance of the tent. The rain was hitting the side of my face. The tall trees around the edge of the garden were shaking violently like wet dogs. I thought the tent would blow away. The white material was swelling like a sail and trying to pull up the ropes.

I bent my head sideways to go through the tent door. At the end, Sophie was walking slowly along the long table, looking at the dishes of food. I walked towards her on the scratchy brown carpet, looking down so I did not trip on the edges. The rain was whipping the waving roof and the wooden poles in the middle were creaking.

As I came closer Sophie stopped and bent over the table. She was looking down very closely into the eye of a dead salmon. Then she lifted her hand and stroked the fish gently from the tail, along the salmon's body, over the slices of lemon and cucumber, until her fingers came to the face. The end of her first finger rested on the surface of the eye. I froze, holding the potato salad, watching her to see what she would do. With her blue-painted nail she dug into the eye hole and pulled out the salmon's eye and held it up between her finger and thumb in front of her face and turned it around. It was black and grey jelly with strings hanging from it. Then she put it into her mouth. She closed her eyes and crunched her teeth down, chewing a few times before swallowing. Her shoulders shook like she was cold.

'What are you doing?' I said.

Sophie turned around and screamed. 'Fuck me. What are you doing?'

'I am carrying a potato salad.'

'Why are you always creeping around like that? You gave me such a fright.'

'Why does everyone put their hand on their chest and say, "Oh, you gave me such a fright," every time I walk into a room?'

Sophie took her hand off her chest. Her eyes were full of guilt and she looked down at her naked feet.

'You have a furtive quality to you. Always lurking in the shadows.'

'I'm just walking normally like a normal person.'

'You aren't a normal person.'

'It is not my fault it is so loud in here.'

'Well maybe we can get you a little bell to wear round your neck so we will all know when you're coming.'

I looked down at the dull grey salmon, the black eye hole full of liquid.

'Why did you eat the fish eye?'

Sophie looked down at the salmon again for a few seconds, like she did not know how to explain. She played with some of the fizzy herbs at the side of the plate with her fingers.

'It used to be my mother's party trick. When we were little, if we had fish, Mum would burrow her finger into the eye socket, pull out the eye and dangle it in front of us. And then she would raise it above her mouth and drop it in. We would scream and she would move it around in her cheeks and then swallow it and go, "Mmm, crunchy!"' Sophie acted like her mother, pushing her tongue around her cheeks and then swallowing. 'For some unknown reason I just felt like trying it, to see what it was like.'

'And what was it like?'

'Pretty disgusting,' she laughed. 'Do you want me to get the other one out for you?'

'No thanks.'

I put the potato salad on the table between a dish of cold chicken curry and a plate of slices of tomato and mozzarella.

Sophie picked up her shoes, lying on their sides on the carpet, and put them standing on their heels. She put one foot in the first shoe and then reached and held my shoulder so she could balance and put her foot in the second shoe. Then, she put her hand out to gently pull the bow straight under my chin and whispered, 'Is it wrong that I find you very attractive dressed like that?'

She looked up at me, waiting for me to say something and I saw in her eyes that she was nervous. We looked at each other for a moment. I wanted to kiss her more than anything.

'Yes, it is wrong,' I said, as strongly as I could.

'I thought you would say that.' She sighed and touched my cheek as she walked past me.

I stayed still, with my eyes closed, taking deep breaths. The place on my cheek where her fingers touched me was burning. I could not believe what had happened.

After a minute I walked back to the entrance of the tent. The rain was falling like a curtain. I saw Sophie, like a silver fish in her dress, slip between two dark bushes.

In the other direction, at the corner of the house, a man was holding his jacket above a woman in a red dress and trying to open the little gate with his other hand. They started running across the lawn. After a few steps the woman stopped and ran back and pulled her high heel out of the grass. Then she bent down and took off the other shoe and ran to the tent holding both shoes. Behind them more guests came through the gate, running across the grass or walking holding umbrellas forward like shields against the wind.

When the first man arrived at the door, he brushed the

dark wet hair from his face, took off his glasses and wiped the drops of water from them with a purple cloth from his jacket pocket.

'Bloody awful day,' he said, sticking his neck forward to look at me through his glasses. 'Now, what does one have to do to get a glass of champagne around here?'

'I can find you one.'

'That would be marvellous. And I don't suppose there are any nibbles going, are there?'

I ran from the tent in the same direction as Sophie and passed two waiters dressed like me in white shirts and black bows carrying bottles of champagne. In the kitchen I wiped my feet on the mat.

'Stay there,' a thin woman in a white apron said to me. Her fingers were shiny with orange oil and she brushed the blonde hair off her face with the inside of her arm. 'Judy, are the mini Yorkshires plated up yet?'

'No, but the smoked salmon blinis are ready to go,' the other woman with the round red face said. 'Shall I give those to him?'

'Good thinking,' the thin woman said.

The second woman put down her knife on to the board next to the onion and passed me a plate of circles of salmon on mini pancakes.

'OK, you can go now.'

As I was walking back to the tent, I tried to decide if I was angry about being called a waiter or being called a man. But I did not really care about either thing. I smiled because it was funny and I wanted to tell Sophie to make her laugh.

When I got to the tent, hands came from every direction

to take the food from the plate. I did not even move. People took two or three pancakes, pushing them into their mouths, and taking more. After ten seconds, all of the food was gone and the people turned around to reach for some prawns on a different plate.

I was holding a plate of little pieces of toast with melted cheese when Richard saw me. He started shaking his head, laughing.

'Told you so,' he said. He took a cheese toast and ut it in his mouth.

'I don't mind.'

'Tell you what, when everyone sits down, you can get under my table and I'll feed you bits of coronation chicken when nobody's looking.'

'It is really OK.'

Richard took the plate from my hands. 'Seriously. Put that down, get a glass of Buck's Fizz or whatever and start mingling.'

I tried to take the plate from Richard but he held it high behind his shoulder. 'Eff off. I'm keeping these,' he said.

As I was leaving, a beautiful woman with pale skin and green eyes bent over the plate, holding her long red hair behind her neck so it did not fall in the food.

'Yum. My fave,' she said. She kissed Richard on the cheek before eating a cheese toast. 'Anyway, Ricky, how are you? I feel like I haven't seen you for literally years.'

'That's because it has been, literally, years,' Richard said in an unusually unfriendly voice.

I went back to the house through the main door so I would

not be given more plates of food in the kitchen. Sophie was on her knees in the entrance hall talking to the two little brides-maids in white dresses with dark red ribbons around their waists. She stood up and took the hand of the smallest girl, who was looking at the floor.

'Why don't we go and find your mummy?'

When the girl looked up I saw her face was wet and patchy. She sniffed and took some jerky breaths. Sophie smiled at me as she walked past, but her smile was sad.

Richard was dancing with his hands frozen like birds' feet next to his chest. He had taken off his jacket and his shirt was soaked with sweat. His expression was serious, with his lips sticking out and his head nodding, like what he was doing was important and he wanted to dance really well. Suddenly, like a man trying to frighten a child by jumping out of a bush, he put his arms above his head with his palms pushing the air away from his body. His eyes became round and his mouth open like he was surprised at himself. Next to him, the woman with long red hair, also with a very serious expression, was dancing by lifting her knees to the side and pushing her palms to the floor as if she was climbing on to a wall.

I sat on the table in the corner of the tent drinking a glass of red wine and watching the guests dancing under the blue and yellow lights. I could watch the dancers for hours. They looked so funny. A drunk woman wearing no shoes fell on the floor and Richard put his hands under her arms and pulled her up. She started dancing again like nothing had happened. But she could not control her feet and she walked in circles with her head hanging down. One side of her dress was broken and kept falling open, showing her bra.

Richard started to dance with an old lady in a blue lace dress. She was about seventy or eighty years old. He held her hand and raised his arm so that she could turn under the arch. Her mouth was wide open like she was having a lot of fun. Richard curled her along his arm in a spiral until she reached his chest and then he pushed her back the other way. But he let go of her hand by mistake and she fell into a tall, hairy man wearing a skirt. He caught the woman with his arm and pushed her towards Richard. The three of them laughed.

After the old woman went to sit down and wave a menu card at her face, Richard took the hand of the woman with the long red hair and pulled her towards him. He put his knees between her legs and his hand on her back and each time he pushed her backwards, he looked down at her body very obviously. The DJ put on 'Twist and Shout' and they danced holding hands, with their knees bent and their feet flat on the floor moving like car wipers. Richard looked up and saw me looking at him. He dropped the woman's hands and pushed through the other dancers as he came towards me. He took both my hands and pulled me from the chair.

'You can't sit there all night and watch, it's not allowed.'

I pulled backwards. 'I'm not a good dancer.'

He waved his arm across all the guests dancing in strange movements and jerking rhythms like they were all dancing to different songs. 'Do you honestly think that matters?'

I could not help smiling and stopped pulling. Richard could

feel he was winning and walked backwards towards the dancers, holding my hands.

'You need to learn how to let loose,' he said.

We stepped on to the wooden floor and stood opposite each other. The song changed.

'Yes!' Richard said, making a fist. 'I fucking love this song. Right, watch and learn.'

He put his hands next to his shoulders and clicked on the beat at the same time as sticking his neck forwards and backwards like a tortoise. I copied him and stuck out my lips. Richard nodded like he was impressed. He swung his arms from his elbows in half circles, clicking his fingers. I did the same. Then I put my arms straight to the sides and rolled my head from one side to the other. Richard laughed and copied me. Then he stuck his chest out and moved his shoulders quickly at the same time as leaning his body forward and backwards. I moved in the same way, so that when he went backwards I went forwards, and the opposite, so we were moving together.

I knew Richard was right, that I needed to learn how to loosen myself. I wondered if I liked to be in control of small things because I had felt for a long time like I had no control over the big things in my life. Now, dancing, I tried to let go of my thoughts. It felt good to let my body move with the music and to be free. I could not stop laughing. I thought I had never felt so happy as that moment. All the fear and uncertainty I had felt before I came to the house disappeared. The singers were calling and repeating the words, *Modern Love, Church on Time* and *God and Man* and I listened carefully so that I would remember the song for ever.

'That's more like it!' Richard shouted. 'You know, you look beautiful when you smile.'

We danced for a few more songs until sweat was running down my back. I walked out of the tent on to the grass, wiping my face with the bottom of my shirt. Outside a woman wearing a man's grey jacket over her dress and the hairy man in the skirt were smoking under the tree covered in little lights. The wind had stopped and the air was cool. I needed to pee so I went behind the big hedge towards the white caravan and walked up the metal steps to the door with the sign, *Ladies Toilets*. Through the door, in the bright light, I saw the bride standing next to the sink, holding her big skirt in her arms and looking over her shoulder at her back. Her eyes were stained with mascara.

'Oh thank God you're here,' she said. 'I'm terrified I'm going to get blue liquid splashback on my dress. Can you help me?'

'Sure,' I said.

'OK, hold this,' she said, putting a big ball of white fabric into my arms. 'Keep it high.'

The bride walked backwards with little steps into one of the toilets and I walked sideways with my back against the wall. She pulled down her pants and sat. I held the material high above her shoulders.

'Have you got it?' she said.

I heard the sound of her pee hitting the water.

'Yes, don't worry. Did you have a good day?'

'Yes and no. I mean, I'm completely shattered. The whole thing's gone by in a blur and I won't remember a single thing tomorrow. Except for the fact that the only thing anybody has said to me all day is how great I look, and it gets a bit boring after a while. Still, at least we had the photos taken outside. That's what really counts at the end of the day, isn't it?' She looked up at me smiling ironically and put her hand with toilet paper under her skirt between her legs.

After she washed her hands and rubbed under her eyes with a tissue, she said, 'I haven't got my dress tucked into my knickers anywhere, have I?'

'You are OK.'

'Thanks. Loo buddies for ever.'

She put her fist out towards me and I realised I was meant to do something, so I put my fist out too. When they touched, she opened her hand and made a noise like a bomb exploding.

'This will probably be my most cherished memory of the day,' she said, turning her head to look at me again as she walked down the steps.

When I was washing my hands in the sink, a lady in a green dress with large breasts was standing at the top of the steps looking confused.

'I think I've got the wrong loo. Is this the men's?'

She leant backwards to look at the sign on the door. When she looked at me again she seemed angry. She opened her mouth as if she was going to say something, but then she quickly shut it and her cheeks turned red.

I took some paper from the box on the wall and laughed, enjoying her mistake. 'No, it's the ladies' toilet.'

'Oh, I'm so sorry,' she said, her eyes moving around, embarrassed. 'I thought—'

'It's OK.' I threw the ball of paper in the bin as I walked past her. 'I don't mind.'

I wanted to find Sophie. I was having fun, but it was not the same without her. I wanted to make her come and dance with me. I walked around, looking for her. She was not standing with the guests near the bar, or sitting talking at the tables or with the smokers. I walked towards the kitchen and looked through the window. There were two waitresses at the sink washing plates and nobody else. It was strange that I had not seen her for a long time. I thought she might have been tired and gone to bed. But I thought of one place she might be and walked around the corner of the house to check the garden. On the bench I saw Sophie's dress shining like moonlight on a lake.

'Sophie,' I said. 'Are you OK?'

'Yes, I'm fine. Sometimes you just aren't in the mood, you know?'

I sat down next to her. She put her arms around her chest and stroked her arms as if she was cold, so I took off my jacket and put it over her shoulders. She put her head on my arm, and her arm around my waist. I could smell mint in her hair.

'Did you have fun?' she said.

'I was dancing with Richard.'

'Richard loves dancing. He won't leave that dance floor now until he is prised off it at five in the morning.'

'I can believe it.'

'Did he rope in some poor unsuspecting old lady to dance with him?

'He did.'

'He always does that.' She was silent for a minute, then she said, 'Was he dancing with a woman with long red hair?'

'Yes.'

'I knew it. That's Georgia, the one I told you about.'

'Sophie, Richard was only dancing with her like he danced with me, with the old lady, with everyone.'

'You are so innocent sometimes.'

We were silent for a minute. Then I felt Sophie looking up at me. She kept looking and I did not look down. I understood what she wanted. But I knew it would change everything. Then she reached up with her hand and touched the side of my face. Her fingers moved under my ear until they were on the back of my neck. Her touch was like silver on my skin. Gently she pulled my head down so that my face was just above hers. Her eyes were looking at mine very strongly. I was afraid, but I could not make myself move away. She lifted her lips so they were touching my lips. I stayed still. She opened her mouth, and I opened my mouth. She tasted of champagne. Our tongues touched. We stayed like that, not moving for what seemed like a long time. I felt that we had joined together, that my blood was flowing through her and her blood through me. Then I pulled my head up.

'This is not a good idea,' I said. 'Someone could see us. We should go.'

We walked along the path towards the tent. When we came to the big green bush, Sophie took my hand and pulled me behind it into the shadows. I pulled back but then I could not resist any more. I followed her and lifted her up so she was sitting on the wall and kissed her hard on the mouth as she put her legs around my waist. I pulled down her dress and kissed her pale breasts like I had been dreaming about for weeks. I thought that if anyone looked behind the bush they would see my back and Sophie's legs and think that I was just a man having a very lucky night.

CHAPTER SEVEN

I picked up the thinnest paintbrush and rolled it in the circle of white paint on the wooden board. With my right hand I held up the little silver laptop and painted a tiny apple with a bite taken and a leaf coming from the top of it. I did this on each of the four laptops and put them on the shelf above the heater to dry. I could not wait for Sophie to see them. She would love them.

It was four days since the wedding and I had spent all the time in the barn. It was difficult to be in the same room with Sophie and Richard because I thought Richard would notice something was different. Luckily he was busy with the baby pheasants. Sophie behaved as if nothing had happened. I thought that what happened was because she had been feeling jealous of Richard and the girl with red hair and needed someone to want her.

I looked at my new scene on the table. The squirrels were already in the café. The female squirrel who worked there was sitting on a stool painting her nails red on the bar next to the plates of cakes and brownies. She had just taken a flat white coffee to the squirrel on the first table. He was looking down into the heart pattern in the coffee foam and wishing that she really loved him. Two squirrels were sitting on the sofa in the corner talking about an interesting design project. The male squirrel was rolling a cigarette and the female was holding her coffee cup with two hands while she listened carefully to his ideas.

When the laptops were ready I put them on the tables in the café. Each one had a different image on the screen. One had a picture of a new bicycle, another was a photograph of a woman in the street wearing crazy clothes on a fashion blog, and another one was the page of the novel the first squirrel was trying to write, but instead was looking out of the window, dreaming. The squirrel on the table near the door was checking his Facebook profile.

The door opened and Sophie came in with a sandwich on a plate. She was wearing her shorts and a vest and no shoes. I put the paintbrushes in the jar of water and the colours floated off them like smoke.

'Can I come in?' she said.

'Of course you can come in.'

'I brought you a sandwich.'

'Thank you.'

Sophie put the sandwich on the table and came over so that she was standing next to me.

'How is *Freelance Squirrels* getting along?'

'It's finished. Caleb is coming tomorrow.'

'I absolutely love it.'

As she bent over to look at the details she put her hand on my shoulder. I could smell her sweat from under her arms, only a little, but it was like a drug on me. Already I felt myself getting hot and wet between my legs. I told myself, *Mirka, be normal.*

Sophie left her hand on my shoulder for a long time, as if she had forgotten what to do with it. I was trying to breathe not too heavily. Then she turned her head and looked at me. I knew she was thinking the same thing. Her lips were open. Slowly, she moved them towards my lips. It seemed like they were never going to touch. But then we were kissing, softly at the beginning, then more strongly.

After a minute I tried to stop. 'Sophie.'

'Don't even start,' she said, still kissing me.

I could not push her because I was still sitting down and wearing my plastic gloves. 'I like Richard. I feel guilty.'

Sophie sighed. 'I knew you would be like this. You're only saying those things because you feel like you have to say them. When actually you want it as much as I do. So either do it or don't do it, but don't do it and talk about how bad it is while you're doing it. It kind of ruins it.'

'I guess you are right.'

'I'm the one who's doing the bad thing anyway. I'm the married one. And I want it.'

I stood up and moved closer to her so that our bodies were touching. I could feel her nipples through my T-shirt. 'What do you want?' I said.

'I want to go and find a bed.'

Outside it was cool and cloudy. Fat bees were flying around the lavender. We walked in silence through the house. As I went up the stairs I could feel my heart beating faster. Sophie went to the blue room and I followed her.

We stood next to the bed and took off our clothes. I had forgotten about her body from the day when I first saw it in the kitchen. She was small, but full, like she was made of cream.

It took her less time than me to take off her clothes and she knelt on the bed while I sat down to take off my socks.

'I can't stop thinking about you,' she said, kissing my ear. 'I can't concentrate on anything. I've got a million emails to write and phone calls to make, but I just sit daydreaming.'

'I'm the same.'

I turned and kissed her mouth, pushing her head down to the pillow. Immediately I could feel myself melting and I had the sweet feeling in my veins like an addict. I kissed her breasts and put my hand between her legs. She was already wet. I put one, then two fingers inside her. It felt like I was touching the most alive part of her, a bloody beating heart.

Sophie was making noises and moving her body against my hand. I closed my eyes and felt the sensations inside my body, as if I was her mirror. It was like the rest of the world had disappeared and I did not know what I was doing until I could hear her cries becoming louder and louder and she started shaking.

I stopped and we lay breathing heavily. Her hair was stuck to her wet face and I brushed it away with my fingers.

'How do you do that?' Sophie said.

'Do what?'

'I don't know. Whatever that was. It doesn't feel like anything else.'

'So you liked it?'

She smiled. 'Couldn't you tell?'

I looked at the gold clock on the shelf. It was already four o'clock.

'Sophie, we need to get dressed. Richard will come back soon.'

'He won't be back yet.' She started to kiss me again. 'I don't want to stop yet.'

I pushed her away. 'We need to be careful.'

'Tomorrow then?'

'Maybe,' I said, and I knew this was going to be my life from that moment. I would not be able to think of anything else.

The next day Richard was in the barn all morning, working on an otter. I watched him gluing the eyes in the wrong position, one higher than the other. The otter looked crazy.

'Fucking thing,' Richard said.

'Why don't you go out, I'll finish the otter.'

'Thanks, but I want to wait for Caleb.'

I had forgotten about Caleb. He was not coming until after lunch. I thought I would never be alone so that I could go to the house and see Sophie.

The yellow chicks that a friend of Sophie's gave to her for me after they became sick and died were lying on the table in a line. I was going to make a scene called *Hen Party in Brighton*. The paper designs were next to them. The back of the box would be painted with Brighton Pier and the chicks would be dressed in pink outfits. The bride would wear a necklace with a red L on a white square and one of the bridesmaids was going to give her a box of penis-shaped chocolates.

I picked up the first chick and started to gently push back the feathers with the knife over the chick's chest, but I could not concentrate. I could not get the picture of Sophie out of my mind. I saw her lying naked like a pale pink starfish on the sheets of the bed and I got hotter and hotter until I felt like I had a fever.

'Mirka, tell me how to make it better.'

'What?' I said, feeling caught. I was holding the chick, staring at nothing.

'The otter. What's wrong with it?'

'Make it lie down on the rock and look to the side.'

'Good plan. Are you all right? You're jolly red.'

'Am I?' I said, feeling myself blushing more. 'I'm just hot.'

At lunchtime Sophie came into the barn with two plates of sandwiches. As she put my plate on the table she gave me a strong look to say, *When are you coming?* I gave her a look to say, *I am trying but I can't come yet.*

All afternoon I could not stop looking at the clock. At last I heard the wheels of Caleb's car on the stones. He came in looking sweaty, his grey shirt full of wrinkles.

'Fucking nightmare traffic.'

'What happened?' Richard said.

'Completely backed up from junction fourteen all the way to seventeen.'

'Should have got off and gone down the back roads. I'll teach you the shortcut. You get off at fifteen, take the first exit off the roundabout and double back on yourself under the motorway—'

'Hi, Caleb,' I said, to try and stop Richard before he spent ten minutes describing every road to the house.

'Hi, Mirka. Where is it then?'

I nodded to *Freelance Squirrels* on the table in the corner. Caleb walked over and had a look.

'That is genius! I can almost hear what they're saying. "Hey, Jasper, check out my new fixie." "Ah yeah, that's totally rad, Felix."'

Caleb and Richard were laughing. I wanted to tell them that the squirrels were not saying that at all, but I said nothing.

'What's next?' Caleb asked me.

I showed him my plans for *Hen Party in Brighton*.

'Love it, love it. When are you going to finish it?'

'I am working as fast as I can.'

'Well, it's not fast enough.' He smiled. Then he turned to Richard. 'What the fuck is that thing?'

'It's an otter.'

'I thought for a second you'd got hold of a sloth. Speaking of which—' Caleb got something out of his pocket and put it on the table near Richard. It was a little square of plastic with some marijuana inside. 'Before I forget,' he said. 'That's for you. New stuff. It's really good. Not too heavy, and kind of sweet.'

Richard picked up the packet and kissed it. 'You absolute beauty. Shall we have a quick one now?'

'Oh, go on then.'

I sighed. It did not seem that they were going anywhere

quickly. I carried on working on the chicks, trying not to think about Sophie, while Richard made a joint and Caleb made some coffee. Then they went outside to smoke it and I could see them from the window, holding their cups and passing the joint between them, talking and laughing.

Finally at five o'clock Caleb left. I thought it might be too late for Richard to visit the pheasants, but he finished his coffee and picked up his car keys.

'Right, better go and check on those birds.'

'See you later,' I said, trying not to sound excited.

After the car had gone, I walked quickly, almost ran to the house. On the path I saw David coming towards me pushing a wheelbarrow full of dark green hedge leaves and sticks. On top there was a dead rat. I was surprised to see him and I did not understand why he was not with Richard, checking on the birds, but then I remembered that he had to cut all the hedges in the garden ready for a wedding. I slowed down so that I was walking normally.

'Hi, David,' I said.

David gave me a long look with dead eyes. It was a look full of hate, like he wanted to hurt me. Then he walked past me without saying anything. It was so unfriendly that I stopped walking for a moment. I stood on the path. I could not understand why he did not like me. I had done nothing to him except come to the house.

Sophie was in the kitchen washing dark red wavy lettuce in the sink. She switched off the tap.

'Oh my God, I thought you were never going to come.'

'I just saw David.'

'Shh, I don't care,' Sophie said, pulling me towards the door. I pulled back.

'He hates me.'

'He doesn't hate you, you're imagining things,' Sophie said, kissing me. 'Come on.'

'He thinks I took his job.'

'Don't be silly, you do completely different jobs.'

She took my hand and I followed her to the blue room again. We took off our clothes and I climbed on top of her, kissing her hard. I had already forgotten about David. All I wanted was to touch her again.

After a while Sophie twisted herself from underneath me and tried to push me down so I would be lying on my back.

'What are you doing?' I said, pushing her down.

'Why do you always get to be the one in charge?'

'I don't know,' I said. 'Because I like to be in control.'

'Is that normal?' she said curiously.

'I don't know,' I said. 'Maybe it's just me.'

'And what happens if you meet someone else like you?'

I held her wrists on the pillow above her head so that she could not move. She struggled but I was too strong. I could tell that she liked it. Her expression was impressed.

'I will win,' I said.

A few days later I was in the drawing room. I was wiping the thick dust from the glass top of the record player with a cloth. I read the names of the songs in the middle of the record, not concentrating until I saw the name, *Matty Groves*. I stopped and opened the lid. I really wanted to listen to it and discover what happened in the story of Matty Groves and Lady Donald. It took me a few moments to switch on the machine and then I put the needle on to the record and listened. The music was unusual, a mixture of guitar and violins. When the woman sang, *A holiday, a holiday*, I closed my eyes and thought of Sophie in the vegetable garden.

Of course Matty Groves went with Lady Donald to have sex with her. But someone, a servant, saw them and went to tell her husband. The words to the song were very beautiful and I realised I was biting my lip because I was so nervous about what would happen next in the story. Matty Groves woke up and saw Lord Donald standing at the end of the bed. I should have guessed, I thought. Now Matty Groves was in a lot of trouble. But I was surprised at how rude he was to Lord Donald, making jokes about how much he liked sleeping with his wife, like he did not care about anything. I would be more frightened than Matty Groves. In the end Lord Donald killed Matty Groves with a sword. Then he asked his wife who she liked more, Matty Groves or him. She said she would prefer to kiss Matty Groves even though he was dead, so he killed her too. I was shocked. They did not deserve to die for what they did, I thought. Or maybe they did. It was a different time when the rules were different. I could not stop thinking about myself, about dying with a sword in my heart for what I was doing. Richard holding the sword at the other end.

I was so lost in the music, which continued after they were dead, and thinking about the poor lovers, that I did not hear Richard come into the room until I saw him standing next to me. I was so surprised and guilty I reached and tried to take the needle off the record but instead it made a horrible scratching sound.

'Great song that,' Richard said. 'Poor old Matty Groves gets it in the end.'

I could not look at Richard. I put the needle back to the side and closed the lid. My face was burning.

'What are you doing now?' Richard said.

'Nothing.'

'Fancy coming somewhere with me?'

'Do you need help with the pheasants?'

'No, no, they're fine.' Richard was hitting his fist into the palm of his hand. I stared at his hands. Then he said, 'I have an uncontrollable urge to kill something.'

I felt the hairs rise on my body. But he was looking very normally at me. He did not seem angry.

'How do you feel about coming to help me?'

'OK,' I said. 'Where's David?'

'He's not working today.'

I was relieved that David was away. I followed Richard through the kitchen. Sophie was doing the crossword and smoking a cigarette. As I walked past, I asked her with my eyes, *What is happening?* She pressed her lips together and lifted her shoulders to tell me, *I don't know, but don't worry.* I realised Richard was just being Richard.

We went to a room next to the living room. I knew it was Richard's study but I had never been inside it. Richard held the door open with his arm so I could walk past him into the room. He was smiling and watching me like he wanted to see my reaction.

The walls of the room were covered in heads of deer. There were about twelve heads, with big horns, looking straight at me with their intelligent black eyes as if they were deciding what kind of person I was. For a moment I thought that they had come to look inside the room through holes in the wall, and their bodies were on the other side. I only realised then how different the taxidermy heads of the deer were to the whole animals, because I did not have the feeling they could suddenly come to life like the fox in the entrance hall. If they did, they would only be bloody heads floating around like a nightmare. Richard was wrong when he told me that taxidermy was to preserve the animal, this was not about the animal at all, only the killer.

'Did you kill them?' I asked Richard, though I already knew the answer.

'I did indeed,' he said, rubbing his hands.

'They are beautiful animals.'

'I know.' He went and stroked the nose of the first deer and looked into his eyes. 'I love deer so much. You have to really love them, otherwise there is no contest. I love to watch them, study their movements, understand how they think. They are incredible creatures.' He stood in front of the next deer, looking up. 'This one, for example, I shot up in the Borders. I followed him for hours. Kept losing him until eventually I came across him in a little copse of trees and I went round the other side and I waited. After a few hours the deer came along through the trees. And finally I got him.' Richard's eyes were sparkling as he told the story of how he killed the deer and his hands were moving dramatically, showing me the positions of the deer and holding the gun up to his eye. Above him the deer's face was peaceful and calm, like he was happy for Richard to kill him. Richard stroked the deer's face. 'Isn't he something?'

'He is something,' I said, though I was not sure what exactly he was.

Richard took a key from the top drawer of the green leather desk and opened the cupboard on the wall, pulling the glass door sideways and taking out a long black gun with a wooden handle. He put the strap over his shoulder and took out some small boxes and put them in his bag.

'Right, are you ready?'

'Are we going to shoot a deer?'

Richard laughed. 'Nothing quite so dramatic as that. You'll see.'

We walked behind the house then over two fields, crossed the stile and then walked along a narrow path between tall yellow flowers. At the end we went through a gate into another field. Richard picked up some grass in his fingers and let it fall, sloping in the wind. He pointed to the corner of the field where there was a hedge.

'OK, silently now. We are going to cross over that hedge and lie down in the grass.'

'OK.'

Richard smiled an evil smile. 'Then it's bunny Armageddon.'

When we were lying down on our elbows, Richard took two bottles of beer from his bag and opened them with his teeth. The sun was strong and yellow on the grass. Twenty metres away about ten brown rabbits were sitting very still like they were listening. The sun in their ears made the skin glow orange. They seemed quite relaxed and not suspicious. One rabbit came from a hole in the grass and sat down, sniffing the air.

Richard put the telescope on the gun to his eye and looked for a long time at the rabbits. The rabbits did not move. Suddenly there was a bang and one of the rabbits fell sideways, his feet jerking. The other rabbits started running across the field or diving down the holes and Richard moved the gun to follow them. The gun fired and another rabbit fell sideways.

We picked up the bodies of the rabbits and went to another field.

'Absolutely infested,' Richard said, looking at all the rabbits in the grass. He put the gun on its legs in front of me. 'Your turn.'

I looked through the telescope. The rabbits were sitting peacefully with no idea that they might die in the next minute.

'Right, put your finger on the trigger.' Richard took my finger and moved it to the right place. 'You want to put the cross below the ear, next to the eye. Don't do anything for now. Just keep breathing, very steady.'

I moved the cross until it was on the head of a rabbit.

'When you're ready, gently squeeze the trigger without moving the gun.'

I had the cross exactly where Richard said, next to the eye. The cross was moving up and down a little. I stopped breathing and pulled my finger against the trigger. But I could not do it, I felt like the rabbit was looking directly at me with his big black eye.

'Sorry, Richard,' I said, looking up from the telescope. 'I can't do it. I can't kill the rabbit.'

'Why not? It's a rabbit, for Christ's sake. It's not going to feel a thing.'

'I don't want to make something die.'

'They're pests. If you don't kill it, David or I will. David positively thrives on the blood of dead bunnies. So it's going to die anyway.'

'OK, but I prefer it if you kill him.'

'That's right, isn't it? Everybody's always happy for someone else to kill things for them, but they don't have the balls to do it themselves.'

'Exactly,' I said.

Richard looked satisfied. 'Glad we are all clear about that then.'

When we were walking back to the house I thought about not wanting to kill the rabbit. I knew that if I ate rabbit I should be able to kill one. But I felt that Richard got some pleasure from killing rabbits, and I did not want to feel it.

'It's the same in Slovakia,' I told Richard. 'I am happy for my father to kill the Christmas carp so I can eat it. But I don't want to kill it.'

'What the fuck?' Richard started to laugh. 'You eat carp for Christmas? Who even eats carp?'

'It's a Slovak tradition,' I said. 'Christmas is the only time we eat it. It's full of tiny bones.'

'But why?'

'I have no idea. Why do British people eat turkey? You never eat it any other time. It's not even from here. Anyway, one year when I was sixteen my father was away working in the Ukraine. He works in an oil company,' I said, to explain to Richard because I never told him about my family before. 'In Slovakia we buy the carp three days before Christmas and put him in the bath to clean.'

Richard looked confused.

'Do you understand?' I said. 'The carp is alive in the bath, swimming. Usually the carp lives in mud so he needs three days in pure water so that he will be clean for eating. Then, on the twenty-fourth of December the man at the top of the family kills the carp by hitting him just above the nose.' I showed Richard with my finger on my nose. 'But my father was not there and I did not have a brother. My grandfather said to me, "Mirka, you must kill the carp because I am too old and sick." I did not want to, because when you kill the carp there is so much blood and it is very violent. I was afraid. Even my father hated killing the carp. Every year my mother and my father had arguments about killing the carp because my father always waited until the last moment on the twenty-fourth and my mother wanted to cook the carp already.

'So I was thinking, there must be an easier way to kill the carp. I took the carp from the bath and put him on the kitchen table. The carp is this big.' I put my palms facing each other with half a metre between. 'You can't take a carp out of water to die, you have to kill it, otherwise it will stay alive for a long time, dying painfully. So I put wires from the car battery on the two wings – what are they called?' I made wings with my hands at the side of my body.

'Fins,' Richard said, putting his hand over his eyes.

'Then I put electricity on the fins to kill the carp.'

'What happened?' Richard looked at me through the gap between his fingers, like he was afraid to hear the story.

'The carp jumped and hit the ceiling and fell on the floor. He was alive and moving around like he was in a lot of pain. Blood was coming from his ears.'

'Oh my God,' Richard said, laughing now.

'My grandfather was very angry with me and he came with a hammer and hit the carp on the head until he was dead. There was blood everywhere on the floor. It was horrible.'

'Sounds like you did the best you could.'

'I don't think I was serious enough about the job, about killing something. Afterwards, for a long time I felt guilty about the carp suffering, but I also felt guilty that I had not done a good job for my grandfather. And I did not want to kill another animal.'

'Fair play to you,' Richard said. 'Wow, I can't believe you tried to electrocute a carp.'

'I should never have tried to kill the carp. It was a bad decision I made, and the truth is it was because I was ashamed of being a girl and I wanted to be the man in the family because my father was not there.'

'OK. Well, I'll kill the animals and you can taxidermy them.'

I smiled. 'Deal.'

The next Sunday was sunny and in the afternoon Sophie and I went for a walk. We walked along the path in the cool woods. The light was soft and green and the sun made sloping stripes of misty air. Sophie walked in front of me with her hands in the pockets of her white shorts.

'Are we walking to the village?' I said.

'What?' She turned around and smiled as she waited for me. 'Sorry, miles away. Yes. I thought maybe we could have a glass of wine or something in the Dog and Duck.'

In the distance, between the trees, two people were walking towards us. Scrabble and Ringo saw their pale yellow dog and ran to sniff it. The three dogs ran in excited circles around the woods. It was a man with a grey beard and behind him a woman with white sticks in both hands that she moved at the same time as her legs.

'Afternoon,' the man said to Sophie as he walked past.

'Afternoon,' Sophie said to the man. Then she said, 'Afternoon,' to the woman.

'Afternoon,' the woman said to Sophie.

'Afternoon,' the man said to me as we crossed.

'Afternoon,' I said to the man. 'Afternoon,' I said to the woman.

'Afternoon,' the woman said, smiling and nodding her head, and I had some satisfaction that every combination of saying 'Afternoon' was completed.

'Scrabble. Ringo,' Sophie shouted when it seemed like the dogs wanted to run away with the other dog. They came running out of a bush and she took biscuits from her pocket and bent down and gave them one each on her palm. 'Good dogs.'

She looked in both directions down the path and, as the couple turned a corner, she stood on her toes to kiss me. Afterwards she looked down, embarrassed, like she did not know what to say. When she was shy like this I liked it because I thought that it meant she must like me.

We started walking again and she took my hand and put her fingers between my fingers. For a moment I forgot that she was married to someone else. We were just like any couple who were at the beginning of a relationship. It was easy to think that we could be together for ever. I had to remind myself to be careful with my feelings and not to get too deep into something that could hurt me.

The path came out into the road in the village next to the red telephone box. We walked alongside the parked cars and houses with their little gardens full of colourful flowers. Outside a small square white house, there were boxes of eggs in a pile on a table and a sign saying, *Happy Eggs from Happy Hens – 25p each*.

On the big square of grass, in the long shadows of the trees, men wearing white clothes were playing a game of cricket. It seemed like a kind of dance they were doing, a performance to the people who were sitting in low stripy chairs drinking beer.

We came to the tall dark green bushes in front of the church.

'My mother's buried in there,' Sophie said. 'Do you want to come and see?'

Sophie opened the metal gate under the little roof and we walked down the path towards the grey church. The clock on the tower said it was five minutes past six o'clock. Sophie went to a tap on the side of the church saying, *Drinking Water*, and bent her head and drank from the stream. Scrabble and Ringo came and drank the water falling from her chin. She wiped her face on her T-shirt, making stains of dark blue.

We walked past the church between the graves. The grey stones were leaning in different angles and covered in spots of pale yellow and white plants. I tried to read the names of the people who had died, but sometimes the writing had disappeared. I thought that the people lying under the stones probably died so long ago that nobody today knew that they were ever alive.

Sophie stopped at a new, shiny stone written with the words, *In Loving Memory of Cristina Sophie Calloway. Greatly missed Wife and Mother. Died 17 February 1999. Aged 52 Years.*

There were red flowers in a pot on the shelf at the bottom of the stone.

I held Sophie's hand and she put her head on my arm. I felt like she was saying something to her mother. I thought that it was a nice place to be for ever, in the grass, under the big tree with white flowers, next to the church. Sophie's mother didn't know this, but it was nice for Sophie to visit. I thought of Misty, the guinea pig.

'It helps, coming to see her here,' Sophie said, as if she could hear my thoughts. 'I used to come every week after she died. But I don't think about her so much now. That's an awful thing to say, isn't it?'

'No, it was a long time ago.'

'She wouldn't want it either. She told me in as many words not to waste a moment of my life moping over her.'

'What was she like?'

'Pretty no-nonsense, my mother. Or rather ...' Sophie paused, thinking. 'What I mean is, she looked death square on. But she made fun of it. When she found out that the cancer was terminal, she always joked she was finally getting to go on the cruise she had always dreamed of going on. Everything was about the cruise. Who she would meet at the captain's dinner table. The unlimited Campari sodas she would be allowed to drink.'

'Why did she never go on a cruise?'

Sophie laughed. 'Oh no, my mother wouldn't have been seen dead on a cruise. That was the joke.'

'It must have been hard for you.'

'My biggest regret is that I didn't say something at the funeral. I was afraid I would cry. But I should have done. She wouldn't have been impressed.'

'I'm sure she understood.'

'You don't know my mother. She had no time for any kind of self-indulgence. The one thing she said to me and Camilla was that under no circumstances were we allowed to cry at the funeral. It would be an embarrassment to our family name.'

'Did you cry?'

'Of course I did. It was my mother.'

I followed Sophie back towards the church. She went inside the entrance house, climbed on to the bench at the side and put her fingers into the corner and pulled out a big brown key.

'How did you know?' I said.

'I used to come and help Mum do the church flowers.'

She unlocked the door and went into the dark church. I went inside slowly. I felt like I was not allowed to be there. Sophie was walking up the red carpet towards the end of the church where there was a table dressed in a green cloth under a colourful window. Next to the door there was a table with papers and books about the church under a piece of plastic. There was a sign that said, *Please help yourself but replace the plastic sheet to protect the table from bat droppings.*

I walked past the stone basin for the holy water. It reminded me of the birdbath. The church was very simple. White walls and arches of dark brown wood holding the ceiling. No statues, or gold or paintings of women crying with circles of light above their heads.

Sophie was sitting down on one of the dark brown benches near the front.

'This was our family pew,' she said. 'We would always come early to sit here.'

I sat down and my knee hit one of the red rectangle cushions and it fell on the floor. I picked up it up and looked inside the blue book on the slope at the top of the bench in front. It was full of the words to songs written like poems on the pages.

As I was looking at the book, Sophie leaned forward to kiss my mouth. She put her hand on my thigh, sliding it up towards my shorts. I pulled my head backwards and took her hand off my leg. Now that I knew Sophie, I knew she would have sex with me in the church. But even I did not want Sophie that much.

'Come on,' she said, trying to kiss me again.

I pushed her away gently. 'Not here, Sophie.'

Sophie clicked her tongue and stood up. I followed her out of the church into the bright light. Scrabble and Ringo were lying on the stone floor of the entrance house, breathing loudly.

Sophie locked the door and put away the key. She walked in front of me and did not look at me or speak to me. I felt like she was angry with me for not playing her game.

We arrived at the pub and Sophie went to the bar.

'You go and find a table in the garden and I'll get the drinks. What do you want?'

'What are you having?'

'White wine.'

'I'll have the same.'

I went through the pub into the garden and sat at a table under a yellow umbrella. People were drinking and talking with their dogs under the tables resting in the shade. Sophie came out holding a wine in each hand and climbed on to the bench next to me.

'Isn't it a gorgeous evening? You can't beat England when it's like this.'

She seemed to have forgotten about the church. She started to tell me about the village fete and all the different costumes she wore as a child for the competition. As she talked, she kept putting her hand on my thigh or stroking my arm. I felt like everyone was staring at us. I did not understand how Sophie could be so obvious. But when I looked again at the people, I saw that nobody was looking. I realised they probably thought we were only two friends who liked to touch each other a lot when they talked.

We were drinking our second glass of wine and I was telling her about my favourite Slovak meal of plum dumplings when Sophie reached out her hand and touched my face and sighed.

'Ah my little Matty Groves,' she said.

'Did you want me to be your Matty Groves when you sang me the song that time in the vegetable garden?'

'Yes, I think I was thinking about it.'

'I thought so.'

'Part of me thought something like this might happen one day. But I never thought it would be with someone like you.'

'A girl?'

Sophie put her head to the side and frowned. 'Mmm. Well, all of it really. But you make a good Matty Groves.' She took a sip of her wine and looked like she was thinking about something. 'There was always something about that name that struck me as being feminine anyway. It makes me think of pubic hair.'

'What?' I said, starting to laugh. 'What are you talking about?'

'Well, Matty can be a girl's name. Short for Matilda. And *Matty Groves*, I don't know, the words are so redolent. A grove is a small forested area and Matty reminds me of matted, as in covered in thick undergrowth. Hence pubic hair.' As she said this, Sophie reached down and put her hand in my jeans into my pants. 'Especially yours.'

'Sophie, stop it,' I said, taking out her hand.

'Oh, you're no fun,' she said, her eyes sparkling.

She was joking, but I felt hurt. I did not like to always be the boring person. I never thought I was like this before. But with Sophie it always seemed to be me who was saying stop, even though she had more to lose. I had a feeling she would become tired of me if I continued.

We walked back to the house holding hands. Sophie sang a song from the church. The song was more about farming than

God, about ploughing fields and scattering the seeds on the land. I felt I was in a magic spell.

In the middle of the woods, Sophie went behind some bushes to take a pee and I waited on the path. Suddenly, from the side of my eye, I saw a young deer standing still between the trees. I turned my head very slowly to look at her so that she would not get frightened and run away. She had white spots on her fur and her big soft eyes were staring at me, afraid but also curious. I tried to tell her with my eyes that I did not want to hurt her, or catch her and keep her for ever. I only wanted to look at her because she was so beautiful and pure. She was frozen, as if she were a taxidermy deer, but there was nothing dead in her eyes. She was so alive. We stayed with our eyes locked together until Ringo or Scrabble came walking along the path and the deer turned and ran, her white behind disappearing between the trees.

'Mirka,' I heard Sophie calling. 'Come here.'

I walked behind the bush. Sophie was lying completely naked on the earth. I could not help laughing. Nobody had ever wanted to have sex with me so much before.

'Do you want something?' I said.

'You know what I want.'

I pushed her legs open and knelt down between them. Then I kissed her skin down her belly until my mouth was between her legs and licked her like I was drinking her. Sophie made a cry of pleasure and Scrabble and Ringo ran out of the bushes to see what we were doing. One of the dogs tried to lick her face like he was worried she was hurt. Sophie reached her arm up to hit the dog to make it go away. She picked up pieces of wood and little stones and threw them at the dogs, but they would not leave her.

'Oh fuck off, dogs,' Sophie said, throwing a stone at them. 'Mummy's busy.'

CHAPTER EIGHT

I was walking through the woods in the silver light when I saw Sophie coming from behind a tree. She was naked, walking slowly and elegantly. She had huge deer horns growing out of her head. Her chin was lifted high and her expression was very serious. When she was standing in front of me, she took off my black sweater over my head and dropped it on to the fire burning next to my feet.

'Sophie,' a man called from somewhere in the trees.

I opened my eyes and I saw Sophie's face next to mine. She was sleeping. There was saliva on the pillow under her lips. I did not understand why we were in the same bed. Where was Richard? I looked around. We were in the blue room and there were clothes everywhere on the floor. Then I remembered that Richard had gone to stay with a friend in Scotland for a few days and there had been another wedding the day before and that I had drunk a lot of champagne. I had a strange metal taste in my mouth.

'Sophie!' a man shouted from downstairs.

I shook Sophie's shoulder hard. 'Sophie, who is that?'

She opened her eyes and lifted her head. When she saw me, she made a small scream.

'What's happening?' she said, looking at me like she was afraid of me.

Below her head on the pillow I saw a red stain. It was blood. I looked down at the sheets and there was blood everywhere, like someone had been murdered. I lifted my right hand and saw that the fingers were covered in dark dried blood. Now I knew what the taste in my mouth was.

'Sophie!' the man shouted.

'Oh my God,' she said, sitting up. 'It's my fucking father.'

She jumped out of the bed naked and picked up her T-shirt. But she put her arm in the hole for the head and then her head would not fit in the hole for the arm. She was panicking like a bird trapped inside a room. In the end the T-shirt was inside-outside with the label under her chin. I did not know what to do and stayed in the bed.

'Coming,' she shouted.

We heard footsteps on the stairs. Sophie froze and looked at me with terror in her eyes.

'Clean yourself,' she said. 'No, get in the wardrobe. Now!'

I realised he was coming to the room. I ran to the wardrobe and pulled the door closed. It would not close completely and I had to hold the metal square lock with my thumb and finger to stop the door from opening. The footsteps were coming up the stairs. Through the thin gap between the doors, I saw Sophie picking up my clothes and throwing them under the bed. She put the covers over the bloody sheets and brushed her hair with her fingers before opening the door and putting her arms out.

'Hi, Dad,' she said, her voice relaxed. 'I wasn't expecting you until next Sunday.'

I could not see Sophie's father outside in the corridor. I heard them kissing on the cheeks. It was difficult to keep holding the lock. I had to put a lot of pressure on it with my fingers to stop them slipping. I could not imagine a worse moment than the door swinging open and Sophie's father seeing me sitting naked inside the wardrobe. My arm was shaking and I held my elbow with my other hand for extra strength.

'We always said August the ninth. Why don't you write anything down?' His voice became suspicious. 'What are you doing, sleeping in this room?'

'Oh, well the window was jammed in ours and it was so hot last night.'

'Where is Richard?'

'He's off stalking. He'll be back tonight.'

'What has been going on in the house? The place looks like a bomb's hit it.'

'We had a wedding yesterday and I haven't had a chance to clean up yet. I would have done, if I'd known you were coming.'

'Whether you thought we were coming or not is totally beside the point. You should have cleaned it anyway.'

'I know, Dad, but it was a really hectic day and I was exhausted.'

'I don't want to see the house looking like this again. I didn't raise my daughter to be a slut.'

'Nice to see you too, Dad.'

'I'm serious, Sophie.'

'All right.'

'What have you got there on your arm? Is that blood?'

'Oh, it's nothing. Just a cut.'

Sophie's father made a suspicious noise. My fingers were slipping on the lock. My hand was frozen like a claw and I was sweating. I closed my eyes and tried to keep my fingers strong.

'Why don't you go and unpack in the green room,' Sophie said. 'It's all made up. I'll go and get Mirka and we'll clear up.'

'Who's Mirka?'

'The girl who lives here who helps us.'

'Then why the hell isn't she down there on her knees scrubbing the floors?' he shouted. 'Honestly, where do you find these people?'

He walked heavily down the stairs. My fingers slipped from the lock and the wardrobe door opened. Sophie was standing by the door with her palms covering her face.

The front door banged. 'Go, go, go,' Sophie said.

I picked up my clothes from under the bed and ran naked along the corridor. As I ran past the big mirror on the wall I saw my reflection. It gave me such a shock that I stopped. My mouth was stained with dark blood. I looked like a monster.

As I was walking up the stairs to my room, memories of the night before came to me. I saw parts of our bodies, flashes of breasts, thighs, hands, hungry mouths with teeth. Everything was moving, twisting together, quickly and violently. The images frightened me. I had never lost control of myself so completely before. I did not know it was possible. We were like animals.

After having a bath, I got dressed and went downstairs. I still had a strange feeling and I did not know what it meant. I moved slowly because I was trying to delay meeting Sophie's father. In the entrance hall I picked up some empty champagne glasses from the shelf above the fire. There were petals on the floor near the door and on the table there were some dirty paper napkins and a plate with a few prawns around a pot of mayonnaise turning yellow around the edges.

Sophie's father was sitting at the kitchen table reading the newspaper. I could see his shining bald head with a ring of pale brown hair above his neck. The newspaper made a scratching noise where his fat belly was pushing it against the edge of the table. A small, thin woman with short dyed blonde hair was wiping the surfaces with a cloth. I put the champagne glasses next to the sink.

Sophie looked up at me from pouring the teapot, and smiled at me politely like I was a stranger who walked into her shop.

'Morning, Mirka. This is my stepmother, Caroline, and my father, William.'

Sophie's father bent down the corner of the newspaper with his hand and looked at me with his small eyes, two blue lakes in a desert of red skin.

'That's Mr Calloway to you,' he said, and the newspaper corner went up again.

Caroline took off the yellow glove and held her hand towards me.

'Nice to meet you, Mirka,' she said, showing two big teeth.

I went to the stone pot next to the toaster, lifted the lid and pulled out the bread.

'Mirka, could you make a start on the great hall, please,' Sophie said in the same polite voice.

I put the bread down and turned to Sophie. Her hands were in front of her chest and she was looking at me, waiting and smiling a strange, empty smile.

'OK,' I said.

I went to the hall and pushed Henry the hoover up and down like I was angry with the floor. Then I remembered it was not my house and I was only someone who worked there. Things were going to be different while her father was staying and I was going to have to get used to it.

That evening I was in the kitchen when the telephone rang. I kept putting the knives and forks from the dishwasher into the drawer, waiting for Sophie to answer it, but it kept ringing so I picked it up and pressed the green button.

'Good evening, Fairmont Hall,' I said.

'Mirka, it's me.'

'Hi, Richard, when are you coming home?'

'There's been an accident on the motorway and it's completely stationary. But I've seen the ambulances and fire brigade go past, so hopefully it should be cleared soon.'

'Sophie's father arrived.'

'What?' Richard said, sounding angry. 'You're kidding me. I thought that was next weekend.'

'Sophie did too.'

'Why doesn't she write things down in her diary properly? This is the last thing I need. I was looking forward to a nice bottle of wine, a spliff and an early night.'

'Sorry to be the bearer of bad news,' I said.

'Very impressive,' Richard said. 'Did you learn that from the crossword?'

'It was a clue yesterday.'

'OK. Well, I'll see you in a bit. I need to start mentally preparing myself. How long are they staying again?'

'Two weeks, I think.'

'Jesus, Sophie, what are you trying to do to me?'

'I'm sure it will be OK.'

'Oh, you just wait. Right, we're moving, I've got to go.'

He hung up the telephone. Sophie came into the kitchen with her skin pink and shining from the shower, wearing a yellow dress with red flowers printed on it.

'You look pretty,' I said.

'I thought it might distract them from how tired and hungover I am. Speaking of which, where's the wine, I need wine.'

She took out a bottle of white wine from the shelf in the fridge door and poured some into a glass. She drank half a glass and breathed deeply as if she was trying to make herself strong.

'I'm sorry about earlier. Ordering you around like that.'

'It's OK.'

'It's not OK. I need to stand up to him and explain that we do things differently round here now.'

'Really, I am OK.'

'You're always OK,' she said, smiling and touching my cheek gently.

We looked at each other for a moment. I knew we were both thinking of the night before. I felt a sudden wave of heat through my body. Then I went to take the glasses from the dishwasher and Sophie sat at the table and rolled a cigarette, looking down at the crossword.

'I'm stuck on the last one. *Illegal gatherings.* Something T, something L, something N. New word, something R, something I. I must be able to get this.' She lit her cigarette and breathed the smoke upwards. 'Ahh, *stolen fruit.*'

'What is stolen fruit?' I asked. 'Why was the fruit stolen?'

Sophie got up and picked up the ashtray drying next to the sink. She came close to me, playing with the sleeve of my T-shirt and whispered, 'They say stolen fruit tastes the sweetest.'

'Why?'

Sophie put her hand around my waist and whispered, kissing my neck, 'You enjoy something more when it is forbidden.'

I stepped away from Sophie and her hand fell off me. I did not understand my reaction, but I was angry and I said, 'What are you trying to say?'

'What? Why are you angry with me?'

'Do you understand what you are saying?'

Sophie was looking at me with a confused and hurt expression.

'I am not enjoying this more because it is stolen,' I explained to her. 'For me this is not a naughty game. I feel guilty all the time. But I can't stop because—'

'Because?'

Only then did I understand the feeling I had earlier. 'Because I love you,' I said. I had not planned to say this, the words just came into my head.

Sophie made a face that was between guilt and pain. I was glad because I wanted her to know. I threw down the drying cloth on to the surface and walked past her towards the door. I needed to be alone to think about what had happened.

As I was passing the corner of the table, William walked through the door, touching the pockets on his navy blue jacket and cream trousers with both hands.

'I've lost the car keys. Where did I put the bloody things?' He saw something by the telephone and his expression changed to relief. 'Oh, there they are. Don't go anywhere, Mirka,' he said as I walked past him. 'I've got a job for you.'

I wanted to walk out of the door, but I was not brave enough. I stopped and turned around. William came towards me and held the keys in front of my face.

'In the boot of my car there are two boxes of wine. Can you bring the one that says, *Château Moncel Lalande de Pomerol*,' he said slowly, as if he was talking to a child.

'What did your last servant die of?' Sophie said.

William turned around. 'Don't you dare talk to me like that. I have a bad back.' He turned back to me. 'Château Moncel Lalande de Pomerol. Can you remember that?'

I took the keys. 'Château Moncel Lalande de Pomerol,' I said, and walked out of the kitchen.

There was a pale circle of the moon in the blue sky. In the field I could see rabbits sitting in the last sunshine on the grass. I wanted to go and sit with them.

It was the first time I had told anyone I loved them and it felt quite serious. It made me feel powerful and weak at the same time. I did not know what it would mean for Sophie and me.

Maybe I had ruined everything. I had made it too heavy and she would be afraid that I could destroy their marriage. Or maybe she would realise that she felt the same way. She would tell Richard she wanted him to leave and we would live together. She could be my wife. I saw images in my mind of Sophie and me eating together in the kitchen, taking a bath, going for a walk, sleeping in the same bed.

I was thinking this as I was taking out the wine from the car and I suddenly stopped and almost laughed. I told myself, *Mirka, don't be stupid. Sophie is not going to leave Richard for you.*

I carried the box of wine and put it on to the kitchen table. Caroline was standing next to Sophie, watching her as she peeled potatoes.

'Do give me a job, Sophie,' she said. 'I hate having nothing to do.'

'You can top and tail the green beans, if you like. They're in the fridge.'

'You know, you only really need to top them, the tail is all right to eat.'

'Whatever you think best, Caroline.' Sophie looked quickly at me and I gave her a look to say, *Be nice.*

William came and cut the tape on the box with a knife and took out a bottle, holding it with two hands.

'Now this is a serious bottle of wine,' he said.

He put the bottle between his knees, pulled out the cork and sniffed it with his eyes closed. Then he went to the cupboard next to the fridge and took three glasses and filled them with red wine.

'Tell me that isn't delicious,' he said, giving a glass each to Caroline and Sophie and going back to the table to pick up his wine.

He held his glass towards them. 'Cheers.'

Instead of touching his glass with her glass, Sophie turned to me and said, 'Mirka, would you like a glass of wine?'

William turned his head towards her, his eyes narrow and his lips thin. Next to his eye I could see a little red worm pumping under the skin.

'That's very kind,' I said, smiling politely. 'But I am OK.'

William was still staring at Sophie. Then he jerked his head away, sat down and picked up the newspaper.

In the silence, Caroline said in a smooth voice, 'Sophie, tell us all about the plans for Richard's fortieth. Are you going to have a party?'

'We haven't talked about it yet,' Sophie said, and something in her voice made me think she was lying. 'But if Richard has anything to do with it then, yes, I imagine that we will have a party.'

'What kind of thing do you think you will do?'

'I don't know. Mirka, can you go and lay the table in the dining room?'

'OK,' I said. I put down the cloth from drying the dishes and went to take knives and forks from the drawer and mats from the cupboard.

'Just lay it for four people,' Sophie said with a bitter smile. 'Apparently we don't eat with the help.'

From the side of my eye I saw William lift his head above the top of the newspaper and stare at Sophie again, his eyes boiling with anger. Sophie kept smiling at me like a robot. The atmosphere was impossible and I went out of the kitchen as quickly as I could.

When I came back down along the corridor after finishing the table, Richard was in the entrance hall, taking off his boots on the mat. The dogs were jumping on his legs, their tails waving.

'Hello, yes, I missed you too,' he said, stroking them. He lifted his head and saw me. 'How's it going?'

'Not good,' I said. 'It is like Sophie is trying to make her father angry.'

'Great,' he sighed. 'That's just great. I keep telling her she needs to bite her tongue for a few days. That's all she has to do. Everyone else seems to manage it.'

I followed him into the kitchen. He walked in with his arms wide and put them around Caroline.

'Caroline, so good to see you,' he said.

As Richard turned to William, Caroline looked down shyly and brushed her apron with her hands.

Richard shook William's hand. 'William, a pleasure as always.'

'Good stalking?'

'Shot a decent stag yesterday.' Richard picked up the bottle of wine, looked at the label and poured it into a glass until it was almost full. Then he took a big sip. 'Beautiful scenery up there.'

'Richard we were just hearing about plans for your birthday party,' Caroline said. 'I do hope we will be invited.'

'Well, that's Sophie's department,' Richard said, looking

down into his wine. Then he looked up and smiled a big charming smile at Caroline. 'Obviously, if it was up to me, your name would be at the top of the list. A party simply wouldn't be a party without you, Caroline.'

Caroline's body twisted like a little girl's. I looked at Richard and he winked at me. He was a pro, I thought.

'This is excellent wine,' Richard said to William. 'Is it local to you?'

'Down the road,' William said, folding the newspaper and putting it on the table. 'We get it straight from the vineyard and they give us a discount.'

'Perfect,' Richard said. 'That's the wonderful thing about France, isn't it? I bet you have some great local cheeses as well.'

'Caroline has banned me from eating cheese. Haven't you, Cee-Cee?'

'I only let him have cheese on Sunday,' she said. 'The doctor has put him on pills for his gout and he still makes a big fuss about changing any of his eating habits.'

'Oh but you should see the cheese stall down at our local farmers' market.' William touched his chest with emotion. 'It's something else.'

'I bet it is. Not like the market here in the town square where you get a few people selling sponges and, if you're lucky, some home-made chutney.'

'I mean, where we are in France, people wouldn't dream of going to the supermarket to buy their food. People are invested in the countryside there. None of these, what I call, pretenders.'

'Quite. And—' Richard began.

But William continued talking. 'What I love most about France is that it's so empty. You can drive for miles and miles, through field upon field. It's so unspoilt. Unlike here, where we feel an uncontrollable desire to stick a housing estate on every available green space.'

'Speaking of which, you know Geoffrey?' Sophie said.

'Geoffrey, yes,' William said, frowning dreamily. 'Funny old cove. Why, what's he done?'

'Sold the Priory,' Sophie said.

'Don't tell me,' William said, holding up his hand. 'To a Russian.'

'An Australian,' Richard said. 'Works in mining. Got seven million for it.'

'Seven million! For that dingy old pile!' William said, shaking his head like he could not believe it. 'The world's gone completely barmy. What's the new guy going to do with the land?'

'We don't know yet. He hasn't said he'll definitely keep David on, or what he will do about shooting.'

'That's the problem with these foreign types, they want to buy into the whole country gentleman thing, but they won't put their money where their mouth is. No interest whatsoever in the work involved. Put on a Barbour and wellies and think they're the real deal.'

'Well, let's see what happens.'

'Right, dinner will be ready in five,' Sophie said. 'Shall I serve in here and we can carry our plates through?'

William looked up at Sophie from twisting the corkscrew into another bottle. 'I'm sure Mirka is perfectly capable of dishing up on her own. Let's go and sit down at the table and she can bring the plates in to us.'

The next day I was ironing tablecloths and sheets in the little room next to the kitchen, watching the maze of wrinkles become smooth under the iron and then folding them in neat piles of squares and rectangles. Sophie came in to take an apron off the back of the door.

'Oh, hi,' she said. 'I was wondering where you were. I thought you might be avoiding me.'

'I am avoiding you.'

Sophie looked down at the bow she was making at the front with the apron's long white strings.

'I'm sorry about yesterday and ...' She was silent, as if she was trying to find the words. 'I do like you, Mirka, but it's so difficult. I'm married.'

'It's OK, I know,' I said quickly, because I did not want to hear any more.

She came towards me and stood on her toes to kiss me.

'Sophie,' Caroline called from the kitchen. 'Do you want me to make a quiche or something for lunch?'

'Great idea,' Sophie said. She kept kissing me and I pushed up her skirt and lifted her up so she was sitting on the edge of the sink. As I put my hand up inside her T-shirt to touch her breasts I thought that maybe she was right about stolen fruit.

'Must go,' Sophie whispered between kisses.

She wiped her mouth and picked up two onions from the basket on the floor.

'Did you sleep well?' I heard her say to Caroline.

'Very well. And you?'

'Like a log. Would you like some tea?'

'Oh, I never have tea in the mornings. Can't stand the smell. I'll take a little coffee if there is some going.'

'Of course.'

They were silent for a while except for the noise of the kettle whistling, cups being taken from the cupboard and put on the table, liquid being poured into them. A knife made a crisp silvery noise as it cut each slice of an onion.

'Let me show you something,' Caroline said. The chopping stopped, there was the noise of feet on the floor, then it started again. 'Now, if you cut them like that, they don't fall apart and you won't cut the top of your finger off.'

'Thank you, Caroline.'

The knife continued chopping for a while, then there was the sound of onions falling into a pan of hot oil.

'You know it's always a good idea to brown the meat first,' Caroline said. 'That way, the onions absorb the flavour.'

'Oh, right. I didn't know. You learn something every day!' Sophie did a little laugh.

'These are the sorts of things you pass down mother to daughter.'

Sophie came into the little room again and took two leeks from the basket.

'I might actually kill her,' she whispered.

'Be nice. It's not for ever.'

She kissed me again and went back into the kitchen.

After about a minute, Caroline said, 'Speaking of children, are you and Richard thinking about trying any time soon?'

'Caroline, I really don't think that is any of your business. That is between me and Richard.'

'It hurts me that you would say that, Sophie. I am married to your father and I'm the closest thing you have to a mother.'

'You aren't my mother.'

'I know nobody can replace her, but your father is worried about you and he asked me to have a little word. See if anything is the matter, whether you needed help. You're thirty-five. This is the age where your fertility falls off a cliff.'

'If he is so worried about me, why couldn't he have the conversation himself? Why did he have to send you as his little emissary?'

'Oh you know what he's like. He's not good at these kinds of things. He thought it would be better to let us women discuss it between ourselves.'

'Oh my God,' Sophie said. 'Do you have any idea what you sound like?'

Then I could hear the sound of choking and I realised Caroline was crying.

'I'm only trying to help,' she said between breaths.

'I know. I'm sorry,' Sophie sighed. 'Oh, hi, Dad.'

'Not interrupting anything, am I?' William's voice was nervous.

'Yup we were just discussing' – Sophie made her voice a sarcastic whisper – 'The Baby Issue.'

'Well, I'll leave you two to it.'

'Why do you find it so difficult to have a conversation with me about it? If you are so burning with concern, why didn't you ask me yourself?'

'It's not really my domain. I merely mentioned in passing to Caroline that I thought there might be a problem in that department, and if so, then money was no object. I wanted to check you were seeing the best people, and if you needed financial help then I was willing to give it. Is that so wrong of me?'

'No, it isn't wrong of you, Dad. Thank you, yes, I am going to see someone about it on Friday as it happens.'

'Good. This is too important to be messing round with. You're not getting any younger.'

'Thanks, Dad.'

'I'm serious. All you women are going about it the wrong way. You should be having children in your early twenties and then getting on with . . .' He paused for a second. 'Whatever it is you want to do afterwards.'

'I don't think many women have the means to have children in their late twenties, let alone early twenties.'

'Well you did. You've been married ten years, for God's sake.'

'OK, enough,' Sophie said. 'This conversation is over. Thank you both for your concern, the issue is being dealt with.'

There was silence, except for the scratching of the newspaper, the sound of knives on the wooden boards and eggs breaking into a bowl. Someone switched on the radio and turned through the channels until it was playing classical music.

I finished the ironing and put away the board. When I came out of the little room holding the pile of folded clothes they were all still there. Sophie was doing the crossword, William was behind the newspaper and Caroline was at the sink with yellow gloves on, washing a saucepan.

'Morning, Mirka,' Caroline said. 'I had no idea you were in there. Quiet as a little mouse. Would you like a tea or coffee?'

I looked at Sophie to see if it was OK. She nodded so I said, 'I'll have a black coffee, please.'

'Sophie,' Caroline said. 'Did you have any plans today?'

'Not really. I've got some paperwork to do.'

'Shall we go into town this afternoon? I need a new pair of shoes and William wants to get some cigars and some handkerchiefs from Brown's. Don't you, William?'

The newspaper corner went down and William stared at Caroline. 'What?'

'I said you want to go to Brown's.'

'Oh yes. You can't seem to get handkerchiefs like theirs in France.'

Caroline turned to me. 'Mirka, you can come too, if you like.'

William frowned. 'Don't be ridiculous, Cee-Cee, we won't all fit in the car. It's full of boxes of wine.'

'Well, we can take them out.'

'All right, if you want to take them out, then fine, but you know I can't touch them.'

'That's OK,' I said quickly. 'Thank you for inviting me but I have a lot of things to do here.'

'Yes, you certainly do,' William said. 'Place is a pigsty. You can start with our bathtub.'

'Dad,' Sophie said. 'Mirka isn't our cleaner.'

'Well who is your cleaner? Because whoever she is, she needs to be sacked.'

Sophie opened her mouth but before she spoke there was a knock at the door.

'Come in,' Sophie said but the door did not open. She got up and opened it. 'Oh, David, it's you.'

William's newspaper dropped on to the table and he stood up smiling. 'David, dear boy.'

David was standing in the door looking embarrassed. 'Better not come in.' He looked down at his boots.

William went over and shook David's hand and hit him a few times on the back with the other hand. 'How are you?'

'Not too bad. Keeping busy.'

'I bet you are. The garden is looking wonderful, I must say. No doubt that's all down to you.'

I looked at Sophie. She raised an eyebrow at me.

'Sophie does a bit too,' David said.

'Does she? I'm surprised she has time between doing the crossword and getting through a bottle of white wine every day.'

William laughed loudly. David smiled nervously. Sophie was staring at William like she hated him, but she said nothing.

'Well, I best be off,' David said. 'Just came to say hello.'

'It's good to see you. We must go and have a pint down the Dog and Duck some time.'

'Yes,' David said.

'Bye, David,' Caroline said.

Sophie watched William waving at David as he walked away. Then she threw the pen on the table and went out of the room.

On the day that Sophie went to London to see the fertility doctor I was coming down the stairs when I heard something smashing in the kitchen. I stopped, listening carefully over the railings. Then I ran down the stairs, afraid of what I would see.

When I came through the door I saw Richard on his knees picking up pieces of a blue-and-white plate.

'What happened?'

'A fox got into one of the pens and killed a load of pheasants. I'm talking a total bloodbath.'

It did not explain the plate. I looked up and saw a yellow stain on the wall from egg yolk.

At that moment, outside the window, two men in dark blue worker suits walked past carrying a metal tube. The telephone rang.

'Leave the plate,' I said. 'I'll clean it.'

Richard picked up the phone.

'David? Can you come in?' There was a pause. 'Afterwards then.'

Richard put the phone down again. 'Typical. The one day I really need him.'

'Do you need some help?' I said.

'No. You shouldn't see it.'

'I'm used to handling dead animals now.'

'This is different.'

'Can you do it alone?'

Richard paused. 'Actually I could use a hand. Can you dig?'

'I can dig.'

Richard suddenly looked panicked. 'Where are William and Caroline?'

'They went into town to go shopping.'

'Thank Christ. Hopefully by the time they come back I'll have it all sorted and nobody will ever know.'

We drove across the field towards the green cliff of the

woods. The car bounced up and down and I held the spade with two hands. Richard was leaning forward and his teeth were moving together. I was nervous about what I would see, but also proud to be helping him when he needed someone. I was thinking that maybe I could save some of the pheasants and make taxidermy with them. They were quite big, but I was used to doing taxidermy with bigger animals now.

'Those little bastards are pure fucking evil,' Richard said as we drove into the shadows of the trees. 'They don't say to themselves, "I'll just kill a few birds and then I'll stop when I've had enough and go home to my wife." No. They don't stop until they've killed every last bird.'

'Did you lose a lot of money?'

'I don't care about the money,' he said, hitting the wheel. Then he sat back and sighed. 'Of course I care about the money. Yes, I lost a lot of money. But I also feel guilty. I'm not daft, I know the birds were going to die anyway, but at least they would have had a bit of a life. I can't even begin to imagine what it must be like being trapped in an enclosed space with a monster raging around ripping the heads off all your friends. Nobody likes to have that kind of blood on their hands, even if it is only pheasants.'

'I'm sure you did everything to protect them.'

He looked at me, nodding his head. 'I'm going to get that fox.'

'How will you know she is the right fox?'

'I'll know.'

After a minute he said, 'Why did you call the fox "she"?'

'In Slovak foxes are female.'

'Even the male ones?'

'The word is female. Pheasants are male. I don't know why.'

'There's no reason why it couldn't have been a female fox. It just sounded funny when you said it. I suppose because we would naturally use "he". And a fox seems like a more masculine animal.'

'It does not mean the animal is more masculine or feminine. It is only the word.' I stopped, thinking. 'But yes, when I think of a fox she is a woman.'

'Interesting.'

We drove through the woods until Richard stopped the car next to a fence of wire diamonds and turned off the engine.

'The shooting season is already completely fucked and I haven't even had a proper chance to cock it up yet,' he said in a tired voice.

We got out of the car and Richard went to the back and took out some black plastic sacks and put on thick gloves. I saw something above me. It was a CD hanging from a tree. I looked around and there were lots of them, twisting and shining.

Richard opened the gate in the fence. I looked through the wire. A metre away there was a pheasant with no head, only a bright red circle at the neck. I looked further into the cage towards the blue plastic barrels. Everywhere, there were bodies of pheasants. But not whole animals. They were twisted piles of feathers and red meat, more like impressions of animals than real animals. I knew I could never make taxidermy from them. They died too violently to come back. All I could make would be pheasant monsters, bodies with different heads, holes in the skin, with missing legs and wings.

'Don't look,' Richard said.

I looked away. Behind Richard I saw a big branch of a tree had pushed down a metal post and bent the fence. The end of the branch was sharp where it had ripped from the tree, leaving a pale scar.

Richard turned his head to see where I was looking. 'Shorted the electrics,' he said, shaking his head. 'Honestly, this stuff could only happen to me.'

I imagined the fox walking over the branch and walking out again later, after the murders, licking the blood from her lips. She would be sleeping heavily now in her hole.

Richard pointed away from the cage to a space between the trees. 'Go over there and start digging a pit.'

The earth was soft under the spade, first dark brown, then orange, then white. I put the mixed earth in a pile next to the hole. There was no sun under the leaves but the air was warm and soon I was sweating under my arms. Richard was walking around the cage bending and standing, putting the bodies in black sacks.

I was digging for an hour. My arms felt tired and sweat ran down my back and between my breasts, but I liked the work. I would sleep well like the fox. Every time I looked towards Richard, there were more swollen black sacks in a pile next to the car. Richard pulled two across the earth towards the grave.

'Go and stand over there,' he said.

I walked away from the car and looked into the trees. The leaves were bright and fresh green. I heard the dull noises of bodies falling into the grave from the plastic bag, then another bag and more bodies. Richard went back to the car and pulled two more bags over. I stood still until he had finished putting all the dead pheasants into the grave. I heard the noise of the spade and the shower of earth and I waited a few more minutes until I thought the pheasants must be covered. Then I walked back towards Richard.

Through the trees I saw a car. It was David's. Richard turned his head. As the car came closer I saw that there were two people inside.

'Oh Christ, no,' Richard said. 'Please don't be William.'

The car stopped and William and David got out. Richard and I did not move. William was wearing cream trousers inside his wellies.

'Morning,' Richard said. 'William, it was awfully kind of you to come down but we've managed to sort it all out. All taken care of. Luckily Mirka was around to help.'

I was too afraid to look at David when Richard said this, but I felt his eyes on me.

'I bumped into David on his way down. What happened exactly?' William said.

'A branch came down on the fence. Just bad luck. But it could have been a lot worse.'

'And how's that?' William said. 'From where I'm standing, it looks like a disaster.'

'I told you we shouldn't have moved the fence,' David said quietly.

'In fairness, David, we discussed it and decided the tree was low risk and we didn't have much of a choice with regards to positioning.'

'I said that branch needed to come down,' David said.

'Did you, David?' Richard said, taking a step towards him. 'Did you?'

'I did.'

'Funny, because I don't remember you saying anything of the sort.'

'Well, what's done is done,' William said. He wiped the sweat from his forehead with a handkerchief. 'I must say, building the pen anywhere in the vicinity of overhanging branches seems like an unpardonable stupidity to me, but there we are.'

'Thank you, William,' Richard said. 'But you weren't here and, as I said, we carefully weighed up the risks and it turns out we were unlucky.'

'By the sounds of things, you seem to have a lot of bad luck.'

'What's that supposed to mean?'

The three men were getting closer and I took a step back, away from them. I noticed that David, who usually stood with his head down, was standing up straight and looking very satisfied.

'I mean that I hear things, and your shoot doesn't have a good reputation.'

'Oh, leave it out, William. We're not Sandringham. People get what they pay for. We are a small shoot.'

'I'm only saying what I've heard. That there are some management issues.'

'Management issues?' Richard looked at William with narrow eyes. 'Who said that? We had a good season last year. I had hardly any complaints. Oh, wait a minute ...' Richard crossed his arms and nodded slowly. 'I know who said that.'

I was waiting for Richard to say who it was, but then I saw that he was looking directly at David. David stared back, but at the same time his body seemed to shrink like a balloon.

'I'm not going to say anything more,' William said. 'But instead of getting defensive you would do well to take some criticism on board and up your game. Come on, David, let's go. I rather fancy a ploughman's at the pub. Shall we do that?'

'All right,' David said.

Richard was silent until the car had driven away. His body was hard and both his hands were fists.

'Fuck, fuck, fuck,' he said. 'That fucking fat pompous cunt. And that oaf standing there like his bloody guard dog or something. They can go to hell.' He shut his eyes and breathed deeply and opened them again. 'Sorry, Mirka. And thank you for helping me. I really appreciate it.'

'It's OK,' I said.

'Do you know what? It *is* OK. This is not the end of the world. It's only some dead pheasants.'

'Exactly.'

Richard put his arm around me. 'Sometimes I don't know what I would do without you.'

I tried to smile. Another time what Richard said would make me feel happy, but now I just felt sick with guilt.

Every day I went to the barn and worked on my new scene, *Guinea Pigs Watching Television with a Takeaway Curry on a Friday Night*. It was a small scene, with only two guinea pigs, a boyfriend and girlfriend, sitting on a sofa. I decorated the living room in a modern style with white square bookshelves and a glass coffee table. I took photographs of the guinea pig couple together and made them small on the computer to put in frames on the shelves and on the wall. In one photograph the guinea pigs were dressed in Halloween costumes carrying a pumpkin they had cut a face into, in another they were standing in front of the Taj Mahal and in another picture they were skiing. For the television screen I printed a picture of Jonathan Ross's face. I was pleased with all the details and I could spend hours and hours making the tiny things for their world, completely absorbed, as if I were inside the scene too.

Every day Sophie brought a sandwich to the barn. We had not had sex since William arrived but she always touched me secretly, behind my ear or on my back, or the side of my hand, so that I knew she still wanted me. She seemed happier after going to London to see the doctor, but she did not talk about it and I was curious.

'What did the doctor say?' I asked her one afternoon.

'It's nothing major, apparently. They've given me something to stimulate my ovaries.' She came and stood behind me and looked over my shoulder. I could feel her breasts against my back and her breath on my neck. 'What are you doing?'

'I'm making a little silver rectangle dish for the curry.'

'Of course you are.' She put her hand inside my T-shirt and touched the side of my stomach.

I shivered from the pleasure, but I tried to ignore it.

'So you can have a baby?' I said. 'That is good news.'

'Who knows,' she said, still stroking my skin gently above my jeans.

I did not say anything else because it seemed that she did not want to talk about the baby. I thought maybe she thought that if she did, she would put a curse on it.

The next day I was in the barn drawing plans for my next

scene. I had an idea to do something at a market in London with sponges and fruit in plastic bowls and DVDs of Nigerian films.

Richard came through the door.

'Still hiding?'

'Yes.'

'Me too. I've run out of things to do. There's only so many times I can go and check on the pheasants. Still,' he smiled bravely. 'Only a couple of days to go.'

He leant over the table and turned the finished scene with the guinea pigs around. His eyes moved around the glass box, looking at all the details.

'This is brilliant. I like the way they've both got their laptops open next to them. How do you think about all these things? It's astounding.'

'Thank you.'

I got up and went to the drawers to find some modelling clay and paint.

'What have we got in the freezer at the moment?'

I went to the freezer and opened it. 'We have one cormorant and the head of the stag you shot.'

'Hmm,' Richard said. 'Maybe I should take one out now so I can do it tomorrow. No, fuck it, it's too nice at the moment for taxidermy. I think I'm going to head back to the house. Is it time for a drink yet?' He looked at his watch. 'Five o'clock. I might treat myself to a beer.'

'OK, see you later.'

'Don't work too hard.'

After two hours I walked back to the house. The grass was

striped dark and light green from being cut that morning. Richard, Sophie and Caroline were sitting on a rug in the middle. Sophie had her head resting on Richard's thigh. Above them, William was sitting on the bench wearing a white straw hat and smoking a cigar. Blue smoke floated away into the shadows of the trees.

'Mirka,' William called when he saw me. 'Mirka, could I borrow you a minute?'

I walked towards them. From the grass next to the bench, William picked up a jug with mint leaves, cucumber and strawberries at the bottom and held it out to me.

'Could you make us some more Pimm's?'

'Yes, of course.'

'I'll do it, Dad,' Sophie said.

'I think Mirka and I have this under control,' William said to her, then turned back to me and put his finger and thumb against the jug. 'You want about that much Pimm's and the rest lemonade. And ice.'

I took the jug and went inside. The bottle of Pimm's was on the table, half-drunk, and the lemonade in the door of the fridge. I put some more ice in the jug first. When I stood up from the freezer, I watched the others through the window for a moment, golden in the evening sunshine. Sophie was talking about something, smiling and her hands were moving. She lifted her chin and laughed. I could make a taxidermy scene of them, I thought. *Rabbits Drinking Pimm's on a Lawn.*

When I came back, William held out his glass and I poured the Pimm's into it. Then I walked around edge of the rug filling everyone else's glass.

'Of course, I forgot you had done that,' Sophie was saying. 'So how was the grand tour?'

I put the jug down next to the bench and started walking back towards the kitchen.

'Wait,' Richard said. 'Come and join us.'

'Yes, come and sit down for a bit,' Sophie said. 'I feel like we haven't seen you for days.'

Caroline got up from the rug. 'You sit here, Mirka.' She went and sat next to William on the bench.

I sat down on the rug opposite Richard and Sophie and put my hands in the grass behind me.

'Well, we liked Rome very much,' William said. 'I hadn't been there since I was twenty and it still had its charm. Equally, Florence is as beautiful as ever. The whole place is absolutely crawling with Septics though. You couldn't move five metres without coming across one of them wearing a pair of trainers and beige shorts shouting at the top of their voice across the street' – William suddenly changed to an American accent – '"Brad, Brad, where's the Starbucks, I need an iced skinny latte."'

William's impression was so good that I could not help smiling.

'I mean, this is Italy, for God's sake!' he continued. 'The home of the best coffee in the world.'

'Thank God I wasn't with you,' Sophie said. 'I know what you're like.'

'We went to the opera at Puccini's house,' Caroline said. 'And he nearly hit one of them over the head with his programme. I had to restrain him.'

William shook his head at the memory. 'A monstrous, obese woman wearing what could only be described as a mumu, talked all the way through *Madame Butterfly*. At a volume that suggested that she thought that everyone in a ten-metre radius would benefit from her insights.'

'Well, it sounds like you had a nice time anyway,' Sophie said.

'We did, we did. And all that art. Those Giottos! And the Brancacci Chapel, which, I tell you, takes your breath away.'

There was a silence. William smoked his cigar, his mind clearly still in the Brancacci Chapel. Richard shook the ice in his glass. I looked down at the daisies in the grass.

'Mirka likes art, don't you, Mirka?' Sophie said.

'Is that right?' William said, making an effort to look interested. 'Who do you like?'

'I like Sophie Calle or Marina Abramović,' I said.

William stared at me. 'Never heard of them.'

'They have interesting ideas.'

'Well, I'm sure they do.' William raised his eyebrows and looked around as if he needed to make a joke because I had said something stupid. 'Anyway, I was thinking, shall we go to the Snooty Fox on Saturday?'

'I was going to talk to you about that,' Sophie said. 'We actually have a big wedding at the house on Saturday and I thought maybe it would be better if you went to Tom's a day early. I'll be running around and I won't be able to spend time with you anyway. Tom won't mind, will he, Caroline?' She was speaking very quickly and playing with the bottom of her T-shirt.

'No, I'm sure he won't,' Caroline said. 'How lovely, who is getting married?'

'I expect it's some awful Stacey and Gavin,' William said. 'And everyone will be wearing grey shiny suits like they are going to the office.'

'Dad, don't,' Sophie said.

'I don't understand why people don't dress properly any more. You wear a morning suit to a wedding. It's quite simple.'

'People don't have morning suits.'

'Then they can hire one. Otherwise nobody knows how to dress and it's a dreadful mess.'

'I think we live in an age where people want to create their own traditions and put their own stamp on their wedding day.'

William was sucking on the end of his cigar and blew out a big cloud of smoke. 'We have some perfectly good traditions. But no, let's all hold hands and sing "Kumbaya". I hate all that.'

The atmosphere had changed. The vein was beating at the side of William's eye. Caroline was watching him nervously. Sophie's jaw was hard and she was staring at him. Richard looked at Sophie strongly, but she did not see. She put her hair behind her ears and took a deep breath.

'Actually, Dad, it's a couple called Christopher and Ben who are getting married on Saturday.'

William leant forward and looked at Sophie like he must have heard the wrong thing. 'Excuse me?'

'They're two really lovely men,' Sophie said. 'They come from—'

William held up his hand. 'I don't care where they come from. They are not getting married in my house.'

'It's not your house any more.'

'Legally, it's still my house.'

'Dad.' Sophie sat up and got on her knees in front of him. 'Come on—'

'Over my dead body.'

'We can't cancel a few days before the wedding.'

'Yes you can.'

'William, be reasonable,' Caroline said, pulling his sleeve.

'Oh, get off me, woman,' William shouted.

Caroline sat back, swallowing like she was going to cry.

'You know we can't do that,' Sophie said quietly. 'Aside from the ethical argument, and not to mention the money, if anyone found out we did it because they were gay, we would get sued.'

'Sophie's right,' Richard said in a serious, calm voice. 'We'd get sued under the European Human Rights treaty, or whatever it's called.'

William's head pulled back and he breathed through his nostrils. Then he said very clearly and slowly, his voice full of anger, 'I don't give a fuck about the European Union or its poxy laws. Nobody from another country is going to tell me what I can or can't do in my own home.'

William leant back on the bench, looking at Richard and Sophie, shaking his head like they were the ones who were crazy.

'Now, William,' Richard said. 'I hate Europe as much as the next man, but that's the way it is.'

'I'll tell you something,' William said, waving his finger at Richard. 'This government had no mandate to change the law. No mandate whatsoever. Nobody wants it.'

'Gay people want it,' Sophie said.

'Well a small group of people don't have the power to

redefine an institution that has been in place for millennia. We are messing with evolution and it's extremely dangerous. It's like we're all being forced to participate in a giant social experiment that nobody has any say in. And we have no idea what the results will be. Absolutely no idea.'

It took me a few seconds to realise what William had said. I could not believe it. Richard and Sophie were both staring at the grass, embarrassed. Sophie looked up at me with a nervous expression and looked down again.

'Dad, things are different now. I know you don't want to accept it, but—'

'Let me tell you, Sophie, what people do in the privacy of their own homes is their business. They can bugger one another to their heart's content as far as I'm concerned. What I object to is them trying to normalise something that patently isn't.'

He sat back and everyone was silent. I knew people thought those things, but I did not think I would ever hear them on a lawn in England. I wanted to say something. Richard and Sophie were obviously not going to say anything.

I stood up. Everybody looked at me. I opened my mouth, but I could not do it. I was not brave enough.

'I am going to finish my work,' I said.

'It's just not natural,' William continued, as if he didn't hear me. 'And nobody is going to convince me otherwise.'

As I was walking away over the grass, I heard Sophie saying quietly, 'OK, Dad, I think we've got the message.'

On the morning of the wedding, I went to the kitchen to make a coffee to take to the barn. Everyone was already awake.

Richard, Sophie and William were sitting around the table reading different parts of the newspaper. Caroline was frying eggs. Nobody was talking. I put the kettle on the cooker and got the milk out of the fridge. Caroline put bits of bacon on to four plates.

'Who's having scrambled?'

'Me,' Sophie and Richard said at the same time.

Caroline put scrambled egg on to two plates and took them to Sophie and Richard.

'Thanks, Caroline, this looks wonderful,' Richard said.

Caroline put one fried egg on to another plate. It fell on to the mushrooms and the yolk burst and flowed on to the beans. Then she picked up the other egg with a spoon and it ripped, dripping on to the sausage.

'Sorry, William,' she said, taking the plate to the table. 'I broke your yolks.'

William pushed the paper sideways and looked down at his plate, frowning.

The Full English was a mess, with the thick yellow yolk all over the beans and tomatoes.

Caroline lifted the plate again. 'All right, I'll make new ones.'

'No, don't. We have to set off in a minute anyway.' He sighed. 'I'll have to eat them.'

Sophie looked at me and smiled like she was saying, *Nearly*. She turned to William.

'You'll have a lovely time at Tom's, I'm sure. What has he got planned?'

'I've no idea,' William said. 'Ask Cee-Cee. It seems I don't know anything any more.'

Sophie rolled her eyes. 'Don't be a drama queen.'

'It's true. And you're right, it's your house. You do what you want with it. You can turn it into a nightclub or a pet rescue centre, for all I care.'

'It's a successful business, that's the main thing. OK?'

William made a noise in his throat and said quietly, 'I suppose.'

I poured coffee into a cup and went out of the kitchen to the barn without saying goodbye. Nobody seemed to notice I was in the room anyway.

Later, in the afternoon, I jumped over the wall and stood next to the tree to watch the wedding. It was a sunny day, with a few big white clouds in the sky. I was so happy that Caroline and William had gone and things would be normal again. I could not wait to be with Sophie.

The photographer was standing away from the wedding guests, in the middle of the grass, looking up at the big cloud that was covering the sun. I looked up and saw the pale circle of the sun moving through the mist at the edge of the cloud until it burst out into the blue sky. The scene suddenly became bright like someone turned on the lights on a stage.

The photographer waved at the crowd and two men in grey suits walked out from the people and stood in front of the fields with their arms around each other. The suits were very elegant and they did not look like they were going to the office. One of the men was bald with a big dark beard and the other was small and handsome with brown skin and black curly hair. They could not stop looking at each other and smiling, completely in love. When they kissed on the lips the guests cheered and clapped. I saw Sophie at the edge of the crowd. She looked beautiful in her red dress. I watched her clapping. Her face was full of emotion and happiness for the men. I felt so much love for her it was like a pain in my chest. I had never felt like this before in my life about anyone and it made me afraid.

Suddenly, as if she knew I was watching her, she turned her head and looked at me. I smiled and waved, and she smiled back. It was a sad smile. She knew exactly what I was thinking. I was thinking about my wedding day with Sophie. We would be having our picture taken with our friends and family. Except that there would be no friends and family. Not my family, not her family, not Richard.

I was lost staring at Sophie until a woman in a big yellow hat asked her something. I realised I was far away in a fantasy world marrying Sophie. My reality was at the house with a woman I loved who was married to a man I also loved but in another way. A man who I was betraying every day. There was no happy end for everyone.

CHAPTER NINE

The pheasants were walking slowly along the bottom of the wall. First a male with his green-and-red head, then two brown females behind. They were all looking around suspiciously. Then they must have seen something dangerous, because they started running, their little legs moving quickly, until they disappeared into the bushes.

As I washed up the dishes from breakfast, more pheasants walked past the window, behaving like they were on a secret mission to escape from prison. There were pheasants everywhere now, in the garden, along the hedges, in the woods. It was like they were growing out of the earth. The weather had changed too, the September air was dry and fresh. The sunlight on the grass seemed thinner, shinier. The apple trees at the end of the garden were heavy with red and green apples.

Sophie brought the kettle to the sink and I switched off the hot tap and switched on the cold tap so she could fill it. She stood on her toes and gave me a kiss on the mouth and smiled dreamily at me like someone very in love. She did not know it, but I could smell Richard all over her skin. It was painful for me, but I could do nothing about it. I had to share Sophie with Richard. It was the only way to be together with her.

'You look tired,' she said, stroking my face.

'What are you doing today?' I said.

'Boring things. Admin,' she said, like she was far away. She sighed. 'Trying to sort out all the accounts from the summer. What are you doing?'

'Taxidermy, I guess.'

Richard walked into the kitchen shaking his keys and Sophie and I both took a small step away from each other. Richard, as usual, did not notice anything.

'No you're not, you're coming with me.'

'Now?'

'Now,' he said, full of excitement. He smoothed his hair back and put on his flat green hat. The dogs stood up and went towards him, waving their tails. Richard stroked their heads. 'I'm afraid you're not coming with me. You're staying here and looking after Mummy. Bye, beautiful,' he said to Sophie, kissing her on the mouth.

'Bye, my love,' she said, stroking his face like she had stroked mine.

I looked quickly away. They were always touching now, and arguing less. It was as if the more Sophie and I were in love, the more Richard and Sophie were in love too. There was a kind of balance between the three of us. But I still could not understand how she could behave the same way to two people, to be in love with both. For me it was impossible. So I tried to ignore them, to pretend not to see, because I wanted to be with Sophie more than I minded the pain.

I put on my wellies and Barbour and followed Richard along the path. On the grass, near the bench, there was a dead pheasant. Richard walked across the grass towards it and picked him up by the feet. A green tube of intestine fell out of the stomach and brushed the grass as he walked to the wall and threw the bird sideways into the long grass on the other side.

'The kites will take care of that,' he said, nodding with satisfaction and wiping his hands on his trousers. 'Look up there.' He pointed to the sky where three big birds were making slow circles. 'Aren't they beautiful?'

'They are beautiful.'

Richard opened the big doors to the other barn. Inside, there was a machine, like a motorbike, but with four wheels. I waited by the door where there was a table covered in onions, their dry skins like brown paper, perfectly curved to wrap them. Richard cut open a big white bag with a knife and poured something that sounded like rice into a plastic box at the back of the machine.

I watched Richard curiously as lifted his leg over the motorbike and bent to press a switch. The engine started and Richard pressed his thumbs on the handlebars, making a loud roaring noise. Then he looked at me and put his hand behind him and stroked the black leather seat, making a face like he thought he was very cool and handsome.

'Need a ride, sugar?' he said in an American accent.

I loved Richard's acting games so I put my hand to my chest and pointed my chin down like I was a shy American teenager in the sixties. 'Who, me?'

'That's right, baby.' He made more roaring noises with the engine. 'I'm going to take you on the ride of your life.'

'My daddy says I shouldn't go on rides with strange men.'

'Do you always do what you're supposed to?'

Richard tapped the seat behind him with his palm and I went and put my leg over the motorbike and my arms around him.

He twisted his head. 'Ready?' he said, in his normal voice now.

'Ready.'

The bike jerked forward and I nearly fell back. Then I got used to the movement and it was easy to sit straight. We went along the track at the back of the house, bumping over the stones and holes. In the field next to us a giant yellow machine was combing the earth. We kept going until the track ended and then we were driving across a grassy field. Richard made the bike go faster. The wind was blowing in my face and I was laughing with excitement.

Richard turned his head. 'Having fun?'

'Yes,' I shouted.

We came to the woods and went along a shady path. The leaves of the trees were not fresh like in the summer, but dull, dark green. Some were turning yellow. The ground was covered in acorns and nuts with furry cases. Crowded bunches of mushrooms grew next to the path and on the ruins of dead trees. Richard stopped the motorbike, walked behind it and pulled something on the box, making the bike shake. After he climbed on again he put his hand in his pocket and passed me a silver whistle.

'Blow that,' he said.

I wiped the end of the whistle and put it in my mouth and blew. It made a high weak noise.

'Louder,' Richard said.

I blew harder as Richard started driving slowly uphill along the path. I turned my head and saw that we were leaving a wavy line of pale brown seeds on the ground. Pheasants started coming from behind the trees to eat the seeds. First slowly, looking around to see if it was dangerous, then running. They were coming from every direction through the trees, like they had heard the noise of the bike and the whistle and knew it was time for food.

'Trick is to feed them exactly where and when you want them for the shoot,' Richard said. 'That way they're more likely to turn up.'

We went slowly, dropping the seeds through the woods until we came out on to a narrow road. Richard shut the door to the plastic box and we drove along the road until we arrived at some black metal gates, where he stopped and switched off the engine.

'I need you to do something for me. The woman that runs the place up there hates me and I don't want to risk bumping into her. Can you go and tell whoever it is on the reception desk that we have a shoot next Friday.' He took a folded piece of paper from the pocket of his coat. 'Give them this – it's the dates of all the shoots up to Christmas.'

I walked through the open gates up a road between two lines

of dark green bushes, until I could see a grey stone house with two towers with pointy roofs. When I got to the big wooden door, I took the metal ring in the lion's mouth and knocked three times. A thin woman with short grey hair opened the door and looked at me in an unfriendly way.

'Can I help you?'

'Hello, I am from Fairmont Hall,' I said. 'I have to tell you that on next Friday there will be a shoot.'

'Ah, I see,' the woman said with a sigh. 'And so it begins again.'

Behind her on the wall there was a wooden rack of square holes with letters leaning diagonally in them. A man with a shaved head and naked feet came and took a letter from one of the holes. As he turned towards me to walk back, I saw he had empty eyes with dark skin under them.

I gave the woman the piece of paper. 'This is for you.'

The woman unfolded the piece of paper and took her glasses from her hair and put them on her nose.

'Right, well, thank you for letting us know, I suppose.'

She started to close the door without looking at me, and I had to step backwards so it would not hit my face.

'What is this place?' I asked Richard when I arrived back at the motorbike.

'A convalescent home for injured soldiers.'

'Why do you have to tell them when you shoot?'

'Because one of them did his nut a few years ago because he woke up and thought he was in the middle of a gun battle.'

'Oh no.' I bit my lip to stop myself from smiling. Not because it was funny, but because of the way Richard said it.

Richard saw and smiled bitterly. 'I know. Just my luck.'

'How many days shooting will you do?'

'Not enough.' He looked worried. 'I won't break even unless I can sell a couple more days. And I lost all those birds to the fox.'

'I'm sure it will be OK,' I said.

'I'm going to give it one more year and if it doesn't work out I've got to come up with some radical new ideas. They've always had shooting here as long as the house has existed, but maybe it's simply not viable any more. The truth is, I don't think my heart is in it.'

'Why?'

'I've never been into it, that's all,' he said, and there was something about how he said it, looking at the floor, that made me think it was not all of the truth, but I did not ask again.

On the journey back to the house Richard stopped the motorbike and walked over to a tree. On the earth there was a box made from metal wire and inside I could see a small animal with grey fur. Richard bent down and opened the side of the box. He took out the animal and came back holding it by the long pink tail. It was a rat.

'Want this one for one of your scenes?'

'Yes, I was waiting for one more rat.'

'There you go then.'

He dropped it into a plastic bag from his pocket and gave it to me. I was still doing my scenes and they were selling for a lot of money in London. Caleb told me there was a list of twenty people waiting to buy one. I could not believe it. Richard let me keep the money from the scenes as long as I also did enough work for him and Sophie. I had enough to travel all over the world. But not yet. I did not want to leave the house. I felt like it was more my home now than my home in Slovakia.

As we drove back home across the field, I closed my eyes and felt the sun and wind on my face, holding on to Richard. Everything was good in my life. I could not wait to get home to tell Sophie about my adventure with Richard and see what she had made for dinner. The three of us would sit and drink wine and talk about the day and laugh together. And maybe if Richard drank a lot and smoked some spliffs he would pass out and Sophie would come upstairs to my room in the night.

Two weeks later it was the first day of shooting. Rain was pouring down the windows in the kitchen.

'Do you want to go with the beaters or come with me to pick up?' Sophie said.

She closed the bottom oven door with a back kick of her foot and carried the pie between two red gloves to the table. It was lunch for the guns.

'I don't know,' I said. 'Which is better?'

'You'll get wetter beating. In fact . . .' She went through the white door and came back holding a pair of folded plastic trousers. 'Put these over your jeans. Otherwise you'll get soaked.'

A short, round woman dressed in navy plastic trousers and coat opened the door. She stood in the rain holding a brown-and-white dog, exactly like Scrabble and Ringo. Only a tiny pink circle of her face showed through the wrinkled hole of her hood.

'I'm taking Ringo, am I?' she said.

'Right. Yes.'

Sophie went and put a lead on Ringo and pulled him over to the woman.

'Mirka, why don't you go with Terri and the beaters? Then after lunch you can come with me.'

'OK,' I said, not moving. I wanted to stay with Sophie in the warm, dry kitchen and then go with her to pick up.

'You might want to put on those trousers now,' Terri said, nodding at the trousers on the table. 'It's pretty wet out here, in case you hadn't noticed.'

'It's such a shame, isn't it? On the first one too,' Sophie said.

I pulled on the trousers and put on my wellington boots. Sophie went into the little room.

'Mirka, come in here and choose a hat.'

I followed her through the door and Sophie was holding Richard's green cap in her right hand and her green hat with feathers in the left. I pointed to the green cap and she quietly stood on her toes and kissed me and stroked my lips afterwards with her thumb.

'We need to get you your own hat.'

I walked with Terri to the barns where a wooden truck, like the ones for transporting animals, was waiting for us. The two dogs climbed the metal steps and Terri followed, turning and holding out her hand to pull me up. In the darkness I saw nine or ten pale damp faces. Terri sat down on a bench near the door and moved up so I could fit. The air was thick with steam and dog breath. In the middle of the truck, on a block, brown-and-white dogs were climbing over each other, breathing heavily with excitement. I had no idea any more which one was Ringo.

'Everyone, this is Mirka,' Terri said. 'It's her first time, so be gentle with her.'

The beaters nodded their heads and said hello then started talking again in quiet voices and stroking their dogs. Then David climbed the steps and leant on the gate. Instead of his usual wool hat, he was wearing a brown suit, flat cap and yellow socks with red ribbons with two points hanging down above the top of his wellington boots like a snake's tongue. He seemed full of energy and importance.

'All right. First up is Flint Field. Got five drives in all today. Someone give the window a bash.'

A man at the end of the benches turned and hit the little window at the front of the truck. Then the truck jerked forward and drove away from the barns, along the track towards the fields.

David continued, 'Terri, John, Andy and Katy, you get out at the east woods and come down that way. Clive, Bronwyn, Sam and Stuart, we'll take you round to the top of the hill so you can flush them down that way. The rest of you can start at the hedge.'

I was surprised at David's new confident personality. I had never heard him say more than a few words, except in the pub. Now he was like the leader of an army.

'Mirka,' he looked down at me like he did not want me there. 'You stay with Terri.'

After we had driven through a few fields, the truck stopped and Terri and three others got out. Terri gave me a white flag and we walked into the woods until we were in a line with a few trees between each person. The man next to Terri said into a radio, 'In position,' and a voice from the radio said, 'Roger.'

The man waved his arm. 'Off we go.'

Everyone walked forward, waving the flags next to their legs in a violent jerking way so that the plastic made a snapping sound. They started to shout different noises. Terri called, 'Ey-up, Ey-up,' as she walked. The man with the radio shouted, 'Hoi-hoi-hoi' and the next man shouted, 'Brump, brump.' A woman at the end of the line made a high noise of 'Argh, argh.' I could not help smiling because they sounded crazy. The dogs ran in circles with their noses on the ground and pheasants jumped out of the bushes and ran away surprisingly fast. We walked, chasing the pheasants, until we came out of the woods and stood in a line along the top of a rectangle of tall corn plants in a field. Below us was a deep, narrow valley.

'Stay back,' the man shouted. He pressed the button on his radio. 'Beaters in position.' He waited for a noise and then turned to us and shouted, 'All right, everyone, move down nice and steady.'

I walked forward, careful to stay in line with the beaters who were waving their flags and shouting. I could hear the pheasants moving under the leaves away from me and suddenly one flew out of the corn making a strange choking noise in his throat. I had never seen a pheasant flying before. He seemed too heavy to fly up high. The long feathers of his tail waved behind him as he swam through the air. Then, when he was above the valley, a gun fired, then another. As I was watching, the bird's neck suddenly seemed to snap and his head went backwards. His wings folded and he fell in a big arch. Poor pheasant, I thought.

When we came towards the corner of the field, closer and closer together in a line, lots of pheasants started flying out of the corn. Now I could see that, in the valley below, there was a curved line of men standing around the bottom of the hill wearing ear protectors, their guns pointed at the sky. They were following the paths of the birds flying above them, twisting around to shoot at any birds who went behind them to the trees on the other side of the valley. It sounded like we were in the middle of a battle. Pheasants were falling from the sky and bouncing on the grass. But some of them reached the trees and were safe. As I watched the birds fly over the valley I secretly wished for them to arrive safely on the other side, even though I knew that was not what Richard wanted.

The beaters came out of the end of the corn and someone blew a horn. The guns stopped banging. We walked in the rain down the field into the valley. On the other side I saw Sophie walking along the edge of the wood with Scrabble. Then she disappeared into the trees. Below us, pale yellow dogs and one black dog were running around, picking up the dead pheasants from the grass in their mouths and taking them to their owners. A woman in a purple hat took a pheasant from the black dog and hung it by the neck on a metal hook she was holding with five or six other pheasants. When she turned around, I saw it was Celia.

There were still pheasants on the grass and the beaters were bending to pick them. In front of me there was a dead pheasant next to a wooden peg with the number 4 written on it. I tried to walk past it, hoping nobody would see me.

'Pick that one up, will you?' a man holding a gun shouted to me.

I looked behind me to see if he was talking to me. There was nobody behind me, and the man was staring at me so I could not keep walking. I bent down next to the pheasant. It was a male and his eye was inside a patch of bright, shiny red feathers. I had no gloves on but I put my hand around the neck and held it. It was warm, so different to the cold animals that came out of the freezer. As I pulled the bird up from the ground I felt the bones in the neck moving under my fingers and I felt sick. I walked quickly, not breathing, to a dark green car where a woman was taking the birds from the people picking up. I gave her the bird and she put his neck next to another pheasant and tied them together with blue string. Then she hung them inside the car, where about thirty birds were hanging from bars on the roof. They seemed suddenly very human, gently swinging by their necks. It was a horrible image, and I was sure it was going to return to me in a nightmare.

At that moment Sophie came out of the trees holding two birds in one hand, Scrabble running next to her.

'How did you find it?' she said, smiling when she saw me. 'I used to go beating when I was a little girl. It's quite fun, isn't it?'

'It was interesting,' I said, thinking that fun was not the word I would use to describe the experience. 'But can I stay with you now?'

'Yes, you can help me with lunch.'

She gave her birds to the woman by the car and bent down and picked up some grass in her hands and rubbed it in her fingers to clean them. At the end of the line of cars, we could see the purple hat coming towards us.

'Quick, let's go now to avoid Celia,' Sophie said.

'Sophie, Sophie,' Celia called.

'Too late.' Sophie stopped and turned around. 'Hello, Celia.'

'Hello, Sophie. My goodness, don't you look well! Something is obviously making you happy.'

Sophie looked shy and said, 'Well, I don't know ...'

It made me smile secretly because I thought that the person making her happy was me.

'Now I wanted to talk to you about something,' Celia said. 'On the seventeenth of November we're having an art exhibition in aid of cancer research at the town hall.'

'How good of you, of course I'll come.'

'Well actually, I wondered if you would say something. I thought you would be perfect, you know, because of what happened to your mother, so I suggested it to the committee and they all thought it was a marvellous suggestion.'

Sophie frowned. 'I'm a terrible public speaker. Honestly, I think it would be better if you got someone else. I will help you in any other way I can.'

'It's only a few words, dear. I'm sure you can manage it for something as important as this.'

Sophie sighed. 'OK.'

'Wonderful. Oh look, there's Richard!' Celia started waving and running after him, calling, 'Richard, Richard.'

Sophie pulled my arm. 'Let's get out of here before I'm roped into something else.'

We walked in the other direction, along the trees past the cars. In one car we saw Monty the angry dog. When he saw us he showed his teeth and started barking behind the glass.

*

On the last drive of the afternoon I was waiting with Sophie at the edge of the trees. The guns were standing by their wooden pegs waiting for the birds to come. The other picker-uppers were at the end of the woods, next to the hedge. Celia was holding Monty and a big black dog by their leads. Monty was barking and trying to pull her towards the guns. Richard was with David, next to his car. David was talking. He seemed angry and Richard had his head down, looking worried. When he saw Sophie and me, he waved and started walking towards us.

'How has it gone?' Sophie said. She jerked Scrabble's rope. 'Scrabble, sit.'

'We're massively under. Which is partly because there are a couple of them that can't shoot for shit. But the rain hasn't helped.' He shook his head as if he was remembering something bad. 'I think I cocked it up by choosing those two drives this morning. I should have gone with one on the other side of the hill where the woods are denser.'

'Do you think you can make it up on this one?'

'Well, we've saved the best until last. But no, whatever happens, we're going to be under to the extent that they'll complain.' Richard sighed.

Sophie rubbed his arm. 'Don't worry about it. You've done your best. The conditions have been terrible. And they all seemed happy enough at lunch.'

'I'll just be so relieved to get the first one out of the way.'

In the distance we could hear the beaters start to move down the hill, whipping their flags and making their noises.

The first pheasant flew across the valley, high above the guns. A man in the middle of the line raised his gun and fired. But he did not hit the bird so he turned around and fired again. This time he hit the pheasant and it fell into the trees behind us.

'Remember that one, Mirka,' Sophie said.

The pheasants were coming thicker now, in waves of four or five birds, and the men raised their guns and fired at the sky. Suddenly we heard a scream and turned our heads. Celia was holding one dog, and one empty rope, looking panicked as she watched Monty running across the grass towards the guns.

'Oh shit,' Sophie said.

Richard started running towards the guns. 'Get that fucking dog out of here,' he shouted, waving his arm.

A pheasant landed on the grass in front of Monty and he picked it up and shook it violently like he was trying to rip open a pillow. Feathers flew everywhere.

Celia started running towards the guns, screaming, 'Monty, Monty.'

Monty ran to the nearest gun and started barking at his boots. The man kicked his leg, making Monty fly. This made Monty bark more and jump on the man's leg. The pheasants were coming quickly and the sky was full of them. The man looked up, not wanting to miss the best part and tried to pretend Monty was not there. He fired twice at the sky and shook his leg afterwards. Monty ran in circles around the man, barking. As the man pushed new bullets into the tubes of his gun, he looked around with an angry expression, to see if anyone was coming to help. Monty saw Richard running towards him and ran away along the line of guns to bark at another man.

Celia was still running and screaming. Richard suddenly changed direction and ran towards her, as if he had decided that maybe Celia was a bigger problem than her dog. He stopped her and held her back with his arm. Now the sky was full of pheasants flying over the valley. The guns were banging and birds were falling like bombs around me. I covered my head with my arms because I was afraid one would hit me. A female pheasant landed in the grass in front of me and she lay jerking on the ground. Sophie walked over to the bird and picked her up and hit her with her stick on the back of the neck. The bird stopped moving.

The birds became less until there were no more. The horn blew. I looked up. The air was full of feathers falling slowly like snow.

'Right,' Sophie said, releasing Scrabble. 'To the trees.'

We walked into the woods and Scrabble disappeared into the trees.

'You go that way,' she told me, pointing in the opposite direction towards the pine trees. 'Pick up anything you see.'

I walked on the soft carpet of needles into the pine forest. It was dark and the air was full of a cold mist. Little sticks came out of the trees and I had to be careful not to scratch my face. I kept walking further into the forest, looking for the pheasant on the ground. Then I heard a noise and looked up. David was standing next to a tree, watching me. I jumped from the shock.

'Oh – hi, David,' I said. 'You scared me.'

David said nothing and made a face of disgust. Then he bent down to pick up the dead pheasant next to his feet.

I felt suddenly angry. 'Have I done something to you, David?'

David did not speak. I continued, 'You don't like me because

I am from Eastern Europe. Is that right? You think I took your job? I did not take your job and I have the right to be here too. There is space for everyone.'

David walked towards me until he was very close. It was the first time I realised how big he was. He looked down at me and twisted his head.

'I know what you are,' he said quietly. 'And I know what you've been up to.'

Then he walked past me into the trees. I stood there, my heart beating hard. David knew about me and Sophie. There was no confusion about what he meant. He must have seen us one day, but I could not think where. He would tell Richard. I saw an image of Richard's face, full of anger and pain. I would have to leave the house, and Sophie. How could I be stupid enough to think that there was a balance between the three of us, and that it could go on for ever?

When I came out of the trees I saw Richard was talking to the man who Monty tried to bite.

As I came closer I heard the man saying, 'But ultimately it's your responsibility. And today was an unacceptable shambles. There were hardly any birds on the second drive. I mean, we're all prepared to be generous, given the conditions, but it's really taking the piss.'

'I know. Look, I'll make it up to you on your second day.'

The man hit Richard on the back. 'Look, I don't want to be an arsehole about it. I just feel it's my duty to be honest.'

Sophie came out of the woods with three birds.

'No birds?' she said to me.

'No, I didn't find any.'

'Are you sure you looked properly? I think that first one went in your direction.'

'David got it.'

She looked suspiciously at me, as if she knew something had happened. 'Are you all right?'

I thought about telling her, but I did not want her to worry so I said, 'I'm fine.'

Celia came running towards us. She looked like she was nearly crying.

'I'm so sorry, Sophie. He's usually so good. I don't know what got into him. I'm so worried I've ruined everything.' She looked over to Richard, talking to the man. 'Do you think Richard will be cross?'

'He's a rescue dog, you shouldn't have brought him.'

At that moment Richard saw Celia with us. He touched the man's arm to say, *Excuse me*, and came towards us.

'What the fuck do you think you're playing at, Celia?'

'Richard!' Sophie said.

Richard ignored Sophie and leaned towards Celia. 'Do you have any idea what you've done? I'm up to my neck in shit already. The last thing I need is you and your psychopathic dog ruining my shoot.'

I forgot that Richard could be so frightening. I never wanted to be the person who made him angry.

Celia's face melted and shook. She breathed, trying to talk. 'I'm sorry. It won't happen again.'

'Damn right it's not going to happen again. You are not coming near another shoot. You're banned.'

Sophie pulled Richard's arm back. 'Celia's been picking up

here since before I was born. It was a mistake. Don't be so harsh on her.'

Richard shook Sophie's hand off him. 'Just get her away from me.'

He walked off. We took Celia, who was now crying, to her car.

'I'm sorry,' she said many times.

'Look, don't worry about it,' Sophie said. 'Things happen. I'll see you at the exhibition.'

As we drove back to the house I forgot about Celia. I could only think about what had happened with David. Maybe, I thought, I could talk to David and try and make him not tell Richard. His relationship with Richard was not good, so maybe he would not feel like he had to tell him. But he might do it to hurt Richard. And he could tell William. I did not know which was worse.

When we were back in the kitchen, Sophie boiled the kettle and filled the teapot. On the table there were plates of biscuits and two cakes, one yellow, one chocolate. I poured milk from the fridge into one of the cow jugs.

The guns started to arrive and take off their boots outside the kitchen door. Sophie and I stood with our backs against the cooker, smiling politely.

A tall, slightly bent man with dark grey hair came through the door. 'I hope I wasn't poaching any of your birds,' he said to the man behind him.

'Not at all, I thought you were actually being very generous,' the man behind said.

The two men stood in their yellow socks, looking down at the table.

'What have we got here?' the first man said to Sophie.

'Chocolate cake and a Victoria sponge,' Sophie said.

'Did you make them?'

'I certainly did,' Sophie said.

'Do you know, homemade chocolate cake is probably my favourite thing in the world,' he said, smiling at Sophie. 'I fall at the feet of any woman who can make a good chocolate cake.'

I felt Sophie gently press her elbow into my ribs so the man could not see and I smiled because I had watched her take out both the cakes from a white paper box from the cake shop in the town.

The other guns came into the kitchen and poured themselves tea and picked up slices of cake. They stood in groups of two or three, talking and holding their plates under their mouths while they were eating. After a while Richard banged a glass jar with a spoon. The jar was full of notes of money. The men stopped talking and turned towards him.

'I've got the final tally,' he said, unfolding a piece of paper from his pocket. 'Ninety-six brace of pheasant and eighteen of partridge. Six hundred and seventy-two shots fired, so that's about a ratio of three. Not quite, but, given the weather, it's not too shabby. Now what have you got?'

A bald man on the other side of the room held up a piece of paper. 'I've got ninety-eight!'

'Anyone else?' Richard said, looking around. Nobody said anything, so Richard went and gave the man the jar of money. 'Well deserved, Freddie.'

Everyone clapped and the man with grey hair turned to the short blond man standing next to him. 'I suppose it wasn't too bad in the end. After this morning I thought we were in for a real stinker.'

The blond man looked up from writing down the numbers in a little book on the table. 'Made up for it on the last drive. Now that's what shooting should look like.'

'Yes, it was good, wasn't it? Apart from that rabid dog, of course.' The tall man shook his head and picked up a brown rectangular biscuit.

'Unacceptable. I don't know why a dog like that was allowed anywhere near a shoot.'

'I'm terribly sorry, I've forgotten your name.'

'Bill Manders.'

The grey man shook his hand. 'Michael Landon. You're Peter's guest, aren't you?'

'That's right. Peter and I know each other from Goldman's, back in the day.'

'Of course. I met him after he'd joined Hamilton, Wells & Pinker.'

'Do you live round here?'

'No, no. I'm up in Norfolk. But I love to get out and shoot in different places. I have a real soft spot for it round here.'

'Yes, it does have something special. You should see it in a few weeks when the beech trees have turned.'

I stopped listening because a man came round the end of the table, took the last piece of chocolate cake and walked towards Sophie and me.

'So do you get dreadfully bored of cooking pheasant?' he said, his eyes moving between me and Sophie. He took a big bite of the end of the cake.

'Unbelievably bored, but I feel obliged to eat as many as possible,' Sophie said.

'Can you sell any?'

'We sell a few to the butcher in town, but we get nothing for them really. A few pence. He just can't sell them.'

'And of course you can't get the supermarkets to take them because of the shot.'

'I know. It's ridiculous. And it's such healthy and cheap meat.'

'My wife makes quite a nice pheasant stew with prunes.'

'That sounds delicious,' Sophie said, nodding politely at the man.

'I'm more of a partridge man myself. Very fond of partridge.' The man closed his eyes as if he was thinking of a partridge coming out of the oven, and Sophie and I looked at each other quickly, trying not to smile. I knew her so well now. I knew that later she would be laughing and drinking wine and saying, 'Oh my God, Mirka, that ridiculous little man banging on about partridge!'

After half an hour the men went to the door and put on their wellington boots. Sophie and Richard kept talking to them as they were leaving, smiling and remembering the good parts of the day while I cleared up the mess on the table. When the last man had gone, Sophie closed the door and put her back against it with her eyes shut.

'Argh,' she said.

'Well done, everyone,' Richard said, coming back to me and Sophie and putting his arms around our shoulders. 'I think this calls for a drink.'

Richard opened a bottle of wine and we sat down around

the table and said 'cheers', banging our glasses gently in the middle.

'Bloody Celia,' he said. 'I could have killed her. And that dog.'

'You were pretty hard on her,' Sophie said.

'She deserved it.'

'Yes, I suppose so.'

'Luckily the guns were pretty decent about it. Another lot and they might have kicked up a fuss.'

Sophie turned to me. 'The word from the beaters' cabin is that you're a natural.'

'They are lying.'

'I half expected to see you running around with your blue latex gloves on,' Richard said. He was burning the corner of a rectangle of marijuana with the lighter.

'Very funny,' I said. 'I was picking pheasants up with my hands.'

'Tomorrow, I'll show you how to pluck one, if you like,' Sophie said.

'It's OK, I have better things to do with my time,' I said, because I knew it would make them laugh.

'You do indeed,' Richard said. 'It's certainly picked up again, hasn't it, after the summer lull.'

'We have a long list of animals,' I said.

'Sophie, we need to sort out everything for the party as well.'

'It's three weeks away, we've got plenty of time.'

'I just want to make sure everyone has a good time. Some people are coming from a long way away.'

'Of course they will.'

We stayed in the kitchen talking and drinking until late. When our glasses were empty and there was no wine in the bottle, Richard said, 'Who wants to take the dogs for their bedtime walk?'

'I'll take the dogs,' I said.

I put the leads on the dogs and picked up the torch from the shelf in the coats room. The dogs were scratching at the kitchen door. I walked along the path, following the light of the torch on the stones. The dogs sniffed the bushes and lifted their legs while I watched Sophie washing the wine glasses in the sink, her lips moving a little like she was talking to herself, or singing. Richard came behind her and put his arms around her and she turned and kissed him. It was a long, sexy kiss and I felt a weight pressing on my chest. Sometimes I was not strong enough to pretend it did not hurt. What was I going to do about my situation? Maybe, I thought, remembering David, my situation would change without me doing anything. I watched them kissing through the window as I waited for the dogs. The strangest thing was that I was also happy to see them in love like that, because I wanted them to be happy. But I was tired of always being the one going to bed alone.

CHAPTER TEN

'Let me guess,' the doctor in the white coat said. He stepped back and looked at me. 'I'm going to go with Saddam Hussein.'

'Wrong,' I said, taking a sip of my champagne.

'You haven't given me much to go on. Generic military uniform and fake moustache. Could be any number of people.'

'Hey, don't be rude. This is not a fake moustache, it is my real moustache.'

The doctor laughed. 'It is a fine moustache. Really luxuriant. May I touch it?'

I let the doctor touch my moustache with the ends of his fingers.

'It must have been difficult for you, growing up with a moustache like that?' he said.

'It was OK because I always knew my power was in my moustache. If I shaved it off, then I would be nothing.'

We were standing halfway up the stairs and I turned and rested my arms on the railings. The doctor did the same and we held our glasses over the heads of the guests below. The noise of laughing and talking was rising to us like hot air.

'So are you going to tell me who you are then?'

'I'm Josef Stalin,' I said.

'Of course.' He clicked his fingers. 'How did I not get that?'

We were silent for a while, watching the party. Below us, a man dressed as the Pope with a plastic inflatable female doll tied to his arm was talking to a man in the costume of the Ku Klux Klan. A waitress brought a plate of squares of smoked salmon and the men reached out and took one each. The Ku Klux Klan man pulled off his pointy white hat and put the food in his mouth. As he was chewing he wiped the sweat from his face and smoothed back his thin wet hair over his head.

'I'm not sure how long I can take it in there,' he said to the Pope. 'I really don't know how they did it. Especially in the Deep South.'

Next to them two Hitlers were shaking hands and pointing to each other's costume.

'I see you've gone for the earlier, Nuremberg Rally era Hitler,' the Hitler in the long grey coat said to the Hitler in the brown suit. He touched the red band of the other Hitler with the swastika on his arm. 'I like what you've done with the armband.'

'My daughter made it for me, bless her. I said, for God's sake, don't tell anyone at your school otherwise Daddy will be in all kinds of trouble.' The man covered his mouth with the back of his hand while he was laughing. 'I'm rather jealous of your coat. Where did you get it?'

'Oxfam. Twenty quid.'

'Can't argue with that.'

'Say what you like about the Nazis, you can't deny they had style.'

'Quite.'

A woman wearing black material over her head with only a rectangular hole for the eyes, like an Arabic woman, came behind the Hitler in the brown jacket and put her hands over his eyes. He twisted away from her hands and turned to see who it was.

'It's me – Suze,' the woman said.

The man put his arms around her. 'Suze! I didn't recognise you. You've done something different, is it your hair?'

'Ha ha ha. You never change, do you, Mully.' She rolled the material over her head, showing her round, pretty face with naughty, smiling eyes. 'Anyway, check this out.'

The woman turned around and bent forward. At the back of her black skirt she had cut a big hole and her completely naked bottom was sticking out.

The Hitler in the grey coat suddenly bent over, holding his chest from laughing so much. The other Hitler laughed leaning backwards and then took deep breaths, wiping away tears from under his eyes.

'Oh that is too good, Suze,' he said, but he could not control his laughing and started again.

I could not help smiling and I saw that the doctor was laughing too.

'I think that one is my favourite costume so far,' he said. 'Obviously Richard's too. He always pulls it out of the bag, Richard.'

'How do you know Richard?' I asked him.

'We went to school together.'

'That's a long time being friends.'

'He's done bloody well for himself, that's for sure,' the doctor said, looking around the entrance hall. 'Anyway, he deserves it. He's a top man.'

'I know.'

'He was best man at my wedding.'

'Which one is your wife?'

The doctor's head fell down. After a few moments, he looked up again and breathed out slowly. 'Divorcing as we speak. The bitch is taking me to the cleaners.'

I quickly tried to think of something different to talk about.

The doctor finished all the champagne in his glass and smiled bitterly. 'Still, at least I don't have to hear her whiny little voice every day for the rest of my life.'

'That's good,' I said.

'I'll tell you what,' he said, pointing at my chest, his face close to mine. 'You women have got it easy. I worked my arse off, growing that business. Why does she deserve a single penny of it?'

Luckily, I looked up and Sophie was walking carefully down the stairs holding the railings to stop herself falling in her high black heels. I could see a little slice of her thighs at the top of the stockings below her short dress. Her hair was covered with black material and she had a white circle around her neck. I realised she was a nun. She turned to the side, smiling and kicking her leg out and I saw that she had put a cushion under the dress to make her look pregnant. I was shocked. I thought of how Sophie cried every time she got her period. How could she make a joke of something so painful to her?

'What do you think?' she said.

'Sophie! So nice to see you,' the doctor said, kissing her on the cheeks. 'God, you look sexy.'

'Nice tache, Mirka. It really suits you.'

'You need a drink,' the doctor said. 'Stay there.'

'So what do you think of my outfit?' She leant against me and touched the side of my hand on the railing with her hand.

'I don't understand you,' I said, looking into her eyes as if I thought I might find something in them to explain. 'How can you wear that?' I was not angry, more interested.

Sophie looked hurt by my reaction. 'It's only a bit of fun. If we can't laugh at things, then what are we left with?'

I watched the doctor walking down the stairs and looking around to find someone with a glass of champagne, but then, as if he had forgotten, he started to talk to a priest. The front door opened and a wheelchair came through the door. Sitting in it was a man dressed as Superman. Behind him, pushing the wheelchair, was a woman wearing a pink shiny tracksuit, her blonde hair tied on top of her head and lots of big fake gold jewellery around her neck. As I watched her push the wheelchair through the guests, I thought how difficult it must be to come to a party in a wheelchair, but then I realised that it must be the costume, but I did not understand why.

'We should probably go downstairs and mingle,' Sophie said. 'Don't worry, I'll introduce you to people.'

When we got to the bottom of the stairs, Sophie disappeared into the crowd. I looked around, not knowing where to go. A man with his face painted black, wearing red-and-white striped trousers and a blue coat, pushed past me. Around me there were lots of people in incredible costumes, all different, but with a lot of care and attention to detail, and I was impressed. But they were all talking very loudly and I did not know anyone. I started to walk towards the kitchen when I saw Richard coming towards me, squeezing sideways between a Saddam Hussein and a man dressed as a Viking. Richard was wearing a tight silver suit with two big curved silver pieces on his shoulders like wings. The front was cut in a deep V shape, showing the black hair on his chest and his nipples. He had put some black makeup under his eyes and his hair was pushed into a greasy curl sticking forward over his forehead.

'Top up?' he said, holding out a bottle of champagne towards me.

I tilted my champagne glass like I had seen Sophie do so many times.

'Are you Elvis?' I asked him.

He laughed. 'Nice try. I could have come as Elvis, I suppose. Late Elvis. On a toilet perhaps. Anyway, no. I'm Gary Glitter.'

'Who's he?'

'You don't want to know.'

'The party is a big success,' I said.

Richard looked proud. 'Everyone loves an excuse to dress up, don't they?'

'I can't imagine William and Caroline dressing up.'

'William could have come as himself,' Richard said. His eyes were shining with laughter. 'Well, thank God they aren't here. Let's cheers to that.'

I held up my glass to his. 'Cheers.'

'Now . . .' He came closer to whisper, looking at me seriously. 'I need you to do something for me later. I'll give you a signal.'

'Richard!' someone shouted. A man wearing a white wig and round pink glasses was coming towards us through the crowd, holding up his cigar above the heads of the guests. He gave Richard a hug and hit him a few times on the back. Richard pointed to the gold square medal on a ribbon that the man was wearing, his eyes wide with shock.

'That's not—'

'It bloody well is.'

'Is it real? Is it yours?'

'Fixed it for me to score a try at Twickenham.'

'What, in the middle of a match?'

'No, they picked me up from school one afternoon and drove me down there. The England side were all there waiting.'

'That is bloody brilliant.' Then Richard put his elbow into the other man's ribs and said curiously, 'Did he, er, have a go?'

The man was taking a breath on the cigar and coughed as he laughed. 'No – obviously not his type.'

'I'd be rather offended, if I were you. He didn't seem particularly discriminating in his tastes.' Richard laughed and hit the man on the back. 'I've got to do something for one second. I'm leaving you with Mirka.'

He twisted the shoulders of the man around with two hands so he was pointing towards me.

'Hi,' I said.

'Hi,' the man said, his eyes looking past my head as if he hoped someone else was coming.

'Who are you?' I asked him.

'You don't know who I am?' the man said, like I was either crazy or stupid. 'Where have you been?'

'I'm foreign.'

'Oh, right. Well, I guess you could say he was—'

At that moment we heard Richard shouting from the stairs, 'If I could have your attention—'

Everyone stopped talking and turned to look at him.

'Just a quick word to thank you all for coming to help me celebrate my fortieth birthday in such style.' He paused, looking around the room and smiling. 'May I say how nice it is to see so many of you honouring our great nation's most eminent paedophiles.' He put his fist to his mouth and coughed. 'Sorry, I mean eccentrics.'

Richard stopped to let the laughing become quiet again. He could not stop smiling, he was so happy with himself. 'In fact, I think you'll agree it's been a bumper year for British paedophilia. So I'd like to raise a glass to all of them, for so willingly sacrificing themselves on the altar of public opinion so that we can make fun of them for generations to come. To Operation Yewtree.'

The guests cheered and raised their glasses into the air, shouting, 'Hear, hear,' and 'To Operation Yewtree.' I saw a woman dressed as a sexy schoolgirl looking at the doctor, biting her lip like she was not sure if she should laugh.

'Anyway, changing the subject,' Richard continued. 'The person I would most like to thank is my beautiful wife for all her hard work in organising this party. Sophie, where are you?' Richard's eyes looked in the crowd for Sophie. In front of me someone held Sophie's arm and put it in the air. Richard smiled down at her. 'Please will you all raise your glasses and make a toast to Sophie. Sophie, I love you.'

He kissed his palm and blew the kiss to her. Everyone said, 'To Sophie.'

I lifted my glass into the air and said the words with them, thinking how happy Sophie would be.

Richard pointed down the corridor. 'Now, if you would like to make your way to the great hall, dinner is served.'

I was sitting on a round table between the doctor and a man dressed as a giant cigarette with his face showing through a hole. Both men were concentrating on eating their sliced duck breasts with mashed potato. There were six tables in the hall and balloons tied to every chair. The noise of talking in the room seemed to get louder and louder.

The doctor finished eating and threw his napkin down on his plate. He reached in front of me, took a half-empty bottle from the table and filled our glasses with red wine.

'So where did you say you were from again?'

'Slovakia.'

'And have you got a boyfriend stashed away back there?'

'Yes, we are getting married soon, when I've saved enough money.'

'Oh?' The doctor laughed. 'You seem a bit young to be getting married.'

'We are very religious,' I said, enjoying the conversation. The doctor was easy to joke with.

'Well, that's interesting, because it's not what I heard.'

'What do you mean?' I said, feeling myself turning stiff.

The doctor bent his head towards me, looking around to see if anyone was listening and said quietly, as if he was telling me a secret, 'Richard told me you were . . .' He stopped like he could not think of the right words. 'More the other way inclined.'

Calmly, I picked up my glass and drank some wine, trying not to look like I cared what he said. I was going to kill Richard when I saw him.

'It is true,' I said, as politely as I could.

'And do you like men as well, or only women?'

'Only women.'

'Interesting,' he said, nodding his head slowly. He put his elbow on the table and turned to me with his chin resting in his hand, staring at me with narrow eyes as if he was trying to understand me. 'I'm intrigued.'

I took some bread from the basket and ripped it into two pieces.

'Can you pass the butter, please,' I said.

'So what I want to know is . . .' He leaned closer. 'How do you actually have sex?'

I smiled with bread in my mouth and swallowed. 'I'm sure you've seen enough porno movies to know the answer.'

The doctor laughed nervously. I turned away towards the man dressed as the cigarette.

'Hello, I'm Mirka,' I said, holding out my hand.

'Paul,' he said.

'Why are you dressed as a cigarette?'

Paul laughed, but then made a face like it was uncomfortable for him to laugh in the costume.

'Try again.'

He moved forward on his chair and looked down behind him. I followed his eyes and saw a white rope coming from under him and falling to the floor at the side of the chair. Then he leaned backwards, showing me a big red stain in the middle of the cigarette. Suddenly I understood.

'You are a bloody Tampax?' I said, not believing that it could be true.

'Bingo.'

'Why is that funny?'

The smile disappeared from his face and he looked down at the table, embarrassed. 'Well, you know, because it's a bit off-key.'

'No, I don't understand. Because it is disgusting for a woman to bleed, so it's funny?'

'Well, that's the point of bad taste, isn't it? To come as something that makes people a little uncomfortable.'

A waitress came to take away our plates. Paul started talking to the person on his other side. The doctor was turned away from me. I stared straight ahead, playing with the lumpy lines of wax dripping down the candle, putting them in the flame to melt again. I got up and went to the toilet. I sat staring at the funny books on the shelf thinking maybe I could go to bed and nobody would notice. I liked Richard and Sophie, but they were busy, and I was not sure I liked their friends. But I did not want Richard and Sophie to think I was having a bad time or worry about me, so I went back downstairs.

When I came into the great hall, Richard was posing for

photographs with his birthday cake. The cake was the shape of two naked breasts with a lacy black bra made of icing that was too small to cover the nipples. Richard was holding the cake and sticking out his tongue to lick one of the nipples.

Sophie was standing watching him, laughing. I went and stood next to her.

'It's not exactly original,' she said. 'But I think he would only have been disappointed if I got him anything else.'

Richard gave the cake to Sophie, who picked up the knife and started to cut the cake into squares. He saw me and waved me towards him with his finger.

'Right, you, come with me.'

We went to the entrance hall where the three waitresses were waiting by the door, putting on their coats.

'I was just coming to find you,' he said. He took three white envelopes from the drawer under the telephone and gave them one each. 'Sterling work, girls. I've put a bit of a tip in there. You've all been absolutely brilliant.' He held the door open for the women to leave and waved at them as they walked to their cars. Then he shut the door and started skipping up the stairs in a strange way, pointing ahead.

'To the Aztec zone,' he said.

I followed him to his and Sophie's bedroom. I waited nervously by the door, waiting to see what he wanted. He went to the drawers on the other side of the room and opened the top one and came back with a white envelope. I thought he was going to pay me some money like the waitresses. As he was coming towards me he took the mirror off the wall, put it on the bed and sat next to it. He hit the covers with his palm so I would come and sit down on the bed next to the mirror.

'What do you think of the party?'

'It's a great party.'

Richard unfolded the envelope and took out a small, sqaure plastic bag, half-full of white powder. I realised it was cocaine. He poured the whole bag into a pile on the mirror and took out a credit card from his wallet.

'What I want you to do,' he said, moving the cocaine around on the silver surface of the mirror with the card, 'is to make about thirty lines so big.' He pointed to the line he had made with a fat middle and thin ends. Underneath it was its own reflection, like a grey shadow. Richard looked at the line with his head on the side, as if he could not decide whether it was the right size, and took another tiny bit of cocaine from the pile and added it to the line. 'That size. OK?'

'OK,' I said.

Richard rolled a twenty-pound note into a tube and bent his head towards the line. 'It would be rude not to, wouldn't it? Can't give it to people without trying it first.'

I watched the cocaine disappear like magic as the tube moved along it, and its reflection also disappeared at the same time, sniffed by another Richard below the mirror. Richard lifted his head, sniffed and shook his shoulders.

'Bloody hell, that's good. Want some?'

'No thanks,' I said.

'You are missing out, my friend. That is grade-A cocaine.'

Richard went to the bathroom and I heard him peeing loudly in the toilet. I put the mirror on my knees and started to take cocaine from the pile and put it to the side so that there would be space for thirty lines. Richard walked past me and leaned over to see if I was doing it right.

'There's more in the envelope, if you need it. Bring it to me when it's done.'

'Richard,' I said.

'What?'

'You told the doctor that I was gay.'

Richard stopped at the door and turned. He looked guilty. 'I thought you didn't mind people knowing.'

'I don't mind people knowing, but I don't like people like him who think it is a disgusting secret. Why did you tell him?'

Richard put his hand on his forehead. 'I'm so sorry. I thought I was doing you a favour.'

'A favour?'

'He came up to me and said he thought you were hot, and did I mind if he had a crack at you.'

I started laughing. Richard sighed with relief and laughed too.

'Hey, watch the coke!' he said, because the mirror was shaking.

'OK, go to your party.'

I quite liked the job of making the lines of cocaine. I had to concentrate to make all the lines the same size. Then I could not believe what I was doing. My life was so strange.

As I came back into the great hall, the man from the wheelchair dressed as Superman walked past me to the door. So it was definitely a costume, I thought. I would have to ask Richard or Sophie. At the end of the room people were dancing. Richard was sitting at the table, smoking a cigar and blowing circles of smoke into the air.

'Ah, there you are. Excellent stuff.' He took the mirror from me and held it towards the woman sitting next to him, who was also dressed as a nun. 'Jane? It's very good, I promise.'

'I can't.' She hit her stomach with two hands. 'Preggers.'

'I didn't know! Come here and give me a kiss.' Richard leant forward and put his arms around her and squeezed her. He looked down at her stomach. 'So you really are a pregnant nun.'

'Properly up the duff. You know me, otherwise I'd be first in line.'

'For a line!' Richard looked around to see who was laughing at his joke. 'Well, I am so pleased for you. George?'

Richard passed the mirror and the note to the man sitting next to the nun. He was wearing tight shorts and a T-shirt made of red plastic material, and a black leather necklace with silver spikes. I had no idea who he was supposed to be and I did not think I wanted to. I had a feeling it was a joke about gay men. He came up from sniffing a line holding his nose with one finger and breathing in deeply.

'Wowee,' he said.

I left them and went to the kitchen to see if there was any mess to tidy. The waitresses had cleaned most things, but there was a pile of dirty plates waiting for the dishwasher to finish. So I put on yellow gloves and started to wash them.

Sophie came into the kitchen with the schoolgirl.

'Poor you,' Sophie was saying. 'It was exactly the same with me and Richard when we first moved down here. I kept thinking, what have I done?'

'And he won't talk about it,' the schoolgirl said. 'It's literally like getting blood out of a stone.'

I saw Sophie go into the little room and come out again.

'Mirka, have you seen the bucket with the ice?'

'It is finished. There is more in the cellar.'

Sophie came to the sink and looked at me like a little cat. 'You wouldn't be an angel and go and get it? I can't go down there in these heels, I'll kill myself.'

When I came back with the ice they were not in the kitchen. I took the bucket to the great hall and put it on the table at the side of the room next to the bottles of whisky, rum, vodka and gin. A lot of the guests had gone but there were still a few people. The Tampax man was dancing, waving his arms up and down, and the Pope was dancing the waltz with his inflatable doll. I could not see Sophie anywhere and I was angry with her for making me do something for her, then disappearing as if it did not matter. Richard was still at the table, talking and laughing and smoking his cigar.

I finished washing the dishes and decided to go to bed. I did not want to be at the party any more with their friends and their jokes that I did not understand or that I did not think were funny. Nobody would notice I was gone.

When I came up the stairs I looked down the corridor and saw that the door to Richard and Sophie's bedroom was open and the light was on. Sophie was sitting on the bed, taking off her shoes. She looked up and waved for me to come to her. I did not move, but she kept waving and it seemed like she wanted to say something important. I went down the corridor.

'Shut the door,' she said. Then she got up and put her arms around my neck. 'I've missed you tonight. Kiss me.'

'This is not a good idea,' I said, pulling my head away from her and looking for the door handle with my hand.

'It's all right, he's literally just gone downstairs with the rest of the coke.'

'I'm going to bed,' I said. I was still a little angry with her.

'Just one minute,' she said kissing me. 'I have been thinking about this all night. I've been trying to corner you, but you keep slipping away.'

I thought about this and I did not think it was true. But her hand was inside my shirt and moving up towards my breast and her lips were sucking my lip and I felt a shiver in my body. I kissed her properly and she walked backwards towards the bed, pulling me with her. I kissed her for a while and she lifted her dress and put my hand between her legs. She was not wearing any pants and I was shocked by the surprise of the soft, wet skin.

'Please,' she whispered. 'I want you to fuck me.'

I could not resist her. I pushed open her legs with my knees and put my fingers inside her. Immediately I was lost in another world. But after a minute I realised what I was doing and stopped. Sophie opened her eyes and frowned.

'Don't stop.'

'This is completely stupid,' I said. 'Richard is downstairs and—'

'Richard is standing right behind you,' Richard said.

My heart stopped beating. I turned my head slowly sideways and Richard was there, leaning on the wall next to the door with a drink in one hand. He raised his eyebrows like he thought the situation was quite funny.

'As you were. Please, don't let me stop you.'

I watched him like it was a dream as he walked to the green chair in the corner of the room. I looked down at Sophie. Her expression was strangely calm, like she was waiting for something. She did not seem afraid at all. Richard sat down in the chair with his legs open and took a sip of his drink, staring at us.

'Carry on,' he said, nodding his head.

I looked at him completely shocked. He looked back at me with an arrogant, joking expression.

'What, do you think I'm just going to let you have all the fun?'

Then I felt Sophie's fingers on the back of my neck, pulling my head down to kiss her, reaching up to my lips with her tongue.

'It's OK, Mirka, he doesn't mind.'

I understood and I felt horror all through my body.

'You told him,' I said.

'Mirka, it's OK,' Sophie said.

I pushed Sophie away and jumped off the bed. Richard was looking at me with an awful smile.

'I've known all along,' he said. When he saw my face he said, 'Did you honestly think she wouldn't tell me? She's my wife.'

I ran out of the bedroom. When I arrived in my room I could not breathe. My legs seemed to break in the middle and my back slid down the door until I was sitting on the floor. I stayed there for a long time, thinking about what had happened. I could not believe it. Richard knew all the time. I felt completely betrayed, even though I knew I was the one who was wrong. I realised that Sophie could not love me if she had told him. I had been stupid to think that she did not have something stronger with Richard than what she had with me. He was her husband. And worse, what did they want from me? Did Richard think he was going to have sex with me too? Or only watch? I felt like I was in the middle of a game they were playing and it made me feel dirty thinking about it.

The next day I worked in the barn without going to the house. I was taking the skin off rats. The day was very slow and I was nervous about seeing Richard and Sophie. Especially Richard. If I was Richard I would ask me to leave the house. I prepared myself for the conversation. I imagined telling him I was so sorry for what I had done and asking him to forgive me.

By seven o'clock in the evening I was hungry and went back to the house. As I was coming towards the kitchen I saw Sophie and Richard sitting at the table reading the newspaper, their dirty plates pushed away from them. I came through the door and took off my shoes. My hands were sweaty from being so nervous. When I finally looked at them, they were both looking at me with faces that were trying to hide the embarrassment.

'We saved you some dinner,' Sophie said, with a bright, helpful expression.

'Yes, you must be starving,' Richard said. He put down the newspaper and went to the cooker, taking a plate of shepherd's pie from the bottom oven. His movements were jerky and he seemed nervous. 'There you go. Sit down. Do you want ketchup or anything?'

I pulled out a chair and sat down, confused about how nice they were being.

'No thanks.'

'How are you feeling today?' Sophie said.

'OK,' I said. 'How are you feeling?'

'Not too bad actually. Richard's suffering though, aren't you, sweetie?' She rubbed Richard's shoulder.

Richard nodded shamefully and looked at me quickly in the eyes before looking away again. 'Had rather a few too many last night.'

I tried to smile but I felt uncomfortable. I did not know why they were behaving in this way, why Richard was not angrier with me, why everything about Sophie's behaviour seemed fake. There was a silence and I ate, staring at my food.

'So did you have a good time last night?' Sophie said.

I looked at her curiously. 'It was a great party.'

'It was, wasn't it?' she said happily. 'I think people really enjoyed themselves.'

'It was so nice to see the old lot again,' Richard said. 'Everyone has changed so much, but at the same time, they're all exactly the same.'

I finished eating and picked up the three dirty plates.

'I think I am going to bed. Good night. Thank you for dinner.'

'No problem,' Sophie said.

'Sleep well,' Richard said.

I walked up the stairs, still feeling uncomfortable and confused.

'Mirka,' Richard called.

I turned and saw that he was running up the stairs behind me. His expression was not angry, but full of regret.

He took a deep breath. 'I wanted to say something about last night. It's been weighing on my mind all day and I feel awful.'

'Don't worry,' I said.

'I'm so ashamed of how I behaved. I was very drunk and I'd had a lot of coke. Honestly, I don't know what came over me. I must have been completely wasted. Anyway I would really like it if we could just pretend it never happened.'

'OK,' I said, but I did not understand why he was saying sorry when I was the one who was having sex with his wife. Maybe he did not know everything, I thought, hoping it was true. Maybe Sophie had told him that it was only one time when we were drunk.

'Great. I've got another shoot on Friday and I could use your help again.' He reached out and touched my arm. 'You were so great last time.'

I looked at his hand on my arm, not believing he was touching me. Then I realised I had to say something.

'Sure,' I said. 'OK.'

I went upstairs to bed. Later, when I was falling asleep, I heard a noise and I jerked awake. I opened my eyes and in the darkness I could see a darker shape moving in my room. I made a small scream.

A hand covered my mouth. 'Shh,' Sophie said.

I was still feeling frightened and confused from the shock. 'What are you doing? Get out of my room.'

'It's OK, it's only me. I need to see you alone.'

'I don't want to see you now. Get out,' I said. I was surprised by my anger.

'Don't be like that. Come here.'

She bent down and I felt her hair fall on my face as she tried to kiss me. I put my hand out and pushed her face away.

'Leave me, please.'

'OK, OK, I'll go,' she said in a hurt voice.

After she left, I felt my eyes get hot. Tears came into them and ran in lines down my face to the pillow.

CHAPTER ELEVEN

Sophie was making apple jelly on the morning the journalist was coming to meet me. The whole house smelt of apples. I watched her stirring the big pot, her face pink with the steam. Before the party I would have thought she looked beautiful, but now I felt nothing. It was two weeks since then and we had stopped everything, but we had never spoken about it, as if nothing had ever happened between us.

'Are you nervous?' Sophie said.

'A little,' I said.

'Do you want some more coffee?' she said politely, like I was a guest.

'I'm OK, thanks.'

Sophie started counting the glass jars on the table. I ate my toast thinking about what the journalist might ask me and what I would say. I was not very good at explaining things sometimes, especially in English, so the more I thought about it, the more nervous I felt.

'I forgot to tell you,' Sophie said. 'Richard sold the last couple of days shooting. He's going to take us out to dinner at the Snooty Fox on Friday to celebrate.'

Richard came into the kitchen wearing his coat and hat. 'Did I hear my name being taken in vain?'

'I just said that your agent sold those two days and we're going to the pub.'

'Yes, I thought we could go to the posh one, not the Dog and Duck. I get a bit bored of it there. Have you booked a table yet?'

'No, I must do that,' Sophie said. Then she looked at Richard and smiled. 'Come here.'

'What?'

Richard stood in front of Sophie and she wiped his mouth with her finger.

'You've got Marmite on your lips.'

Richard wiped his face with his sleeve. 'Oh, thanks.'

Then she kissed him. 'Love you.'

'Love you too.'

I looked away. I felt like it was all some kind of performance, but I did not know who for. For the two of them, more than for me. Was Sophie trying to make herself believe she was the perfect wife? Or was she trying to punish me for making her leave my room that night?

'Great,' I said, getting up and putting on my trainers. 'That will be nice.'

'Good luck,' Sophie said.

'Oh, it's the big day,' Richard said. 'You really are going to be famous after this. I hope it goes well.'

'Thanks.'

I carried my cup to the barn and drank the coffee, sitting and staring at the rats that were melting on the shelf. I had a strange, empty feeling. I thought of going to dinner with Richard and Sophie at the pub, and I did not want to go. I knew they were being kind. That was the problem. There was something wrong and fake between us all. But I pushed the thought away, picked up the first rat and cut open his belly. Caleb was waiting for my next scenes and I could not work fast enough. I spent all my time in the barn, which was good because I did not like to be alone with Sophie or Richard.

At twelve o'clock Sophie knocked on the door. A man walked into the room behind her. He was thin, and young, only a few years older than me, with a big orange beard and long dirty brown hair. He looked like he had been outside in the forest for weeks, trying to survive.

'Mirka, this is Otto,' Sophie said.

She had a very proud expression and I was embarrassed, like she was my mother. I peeled off my blue gloves and walked around the table to shake his hand.

'Nice to meet you,' I said.

Sophie was still standing next to the door so I looked at her strongly to make her go away.

'Right, I'll leave you to it,' she said, as if she remembered something.

'Come in, please,' I said.

'So this is where you make all your stuff,' Otto said.

His accent was not English, but I did not know what it was. He was wearing a red shirt with a pattern of squares, jeans and brown boots. He looked down at the rat on the table.

'Cool,' he said.

I stood silently, not knowing what to say as he walked around the room looking at the stuffed animals and boxes of tools and reading the labels on the drawers. He came back and bent down and looked closely at the rat.

'Do they smell?'

'No, they don't smell.'

'Does it make you feel strange, spending all day cutting up dead animals?'

'Yes and no. It is a little strange, yes.' I realised this was not a very satisfying answer and I tried to think of something better to say. 'Most things that people do all day are strange to other people.'

'Hang on.' He took his mobile phone from his pocket and put it on the table as he sat down. 'We might as well start the interview. Do you mind if I record this?'

'Sure.'

He pressed the screen of the phone. I sat on the stool opposite him.

'OK,' he said. 'So tell me, how does it make you feel, working with dead animals?'

'At the beginning I thought it was disgusting. But it is not disgusting if you work carefully. And I find it satisfying work.'

'Oh yeah, why's that?'

'I like working in something so small and detailed, because you have to concentrate very hard. Not everyone can do it.'

'What scene are you working on at the moment?'

I pointed to a big glass box on the other side of the room. Otto walked over and looked inside.

'It's called *Rats at the Office Party*.'

I had already put the white plastic desks and tall black chairs in the scene. The walls were white and I had put squares of bright lights in the ceiling. The boss rat was going to sit in the glass office in the corner. Every desk had a computer, some files, or stationery, and personal objects like a family photograph in a frame, or a cactus.

'I'm making a photocopier,' I said. 'It is difficult to get the perfect pale grey colour. And I want to put green light inside, so when the rat takes his trousers down and sits on it, it will glow underneath him.'

Otto laughed. 'Nice.'

'Where are you from?' I said, curious.

'Finland,' he said. 'Where are you from?'

'Slovakia.'

'Cool. How long have you been here?'

'Nearly a year. And you?'

'Three years.' He picked up his phone and checked the screen and put it down again. 'So, decorating the scenes must be the fun part.'

I was not sure what the question was. 'Yes, it is very fun.'

'But you like the taxidermy part as well?'

'Yes, I get pleasure from taking away the insides, which are messy and rotting. Afterwards the animal is clean and can live for ever. It makes me feel good.'

'But the animal doesn't know it is living for ever.'

'Yes, but I know.'

Otto nodded slowly. 'And why do you think people like these scenes so much? Instead of, like, an owl sitting on a branch, in its natural home. Like that one.' He pointed to Richard's tawny owl.

'I think they like the detail. Everyone likes stories about themselves that they can recognise.'

'Yeah, and I guess animals behaving like humans has always been a thing, like a wolf who gets dressed up in ladies' clothes and stuff.'

'Maybe we can see that the animals are like us, or we are like animals.'

'Cool, yeah. I think you're right,' he said, bending down to look Richard's raven in the eye. 'OK, let's take some pictures.' He went to his bag on the floor by the door and took out a big camera with a long lens. 'Just do what you do and ignore me.'

I put on my gloves and picked up the rat to cut the skin around the ears and eyes. Then I gently pulled the skin over the head. Otto was moving around the room, bending his knees and taking pictures of me, then checking the screen of his camera. He came very close, with the lens only a few centimetres from my face and it was difficult to keep my expression normal.

'OK, can I get a couple of photos with you working on the scene? Put your arm inside like you are doing something to it.'

I looked into the scene and put my hand on the water cooler as if I was moving it.

'So what's next?' he said.

'I will keep doing the scenes until I have no more ideas. But at the moment I have hundreds.'

'Do you think you'll always be a taxidermist?'

'That is an impossible question,' I said, smiling. 'But for now, yes.'

'Perfect. Well, I think I have everything,' Otto said, looking through the pictures on the camera screen. He looked up at me and smiled. 'So will you make it up to London some time?'

'I hope so.'

'Well, we could maybe go for a drink or something.'

I didn't understand if he was asking me out for a date, so I said quickly, 'You know I'm gay, yes?' Immediately I blushed.

Otto laughed. 'Yeah, I guessed. I just thought you seemed cool and we could hang out.'

I wondered if it was the truth or if he was lying to save the situation. But it did not matter.

'I feel like an idiot,' I said.

'It's cool, don't worry. Anyway, you have my number.' He put his camera in his bag and stood up. 'The magazine puts on parties sometimes. They're pretty fun. I'll let you know when the next one is happening.'

'I'd like that.'

I walked with him to the door then stood and waved from the entrance to the barn as Otto walked along the path to the little gate, thinking about everything, still feeling embarrassed about what I had said.

Five minutes later, Richard came into the barn carrying a dead fox on his shoulder. He swung it off into a plastic box on the floor. There was blood on the white fur around the fox's mouth.

'So your hipster boyfriend from his wanky magazine's

gone then?' he said, with a mean expression in his eyes. 'Saw him from the window. Looks like he missed his calling as a lumberjack.'

I thought Richard was being horrible for no reason. It seemed like he was jealous. Maybe he thought I thought Otto was cool and we would be friends and he did not like it.

'The article and pictures will be in the magazine next month,' I said with no emotion.

Richard looked down guiltily and sighed. 'Sorry. I didn't mean to be a twat.' He smiled, though it looked like it was difficult for him. 'Congratulations. I'm excited about reading it. You deserve it.'

Behind him in the door, I saw David. He was holding a gun and staring at me. Richard turned to where I was looking.

'Oh, there you are, David. How's everything looking for Saturday?'

I sat down and picked up a paintbrush and looked for something to pretend to work on. David and Richard talked about the shoot. My hands were shaking and I could not look up. Even though I was not with Sophie I was still afraid of David. There was something in his eyes that made me think he would hurt me if he had the opportunity. He looked at me like he had power over me and I hated it.

On the Friday night I had a shower after I finished work. I put on my best shirt, made from a black silky material, then my sweater. I looked in the mirror and combed my hair. It was the first time I had gone out at night with Richard and Sophie and not just driven them to a dinner at someone's house.

'Taxi'll be here in ten minutes,' Richard shouted from below.

I took my jacket from the chair and went down the stairs. Richard was coming out from his room with his arms through a green jumper, pulling it over his head.

'I thought I was going to drive,' I said.

'I thought it would be nice for you to enjoy a few drinks, have a night off being designated driver.'

'Now, thanks to you, I can get completely smashed,' I said, remembering.

Richard laughed. 'Taxi's actually coming in twenty minutes but I thought if I lied, I might have an outside chance of Sophie being on time.'

I thought of something. 'OK, then can I check my emails?'

'Course, go and hop on Sophie's computer.'

I went down the corridor to the living room. I opened the computer and logged into my inbox. There was one email from Caleb and nothing else. I had a sudden feeling of loneliness so strong that it was difficult to breathe. Nobody thought about me. I closed the computer.

When I got back to the entrance hall, Richard was standing with his hands in the pockets of his jacket, looking up the stairs. The lights of the taxi shone through the window.

'Taxi's here,' Richard shouted.

After five minutes Sophie was still upstairs.

'Where is she?' Richard said. 'Why is she incapable of being ready on time? She does this every single time. What is she doing? I can't stand it, it drives me fucking crazy.'

'Sorry sorry sorry,' Sophie said, running down the stairs. She saw Richard's face. 'What?'

'Why can't you be on time?'

As the taxi drove up the hill, Sophie said, 'Well, this is nice,' but nobody said anything.

We drove down the other side of the hill to a village I had never been to before. There was a small river with a wooden bridge and some willow trees growing next to it. We turned into the car park next to the pub. Above the door, there was a sign with a picture of a fox with his nose lifted high, wearing a jacket and black hat, holding a stick under his arm.

The pub was full of people eating and talking, their faces lit by the candles. We followed a waitress to a table in the corner. The waitress was wearing black jeans and a grey T-shirt with her sleeves rolled up on the shoulders to show her completely tattooed arms. When she turned around and gave me a menu on a piece of paper, I thought how pretty she was. She had shiny black hair, soft curvy lips and skin the colour of milky tea.

'Thank you,' I said, looking into her dark eyes with long lashes.

'That's OK,' she said, looking back at me for a long time, with a lot of energy and curiosity. I had a feeling that she was testing me somehow. Then I realised why she was looking at me like that. I was so surprised, my cheeks burnt and I looked quickly down at the menu. I never thought I would meet another girl who liked girls in the countryside. Now I had met two.

'So shall I tell you about the specials today?' she said.

'Please do,' Richard said.

'For starters we have scallops served with a cauliflower cream or chicken liver pâté. And for mains we have a braised ox cheek stew with mashed potato, which I can highly recommend. And we also have Dover sole served with buttered leeks.'

'Ooh, those sound so good,' Sophie said. 'I might have the Dover sole.'

'Any questions, just let me know,' the waitress said.

I made myself look up. She was still looking directly at me with a small smile at the side of her mouth. I smiled back a little. Then she turned and I watched her body moving as she walked towards the bar. She was tall, with wide shoulders and a long body. She moved elegantly, with a lot of confidence.

I realised what I was doing, and stopped staring. When I looked back at Richard and Sophie I saw that Sophie was looking at me curiously. I tried to smile normally but I saw in her eyes that she knew something. Good, I thought, I hope she knows. I did not have to hide anything from her. We were not together. Richard was busy reading the menu. I looked down and tried to decide what I was going to eat. Richard put his menu on the table and picked up a thin, black leather book.

'Red or white?'

'White,' Sophie said.

'Mirka?'

'Red.'

'Well, we can have a bottle of each since nobody has to drive.'

Richard read every page of the wine menu. Sophie put down her menu and started to roll a cigarette.

'What are you having, Mirka?' she said.

'Steak.'

'And for a starter? Richard, are we having starters?'

'I'm having a starter, you do what you like.'

'OK, I'll have scallops,' I said.

'Richard, shall I make you a cigarette?'

'Please,' he said, not concentrating. He was leaning back in his chair with his neck twisted, watching the waitress at the bar, waiting for her to look at him. She saw him and came over.

'I think we're going to try the Fleurie. And a bottle of the Sancerre.'

'Excellent choice,' the waitress said, smiling. 'Are you ready to order food as well, or shall I come back?'

'I'm ready, are you guys ready?' Sophie said. 'Mirka, you start.'

I watched the waitress as she wrote down our orders on the notepad. I liked how strong her arms looked, the way you could see the shapes of the muscles under the skin. The tattoo on her left shoulder was a picture of a pirate ship sailing out of her arm. She had two black-and-white flying birds on her right shoulder, and a pretty pattern of flowers from her hand to elbow. I could feel Sophie watching me watching her. I looked at her directly to say, *Yes, I am looking at the waitress.*

She looked away quickly and turned to Richard. 'Shall we go outside?'

'Let's wait for our drinks,' Richard said.

There was another silence and Richard picked up the wine menu again. Sophie looked around the room. It was uncomfortable. I felt like I was with my parents. And not in the same way as when I arrived at the house, when I felt protected and safe. Now it was more like I was their teenage daughter, trapped in a car with them on a long journey, wanting to escape.

'It's a lovely pub, isn't it,' Sophie said. 'Cosy.'

After ten minutes Richard was looking over his shoulder towards the bar every few seconds.

He frowned. 'We are still notably untroubled by anything resembling a drink.'

'I'm sure it will be here any second,' Sophie said. 'It's so busy tonight.'

'Let's go and have a fag and hopefully it will be here by the time we get back.'

I was feeling relieved to be on my own when the waitress came to the table with a bottle of white wine in a silver bucket. Then she went to the bar again and brought a bottle of red wine and wine glasses.

'I guess you'll have to try the red and the white then,' she said.

She twisted the opener quickly into the cork of the white wine. Then she poured a little white wine into my glass and stood up straight, holding the bottle with a white cloth wrapped around it, waiting for me to say something.

'What do I do?' I said.

'Put the glass to your nose and smell it. Then take a sip and look into the distance as if you are thinking hard about all the complex flavours.'

I picked up the glass and drank the wine. 'Tastes fine.'

She poured some red wine into the bigger glass. 'OK, now swirl it round as you hold the glass up to the light.'

'It's red,' I said, smiling. 'What am I looking for exactly?'

'I have no idea. You just have to look really important about it.'

'Absolutely delicious,' I said, putting down the glass and wiping the red wine from my mouth.

The waitress laughed and she looked even prettier. I gave her the same strong look that she was giving me.

'So, do you live round here?' she said.

'I work at a house close to here. Do you live round here?'

'My parents run this place. They live upstairs. I've come home for a few months to save some money before I go travelling in January.'

'Where will you go?'

'I've got a friend in Mexico City, so I thought I'd start there. And then we'll see.' She lifted her shoulders. 'What's your name?'

'Mirka.'

'I'm Alice.' Her lips were open so I could see the white ends of her teeth with a little gap between them.

Sophie and Richard were walking towards the table. Alice gave me a smile like she would have liked to talk for longer, and then turned to go.

'Excellent, some booze,' Richard said.

The wine seemed to get drunk quickly. Sophie and Richard were talking about the house, the weddings, the guests, plans for next year. I was not listening. I could not stop looking at Alice. She was good at her job, I thought. The way she moved around the pub, carrying a lot of heavy plates and trays of glasses as if they were nothing.

After Alice took away the plates from our main course, Sophie went to the toilet. Richard poured some more red wine into our glasses.

'I had an email from Caleb,' I said.

'Oh?'

'He invited me to London. He is going to put *Rats at the Office Party* on display in his shop.'

'You should go.'

'I think I will.'

Sophie came back and held out her wrists towards Richard. 'Smell that. Isn't it nice? It's mandarin and grapefruit.'

'Lovely, darling,' he said, jerking his head away like the smell was too strong. 'He did mention actually last time that we spoke that he wanted to do an exhibition of your work. Wouldn't that be great?'

I noticed that as Richard and I were talking, Sophie kept turning her head towards the bar. Suddenly someone switched off the lights so that there was only candlelight in the room. People stopped talking. The kitchen door opened and Alice came through holding a cake. She walked with her hand in front to stop the candles from going out. She was looking at me, smiling a lot.

'*Happy birthday to you*,' she started singing. Sophie and Richard sang too. Then most of the people in the pub started singing as she walked towards our table. '*Happy birthday, dear Mirka, Happy birthday to you*.'

She put the cake down in front of me. I blew out the candles and everyone clapped and my throat got tight from the feeling of all the strangers singing and clapping for me. Then the lights came back on and everybody started talking again. Alice brought a knife and plates.

'You were keeping that secret,' Sophie said. 'I thought you were going to tell me, but you didn't.'

I did not say that I had not told her about my birthday because I was still upset and I did not want to give her a reason to be nice to me. A part of me wanted to feel lonely. Until I checked my emails, and then I really did feel alone.

'How did you know?' I said.

'I found your CV again the other day and it was on that. I'm clever, you see.'

'Thank you so much,' I said, and I meant it.

'The big Two O,' Richard said. 'Oh, to be twenty again! All those young, sylphlike girls ahead of you.' Richard winked at me and I could not help smiling.

'All right, Richard, don't get carried away,' Sophie said. 'Mirka, I got you a little pressie.' She pulled something soft wrapped in wrinkled gold paper from her handbag. 'You can change it if you don't like it.'

I ripped the paper and inside there was a scarf, hat and gloves made from soft black wool. I put on the gloves. They were cut so the ends of my fingers were naked.

'They're cashmere,' Sophie said.

'They are very beautiful. Thank you.'

'I was tempted to buy you orange or something, but I thought, better play it safe.'

'Hey, this means we're both Scorpio,' Richard said. 'The most powerful sign in the Zodiac.'

'Oh please,' Sophie said and hit his arm.

Richard moved away from her as if he was really hurt. 'Ow, it's true. I read it in the horoscope section of the paper. Passionate, determined, resilient. We lead dramatic, fate-filled lives, apparently.'

'Well, it must be bollocks,' Sophie said. 'Because I can't imagine two more different people.'

'Hmm, I don't know,' Richard said, smiling at me. 'We have certain things in common.'

I tried to smile. I realised he meant Sophie, and he was trying to make a joke about what had happened, but I could not joke about something like that.

The cake was delicious. I forgot my negative feelings and felt happy that Sophie had discovered about my birthday. We talked more about the house, and which were the best weddings and shooting days. Then Alice brought the part of the cake that we could not eat in a box to take home with the bill.

'I hope you had a good birthday,' she said.

'I did,' I said. 'Thank you for singing.'

Out of the side of my eye I saw Sophie rolling her eyes.

'Come on then, let's go,' she said.

As we were leaving, Alice held the door open for us.

'Goodbye,' Alice said to Sophie and Richard.

'Nice to meet you,' I said.

'Maybe see you around some time,' she said, looking at me very directly.

'I'd like that.'

'Well, you know where I am. I'm always here and to be honest I could do with some distraction.'

'I'm sure I can think of something to distract you,' I said.

I thought Richard and Sophie were too far to hear anything but I looked up and saw they were watching. As we came out of the pub and the door closed behind us, Richard turned and put his arm around me.

'Think you might have scored there,' he said, squeezing my shoulder. 'She was pretty sexy too.'

'Richard,' I said, to make him stop.

As Sophie was getting into the taxi she gave me one of her cold, hard looks.

'Richard, you come in the back with me,' she said, smiling at him. 'Mirka you go in the front.'

All the way home Sophie and Richard were laughing and kissing in the back of the car. I knew Sophie was trying to make me jealous. I just looked out of the window at the dark trees and tried not to listen. I thought about how much I enjoyed talking with Alice. She was like me. We were approximately the same age. And most important, she probably was not married. We could be friends at least. It would be good to have a friend. And maybe one day we could be more. But my life at the house was too complicated already. I needed to think about what I wanted. Things were not right.

When the taxi arrived outside the front door, I took a twenty-pound note from my wallet and gave it to the driver.

'Call it sixteen,' I said, copying Richard from the journey to the pub.

'Put that away,' Richard said. 'Don't under any circumstances take that. Here, look, take this.' Richard took a note from his wallet and gave it to the driver. 'Keep the change.'

'Please, Richard, let me pay for something,' I said. 'You paid for the meal.'

'Don't be silly, this is my treat. You hold on to it.'

I put my money away. I was angry with Richard. It would have been more generous to let me pay, I thought.

Sophie tried three times before she got the key inside the lock. She was bent over, her face next to the lock, shaking because she was laughing. Richard was laughing too. I felt impatient with them. They were always drunk.

'Who wants a nightcap?' Richard said when we were in the kitchen.

'I am going to bed,' I said.

'Come on, it's your birthday. Just one,' Richard said.

'Really, I'm going to bed,' I said.

'Let her go, Richard, you know she doesn't like drinking,' Sophie said in a bitter voice, her words blurry from the alcohol.

'Good night,' I said.

I walked away and I could feel them watching me. Then I heard their laughter as I walked up the stairs. I was tired of them. It was true they had been kind and they had given me a lot. Especially on my birthday. But sometimes it seemed that they both wanted something from me and they did not like it when I gave what they wanted to other people.

The next day I got up and went to the barn. I felt strange and sad, as if I had no energy left any more. I lifted the lid of the freezer and stared for a long time at the animals until I remembered what I was supposed to be doing. The animals were mixed, with no two animals of the same kind, and I wrote them down on a list. Then I sat down and started to draw the plans for my next scene.

I could not concentrate on my work and kept looking out of the dirty windows into the rain. Brown leaves were blowing from the trees. I needed something to change. I thought of Otto in London and Alice going to Mexico City. I imagined myself walking along the streets looking at all the new things with them. I knew the best of my experiences at the house were in the past. In the summer I had been so happy, happier than I had ever been. But that was because I was in love. And now it was over. There was no reason for me to stay. The only reason I was staying was because I had so much work to do for Caleb. But, I thought, I could work somewhere else.

I decided I should tell them immediately. I put down my pencil and walked quickly to the house. I was afraid if I did not do it, I would change my mind.

Sophie was not in the kitchen or at her desk. I went to Richard's study and gently pushed open the door, knocking at the same time. He was talking on the telephone with his feet on the desk, winding the curly line around his fingers. He waved for me to come in. I sat on the chair opposite him and waited. On the wall there was a new deer head, the one that Richard killed in the summer.

'OK, bye bye now,' Richard said.

He smiled at me and put the telephone down. I could tell he was in a good mood, full of energy.

'Well, if it isn't my favourite Slovak taxidermist,' he said. But he frowned when he saw my expression. 'Is everything all right? You've been a bit quiet recently.'

'I'm OK,' I said.

'Come on, tell Uncle Richard all about it. Are you happy? Is there anything we can do to make you happy? Because your happiness is my number one concern. Numero uno.'

He was smiling so honestly at me that I felt bad.

'It's nothing to do with you.'

'Good, because quite frankly we couldn't survive without you. Seriously, Mirka, we love having you here. We really do.'

I realised I could not say it. I did not want to leave them, not yet. Even if it would be more painful in the end. I felt like something was not finished.

'So tell me,' Richard said. 'What's up?'

'Well, I wanted to ask if I can go to London to see Caleb.'

I only thought of it at that moment, but I realised it could be a holiday that I needed.

'Of course you can, you don't even need to ask.'

'Thanks.'

'So tell me something. If you could live any place at any time, where would you live?'

'Hmm,' I said. 'Why do you ask?'

'No reason. I was just listening to the radio this morning and it made me think of it, that's all.'

'I don't know, probably Berlin in the twenties and early thirties. Before the Nazis ruined it.'

'Why?'

'Because in my imagination it is a paradise full of artists and gay people and interesting nightclubs. You can be very liberated and sunbathe naked in the parks.'

'Funny,' Richard said, stroking his chin to tease me. 'Hadn't got you down as a sunbather.'

'OK, maybe I am more in the bars talking with the gay people.'

'Well, I get it. I can see you there, actually. Hanging out at the Kit Kat Klub, cigarette holder between your fingers.' He put two fingers to his mouth and took a breath on an imaginary cigarette.

'And you, where would you live?' I asked.

'Well, I know it sounds stupid, but I would have liked to have been alive during the War. The Second World War, I mean. I think it was an interesting time. And I would have liked to have fought for my country. The radio programme was about soldiers who fought in Burma. That's what made me think of it.'

'Yes, that does sound stupid,' I said.

Richard jerked his head back. 'Why do you say that? I think there are lots of people who feel the same. It seems a perfectly normal and noble sentiment to me.'

'You want to live in a war so you can kill people and have your legs exploded by a bomb?'

'Well, obviously not. But to me it seems like a time when everyone knew what was good and what was evil and they were prepared to fight for what was good. And to die for it.'

'What about the men in the convalescent home? Do you think they are happy? Walking around with naked feet and afraid of the noise of guns?'

Richard looked at me like he was annoyed that I was not more impressed with his choice. 'I just wish I had had the chance to do something truly great in my life,' he said. 'My grandfather was involved in the D-Day landings.'

He reached behind him and took a silver frame off the top of the shelf and passed it to me. It was a black-and-white picture of a man who looked like Richard, but with a smaller mouth, wearing a uniform with some medals on the chest.

As I looked at it, Richard continued talking.

'They were trying to stop the Germans getting reinforcements to the beaches in Normandy, so they made a plan to blow up the bridges along the canal that ran behind them to stop the tanks. They couldn't fly planes over and parachute the men out because of the noise of the engines. So they used gliders. My grandfather was in one of them.'

I passed him the photograph and leant back in my chair with my arms crossed.

'They were called flying coffins,' Richard continued. 'No wheels, just rails. The first one had to land on the barbed wire so they could get over the fence. And they did all of this in the dark. Can you imagine doing anything like that in your life?'

'No,' I said. 'But just because you are not killing people in a war it doesn't mean your life is not a good life. War is not a stupid game with guns and radios running around the woods.'

'OK, fine. But in your little paradise of queers and degenerates you don't particularly like the Nazis either. And they certainly don't like you. So someone needs to stand up and fight for your way of life.'

'You forget you were not very enthusiastic about protecting my country from the Nazis.'

'What do you mean?' Richard said, frowning.

'When they invaded Czechoslovakia I think what Britain said was, "No, it's OK, Mr Hitler, you can have it."'

'Oh, touché!' Richard said. 'But that wasn't really Slovakia, was it? Wasn't Sudetenland up the Czech end? What happened to Slovakia? Do you know, I did A-level history and I can't remember any of this stuff.'

'Slovakia became independent in the war and fought with

the Germans. One country became two countries on opposite sides. That is why I think war is stupid. One village further and you can be on a different team.'

'I never knew that.'

'It is more complicated because there was a big rebellion. But we do not have the same proud relationship with war like you do with your poppies.' I nodded to the paper poppy Richard was wearing on his jumper.

'Point taken. All right, you can go now,' he said. He took his feet off the desk and picked up a pen. 'I need to get on with my work.'

I left his study and went back to the living room to Sophie's desk. I opened the computer. There was an email from Otto. The magazine was having a party the next week and I was invited. I wrote back and said I would love to come. On the same day I could go and see Caleb in the shop and then go to the party. I was excited.

I took the train to Paddington and then the pink tube line to Liverpool Street. It was the middle of the day and the tube was not so full. There were some Italian tourists wearing the same puffy coats with horizontal lines of stitches and fur around the hood. They were talking loudly and I heard one of them say 'Tate Modern'. A woman with dyed pink hair was listening to music on her headphones. The boy sitting next to me was playing a computer game on his phone. An old woman came in and the businessman opposite me got up so that she could sit down. I watched everyone coming through the doors like I had not seen people for months. I had not seen people like these for months. Everyone was different and I knew they all had interesting stories.

At Liverpool Street I changed tube and took the red line one stop to Bethnal Green. I did not know which exit was the right one, but I walked up the nearest stairs and came out on a busy road junction next to a pub. The sky was bright blue. There was a man with a blanket sitting on the pavement with a dog asleep next to him.

'Spare any change, love?' he said.

I took out my wallet and gave him a pound coin. Then I looked at the map I had drawn on a piece of paper to find Caleb's shop. I saw the sign, *Bethnal Green Road*, on the wall above me, so I walked under the bridge along the street.

The shop was very close but I felt like I never wanted the journey to end. As I went past all the different places – estate agents, kebab shops, pubs, shops with vegetables outside, betting shops, markets selling clothes and towels and rolls of wallpaper   I stared at the people. They were all making their lives in London, I thought. I realised I was jealous. I had been sad and lonely and so I had run away.

In front of me I saw a young woman and a man, obviously a couple from the way they were laughing and touching each other, looking at something in a shop window. They were bent over, pointing at something. When I got closer I saw that it was *Rats at the Office Party*.

'Hey, would you mind taking a picture of us,' the woman said.

'No problem,' I said.

The woman got out her mobile phone from her rucksack and

gave it to me. She brushed her blonde hair a few times with her fingers so that it flowed over her coat shoulders. They stood with their arms around each other next to the window posing and smiling, and I took a few pictures.

'It's cool, isn't it?' the woman said.

I could not say anything, so I just nodded, but I felt proud. I liked that all the people of London could see something I made when they were walking past on the street. After the couple had gone, I looked at the scene for a moment. It was my best work, I thought, especially the two rats having sex against the wall in the stationery cupboard.

I opened the door to Caleb's shop and went inside. It was full of taxidermy animals and heads. Many were exotic animals I did not know the names of. I recognised the parrots and the heads of the zebra and the gazelle. On the walls there were frames full of butterflies and beetles. There were some skulls in piles. Some of them looked human. A taxidermy cat with the wings of a white bird was flying above them. There were also some small animals like a lizard and a baby pig in glass jars full of liquid. If anyone wanted to be reminded of dying, this was the shop.

Caleb came up the stairs wearing a black cape. He kissed me on each cheek.

'Hello, hello. Doesn't it look grand? I've sold it, but I've asked them to let it stay on display for a bit.'

'I'm very happy,' I said.

'Good. Now what about this exhibition? I was thinking the end of February. Do you think you can make eight pieces or so by then?'

'I think so, if I work very hard. I have enough ideas. But could you help me find animals? Only ones that would be dead anyway.'

'I'm sure I can accidently gas a few rabbits.'

'I'm serious.'

Caleb put his hand on his chest. 'I promise no animals will be harmed in the making of your art. And any help you need with procuring materials, just let me know. I can get anything.'

'Thanks.'

'I mean *anything*.' He put his finger to his nose.

'OK.'

'Now, can I buy you lunch? There is a great pie and mash shop down the road, a real Edwardian East End one.'

'I would love lunch,' I said. 'But I feel like I have eaten pie and mash nearly every day for months. Can we eat something different?'

Caleb laughed. 'Fair enough. Right, a challenge.' He rubbed his hands. 'What do you want? We've got Vietnamese, pizza, kebabs – not crap ones. I mean, proper Turkish ones – there's a curry house on the corner. I think that's about it.'

'Can we have Vietnamese, please?'

'We certainly can. I think you've made the right choice there. The one down the road does an excellent salt-and-pepper squid with a purple basil dipping sauce.'

'Yum,' I said.

We walked down the road for about ten minutes and went into a restaurant with a picture of a waterfall that was lit by special lights so that the waterfall seemed to be really flowing. The waiter behind the bar smiled and waved us towards a table next to the window. He came over with two menus.

'All right, Duong. How's tricks?'

'Not too bad. You?'

'Can't complain. Now, what am I going to have? Can I have a green tea?' He looked at me. 'Do you want a green tea?'

I nodded.

'Actually,' Caleb said, 'shall I order? Do you trust me?'

'I trust you.'

'OK, we'll have the Bo Nam Beef, soft shell crab, salt-and-pepper squid, a green papaya salad and the summer rolls. And some spring rolls – fuck it, why not?'

After the waiter had gone, Caleb said, 'I have the same stuff every time. If you deviate, it only leads to disappointment.'

'It sounds delicious.'

'So how is everything down at the house?'

'It's OK,' I said.

Caleb looked at me with narrow eyes as if he could tell I was not saying something. 'Just OK?'

'It's complicated.'

'Well, you can tell me anything. I shan't breathe a word to anyone.'

'I had an affair with Sophie,' I said.

'Whoa there,' Caleb said, breathing out. 'I was not expecting you to say that. Though I must admit, I can see the attraction.'

'I said it was complicated.'

'Does Richard know?'

'Richard knows something. But he does not seem to mind, which makes me think he does not know everything.'

'Sounds like a messy situation. What are you going to do?'

'I need to leave the house. But I can't. It's like I'm stuck.'

The waiter brought the squid rings and the soft shell crab. Caleb took a bite of one of the legs.

'Fuck me, that's delicious. Anyway, you were saying?'

'I betrayed Richard. Things will probably not get better. I should leave before I cause more pain to everyone.'

I took a squid ring and dipped it in the green sauce. It tasted a bit like soap, but in a good way.

'Look, don't be so hard on yourself. All's fair in love and war and all that. You can't stop people falling in love. The most important thing is to protect yourself. From the sounds of things, I would say you need to get the hell out of there.'

'You are right.'

'Come to London. Find your own people. Richard and Sophie, I love them dearly, but they live on another planet.'

After I said goodbye to Caleb I walked all the way down the Bethnal Green Road. I felt so much better from talking to someone. Ahead of me the sun was going down and the sky was pink. There were a few hours until I had to meet Otto at the party so I had a coffee in a coffee shop and then walked around the shops near Brick Lane and Spitalfields market. In the window of one shop I saw a beautiful grey shirt hanging. It was probably too expensive, I thought. But then I remembered I had money, so I went inside.

The shop was full of beautiful, simple clothes. Mostly black or grey. It was like my heaven. I found the shirt and looked at the label. It was not too much and I had not bought anything since I came to England.

I went over to the man behind the desk. He was tall and thin, with dark brown skin and his hair shaved at the sides so it was like a cube on top of his head. He was very handsome and I wondered if he was a model.

'Can I try this, please?'

'Of course! Have you got the right size? Let me see.'

I passed him the shirt and he looked at the label.

'Uh huh, that should work.'

I went into the little room and pulled the curtain closed. As soon as I put on the shirt I knew it was perfect. I looked in the mirror and made some poses. Suddenly I remembered Sophie from that day when she bought me the Barbour and wellies. I had been so happy that I had made her laugh. I felt a little sad that she was not there with me.

'Let me see, let me see,' the man said behind the curtain.

I came outside the little room and posed for the man. Then I turned around.

'Oh my gosh, you look fabulous!'

'Really?'

'Darling, you have a figure to die for, you could wear a bin bag and you'd still look gorgeous. But that shirt, seriously, nobody is going to be able to take their eyes off you. Now, if I can make one suggestion . . .' I stood still while the man came and closed my top button. His face was very close to mine and I looked away so that I would not be staring at him. He smelt of expensive perfume. He turned me around to the mirror. 'You can wear it open, but I think it looks more elegant like that.'

'Thanks,' I said smiling. He was right about the top button. 'OK, I'm going to buy it. Can I wear it now?'

'Of course. Going anywhere special?'

I got out my bank card from my wallet. 'A magazine party.'

'Well, get you! You are going to be the belle of the ball.'

'Oh stop!' I said, joking with the man. I picked up my bag and went to the door. 'Anyway, thank you for your help. I hope you have a nice day.'

The man smiled. 'You too, honey.'

The party was in a bar near Old Street. I had made another map to get there from Caleb's shop and it was not too difficult to find where I was. It was dark as I walked up Great Eastern Street. Ribbons of white and red car lights went past. Then I turned down a street to the left and I could see the bar ahead with a group of people smoking outside. I went to the woman on the door holding a board with a piece of paper.

'I'm here for the Craven party,' I said. 'My name is Mirka Komárova.'

The woman looked down the list and turned the page. 'There you are. Go straight downstairs. Cloakroom's on the right.'

As I pushed open the door at the bottom of the dark stairs I could hear the music and the noise of people shouting. I was suddenly quite nervous. I walked through the groups of people looking for Otto until I saw him in the corner talking to another boy with a beard and a girl in a black vest and jeans. They were all drinking beer from bottles. Otto waved at me.

'Mirka, great that you could make it. This is Matt and Jess.'

'Hi,' I said, shaking their hands.

'Mirka is the one I told you about, who makes the taxidermy scenes.'

'Oh yeah, I saw the photos,' Matt said. 'Those are so cool. They must take you hours.'

'Yes, they take quite a long time,' I said.

'I loved the one with the chicks,' Jess said.

'You haven't got a drink,' Otto said. 'Come with me, I'll take you to the bar.'

We leant on the bar and talked while we waited for the barman to bring us beers. I told him about the exhibition. He told me about the next issue of the magazine, which was going to be the biggest ever. It would be finished before Christmas.

'Two Blue Armadillos,' the barman said, putting the bottles down in front of us.

I got out my wallet from my pocket.

'No, it's cool,' Otto said. 'We've got a tab. Drinks are free until it runs out.'

We went back to Matt and Jess and stood talking loudly about different things: films, music, art exhibitions and new restaurants. I spoke to Otto about what it was like to live in Peckham. He had a French bulldog called Omelette who his girlfriend left him with when she went back to Berlin. Secretly, he wanted to write film scripts. But it was hard because he had so much work for the magazine. Matt was studying for a Master's degree in psychology. Jess was a spoken-word poet.

'By the way,' Jess said. 'I love your shirt. Where did you get it?'

'A shop called Philocaly near Brick Lane,' I said.

During the night I met many more people. A man called Christian who was a tattoo artist. A woman called Roxy from Detroit who sang in a jazz band. Amit, who was developing an app that would tell you if a medicine was genuine or fake. I told them about my life at the house and the weddings and the shooting.

'Wow, it sounds so different,' Amit said, looking impressed. 'Such a unique insight into a culture for you.'

I suddenly realised it must be late. 'What's the time, please?'

'Nine thirty,' he said.

'I have to go or I will miss the last train.'

I said goodbye to Otto and waved at everyone. I went upstairs and ran past the queue of people waiting to get into the bar in the direction of the station.

On the tube back to Paddington I thought about everything that had happened. My brain was full of all the pieces of information and stories that people had told me. I had never experienced a day like that before in my life or met so many different people. I realised I had been living in a very strange world. An interesting world. But a small one, with only a few people living in it. I was not sure that I could do it for much longer. I thought about what Caleb said about finding my people. I felt like maybe I had found some. I could come and make a life in London like them. I decided I would work hard for the exhibition and then I would leave. And I would ring Alice.

CHAPTER TWELVE

Sophie knocked on the door of the barn and came in quietly. I was in the middle of dressing a squirrel in a mumu. Sophie pushed down the hood of her blue coat as she came towards me.

'Are you ready? We should probably get going to the exhibition. I mean, you don't have to come with me if you're too busy, I know how much work you have to do. I just thought it might be nice to spend some time together. And it will be really boring if you don't come.' She smiled nervously.

'It's OK, I'll come.'

'It's not going to be anything special. It will be full of old people and—'

I interrupted her: 'I said I would come.' I sounded more impatient than I wanted to.

Sophie just nodded. I put the scissors back in the box and

moved the pink paper to the side. She looked down at the little roses I had made for the bouquets.

'What are you making?'

'Roses.'

'What for?'

I pointed to the glass box at the side of the table. She went and looked inside. The scene was decorated like an English country garden with flowerbeds of foxgloves and hollyhocks, delphiniums and peonies. At one end of the garden the squirrel and the rabbit, both wearing white dresses, were looking at each other, very in love. The wedding guests, a mixture of mice, rats, squirrels, rabbits and one guinea pig, were standing in a circle holding hands.

Sophie laughed. 'Lesbian wedding?'

'*Humanist Lesbian Wedding.*'

'Ha, very good. I should buy it and give it to my dad for Christmas.'

'He was my inspiration, actually.'

'Yes, well . . .' She looked down. 'Come on, let's go.'

We were silent as we drove to the town. I could feel Sophie next to me was trying to think of something to say. I looked out of the window at the naked winter trees, black against the sunset.

'Where is Richard?' I said, remembering that we did not see him in the house.

'Gone to the pub. He's drowning his sorrows after yesterday's debacle.'

'He is very unlucky with the shoots. Yesterday the weather was terrible.'

Sophie nodded slowly. 'Yes, but sometimes I wonder if it really is all down to luck. Obviously he can't control the weather. But there always seems to be something wrong: birds not behaving as they should, crazy dogs, foxes getting in the way, demanding people who aren't sporting when things go wrong and want their money back.'

'Poor Richard,' I said and Sophie was silent.

We parked in the car park behind the supermarket and walked along a tunnel through a building towards the square. Outside the town hall the trees were full of little blue lights. The circles of poppies were still leaning on the tall stone rectangle in the middle of the square. I followed Sophie as she walked to the big brick building.

There were not many people in the bright hall, only ten or eleven, mostly women holding wine glasses and talking quietly. Some were looking at the paintings on the walls. Sophie went towards the woman in a pale blue suit and pearl necklace sitting behind a desk.

'Sophie Parker plus one.'

'Ah, Sophie Parker, of course. You are most welcome.' The woman crossed out Sophie's name on a list and gave her a piece of paper. 'And there's your list of prices.'

I went towards the wall behind the desk. The first painting was of two oranges on a table with a white tablecloth. The artist had used a lot of blue in the shadows and in the wall behind the table.

Sophie came and stood next to me. 'Do you like that one?'

'I like the colours.'

'Well, I've got to buy one. So you can choose. You can keep it, if you like, as a souvenir.'

'So I can remember you after I leave?' I said, and was surprised by the bitterness in my voice.

'I didn't mean that.' Sophie sighed. 'Let's look at the others.'

We walked slowly around the room, looking at each painting. They were mostly of fruit and vegetables or the sea. We stopped in front of a picture of a dog and a monkey sitting on a piece of wood with some grass behind and some swings in the distance. The big grey dog with long black ears was smiling strangely. He had a confused expression in his eyes, which were looking in different directions. The monkey was smiling evilly.

'I think I can safely say that even I could do better than that,' Sophie whispered. 'And I have no artistic talent whatsoever.'

'The dog looks crazy and the monkey looks like he is masturbating.'

Sophie started laughing. 'That's not a monkey.'

'What is it?'

Sophie showed me the piece of paper with her finger. 'The painting is called *Two Dogs in the Park*.'

Sophie and I started laughing and then we could not stop. A woman in a purple dress standing next to us turned her head quickly and gave us a sharp look as if we were behaving badly. I thought how good it felt to share a joke with Sophie again after so long. I had missed her friendship.

'Shh,' Sophie said, holding my arm and pulling me towards the next painting. 'We mustn't laugh. It's for charity.'

The next picture was of a woman in a bath with her knees and breasts sticking out of the water, painted in thin, watery paint.

'I like this one,' I said.

'I bet you do,' Sophie said. 'Anyway, you can't have it – it's sold.'

'How do you know?'

'Look for one without a red dot.'

We walked past more paintings. I stopped next to one of the English countryside with a pattern of fields and trees stretching to the sky. It reminded me of when I first came to the house. Except that the fields were red and the trees were purple.

'This one,' I said.

Sophie looked at the painting with her head on the side. 'It's a bit garish.'

'I like it.'

'Yes, maybe you're right. It could be a forgotten expressionist masterpiece. Go and give the woman on the desk my name and get a red dot.'

When I came back from putting the red dot on the wall next to the painting, Sophie was talking to a glamorous woman in a tight, short black dress and diamond earrings.

I did not want to interrupt so I stood pretending to look at the paintings again. Then I saw Celia coming towards us. She was trying to get to Sophie but she had to pass me first.

'Hello …' Celia paused. 'I'm terribly sorry, I've forgotten your name. How dreadful of me!'

'It's Mirka,' I said.

'Of course it is. Did you come as Sophie's plus one? Is Richard here?'

'No, only me.'

'What a shame. I wonder why he couldn't come. And how are things at the house? I heard that not everything was going so well. Richard has been seen a few times a bit worse for wear in the pub.'

'He's fine.'

Celia did a little laugh. 'Yes, well, dear, I don't really know why I'm asking you this sort of thing, it's not like Richard and Sophie are going to make you privy to all the ins and outs of their lives.'

I lost my patience. 'You're right, Celia. Richard is at the pub. He's probably completely drunk.' I nearly said that we invited him to the exhibition and he said that he would rather eat his own scrotum, but I did not. 'He had lots of problems with the shoots, but the worst was your dog.'

I left Celia with her mouth open and walked off to look at the paintings. After a while I felt bored and went and stood on the steps outside in the cool air. In the square, an old man with a grey beard was sitting on top of a bench with his feet on the seat, smoking a cigarette and staring down at his can of beer. There was nobody else. It was a sad scene.

When I came back into the room, Sophie was standing on the stage. Everyone was looking at her. She bent her head and put her lips to the microphone.

'As many of you know this is a charity very close to my heart. My mother died of cervical cancer in 1999 and since then we have made huge advances in the treatment and detection of this disease, thanks in large part to the work of this charity. So I wanted to thank you for coming tonight and lending your support.'

She talked for a few minutes about the screening programme for the cancer and the increased numbers of women who were cured thanks to the research paid for by the charity. I was surprised at how elegantly and passionately she spoke. But underneath, I could see how nervous and emotional she was. Her hands were shaking and she had pink patches on her neck and the side of her face.

As I watched her, something happened to me. My heart filled with old feelings. It was like I had forgotten what she looked like and now I could see her again, beautiful and glowing, as I did before.

At the end of the speech, everyone clapped. Sophie came towards me.

'Let's go,' she said, taking my arm.

We started walking towards the door but Celia was there. She was smiling and holding her hands in front of her chest. She did not look at me as we came closer.

'Sophie, you were wonderful. Thank you so much.'

Sophie sighed loudly. 'I warned you I wasn't a good public speaker.'

Celia took Sophie's hands. 'Your mother would have been so proud.'

I looked at Sophie. I thought she would be angry with Celia for always talking about her mother as if she knew her better. But Sophie smiled. She was swallowing, trying not to cry.

'Thanks, Celia. I did my best.'

'You did, dear.'

Sophie was silent as we walked back through the car park. I could tell she was far away somewhere.

'I'll drive,' I said when we got to the car.

'It's OK, I only had one small glass.'

'Yes, but you are still shaking.'

Sophie looked down at her hands as if they were not hers. 'You're right. You drive.'

I drove out of the town along the main road and turned on to the narrow road through the woods. It was very dark.

'Well, at least that's over with,' Sophie said, sounding happier. 'I think I did all right. It felt like I was speaking too quickly and all I could hear was my heartbeat in my ears from being so nervous.'

'You were good. And you didn't seem so nervous.'

'Thanks.' She looked at me, smiling. 'And thank you for coming with me tonight. I know you've got all your exciting things going on with the exhibition and the magazine, but it meant a lot to me.'

'It's OK.'

She reached her hand towards me and brushed my hair gently behind my ear with her fingers. It was like electricity in the nerves of my ear.

'I've missed you,' she whispered.

I kept my eyes on the broken white line ahead. I was not driving quickly. Sophie pulled her seat belt to move closer towards me and kissed my neck. I put my head sideways so that she could not do it. Sophie acted like it was a game and put her hand on my thigh and started moving it upwards. This was exactly the reason I was angry with her, I thought, but at the same time, it was the reason why my body suddenly felt alive everywhere, like it had woken from a long sleep.

'Sophie, stop,' I said. 'It's dangerous.'

'Why are you angry with me?'

'I'm not angry with you. I'm trying to drive safely.'

She kissed my neck again and at the same time lifted up my sweater to stroke my stomach. I felt her fingers moving downwards into the top of my jeans. I reached down and took her hand out even though all I wanted to do was close my eyes and let her continue.

'Stop it, Sophie,' I said.

'I never know what you're thinking,' she said. 'You're completely impenetrable sometimes.'

She put her hand into my jeans again. I looked down quickly and put my hand on hers to take it out. When I looked up again, I saw two silver lights floating in the darkness. A deer was running across the road. Its white behind disappeared into the trees on the other side. I froze. Then another deer, even closer, bright in the lights of the car, crossed the road in front of us. I put my foot heavily on the brake. At the same moment, a deer jumped from the side of the road and hit the car. It made a screaming, not-human sound of flesh against metal, bounced over the front of the car and hit the window. I saw a flash of brown fur and a thin stick of leg. Then it fell over the side of the car.

The car stopped. Sophie and I were bent forward violently. Sophie had one arm over her head to protect herself, and the other hand still inside my jeans. She took her hand away and put her face in her hands. Then she started crying loudly, taking big breaths.

'Are you OK?' I said.

Sophie was still crying.

'Are you hurt?'

Sophie wiped her face with her hand. 'No, I'm fine. It's just the shock.'

I got out of the car and walked slowly back towards the deer. It was lying at the side of the road. I was afraid there would be a lot of blood. I hoped it might be alive and I could take it to a doctor, but I knew that was not going to happen.

When I got closer I saw that it was a female, still young. Her soft white belly was pink in the red lights of the car. There was no blood on her fur but her thin legs were bent unnaturally under her body like a spider's. When I saw her eyes, black like stones, I knew she was dead. I put my hand on her neck to see if I could feel her heart beating. Her body was warm and strong under my palm but there was no life. I sat down on the road next to the deer and stroked her head.

'I'm sorry,' I whispered, and tears came into my eyes.

The car door opened and Sophie's boots stepped on to the road. She walked slowly towards me with her hand on her mouth and got down on her knees.

'Is it dead?'

I nodded my head.

'I'm sorry.'

'She would be alive if you were not being so stupid.'

Tears ran down Sophie's cheeks making shiny red lines. 'I'm sorry.'

I was suddenly angry. 'You are a dangerous person, Sophie.'

'Don't say that. I didn't mean to hurt anything.'

'You don't care about other things. Everything is a game. Everyone is a toy for you to play with.'

Sophie looked hurt and confused. 'Why are you being like this?'

'You have no idea?'

'No.'

'Sophie, I loved you. I thought we were together. And then at the party I realised that I was just a toy for you and Richard. He knew about us all the time. Did you tell him everything?'

'Not everything,' Sophie said.

'But you told him we were having an affair?'

'I told him we had sex now and again when we were drunk.'

Now I was confused. 'Why wasn't he angry? Why does he not want to punch me in the face? Why hasn't he asked me to leave the house?'

'He wasn't angry.'

'I don't understand why he didn't care. What kind of husband does not care if his wife is fucking someone else?'

'Because you're a girl Mirka,' Sophie said. 'Not another man. He doesn't feel threatened by it. I don't know, maybe he doesn't think it's real or something.'

'But why did you tell him?'

'I don't know. Because he's my husband. It came up in conversation. Richard knows I had sex with girls at uni and then I told him about you. The possibility was there. If anything, he thought it was sexy.'

'That is disgusting,' I said. 'It is an insult.'

'Don't be stupid. You are blowing this all out of proportion. And frankly, you're not exactly innocent in all this. Richard isn't the one in the wrong here.'

I was silent. Sophie was right.

'Look,' she continued. 'The only reason Richard might have turned a blind eye to what was happening was because he knew

I was happy, when before I had been miserable. And the reason I was happy was because of you.'

Sophie was kneeling in front of me and she reached out her hand and touched my face.

'I love you, Mirka, I really do. I'm sorry for everything, for taking so long to realise how I felt. I've been an idiot.'

I looked into her eyes and saw that it was true. My heart melted. She leant forward and kissed me and I let her. It felt so good. I had forgotten what it was like to kiss her. Then I remembered that we were kneeling in the road with a dead deer next to us. It was typical of Sophie, I thought, for her to say the thing I wanted more than anything, at the worst time.

I pushed her away and stood up. 'Help me pick up the deer.'

Sophie looked confused. 'What are you going to do with it?'

'Take her to the house.'

'No, Mirka, we leave it here and report it. It's dead.'

'I'm not leaving her here at the side of the road for birds to eat her eyes. I will dig a grave and bury her.'

I got on my knees and put my hand under the neck of the deer. The body was heavy but I got my other arm under her stomach and lifted her. Sophie went and opened the boot of the car.

When we arrived at the house I drove to the barn and carried the deer to the freezer. It was empty and I put her inside on the floor with her legs under her like she was sleeping.

Sophie looked at me from the door of the barn with narrow eyes. 'Why are you putting it in there?'

'Because she can stay fresh while I dig her grave,' I said.

I looked at the deer for a moment before I shut the door.

Her eyes were sad, but peaceful. I decided then I could not put her in the cold, dark grave. I would taxidermy her. I would make her a beautiful, natural home with ferns and grasses to live in for ever. I had to do something for her after what I had done.

Sophie walked in front of me back to the house. We passed Richard's car parked at the back. In the kitchen there was a half-drunk bottle of red wine on the table and a dirty glass.

'I'll go up and check on him,' Sophie said.

I washed my hands in the sink, then poured myself some wine in a clean glass. After a couple of minutes Sophie came back. She took off her coat and scarf.

'He's out for the count.'

We looked at each other, knowing what this meant. Then she came to me and kissed me and pushed me backwards so that I was sitting on the table. She was kissing me very hard with her tongue deep inside me. I felt her pulling open the buttons of my jeans. For the first time I did not try and stop her, I just let her have control. She put her hand inside my pants and her fingers into me, moving them gently. After a while I opened my eyes and I saw my reflection in the window, the back of Sophie's head as she was kissing my breasts, my foot on the sink. Then I could feel myself coming and I shut them again.

'That was the best breakfast I've had in a long time,' the man said, putting his hands on his red jumper and stroking his belly.

The man was about thirty, with a small patch of thin blond

hair left at the front of his head and big soft lips. His wife or girlfriend was pretty, with blue eyes full of kindness and thick brown hair falling over her shoulders.

'I'm glad you enjoyed it,' I said.

'Far too big, though. I think I'm going to need a rest before I walk anywhere.' He twisted his head and looked behind him out of the window. 'What's the weather doing?'

It was raining sideways lightly, almost like a mist.

'Could you recommend a walk?' the woman said.

'Of course,' I said. 'If you walk down the drive there is a footpath opposite the gate. You follow it all the way up the hill and there is a pretty village on the other side. The pub there, The Snooty Fox, is good for lunch too.'

I thought of Alice. I was going to ring her after I came back from London, but then I had started things with Sophie again. It was a shame. I wished we had met at a different time.

The man was saying, 'That sounds like an excellent plan, shall we do that then?'

'Sounds perfect.'

'Where are you from?' I asked them.

'We're from London,' the man said. 'Just thought we'd take a few days off work and soak up some nature. We hardly seem to see each other because we both work so late. So it's nice to have a proper break, get out of town.'

The woman suddenly stuck out her hand towards me, her thin fingers bending upwards at the end. There was a ring on her fourth finger with a big, sparkling diamond.

'Jamie proposed to me yesterday,' she said proudly. 'We were walking across a field and suddenly the clouds cleared and the sun came out. I turned around, and there was Jamie, down on one knee.'

I held the end of the woman's fingers and looked closely at the ring. 'It's beautiful,' I said. 'Congratulations.'

'Thank you,' the woman said, taking her hand back. She twisted the ring, looking at it again, her eyes sparkling.

When I got back to the kitchen I put two pieces of bread in the toaster and took out the dish from the bottom oven with two sausages and some tomatoes for my breakfast. As I put the sausages on to the plate with a spoon, one of them rolled on to the floor.

Scrabble and Ringo, lying sleepily in their basket, immediately woke up. They stood up, treading on each other, racing to be the first to get to the sausage. One of the dogs got in front and ran towards my feet, but I bent down and picked up the sausage. I held it in front of him.

'Not for you . . . ' I looked at the white stripe in the dog's face. Scrabble's stripe went all the way down his face, separating his brown ears. This dog's white stripe was cut by brown in the middle. 'Not for you, Ringo.' He walked slowly back to the basket, his head hanging low.

I looked closely at the sausage, blew on it to get any dust or hairs off and put it on my plate.

Sophie came into the kitchen, wearing her coat and red gloves, and picked up her purse from the dresser.

'I've got to go shopping and then the garden centre. Can you do lunch?'

'Sure,' I said.

She bent down and kissed me on the mouth as she walked out of the kitchen.

Terri came to collect the dogs for the shoot. I washed up the dishes from breakfast, listening to classical music on the radio. Then I made a chicken pie and decorated it with a rose and two leaves made from pastry like Sophie did. While it was in the oven I carried the recycling to the bin near the gate and went to the barn to feed Sammy Twinkle.

The guns came at two o'clock and took off their wellington boots outside the entrance hall. I was carrying logs in my arms towards the fire as they came in.

'Hello,' I said to one man with thick white hair and a moustache. 'How did it go?'

'Not great,' he said. 'Only eighty-five.'

'I'm sure it will be better this afternoon,' I said. 'Hawthorns is the best drive.'

I turned the burning logs in the fire with the metal scissors and put the new logs on the top. From the shelf over the fire I took the little bell and rang it. The men who were standing around the entrance hall in their socks turned to look at me and stopped talking.

'If you would like to make your way to the dining room,' I said, pointing down the corridor. 'Lunch is served.'

When the men had gone, Richard came through the door rubbing his eyes with the end of his fingers.

'How's lunch?' he said, looking worried.

'Everything is perfect,' I said.

'You're a star,' he said. 'I can't hack anything else going wrong. The birds are not flying today. It's like they know what's going on.'

'Oh no.'

'It's not a disaster. I just wish it would go smoothly for once.' As he walked past me towards the dining room, his eyes looked up and down my body. 'Nice apron, by the way, it suits you.'

'Don't get used to it,' I said.

I put down the pie on the dining room table and cut into the brown pastry with a big spoon. Steam came from the hole. I could feel the men watching me hungrily as I put a piece of pie and some mashed potato on a plate and passed it to the man sitting to my side.

'Did you make this yourself?' he said, looking up at me.

'From scratch,' I said, even though all I had done was roll pastry from the packet.

'You must get very bored of pheasant,' he said.

'Yes,' I said. 'Personally I prefer partridge.'

'Me too!' the man said, looking excited. 'Great little bird, the partridge.'

I looked across the table and saw Richard shaking his head at me, trying not to laugh at my performance. I winked at him. It was fun to play our acting games and to share jokes together again. I felt completely comfortable with him, as if nothing had happened.

When the guns had gone home and I was clearing away the plates and cups from tea, someone knocked on the door. It was Terri. She was holding the dogs, who were completely covered in mud.

She passed me the leads. 'I'll leave these two reprobates with you.' She bent down and stroked their heads. 'That's right, I'm talking about you, you naughty dogs. But you enjoyed it, didn't you? Yes, you did.' She stood up again and gave me two pheasants tied with blue string. 'Those are for you too. See you round, Mirka.'

'Bye, Terri.'

I pulled the dogs to the little room and hung the pheasants on the hook on the back of the door. When I switched on the taps, the dogs started howling and walking in circles.

'Don't be silly,' I told them. 'You know you have to have a bath.'

When the sink was half-full of water I went to pick up Ringo but he ran in a circle around me. I turned around and trapped him in the corner.

'You think you are going to escape from me? I don't think so.'

I picked him up with his legs still trying to run and put him in the sink. He stopped moving and let me splash water on his legs and belly with my hand.

'Good dog,' I repeated.

I washed Scrabble and rubbed both the dogs with a towel. Then I gave them a biscuit each on my palm and opened the door. They ran away, their nails scratching on the floor.

All the work was finished so I poured some wine into a glass, took the blue pen from the pot next to the telephone and sat down with the crossword in front of me on the table. I read every clue looking for words to show me it was an anagram or double meaning, but I did not see any. As usual, the crossword was too difficult. But then I saw one clue, *Clean fixture for our feathered friends (8)* and I knew the answer immediately. I remembered Sophie showing me the bath on the day I arrived at the house. She had called it a fixture. *Feathered friends* was obviously *birds*. I picked up the pen and wrote *BIRDBATH* neatly in the boxes.

The next morning I went to the barn. The deer was defrosted and waiting for me. Before I cut her open, I measured all the distances on the body with the callipers and wrote the numbers in a notebook. I had never cut open such a big animal before and I was afraid I would not be able to do it right.

I took the sharp knife from the table and made a cut in the skin under the neck. I cut down the middle of the stomach. The fur was breaking apart and I could see the organs, fat and swollen, under a thin white shiny fabric. They looked like they were going to burst. I felt suddenly sick. It was very different to cutting open a mouse. I took a deep breath and pushed the hair from my face with my elbow.

At that moment Richard came into the barn. He put the gun against the wall and stood looking down at the deer, drinking his steaming coffee.

'You need to get rid of the guts,' he said.

'I know.'

He brought a plastic tray from under the sink and put it on the floor. Then he put his cup down on the table and picked up the deer.

'No,' I said. 'I want to do it.'

'OK,' Richard said, his voice warning me that I did not know what I was doing. 'I'll hold it. You pull them out.'

He picked up the deer and put her in the plastic tray with her legs open. With one hand he held her head against his thigh, and with the other hand he took his cup from the table and drank some coffee.

'You aren't wearing gloves,' he said.

I looked down at my hands like I was in a dream.

'I think you might want to put them on for this bit.'

The box of blue gloves was on the table and I took two and put them on. The organs were falling out of the cut in the stomach. At the bottom, grey tubes of intestine were bursting out in a bag made of white web. The red organs were above. Richard held open the top of the cut next to the ribs.

'You need to cut around the diaphragm. See that flap there,' he pointed to some material stretching around the ribs. 'Cut that.'

It was like a barrier holding up the organs and when I cut it, they fell down on top of the stomach. I cut up into the ribs to free the lungs and heart.

'Now cut the oesophagus.'

I cut across the white rubber tube in the neck.

'OK, get your hands in there at the top and drag the insides downwards.'

I did it quickly. It did not smell but the sound of it gave me needles under my skin. Afterwards there was a lake of thick red blood still inside the deer. Richard held her higher and I pushed back the legs and opened the cut so it could flow out into the tray.

Richard picked up the tray. 'I'll put this out for the kites.'

'No, I want to put it in her grave,' I said.

Richard shook his head. 'OK, you do what you have to do.'

It took all day to take off the skin. With one hand I cut

between the white fat and the skin, and with the other hand I pulled the fur back. I peeled the skin carefully over the head. At the end of it, the body of the deer lay on the table, white fat and patches of red muscle. Her skin was lying next to her. Her eyes of round black jelly were sticking out of the skull. It was disgusting. I was making the situation worse, I thought. But I could not put the skin back on the deer, or the insides back inside. Or drive the car backwards from hitting her.

We buried the deer's body the next day. It was a cold grey afternoon. Richard had dug a grave next to the big pine tree at the front of the house and we carried the two bags from the freezer there, one bag with the organs, one with the body. The legs were too hard to bend so we put the deer on her back with her legs sloping against the wall. At the end of the grave we put the frozen lump of intestines and organs. Richard started to throw earth on top of her with the spade. I took some earth in my hand and threw it into the grave.

Sophie walked over the grass towards us and stood next to me, rubbing the top of my arm. Richard kept putting earth on top of the deer until the grave was full.

Richard stood back and leant on the spade. 'Do you want to say anything?'

I looked down at the grave. 'I'm sorry I killed you before you could experience your life.'

'I'm sorry too,' Sophie said. 'For the part I played in your death.'

We stood for a minute in silence, looking at the grave. I was thinking that the skin of the deer was in the barn, curing.

When it was finished I would make the deer whole again, and put her in a beautiful home. But now I was not sure which part of the deer was really the deer. The important parts of the deer – the heart, the eyes, the brain – were in the grave. All I had was the skin. What was I doing?

Sophie put her hands together. '*Our Father*,' she said. '*Who art in heaven. Hallowed be thy name.*'

Richard looked at Sophie and rolled his eyes. But then he joined her. '*Give us this day our daily bread.*'

I did not know the words and listened silently. It felt right to say something serious like the prayer and I was grateful to them.

When it was finished, Sophie looked up at the sky and put out her palm. 'Let's go in. I think it's going to rain.'

Richard looked down at the grave. 'Rest in pieces, little deer.'

'Richard!' Sophie hit him on the arm. 'You always have to lower the tone.'

'I can't help it!' Richard started laughing.

Sophie tried to hit him again and he stepped back, holding his arm.

'Ow. Come on, how could I resist that? It was a gift.' He stopped laughing and looked at me. 'Sorry, sorry.'

I could not help smiling. For a moment I felt that we were back to the old times, when the three of us were always together laughing. Maybe things could be the same again, I thought. We could all be happy together. But then I thought that maybe the reason that we were balanced again was because he knew Sophie and I were together. He knew, and he did not mind. This made me feel strange.

There were plates of sandwiches and biscuits on the kitchen

table, covered in plastic film. We took off our boots on the mat and Sophie hung our jackets in the little room. Richard sat down and crossed his feet in red socks on a chair.

'Tea, anyone?' Sophie said.

'I think I'm going to need something stronger than tea after that little performance,' Richard said.

I sat opposite him at the table. 'Thank you for doing that,' I said. 'It was important to me.'

Sophie opened a bottle of red wine and poured two glasses. She gave one to Richard and one to me. I took a ham sandwich from the plate. Sophie was chopping some carrot into long sticks and she brought the plate of them to the table with a glass of lemonade.

'David was in today,' Richard said.

'Oh?' Sophie said.

'The Australian who bought the priory is bringing in his own guy. Wants to do a massive overhaul.'

'Is he keeping David too?'

Richard shook his head. 'No.'

'Oh no,' Sophie said. 'Poor David. Can we find him some more hours?'

'You know we can't. He'll be fine. There'll be something.'

'That's bad form though. Not a great way to ingratiate yourself with a community.'

Richard shrugged. 'That's life,' he said. He turned to me. 'So we need to talk about something.'

My stomach felt empty. I tried to look normal. 'What?'

'Christmas.'

I felt myself breathing out heavily. 'What about Christmas?'

Richard looked at Sophie. 'We were thinking that maybe we could have carp for Christmas. Would you like that?'

He looked at me with a hopeful expression that made me smile. I loved him so much sometimes. He could always surprise me with his kindness.

'Only if I don't have to kill it.'

'Excellent news. I've never really been a big fan of turkey anyway.'

'You have never eaten carp.'

Richard put his head back and laughed. 'I can't wait.'

Sophie looked happy. 'It will be just the three of us. You'll be pleased to hear that my father is staying in France.'

'Your first Christmas in England,' Richard said.

'No, I was already here last year,' I said. 'I had Christmas Day alone. I walked along the Holloway Road. It was raining and I found a McDonald's that was open so I went in there and—'

'Stop,' Richard said, holding up his hand. 'I can't bear it. That is the most depressing thing I have ever heard.'

Sophie was laughing. 'We will try and do a little bit better than that. You poor thing. I literally can't think of anything worse.'

'Thanks,' I said. 'I am very excited about having Christmas here with you.'

Sophie and I were lying in bed after sex. It was the afternoon and Richard was out in woods on the bike feeding the birds. I pulled up the covers over our bodies and put my head next to hers on the pillow so that the ends of our noses were almost touching. Her eyes were closed and I watched the curvy line of her white eyelashes move against her skin like the hairs of a moth.

'Sophie,' I said.

She opened her eyes. 'That sounds ominous.'

'Something is not right.'

'What do you mean?'

'I mean us. I can't enjoy being with you because I know I have to leave you. So it's painful.'

'You didn't care in the summer.'

'I know. I was more . . .' I could not think of how to say it.

'In love? Have your feelings changed?'

'No. Of course not. But now, after everything, I know what will happen.'

'Look, we both love each other. Why can't we just enjoy it?'

'Because I can't stay here for ever with you.'

Sophie lifted her head and rested it on her palm. She was smiling and leaned forward and kissed me. 'Why not?'

'I have to go one day. I can come and visit you.'

'Yes, but don't. Stay here for ever.'

'You know it's impossible.'

'Stranger things have happened.'

'Are you going to take me to your dinner parties? Hello, everybody, this is Richard's other wife.'

'Hey, you would be my wife, not Richard's!'

'And they would think that was normal?'

'I don't care what anybody else thinks.'

'That's not true. And it's not right for Richard.'

'Oh, Richard doesn't care. He just wants an easy life.'

'He knows, doesn't he?'

'No.'

'You're lying.'

'I don't know. Maybe. I haven't said anything.'

I said nothing. I still thought she was lying. There was something about Richard knowing that made me uncomfortable. I did not like feeling that I was the one with the least knowledge in the situation.

Sophie put her palm on my cheek. 'All I know is that before you arrived I was unhappy. I was lonely. Richard and I fought all the time. I don't know how or why, but you've brought happiness to the house. And when something like that happens maybe it's better to just be thankful and not question it.'

We lay in silence for a minute. Sophie was stroking my arm. Behind the curtains I could hear the sounds of the rain hitting the glass.

'Sophie, you don't understand,' I said. 'I love you, but—'

Her blue eyes looked at me. 'What don't I understand?'

'One day I want to find someone I love who is only for me. I want to live with them until I am old. Maybe I want children, maybe not. But if I have children it will be for two of us. I can't be in a relationship with three people.'

Sophie put her head under the covers between my breasts like she was trying to hide. I kissed her hair and put my arms around her head. The gold clock said five minutes past three o'clock.

'I'll leave Richard then,' she said.

'What?'

Sophie's head came up out of the covers. 'I said I'll leave Richard.'

'Don't say that,' I said. 'I know it's not true.'

319

She opened her mouth to argue and then closed it again. She looked at me with an expression like a child. Then her eyes filled with liquid. 'Please don't leave me,' she said. 'Not yet.'

I kissed her forehead. 'I'm not going anywhere yet.'

The conversation was exactly like I knew it would be. There was no solution. I would stay for Christmas and then I would go. It made me sad thinking about it, but the sadness was already everywhere. Every time I touched Sophie, every time I kissed her, I did not feel alive like I did before. I still loved her, but our bodies were dirty with the lies of the past and the pain of the future.

The glass box for the deer was ready. I had painted a waterfall on the back wall, with trees around it and the sun shining in the blue sky. And on the green floor I had put rocks, grasses, soft moss, and ferns.

I was working late in the night because I wanted to finish it. The deer had the new body inside her. I sewed the cuts in the skin carefully with white cotton, putting extra wood wool inside so the deer would not be too thin. I had not put the eyes into the holes yet, so it looked like her eyes were closed. I could not decide on the best pose. I tried putting her lying down with her legs under her like she was resting, but it reminded me of her death, so I put her standing up, with her head lifted as if she had just heard a noise. This made her seem the most alive, I thought.

As I was moving one of her legs forward, the deer suddenly opened her eyes. She had an expression of pure evil, like she hated me and wanted to hurt me. Her eyes were unnaturally big and glowing black. She opened her mouth and growled, showing me her sharp teeth. I stepped backwards into the chair behind me. It fell over making a loud noise. The deer stepped towards me, her head bent down like a bull, still making a frightening growling noise and scraping the table with her foot like she was going to jump on me and kill me.

I screamed and my own scream woke me up from the dream. My face was covered in sweat and I felt like my heart was about to explode. I lay breathing, trying to calm myself. The dream seemed so real. I could not get the image of the evil deer out of my mind or push away the feeling that I had done something very wrong.

Light was escaping into the room at the edges of the pink curtains. I pulled the fabric. For a second I thought that the world had disappeared and there was only a thick grey material pressing against the window. But it was just a cloud, I realised. I got out of bed, put on my clothes and went to the barn.

The deer was finished, standing in her new home. I sat down in front of her. Her eyes stared back at me, dead and cold, with no life inside them, like they would stare back at every person who looked at them for ever. It was nothing like the look between the deer and me that summer evening in the woods when I had been walking with Sophie, a look between two pairs of eyes, human and animal, so quick, full of energy and surprise.

Around the eyelashes I could see some glue. At the corner of one of the eyes there was a small hole showing the fake white skull underneath where I had not put the skin in the right position. I had told myself I was doing it for the deer but I had only done it for myself, to give me comfort and make me feel less guilty. But it gave me no comfort to see her in the box. I did not understand how the stuffed Misty could have helped the man. There was nothing left of the real animal. Everything important was in the grave. This was just the skin. All I could see in front of me was a fake scene with a fake deer inside and all I felt was guilt for the terrible violence that I had done to her dead body.

I took a pair of scissors and cut along the lines where I had sewed her skin. Then I peeled the skin off and took it outside, picking up the spade that was leaning against the wall at the entrance to the barn.

The cloud was so thick I could not see the house as I dug into the grave next to the pine tree. The soil was still loose and easy to dig. When the hole was deep enough, I put the deer's skin inside so that it could be with the rest of her body and it could rot into the earth like it was supposed to.

'I'm sorry,' I said again.

I walked back towards the house with the spade resting on my shoulder. The cloud was getting thinner and glowing in the sunlight. I decided that I would never taxidermy anything again. I felt sick thinking about it. I would find something new to do. There would always be new ideas. This one was finished. Ahead of me the sun shone on the grass through the mist that seemed to be flowing away, trying to escape the light.

CHAPTER THIRTEEN

I held the wooden box while Sophie took out the shiny red and gold balls to hang on the Christmas tree. The white lights in a spiral around the branches shone like tiny stars in their curved mirror surfaces. In the box, lying in the paper, there were also snowflakes made from pearls and small painted wooden statues of kings and shepherds with red ribbons coming out of their heads. I pulled out a glass ball with a reindeer inside. I shook it so that it snowed.

'What is this one?'

Sophie was standing on her toes to put one of the balls on the highest branches. She put her arm down and looked at the reindeer and smiled.

'One year Camilla and I were allowed to choose a decoration for the tree and I chose that one.'

'It's pretty.'

'Grab me that chair, would you?'

I put down the box and went to pick up the wooden chair next to the fire.

Sophie climbed on to the chair. 'I need the angel now.'

I passed her the paper angel and Sophie put her over the top of the tree with the branch pointing up her skirt. Richard came down the stairs.

'Hey, what's going on here? Don't do that,' Richard said when he saw Sophie. 'You shouldn't be standing on chairs.'

Sophie twisted her body to look at him. 'I'm fine, don't be ridiculous.'

Richard walked over to her, put his arms around her and lifted her from the chair.

'What are you doing?' she said, laughing and kicking her legs.

'I'm looking after you like a responsible husband.' He kissed her and put her feet on the floor. He looked up at the tree. 'It's enormous.'

'You can blame Mirka for that, it was her choice.'

'Why can't Sophie stand on a chair?' I said. As soon as I spoke, I knew the answer.

Sophie looked at the floor with a shy, almost guilty expression and then looked at Richard. Richard nodded.

'Actually, we have something to tell you,' she said.

Richard put his arm around her. 'Sophie's going to have a baby.'

Even though I knew what he would say, the words were strange to hear. Then I realised I had to react, so I made myself smile. 'That is very good news. I'm happy for you.'

They were looking at each other, smiling. I had never seen them looking so happy. And I was happy for them, they wanted a baby so much. But at the same time I knew this was the end. Everything was over. Me and Sophie, my time living at the house. There was no confusion now.

Richard looked at me as if he could hear my thoughts. 'Of course we want you to stay with us. We are going to need you more than ever.' He put his palm on Sophie's stomach.

'Yes,' Sophie said. 'Nothing has to change at all.' But then she looked quickly at the floor.

'When will it be born?' I asked.

'Not until May,' Sophie said.

'How long have you known?'

'I've had my suspicions for a while now, but then I took a test a couple of weeks ago.'

I thought of all the times we had been together. She had known she was pregnant and she did not tell me. She had probably known since the night we hit the deer and she let me fall in love with her again.

I thought of something. 'But you've been drinking and smoking.'

'No I haven't,' she said, smiling. 'You just haven't noticed that I've stopped.'

I tried to remember the last time I saw Sophie smoking a cigarette or drinking. It was true, she had not been smoking.

'You were drinking at the exhibition.'

'I only had a glass of wine.'

Sophie looked very pleased with herself and Richard looked up proudly at her. She had known then, I thought.

'Will you stay?' Sophie said. 'It would mean so much to us if you did.'

'Think about it anyway,' Richard said.

'I'll think about it,' I said. 'Anyway, congratulations.'

'Where are you going?' Sophie said.

'I need to do some things in my room,' I said.

I went upstairs and lay down on my bed, looking at the ceiling. I felt sad. What had I expected? I had been stupid to start things with Sophie again. I thought about packing my bag and leaving immediately. But then it would be obvious it was because of the baby. I decided I would stay until Christmas and then I would leave. I could not have another Christmas alone like the year before. Anything would be better. But then it was time to go and make my life somewhere different.

I went and sat at my desk. The pale blue wool scarf I bought for Sophie and the shirt with red and yellow squares I bought for Richard were folded next to a tube of gold paper and a ball of red ribbon. I rolled the tube across the desk and started to cut a piece to wrap the presents. There was a knock on my door.

'Wait,' I said, looking around for somewhere to put the presents. I put them under the covers.

'It's me,' Sophie said.

'OK.'

She came in and stood with her back against the door. I did not say anything.

'I'm sorry,' she said. 'I was going to tell you.'

'I'm used to it.'

'Nothing has to change.'

'You're completely crazy. Do you really think I will stay with you and Richard and the baby?'

Sophie looked down at her hands. When she looked up again, her eyes were full of tears. 'I love you, Mirka.'

I wanted to say, *I love you too*. But it would make things worse.

'I'm leaving after Christmas,' I said. 'Now please go. I have things to do.'

Sophie opened her mouth like she wanted to say something, but instead she just turned and went out of the room.

The next morning I was at the kitchen table, drinking coffee. Otto had sent me the magazine. On the cover was a picture of a man with a beard and black hat and a woman with long blue hair and a ring through her nose. Both were wearing fashionable black clothes and not smiling.

I looked through the pages until I saw a picture of me with my hand inside *Rats at the Office Party*. It was strange to see myself in a magazine. The article was called 'Death Becomes Her', with Otto's name below the title. Between the words there were more pictures of other scenes I made, like *Mice Raving* and *Freelance Squirrels*. The article was about the history of anthropomorphic taxidermy and there was the same picture of Walter Potter's *The Kittens' Wedding* that I saw with Sophie.

I read: *Mirka is someone who understands the philosophical nature of her art. How, in our strange condition of being simultaneously within and outside of the animal kingdom, we invest taxidermy with our longing for permanence.*

I closed the magazine. I did not want to read any more. It felt like it was about a different person who was not me, a person in the past. I drank some coffee watched the rain zigzag down the window. I could not stop thinking about what happened the day before. Did Sophie really think that the baby was a small detail and we could continue, all of us together, at the house? I did not understand her sometimes.

Without deciding to, I got up and went to the telephone. On the board next to the phone there were lots of cards for taxis, restaurants, plumbers and other services stuck with pins. I looked at them until I found the one that said, *The Snooty Fox*. I pressed the numbers.

'Hello, The Snooty Fox,' a man said.

'Hello,' I said. 'Is Alice there, please?'

'Yes she is. Just give me a minute.' There was a noise as he put the phone down. Then I heard him shouting, 'Alice.'

I changed hands and rubbed my palm on my jeans because I was sweating. I did not know what I was doing or what I would say.

After a few seconds someone picked up the phone. 'Hello,' Alice said.

'It's Mirka, I met you a few weeks ago at the pub. It was my birthday.'

'Oh hi, I was wondering if you were ever going to call me.'

'I'm sorry. I wanted to. So many things happened.'

'Well maybe you can tell me all about it over a drink some time.'

'I'd like that,' I said.

'You've certainly picked your moment. I don't have any time off until after Christmas now. But we stay open all the time, so you can drop in. Everyone mucks in and helps themselves to drinks. It's usually pretty rowdy.'

'That sounds fun.'

'Yes, come! I'd better go. Hopefully see you some time.'

'Bye,' I said as she hung up.

After I put the phone down I did not know why I called. I could not go to the pub on my own. What would I tell Sophie? And what was I hoping for? Alice was going to Mexico soon.

My coffee was cold and I threw the rest away. I took Henry from the cupboard and went to hoover the entrance hall. The Christmas tree had dropped a lot of needles. After a while I realised the phone was ringing. Then I remembered I was alone in the house. I switched the hoover off and went to pick up the phone.

'Hello, Fairmont Hall,' I said.

'Oh, it's you,' William said. 'Is my daughter there?'

'She went shopping,' I said.

William sighed angrily. 'Well, tell her to call me back as soon as she gets in.'

'Would you like me to give her a message?'

'Yes, tell her Tom isn't coming to France any more so we are coming over for Christmas. We're going to his on the twenty-second and then we'll come to you on Christmas Eve. Camilla gets into Heathrow early, so we'll pick her up on the way.'

'OK,' I said.

'Tell her to get a decent turkey. I know what's she's like.'

'OK.'

'And make sure the house is tidy this time. I want all the beds made up and the place looking jolly. Has she got a tree?'

'She has a tree.'

'All right, see you on the twenty-fourth.'

I put down the phone. This was the worst news. I was still excited about Christmas with Richard and Sophie, even after the news of the baby, but now I did not know if I wanted to stay. I would be a servant bringing them plates of mince pies and filling their wine glasses. William would say lots of things that would make me uncomfortable or humiliate me. But, even as I thought this, I knew I would not leave. At least, I thought, I could go and have a drink at the pub with Alice if I needed to escape.

After an hour, Richard and Sophie were still away from the house. I made the beds in the red room and the green room. Now the doorbell rang. I went downstairs and opened the door.

'Good morning,' I said.

It was Celia's purple hat and long blue wax coat. She looked up and I saw that her eyes were red from crying and moving around in a panicked way. She was holding some pieces of paper.

'What is wrong, Celia?' I said.

'Monty's gone missing,' she said. 'It's been two days and I'm beside myself with worry.'

'I have not seen him, I'm sorry.'

'I've been around high and low, looking for him. I've not slept or eaten. Whenever he's run off before, he's always come back. I don't understand it.'

She held the pile of paper towards me and I took one. In the middle of the page there was a big photograph of Monty. At the top it said, *MISSING. Can you help me find my beloved dog Monty. Jack Russell. Cash Reward*. Under the picture was Celia's address and telephone number.

'Can you help me put these up on your land?' she said. 'On stiles and gateposts. So that walkers will be on the lookout.'

'Of course I will.'

'He just disappeared from the garden. I'm terrified he's been dog-napped.'

'I am sure you will find him.'

'I heard that Romanian gangs are targeting terriers,' she continued. 'They sell them to people who run dog-fighting rings. They put them in with the big pit bulls to warm them up. As a starter.' Celia started to cry and sniffed loudly. She took out a tissue from her coat pocket, blew her nose and pressed the corner into her eyes. 'Apparently they like Jack Russells the most. Because they're such brave little dogs.'

'Celia, I am sure this is not what happened to Monty. We will find him.'

'My friend Edith said they are in town. The Romanians. They have been seen in the supermarket, asking for directions.'

'That doesn't mean they are stealing dogs.'

Celia looked at me angrily, like I did not understand. 'They spread out a big map and while you are distracted, they take your purse from underneath.'

'OK, but I think we will find Monty. I will put up the signs.'

Celia touched my arm. 'Thank you, dear.'

I went to Sophie's desk. I opened it and found some tape in one of the wooden holes and plastic envelopes in the top drawer to protect the paper from the rain. As I was closing the desk I saw a small *M* in the wood written in blue pen. Had Sophie written it there because of me? Because she had been dreaming about me? If she had, I thought, it was probably a long time ago when we were happy.

When the dogs saw me putting on my wellies, they got out of the basket and barked with excitement.

'Come on then,' I said, opening the door and letting them go past me.

Outside the earth was muddy from the rain and the pools of water in the road were the same pale yellow as the sky. I walked along the path up the hill. I put a piece of paper on every gate or stile. When I came out of the woods on to the road I saw a huge dark grey cloud moving across the sky like someone was shutting a lid. As I put a notice on the brick gatepost of the home for injured soldiers I felt the rain on my face.

The rain was thick. I started to run back to the house, first along the road, then across the field. Between my jacket and the top of my boots, my jeans were completely wet. Water ran down my face. The dogs were running in front of me. I had to look at the ground so I would not fall. One time I looked up to check my direction. Rain was hitting my eyeballs. Suddenly I saw something in the distance. At the edge of the woods there was a man sitting in a high chair half way up a tree. He was pointing a gun at me. My blood froze. I started to run faster. As I ran, the man followed me with the gun, always keeping it pointed directly at me as I moved. I thought he was going to shoot me. I got down on the ground and covered my head with my hands, hoping I was hidden enough in the earth. I did not know what else to do. I stayed there for a minute. Then I looked up and the man was gone. I got up and ran to the house. I tried to remember what the man looked like. I was sure it was David.

I arrived back at the house covered in mud. I took off my coat and my wet clothes and washed my face in the sink in the little room. I was cold so I wrapped myself in one of the dogs' towels and stood next to the cooker, pressing myself against the warm metal. My heart was still pumping quickly from the fear.

Suddenly I saw David outside in the garden walking along the path. I ran outside into the rain, still wearing only a towel.

'David,' I shouted. 'What were you doing?'

David turned around. He looked annoyed, but he did not seem guilty. His eyes looked down at the towel. I walked up to him until I was very close.

'What were you doing?' I said again.

'I don't know what you mean,' David said.

'You were pointing a gun at me. I saw you.'

'I don't know what you are talking about.'

'I'm not afraid of you,' I said. 'You think you know something and you have power over me. But you don't. You can tell Richard if you want. But it won't change anything because he already knows. And you can tell William if you want. I don't care if he knows. I want him to know.'

David made an expression of disgust, like he did not want to hear anything about it. He was silent, looking at me with his small black eyes.

'Well in that case,' David said slowly, 'you should talk to Richard. He was the one who took his gun down to the woods earlier. By the sounds of things, he has reason enough to be pointing it at you. I told him he should keep his eye on you. I knew something was up that time I saw you two in the garden singing to one another. Right from the beginning I told him to watch out.'

'Does it feel good to be right?' I said.

He stared at me with eyes like holes. 'You don't belong here,' he said, and then turned and walked away.

I thought about what he said. Maybe Sophie had not betrayed me like I thought. It was David who told Richard. But then I remembered the important thing. It was Richard with the gun. I was shocked. I never thought that it would be Richard. Now I was more afraid than angry. Did Richard want to hurt me?

I looked down and realised where I was. The towel was soaked. My body started shaking. I went upstairs and had a hot bath. When I came downstairs again I saw Richard's car through the window. His muddy boots were on the mat. I went to the kitchen. He was drinking tea and eating cake left from a shoot. When he saw me he got up quickly from the chair wiping his mouth.

'Mirka, I'm so sorry.'

'What were you doing?'

'I was practising keeping you in my sight, and then I realised you had seen me. I tried to drive round and get you, but you were gone.'

'I thought you were going to shoot me.'

'It wasn't loaded.'

'I didn't know that. I was frightened.'

Richard looked down. 'I know. I'm sorry.'

'What are you doing in the chair in the rain?'

'I went to watch the deer and think.'

'You need a gun to do that?'

'Well, I can watch them through the scope and study their movements. It calms me down. Anyway, what were you doing out there?'

'Celia's dog Monty disappeared, so she asked me to put up notices around the land.'

I went to my coat hanging on the back of the door of the little room and took a piece of paper from my pocket. I gave it to Richard. As he looked at it something happened to his face, as if he was thinking many things at the same time.

'Can't pretend I'm that upset to hear he's gone AWOL. He's a nasty little piece of work.'

'He's just a dog.'

'Well, anyway, you're a good person for helping. Sophie back?'

'I don't think so.'

Richard sat down again and drank some tea. 'I was thinking about the deer.'

I put the kettle on the cooker and took a cup from the cupboard.

'What about the deer?'

'I was thinking maybe we could offer some deer-stalking here. I've seen other places doing it. You can do a one-day course where you learn how to stalk in the morning and then in the afternoon you butcher a deer that's already been hung for a while.'

'But you had so many problems with the pheasants.'

'Exactly,' Richard said. 'I need to diversify. We could even offer a package where you could learn to cook venison. Sophie could get involved with that bit, perhaps. Now here's where you come in—'

I knew what he was going to say and I shook my head.

Richard frowned. 'Hear me out,' he said. 'We all know I'm not the world's greatest taxidermist. But you are.'

'No, Richard,' I said.

'We can also offer to taxidermy the head of the deer for them. It's perfect.'

'Like a factory of death,' I said, imagining myself making taxidermy deer heads, again and again, for ever.

Richard looked angrily at me. 'There is absolutely nothing wrong with killing an animal in the wild and eating it. It's better than rearing cattle in inhuman conditions and killing them out of the way where nobody can see.'

'This is not about meat. This is about people paying money because they want to kill something for pleasure. They can buy meat in the supermarket. We aren't living in the medieval world.'

'Mirka, you are being deliberately obtuse. We should be encouraging people to be more in touch with the way in which meat ends up on their plate.'

'I understand. OK. But if it is about meat, why do you want to keep the head? When I eat some lamb I don't want to put the head of a sheep on my wall and say, "Look, everybody, look at the sheep, I ate it." They want to put the head of the deer on the wall to show everyone how powerful they are because they killed a fast, clever animal. That's why you don't shoot cows and sheep. Because they are too easy. No fun.'

While I was talking, Richard got up and came and stood opposite me by the cooker. 'You don't know what you're talking about. Hunting is a way of life for millions of people around the world and has been since the dawn of time.'

'A way of life?' I said. I was surprised at the violence in my voice. 'You told me they worked in banks and hedge funds.'

I realised I should stop. Richard's face was shocked. Then his expression turned hard. He came closer to me, raising his shoulders. I could feel myself leaning backwards a little, afraid.

'Look, I need to make some money somehow,' he said between his teeth. 'And if you want to look at it that way, offering rich city cunts the chance to come and kill things for kicks seems to me to be as good a way as any. And you—' He pointed his finger at my chest. 'You've been busy making a load of cash on my time and I've let you. And now, when I need you, you decide to get all moral about it.'

'Richard,' I said in a smooth voice, trying to calm him, 'I will help you if I can. But I am never going to do taxidermy again.'

Richard stepped back and his shoulders relaxed. 'Just don't think I'm stupid,' he said.

I did not know if he meant about the taxidermy, or about Sophie.

'What's going on?' Sophie said.

Richard and I turned our heads. Sophie was standing at the kitchen door holding a basket full of shopping. She looked at us suspiciously.

'Nothing, darling. I was just discussing a business idea with Mirka.'

Sophie put the basket on the table. 'Why do you both look so guilty then?'

'We don't,' Richard said. 'How was town?'

'Mayhem. Anything exciting happen here?'

'Not much. Do you remember Celia's horrid little dog? Well, Mirka was here and she came around and apparently he's gone missing. Mirka kindly went and put up some notices for her.'

'Oh no. Poor Celia. Well, I'm sure he'll turn up. Well done, Mirka, that was very nice of you.'

'That's OK,' I said. My face was burning. I was feeling guilty about Richard. I did not mean to speak to him so strongly. He was right, I could not be moral. 'Oh,' I said, remembering. 'Your father rang. He is coming on Christmas Eve and he said I should tell you to get a turkey.'

'What?' Richard and Sophie said at the same time.

I nodded, apologising.

'Oh my God, you are fucking kidding me?' Sophie said. 'He can't come. I don't want him to come.'

'Sophie, we can't say that.'

'I know we can't say that,' Sophie shouted at Richard.

Richard held up both palms. 'Sorry.'

'It's fine. It will be fine. I'll order a turkey from the butchers. Wait, no, I won't. We are having carp for Christmas.'

'I'm not sure that is the best idea,' Richard said.

'It's my house and he has to accept that we do things differently now. We're having carp and Mirka you are eating at the table with us. He must understand that you are part of the family. He can go and have Christmas somewhere else if he doesn't like it.'

'Camilla is coming too,' I said.

Richard closed his eyes. Sophie stared at me, her mouth open.

'Well that's just absolutely brilliant.' She started laughing, but it was not a real laugh. 'Let the good times roll.'

A week after Celia came to the house, Sophie and I were sitting at the kitchen table doing the crossword together. The dogs were asleep in their basket. It was dark outside and our reflections were yellow in the black window.

'Three words. I'll give you a clue. It's an anagram.'

'How do you know?' I said.

'*Scrambled.*'

'Oh yes.' I thought for a while. I wrote all the letters in a circle on the edge of the newspaper like Sophie taught me. 'Stamp pen hum.'

Sophie frowned. 'That's not really a thing, is it?'

'Do you know the answer already?'

'Yes.'

'Hump mans pet.'

Sophie started laughing. 'No, but I like that one.'

'Hats pump men.'

Sophie bent over, she was laughing so much.

I was laughing too now. 'Thump pans me.'

'Stop. These sound so weird.'

'Hum spent map.'

Sophie wiped her eyes. 'Do you give up?'

'I give up.'

'It's *man the pumps*, silly.'

'Of course it is. How did I not guess immediately.'

We smiled at each other.

'I'm going to miss you,' she said. She reached out and held my hand. I squeezed it.

'Seriously,' I said. 'Who is man the pumps?'

Richard came into the kitchen. Sophie and I took our hands back quickly, but he did not see anything. He seemed excited.

'I've got something to show you. Come with me.'

Sophie and I followed Richard up the stairs and along the corridor to the blue room. He went into the bathroom. As I went into the room I saw the bath was full of water and there were two big grey carp swimming lazily at the bottom.

'What do you think?' Richard said, looking pleased. 'I thought I better get two because I know how much your father eats.'

'Oh God,' Sophie said.

'What, do you think I should have got three?'

'No, two's fine. I just can't believe I'm going to feed my father carp.'

'He'll be fine.'

At that moment the doorbell rang and the dogs barked. Sophie and Richard looked at each other with confused expressions.

'I bet it's Celia,' Sophie said.

We went down the stairs again and Sophie opened the door. It was the same policewoman from my first night in the house.

'Good evening,' she said.

'Hello,' Sophie said. 'Has something happened?'

'I'm here to inform you that Monty, the dog belonging to Celia Atkinson that was reported missing last week has been found dead on your property. Celia found his body this afternoon in a hedgerow.'

Sophie put her hand over her mouth. 'Oh no, poor Celia, how terrible.'

'He was shot.'

'Oh God. By who?'

'We don't know yet, ma'am.'

Richard came and put his arm over Sophie's shoulder, looking at the policewoman with a worried expression.

'When did this happen?' he said.

'From the level of decomposition, the vet estimated that Monty was killed soon after Celia realised he was missing.'

'And what was he shot with?' Richard said, leaning towards the woman with his eyebrows together.

'Multiple gun-shot pellets were found in his abdomen. Again, we need to run some tests to be able to say exactly what kind of gun.'

Richard shook his head. 'How awful. And what kind of involvement do the police have in these kinds of cases?'

'Monty's tags and freedom collar were removed and he was thrown at the bottom of the hedgerow. His identity has been confirmed, however, by his microchip.'

'Yes, but he's a dog not a human. It's not murder.'

'It comes under the crime of damage to property, sir, so we will be investigating his death thoroughly.'

'Of course, of course,' Richard said.

'Anything we can do to help,' Sophie said.

The policewoman looked very directly at Richard. 'You do know it is perfectly legal for a landowner to kill an animal that is worrying livestock or game, as long as you report it within forty-eight hours.'

'Yes, I know. He probably disturbed some poachers,' Richard said, looking at the floor. 'Sadly we get a lot of them here.'

'Were you out working on the land last Tuesday and Wednesday?'

'Yes, of course,' Richard said quickly.

'Were you alone?'

'What are you trying to suggest? That *I* killed the dog?' Richard pointed to his chest.

'We have to look at all the possibilities. And the fact is that Monty died on your land. I believe you have a David Ford who works here? Was he with you on those days?'

'He was with me on Tuesday, and my assistant here, Mirka, was with me on Wednesday.'

The policewoman turned her head to me. I smiled and nodded my head dreamily, even though I knew it was not true.

'OK, well I'll be off. I will let you know as soon as the results of the tests come through. I may be back to collect statements.'

After the door closed we were silent, listening to the sound of the policewoman's feet on the gravel. Richard still had his arm around Sophie's shoulders. I could see the anger in his eyes but I thought I could see fear there too.

Sophie stepped away from him. 'Tell me you had nothing to do with the death of that dog.'

'Of course I didn't,' he said. 'What do you take me for?'

'That's exactly why I'm worried.'

'Look, I didn't kill that little rat.'

Sophie looked at him with narrow eyes. 'No, I suppose not even you would be stupid enough to kill a dog with your own gun, on your own land and think that nobody would ever find him and put two and two together.'

She walked past him towards the kitchen. Richard breathed out slowly and wiped his forehead with his palm.

'It will be OK,' I said.

'I know it will,' he said in a sharp voice. 'I just want to get it cleared up.'

The day before Christmas Eve Richard and Sophie went to a drinks party at another house. I thought about walking to the pub. But in the end I thought that it was too much. I just wanted to relax and try to enjoy my last few days at the house. So I lit a fire in the drawing room and watched television with the dogs.

The computer was on Sophie's desk. I kept looking at it. Part of me wanted to check my emails, but another part remembered how bad it made me feel when nobody emailed me on my birthday. But after a while, I could not resist and I got up and opened it.

There was an email from my father. I opened it nervously. *Happy Christmas, dearest Mirka,* it said. *I hope you are well and happy wherever you are. I am thinking of you. Love Dad.*

It was not much. But I felt my heart glowing in my chest. My father was thinking about me in Slovakia. It meant a lot.

Happy Christmas, I wrote back. *It is good to hear from you. I am well and happy. I have been living in England. I have a lot to tell you! I am thinking of you too. Love Mirka.*

Then I fell asleep watching an episode of *Dad's Army* and woke up to the telephone ringing. I ran to the entrance hall.

'Hello, Fairmont Hall,' I said.

'Is Mr Parker there, please?'

I recognised the policewoman's voice.

'He is not here.'

'Will you tell him that I'll be coming tomorrow to the house to inspect his guns.'

'OK.'

'Monty had over forty gunshot pellets in his abdomen. If Richard shot him, he could face a fine of twenty thousand pounds or six months in jail.'

The policewoman sounded as if she knew it was Richard.

'OK,' I said.

Richard and Sophie did not come back until midnight. When I heard the car, I went to the hall and opened the door. Richard was standing next to the car peeing into the grass. His body was waving backwards and forwards and he looked like he was going to fall over. Sophie walked towards me up the stairs. She was wearing her coat over her shoulders and for the first time I saw the small curve of her pregnant belly in her tight red velvet dress.

'I didn't think you would still be up.' She turned and stood next to me on the top step. 'Look at the state of him.'

Richard was walking sideways, pulling up the zip of his trousers.

'How was the party?'

'As fun as any party can be when you're stone-cold sober and everyone else is completely shit-faced. And Richard decided to tell anyone who would listen how much he hates all of the rich cunts who come pheasant shooting every year. Thereby ensuring that nobody will come next year. Well done, Richard, you've solved your own problem,' she shouted at him.

'I stayed awake because the policewoman called to say she is coming tomorrow to look at the guns.'

'Oh God,' Sophie said, looking at Richard again. 'I hope he didn't do anything stupid.'

Richard walked up the steps. 'You missed the world's greatest bore-off,' he said. 'In the blue corner, Sir Bore of Boringham, and in the red corner, Lord Dull of Dullington. Going at it, tooth and nail.' He did some punches with his arms.

We went inside and Richard put his jacket over the end of the railings but it slipped on to the floor. I picked it up. Sophie walked to the table to put the car keys in the bowl and turned around.

'Richard, the policewoman phoned. She's coming back tomorrow to look at the guns. This could be serious.'

Richard was walking up the stairs slowly, holding the railings. He looked down at Sophie. 'What? Why can't she leave us alone? Haven't they got anything better to do?'

'I guess they must think that the brutal killing of a dog and the attempt to cover up his death is a pretty big deal.'

'Oh, shut the fuck up,' Richard said, pulling himself up the steps. 'I'm not listening to any more of this crap.'

'You could go to jail. It's murder.'

Richard leant over the railings and whispered, 'It's not murder, Sophie, it's a fucking dog.'

Sophie followed Richard up the stairs. 'You killed him, didn't you?'

'Of course I didn't.'

'Admit it. I know you did.'

Richard turned on the top step. 'OK, fine. Yes, I killed him. Do you want to know why I killed him? Because he was on our land, running around trying to rip the heads off the pheasants, scaring the shit out of them, and I was completely within my rights to do so. Happy now?'

'Then why didn't you report it?'

'Because I was busy and didn't want to deal with all of this bollocks.'

'You fucking idiot!' Sophie shouted. 'What have you done?'

I was still standing next to the tree. Sophie followed Richard down the corridor to their bedroom. I did not know what to do. After a minute I went to the kitchen and took the dogs outside for their last walk. Richard and Sophie were still shouting when I brought the dogs back inside. I remembered the first night in the house when Richard had been drunk and pushed Sophie on to the floor. He was as drunk tonight as he was then, but this time Sophie was pregnant. I felt suddenly afraid for her and I ran up the stairs to see what they were doing.

Their bedroom door was shut. I could hear Sophie crying loudly.

'I don't know who you are,' she was saying. 'I don't want to be married to someone who does things like this.'

'For God's sake, Sophie, why are you making such a fuss? Get over it.'

'I won't get over it. I won't ever get over it.'

'I don't understand why this is such a big deal.'

'You took off its collar. You tried to hide the body. You lied.'

'Come on, Sophie,' Richard said more gently.

'Poor Celia.'

'Oh, don't go all "poor Celia" on me. You hate Celia. You think she's a meddling old cow.'

'She was my mother's friend.'

'Sophie, come here. You are blowing this all out of proportion.'

'Go away. Get away from me. I want you to go. I don't want you in my house any more.'

'Oh, it's your house now, is it?'

'I want you to leave.'

'Well, guess what? We're married and it's my house too.'

'I don't love you any more.'

As Sophie said this I felt a pain in my heart for Richard.

'Don't say that,' Richard said, sounding afraid.

'It's true. I realise now that I haven't loved you since you cheated on me with that woman. Something broke between us.'

'What woman? What are you talking about?'

'You know perfectly well who I mean.'

'I've never cheated on you. Never.'

'It's too late, Richard. I don't love you any more. You embarrass me.'

'Me, embarrass you? Me, embarrass you? You're the one going on about the merits of organic sausages for eight hours until everyone is ready to slit their throats.'

'I'd rather be with Mirka than with you.'

Another time I would be happy to hear this, but the way Sophie said it did not make me feel good. Like I was the last person. But then I heard a loud clapping sound. Sophie screamed. There was a noise of furniture moving and something hitting wood. I quickly pushed open the door.

Sophie was lying on the bed and Richard was above her, with his knees either side of her body. 'Get out, get out,' she was screaming, trying to hit him with her fists.

Richard caught her hands with one hand and hit her face

with his palm. He put her hands down on the bed so she could not move. She was crying so much she could not breathe.

'Sophie, stop it, stop it,' he was saying. 'You're hysterical.'

'Get off her,' I said. My voice sounded strange to me.

Richard twisted his head and saw me. 'This has nothing to do with you,' he said. 'So you can fuck right off.'

'Richard, get off Sophie please,' I said.

Richard stood up off the bed and started to walk towards me. 'Get out of my bedroom.'

As he came closer, he seemed to get bigger. I realised I was walking backwards out of the room. Richard swung the door violently and it closed just in front of my face. I did not know what I should do. I could not leave Sophie. I ran down the stairs, along the corridor to Richard's study and took the keys out of the top drawer of his desk. I took one of the guns out of the cupboard and ran back along the corridor and up the stairs again.

I did all of this without thinking. It was very quick. But when I opened the door to the bedroom and stood there holding the gun in my hands I felt really frightened. It was heavy and cold. I felt like I was making a mistake.

Richard was bending over Sophie on the bed again with his hand around her neck.

'I'm not leaving this house,' he was saying. 'It's my house too. I've worked my arse off for this place. How fucking dare you try and throw me out?'

Sophie saw me. Then Richard turned his head to see what she was staring at.

'Get off her,' I said.

Richard stepped backwards and put his palms next to his shoulders. 'Easy, Mirka.'

I walked to the bed, towards Sophie's head, keeping the gun pointed at him.

'Get out of the house,' I said.

Richard walked sideways towards the door. I followed him with the gun. I was terrified. I did not even know if the gun had bullets inside or not. If I pulled the trigger by mistake, I could kill him. I realised Richard did not know either. There was fear in his eyes, but also a kind of satisfaction.

'This is nice,' he said as he walked backwards through the door. 'Being thrown out of my own house by my Slovak assistant. This is going to make a great story one day.'

'I'm serious,' I said, walking towards him. 'Get out of the house.'

Richard walked backwards down the corridor, and I followed him slowly, trying not to show my fear.

'So this is your little plan?' he said. 'You think she's going to leave me and shack up with you, do you?'

I said nothing and walked slowly forward. Richard looked behind him and stepped down the stairs, holding the railings.

'You think she's going to marry you, do you?' he said. 'You think she's going to introduce you around to all her friends and family?'

'Why is that so impossible? You think she can't love me as much as she loves you? You never thought it could be anything serious. Well, maybe you were wrong.'

Richard smiled a mean smile. 'You think it's going to go

down well with William when he finds out his favourite daughter has gone off with an Eastern European dyke?'

'You think it's going to go down well with William when he finds out you hit his favourite daughter when she was pregnant?'

He stepped forward. 'You fucking bitch.'

I held the gun higher and he stopped.

When I got to the bottom of the stairs I put the gun under my arm and held it with one hand as I put my other hand in the bowl of keys on the table. I took out the car keys, watching Richard at the same time. I threw them to him and they hit his jumper and fell on the floor.

'Pick those up, get in the car and drive away,' I said.

Richard looked at me with pure hatred in his eyes. It hurt but I did not look away.

'I can't believe we welcomed you into our house,' he said, shaking his head with disgust.

He turned and walked out of the door. I stood on the top step, still pointing the gun at him as he got in the car and closed the door. The lights switched on and the car moved backwards. I stayed at the door and watched the lights move up the road until they disappeared over the top of the hill. Then I ran back up the stairs to Sophie.

'Are you OK?' I put the gun on the floor and ran to the bed. 'Is the baby OK?'

Sophie was lying on her side crying. I put my arms around her and stroked her hair and kissed her forehead.

'Are you sure you are OK?' I asked again.

'Yes, I'll be fine. Thank you. I don't know what would have happened if you hadn't been here.'

'You are safe now,' I said.

'I was so frightened. He's taken complete leave of his senses. You can't just go around killing dogs. Honestly, if he's capable of doing that, what else is he capable of? I feel like I've been married all these years to someone I don't even know.'

'It's OK now,' I said.

Sophie looked at me like I did not understand. 'I don't want him to come back, Mirka. I want you to stay here with me. You make me happy. We can be together.'

'OK,' I said and I pressed her head against my chest and kissed her forehead. The words were too much for me. I did not know if I believed her. My heart was afraid.

'We can bring up the baby together,' she said in a sleepy voice.

'Shh,' I said.

I stayed holding her until I knew from her heavy breathing that she was sleeping. Then I went to sit on the chair by the window, to watch in case Richard came back. The gun was resting on the wall. I felt sick looking at it. I could not believe what I had done. It was very dramatic and nothing could be the same now. It could never be the three of us in the house again. It was Richard or me. I thought about Sophie's words. I tried to imagine our future together, the two of us with the baby in the house. We could be happy. But the image kept waving and bending like it was under water.

'Mirka, wake up,' Sophie was saying.

I opened my eyes and lifted my head. My neck hurt from sleeping in the chair.

'What is happening? Is everything OK?'

'You fell asleep.'

Sophie was dressed in jeans and a red sweater. She had put on a lot of make-up, but I could still see the bruise around her eye and the pink mark across her cheek.

'How are you?'

'I'm fine, it was only a slap.' She walked to the mirror and put her fingers to the mark on her cheek. 'Idiot bastard. What is wrong with him? Am I the only person who thinks he has completely lost it, killing that dog?'

She seemed different. Not shaky or upset, or relieved that Richard was gone. She was behaving as if it was just a small thing he had done to her.

'No,' I said, trying to hide my disappointment.

'I can't believe I said those things to him. I guess they must have been building up in me. Well, at least that should teach him a lesson.'

I turned and looked out of the window. Everything outside was frozen. The grass, the earth, the trees, the fields and hedges were all white, like all the colours had gone from the world. I understood what Sophie said. What happened meant nothing. Richard would be back when he had learnt his lesson.

In the distance I saw something moving. It was a car coming down the hill.

'They're coming,' Sophie said.

'Who is coming?'

It was William's green car. I had forgotten that it was Christmas Eve. I suddenly felt panicked. They could not come now. What would we say about Richard?

The car stopped outside the house. I watched William and

Caroline sitting in the front seat talking about something. The back door opened and a foot in a high-heeled black boot stepped out on to the stones. A woman wearing a fur coat and sunglasses stood up and shut the door behind her. She had a pointy chin and strong jaw like Sophie, and when she pushed the sunglasses up on to her blonde dried hair I saw she had those same long blue eyes. Her lips and nails were painted bright red.

'That is your sister?'

'No shit, Sherlock.'

'She's like you, but in another universe.'

'That is a good way of putting it.'

We stood back from the window so they would not see us.

'I better go down,' Sophie said, kissing me gently on the cheek. Then she held my shoulders and looked at me very directly. 'This will be OK, I promise. I'll tell them Richard and I are having a little bit of time apart or something. It will be fine.'

I walked along the corridor towards the stairs to my room. I heard Sophie open the front door. I did not understand how she thought everything was going to be OK. It was not OK for me.

'All right, Sophs. Long time no see,' Camilla said. 'You look like shit. What happened to your face?'

'Oh nothing. I bumped into the door.'

'That old chestnut? Sophie—'

'Don't be stupid, Camilla.'

'All right, all right. So where is Ricardo?'

'Um, he's out somewhere doing stuff. How are you?'

'Moving back from New York.'

'I thought you loved it.'

'I miss English men.'

'My number one daughter,' William said loudly, sounding excited. 'Come here and give your father a kiss. Don't look at me like that, Camilla. I mean in seniority.'

'Hello, Sophie,' Caroline said. 'Oh, it's freezing in here. We need to get that fire going.'

'Where's Richard?' William said.

'Out, apparently,' Camilla said.

'Are you alone?'

'Er, yes. I mean no. Yes,' Sophie said. She sounded completely lost. 'Sorry, I'm just feeling a bit under the weather.'

'You got rid of that girl then?' William said.

'What girl?' Sophie said, and I felt like she had put a knife in my heart.

'That dreadful, sullen-looking Eastern European girl who was always creeping around eavesdropping on our conversations. I don't know how you could stand to have her in the house.'

'Dad, please.'

'You do look poorly,' Caroline said. 'Maybe you have the flu. Or maybe ...' There was a pause. 'Sophie, have you got something to tell us?'

'Oh right, yes,' Sophie said in a dreamy voice. 'I was going to tell you later. As a Christmas surprise. That's what it is. Surprise!'

'Oh, Sophie!' Caroline said, her voice full of happiness. 'I knew it the moment I saw you. Oh, that is wonderful news. How many weeks are you?'

'Congratulations, darling,' William said. 'I am so happy to hear it.'

'Nice one, Sophs,' Camilla said. 'About bloody time.'

I walked quietly up the stairs. Sophie was with her family now. She would not tell them anything and Richard would come home and everything would be normal again. I was angry with myself. I had been so blind after I promised myself I would not be again. From the beginning I had not seen Sophie how she really was. She wanted everything. She wanted everyone to love her. She wanted the husband, the father, the house, the baby and the lover. But sometimes you had to make a choice.

I took my rucksack out from underneath my bed and started to put my things into it. I suddenly thought about David. He was right in the end, I did not belong at the house. Then I put on my black boots and black half-finger gloves and picked up the presents for Sophie and Richard from the desk. Before I switched off the light I looked around. I had got used to my bedroom and I liked it. But now, looking around, I felt nothing.

As I came down the stairs I heard a woman scream. Then there were loud footsteps running. A door opened and someone heavy walked along the corridor.

'What the fuck is in my bath?' Camilla shouted.

'Are you all right, Camilla?' William shouted.

'What is it?' Caroline said.

'Oh, sorry, I completely forgot about the carp,' Sophie said.

'Carp?' William said. 'What on earth are you doing with carp in the bath?'

I put my head around the wall at the bottom of the stairs and saw Caroline going into the blue room, with William ahead of her, crossing the room towards the bathroom. I left my bag in the corridor and followed them inside.

William, Caroline, Camilla and Sophie were all looking down into the bath.

'Is this some kind of a joke?' William said.

'We were going to eat them for Christmas,' Sophie said.

'Sorry, what?' Camilla said. 'Why?'

'It was my idea,' I said.

All of them turned around. They stared at me, looking confused.

'It is a Slovak tradition to have carp for Christmas,' I said. 'I remembered how much you loved European food, William, so I thought it would be a nice surprise.'

'Well, that's jolly thoughtful of you,' William said. 'But we eat turkey at Christmas.'

'Maybe this year you can eat something new,' I said.

Sophie gave me a warning with her eyes. I ignored her.

'I don't want something new. In this country we eat turkey.'

Sophie stepped forward. 'There's still time to get a turkey. Maybe we can have both.'

Now I looked at Sophie. 'No, I don't think you can have both turkey and carp together. You have to choose, turkey or carp.'

I could see in Sophie's eyes that she understood. She said nothing.

William looked at Sophie angrily. 'I'm sorry, Sophie, but what is going on? Why is this girl trying to dictate what we eat for Christmas dinner?'

'My name is Mirka,' I said.

Then I turned and went out of the room.

'Mirka, wait! Dad, look, I can explain,' I heard Sophie saying.

I picked up my rucksack and put it on my back as I went

down the stairs. In the entrance hall I went to the tree and put the two presents at the back, hidden behind the leaves. When I saw my writing, *To Richard, thank you for everything, love from your favourite Slovak taxidermist, Mirka*, tears came into my eyes. I stood up again, wiping my tears.

Sophie was standing on the stairs. She looked at the rucksack.

'Where are you going?'

'I'm going,' I said.

We stared at each other for a long time until my heart felt like it was breaking apart. Our eyes communicated all of our history, the happiness and the pain. Then she changed her expression and looked at me politely like I was a B&B guest who was leaving after one night.

'Well, come back and visit us one day.'

I nodded and then went quietly out of the door.

It was cold outside. My feet cracked the ice of the pools in the road and my breath was like smoke. I walked along the path up the hill. Every leaf of grass, every tiny branch of a tree or hedge was frozen white. When I got to the top I could see the village in the distance. The Snooty Fox was at the end of the line of willow trees. I would find something for myself, I thought.

I turned to look one more time at the house. The sky was pale blue and the house was pink in the middle of the frozen land. It was a beautiful scene, so perfect and still, that I felt like it was behind glass. Already, I could not believe I had really lived there. I turned around and started to walk down the other side of the hill towards the white fields that rolled like waves into the distance.

Acknowledgements

I would like to thank the following people who helped me in writing and researching this book and to whom I am so grateful: Clare for being an incredible and perceptive editor; Elinor for being the best agent anyone could hope for; Derek for his help in researching taxidermy; Chris and Pope for help with matters relating to pheasant shooting and gamekeeping; Paula for being a reader and M for being the inspiration I needed. I want to mention Rachel Poliquin's beautiful and insightful book, *The Breathless Zoo: Taxidermy and the Cultures of Longing*, for making me look at taxidermy in a new light. Lastly I would like to thank my parents for all their support and love.

To buy any of our books and to find out
more about Abacus and Little, Brown, our authors
and titles, as well as events and book clubs,
visit our website

www.littlebrown.co.uk

and follow us on Twitter

@AbacusBooks
@LittleBrownUK

To order any Abacus titles p & p free in the UK,
please contact our mail order supplier on:

+ 44 (0)1832 737525

Customers not based in the UK should contact
the same number for appropriate postage
and packing costs.